WOLFHOUND
CENTURY

By Peter Higgins

Wolfhound Century

PETER HIGGINS
WOLFHOUND
CENTURY

orbit

www.orbitbooks.net

Orbit
Hachette Book Group
237 Park Avenue, New York, NY 10017
www.HachetteBookGroup.com

First U.S. Edition: March 2013
First published in Great Britain in 2013 by Gollancz, an imprint of the Orion Publishing Group, Orion House, 5 Upper St Martin's Lane, London WC2H 9EA

Orbit is an imprint of Hachette Book Group, Inc. The Orbit name and logo are trademarks of Little, Brown Book Group Limited.

The Hachette Speakers Bureau provides a wide range of authors for speaking events. To find out more, go to www.hachettespeakersbureau.com or call (866) 376-6591.

The publisher is not responsible for websites (or their content) that are not owned by the publisher.

The characters and events in this book are fictitious. Any similarity to real persons, living or dead, is coincidental and not intended by the author.

Library of Congress Control Number: 2012951502
ISBN: 978-0-316-21967-9

10 9 8 7 6 5 4 3 2 1

RRD-C

Printed in the United States of America

The wolfhound century is on my back —
But I am not a wolf.

OSIP MANDELSTAM (1891–1938)

Part One

1

Investigator Vissarion Lom sat in a window booth in the Café Rikhel. Pulses of rain swept up Ansky Prospect, but inside the café, in the afternoon crush, the air was thick with the smell of coffee, cinnamon bread and damp overcoats.

'Why don't you go home?' said Ziller. 'No one's going to come. I can call you if anything happens. You can be back here in half an hour.'

'Someone will come,' said Lom. 'He's not sitting out there for no reason.'

Across the street, a thin young man waited on a bench under a dripping zinc canopy. He had been there, in front of the Timberworkers' Library and Meeting Hall, for three hours already.

'Maybe he spotted us,' said Ziller. 'Maybe the contact is aborted.'

'He could have lost us straight off the boat,' said Lom. 'He didn't even look round. He's not bothered about us. He thinks he's clean.'

They had picked him up off the morning river-boat from Yislovsk. Briefcase – that was the cryptonym they gave him, they didn't know his name – had hung around the wharves for a while, bought himself an apricot juice at a kiosk, walked slowly up Durnovo-Burliuk Street, and sat down on a bench. That was all he had done. He carried no luggage, apart from the small leather case they'd named him for. After an hour he'd taken some bread out of the case and eaten it. Except for that, he just sat there.

Ziller picked up his glass of tea, looked into it critically, set it down untouched.

'He's an arse-wipe. That's what he is.'

'Maybe,' said Lom. 'But he's waiting for something.'

The truth was, Lom rather liked Briefcase. There was something

3

about him – the way he walked, the way his hair was cut. Briefcase was young. He looked … vulnerable. Something – hatred, idealism, love – had driven him, alone and obviously frightened, all the way across the continent to Podchornok, his ears sticking out pinkly in the rain, to make this crude attempt at contact. The call from Magadlovosk had said only that he was a student, a member of some amateurish break-away faction of the Lezarye separatists. The Young Opposition. The Self-Liberation Will of All Peoples. He was coming to meet someone. To collect something. Magadlovosk had sounded excited, unusually so, but also vague: *The contact, Lom, that's what matters, that's the target. The contact, and whatever it is he's bringing with him.*

'You really should go home,' said Ziller. 'What time did you finish last night?'

'I'm fine,' said Lom.

'Fine? You're over thirty, you do twice the hours the others do, you get no promotions, you're on crappy pay, and you need a shave. When did you last eat something decent? '

Lom thought of his empty apartment. The yellow furniture. The unwashed plates and empty bottles. Home.

'Why don't you come round?' Ziller was saying. 'Come tonight. Lena's got a friend. Her husband was killed when the *Volkova* went down. She's got a kid but … well, we could invite her—'

'Look,' said Lom. 'I had some paperwork last night, that's all.'

Ziller shrugged. He lit a cigarette and let the smokestream drift out of his nose.

'I just thought …' he said. 'Maybe you could use a friend, Vissarion. After the Laurits business you've got few enough.'

'Yeah. Well. Thanks.'

They sat in silence, awkwardly, staring out of the window. Watching Briefcase staring at nothing.

'Shit,' said Ziller, half-rising in his seat and craning to see down the road. 'Shit.'

A line of giants, each leading a four-horse dray team and a double wagon loaded high with resin tanks, was lumbering up the hill from the direction of the river quay. They were almost in front of the Rikhel already – the rumbling of the wagons' iron wheels set the café floor vibrating faintly – and when they reached it, Briefcase would be out of sight. The teams were in no hurry: they would take at least ten minutes to pass.

'You'll have to go outside,' said Lom. 'Keep an eye from the alley till they're gone.'

Ziller sighed and heaved himself reluctantly to his feet, trying to shove the loose end of his shirt back under his belt and button his uniform tunic. He took a long, mournful, consolatory pull on the cigarette and ground the stub into the heaped ashtray, squeezed himself out of the booth and went out into the rain with a show of heavy slowness. Theatrics.

Lom watched the giants through the misted window. They walked patiently under the rain: earth-coloured shirts, leather jerkins, heavy wooden clogs. The rain was heavier now, clattering against the window in fat fistfuls. Only one person was standing out in the street. A soldier, bare-headed and beltless, grey uniform soaked almost to black, left sleeve empty, pinned to his side. He had tipped his face back to look up into the rain and his mouth was wide open. As if he was trying to swallow it down. He had no boots. He was standing in a puddle in torn socks, shifting from foot to foot in a slow, swaying dance.

Two kinds of rain fell on Podchornok. There was steppe rain from the west, sharp and cold, blown a thousand versts across the continental plain in ragged shreds. And the other kind was forest rain. Forest rain came from the east in slow, weighty banks of nimbostratus that settled over the town for days at a time and shed their cargo in warm fat sheets. It fell and fell with dumb insistence, overbrimming the gutters and outflows and swelling the waters of the Yannis until it flowed fat and yellow and heavy with mud. In spring the forest rain was thick with yellow pollen that stuck in your hair and on your face and lips and had a strange taste. In autumn it smelled of resin and earth. This, today, this was forest rain.

Ziller was taking his time. The giants and their drays had gone, and Briefcase was still on his bench. The soldier wandered across to him and started waving his one arm. He seemed to be shouting. He had something in his hand and he was trying to show it to Briefcase. Trying to give it to him. Briefcase looked confused.

Shit. This was *it.* This was the *contact*!

Lom crashed out into the rain and across the road.

'Hey! You! Don't move! Police!'

5

Where the hell was Ziller?

Briefcase saw Lom coming. His eyes widened in shock and fear. He should have waited. Showed his papers. Said he had no idea who this soldier was, he'd just been sitting there eating his bread and watching the rain. Instead, he ran. He got about ten paces across the road, when Ziller came out of the alleyway by Krishkin's and took him crashing down into the mud.

The soldier hadn't moved. He was staring at Lom's face. His eyes, expressionless, didn't blink. They were completely brown: all iris, no whites at all. He opened his mouth, as if he was going to speak, and Lom smelled the sour, earthy richness of his breath, but he made no sound. His one hand worked the small cloth bag he was holding as if he was crushing the life out of it. Lom snatched it out of his grip.

'Give me that!'

The man's fingers felt cold. Hard. Brittle.

Lom undid the cord and looked inside. There was nothing but a mess of broken twigs and crushed berries and clumps of some sticky, yellowish substance that might have been wax. It had a sweet, heavy, resinous perfume.

'What the fuck – ?' said Lom. 'What the fuck is this?'

The soldier, gazing into him with fathomless brown eyes, said nothing.

2

Five time zones to the west of Podchornok, on the roof of the Grand Hotel Sviatopolk in Mirgorod, Josef Kantor waited. Despite the ragged fingernails of wind scraping at his face, he was immovable: a pillar of patient rock in a dark and fog-soaked coat. The fog had come and gone. Drifting in off the river before dawn, it had enfolded him in blankness and sifted away at the cold rising of the sun, leaving him beaded with dull grey droplets. He had not moved. He was waiting.

Kantor teased the cavity in his tooth with the fatness of his tongue. The hurting was useful. It kept him rooted in the true present, the only now, the now that he was making come to be. He only had to wait in the cold and it would happen. He only had to not be deflected. Not be moved. And it would happen.

Far below him, Levrovskaya Square, transected by tramlines, was monochrome with yesterday's snow under the blank white dawn. Twelve floors beneath his feet the lobby roof projected, taking a small trapezium bite out of the squareness. Pavement tables were set in two neat rows, penned in by a rectangle of potted hedge. Empty. Sellers were setting up next to the tram stop: a woman putting out a stall of old clothes, linen and dressing gowns; another, wearing a sheepskin coat, lighting a stove for potatoes; an old man arranging his trestle with trays of pancakes, bowls of thin purée, cans for kvass. For the first time, Kantor consulted his watch. Exactly nine a.m.. It was time.

The iron car rattled around the corner and into the square, drawn by a pair of horses, stepping carefully, leaning into the weight, heading for the Bank of Foreign Commerce. His people would begin to move now. He looked for the women first, and there they were, Lidia and

Stefania, the edges of their skirts wet with melting snow, crossing to the gendarme in his kiosk on the corner. The women were laughing, and soon the young gendarme was laughing too. He would be smelling their heavy, promising scent. Kantor used the women to ferry explosives, and they soused themselves with perfume to cover the clinging smell of dynamite strapped against their sweating bodies.

Lidia drew the revolver from her skirts and shot the young gendarme twice. His legs gave way and he crumpled into a sitting position, hunched over his burst belly: blood in the slush; crimson in pale grey. He was still alive, moving his body from side to side, pawing weakly at his face. Lidia stepped in close and shot him in the side of his head.

In Levrovskaya Square, no one noticed.

No, that wasn't correct. An old man in the uniform of the postal services was staring across from the opposite pavement. He took his bag from his shoulder and laid it on the ground, gazing at the dead boy. That didn't matter. The strong-car had reached the middle of the square. But where was Vitt? He should have come out of the Teagarden by now.

And there he was, but he was running, his grenade already in his hand. He dropped it hastily into the path of the horses. It didn't explode. It simply lay there in the snow, inert, like a round black fruit. Like the turd of a giant rabbit. Yelling, the driver hauled on the reins. Kantor watched Vitt stand, uselessly, eyes blank and mouth slightly open, gazing in abstraction at his hopeless failure of a bomb.

Vitt turned and ran out of sight down the alley between the Teagarden and Rosenfeld's. The driver was still screaming at the horses. They stood confused, alarmed, doing nothing. The back of the car opened and soldiers climbed out, looking around for something to fire at. Kantor saw Akaki Serov saunter towards them, smiling, saying something jaunty. When he was close enough he lobbed a bomb with casual grace, going for the horses, and another that rolled under the car. The double flash came, and sudden blooms of smoke and flying stuff, and then the sound of the concussions. The force of the double explosion disembowelled the horses and tore legs and arms and heads off the men. Akaki Serov, who was too close, was burst apart also.

Into the silence before the screaming began, the rest of Kantor's people surged forward, the giant Vaso wading among them like an adult among small children. Lakoba Petrov, Petrov the Painter, hurried along beside him, taking three steps for his one. Petrov was bare-headed, his face flushed pink, firing his Rykov wildly at groin level. The pair ran towards the burst-open strong car, out-distancing the others. Petrov shot a soldier who was rising to his knees, while the giant wrenched at the doors of the car, tearing the metal hinges, and climbed inside. It seemed improbable that he could fit himself inside such a small space, but he ducked into it as if it was a cupboard to hide in.

The others spread out across the square, firing and lobbing grenades. Pieces of flesh, human and horse, spattered the cobbles. There were soft messes of blood and snow and fluid. The screams of the injured sounded as remote to Josef Kantor as the distant cries of the gulls in the bay.

The revolutionary is doomed, he whispered across the Square. *The revolutionary has no personal interests. No emotions. No attachments. The revolutionary owns nothing and has no name. All laws, moralities, customs and conventions – the revolutionary is their merciless and implacable enemy. There is only the revolution. All other bonds are broken.*

The potato seller lay on her face in the middle of the square, her leg somewhat apart from the rest of her, her arm stretched towards a thing she could not reach.

A kind of quiet began to settle on the square, until the tall bronze doors of the bank were thrown open and a mudjhik came lumbering out, twelve feet high, the colour of rust and dried blood. Whatever small animal had given its brain to be inserted inside the mudjhik's head-casket must have been an exultant predator in life. This one was barely under control. It was smacking about with heavy arms, bursting open the heads of anyone who did not run. Behind the mudjhik, more militia came out of the bank, firing.

Whether it was the shock of the mudjhik or some more private and inward surge of life-desire, one of the horses attached to the strong-car twitched and jerked and rose up, squealing. Still harnessed to the car, its comrade dead in the traces alongside and its own bowels spilling onto the pavement, the horse lowered its head and surged towards the empty mouth of East Prospect. With slow determination it widened the distance between itself and the noise and smell of battle, pulling behind it thirty million roubles and Vaso the giant, who was still inside.

9

Kantor breathed a lungful of cold, clean air. The chill hit his hollow, blackened tooth and jolted his jaw with a jab of pain. Time to come down from the roof.

3

When Lom got back from placating Magadlovosk on the phone, Ziller was already in the office, writing up his report. Ziller wrote carefully, word by meticulous word, holding his chewed pencil like a jeweller mending a watch.

'Where are they?' said Lom.

'Who?'

'Briefcase,' said Lom. 'The soldier.'

Ziller put down his pencil. 'Oh,' he said. 'Them. Lasker had them taken across to the Barracks. The militia are going to sweat them a bit and then send them to Vig.'

'What?' said Lom. 'I'd have got what I needed in an hour. They won't survive a week at Vig. You saw them—'

Ziller looked awkward.

'Lasker wanted them off the premises. He said they were an embarrassment.'

'It was a contact,' said Lom.

'Yeah,' said Ziller. 'Well. Lasker thinks you fucked up. Actually, he just doesn't like you. But forget it; it doesn't matter anyway. You're going on a trip. There's a wire on your desk. There was no envelope, so I read it. So did Lasker.'

Lom spread the crumpled telegram out on the table, trying to flatten the creases with the side of his palm. A flimsy sheet with blue printed strips pasted down on it.

INVESTIGATOR VISSARION LOM MUST MIRGOROD SOONEST STOP
ATTEND OFFICE UNDER SECRETARY KROGH STOP 6PM 11 LAPKRIST
STOP LODKA STOP MANDATED REPEAT MANDATED ENDS

Lom read it three times. It wasn't the kind of thing that happened. A provincial investigator summoned halfway across the continent to the capital. They never did that. Never.

'Maybe they want to give you a medal, Vissarion Yppolitovich,' Ziller said.

'Or shoot me in the throat and dump me in the Mir.'

'Don't need to go to Mirgorod for that. There's plenty here would do it, not only Lasker, after what you did to Laurits.'

'Laurits was a shit,' said Lom. 'I saw the room where she was found. I saw what he did.'

'Sure. Only she was a non-citizen and a tart, and Laurits was one of *our* shits. He had a wife and daughters. That makes people feel bad. You're not a popular guy any more.'

'It wasn't a career move.'

'Better if it was,' said Ziller. 'They'd understand that.'

'I did it because he was a murdering bastard. That's what policemen do.'

'You shouldn't joke about this, Vissarion. Things could get serious. People have been asking questions about you. Turning over files. Looking for dirt. You should be careful.'

'What people?' said Lom.

Ziller made a face. 'You know,' he said. 'People.' He hesitated. 'Look, Vissarion,' he said. 'I like you. You're my friend. But if they come after me, I won't stand up for you. I can't. I'm not that kind of brave. I won't risk Lena and the children, not for that. It might be a good thing to be away for a week or two. You know, let things settle down.'

Lom folded the telegram and put it in his pocket. A trip might be good. A change of scene. There was nothing here he would miss. Maybe, just possibly, in Mirgorod they had a job for him. A proper job. He was tired of harassing students and checking residence permits while the vicious stuff went on in this very building, and they fucked you over if you did anything about it. He looked at his watch. There was time: an hour to pack, and he could still catch the overnight boat to Yislovsk.

'You can take the Schama Bezhin file,' he said to Ziller. 'Call it temporary promotion.'

Ziller grinned. 'And I thought you didn't appreciate me,' he said. 'Don't rush back.'

4

A messenger was standing near the back exit of the Sviatopolk, white-faced, gripping his bicycle. Kantor dragged the machine out of his hands and rode off in pursuit of the dying horse, the money and the giant. He found them in a lane off Broken Moons Prospect. Vaso had begun to unload the satchels of roubles, stacking them neatly in the gutter. The horse was dead. Vaso was inside the back of the car, filling it almost completely. Kantor leaned his bicycle against the wall and peered in.

Vaso looked back over his shoulder.

'They were waiting for us,' he said. His huge blue eyes peered into Kantor's face as if from deep under water. 'Inside the bank. They knew we were coming.'

'Yes.'

Kantor looked away a fraction too late. In some odd instant of rapport, some unprotected momentary honesty, there was a flash of communication between the giant and the man which neither had intended. Kantor saw the start of it in the giant's huge eyes and the changed way he held his massive shoulders.

'You,' said Vaso. 'It was you that told them.' He began to pull himself backwards out of the strong-car.

'Vaso,' said Kantor quietly, 'wait. It's not how you think.'

But even as he spoke, Kantor had already taken the grenade from his pocket and shoved it hard into the crevice between the thighs of the giant.

Three pounds of explosive filler encased in a sphere of brittle iron.

The release lever of a standard grenade is held in place by a pin. Once the pin is removed, only the grip of the bomber prevents the lever from springing open, firing the primer and igniting the fuse, which detonates the main charge with a ten second delay. But when Kantor thrust the grenade between Vaso's legs, it was squeezed tight. The lever couldn't spring open.

Vaso, alarmed but uncertain what had happened, hastily tried to back out. Kantor retreated until he was pressed against the wall of the building behind him, watching the giant reversing into the light. At the last moment, the bomb dropped free, rolled forward into the vehicle, and exploded. The force of it struck Kantor like his father's fist used to. It cracked his skull backwards against the wall and the world slipped sideways. When it righted itself, the remains of Vaso were on the ground in front of him. The giant's head, as big as a coal bucket, was smouldering. There was no skin on his face, but his lidless eyes still had life in them. He looked up mutely at Kantor and the big gap of his mouth moved slightly.

Kantor reached inside his coat for the revolver tucked in his belt. He brought it out, showed it to the giant, and fired two shots into his head.

5

*T*he light of the broken moons, circling one another in their slow, wobbling dance, floods the forest. Archangel dominates the empty landscape, a thousand feet high, like a solitary hill. The huge slopes of his body have accumulated a thick covering of snow. When he struggles to move, he dislodges avalanches and rumbling slides of ice, but he cannot shift himself. His body is irredeemably stuck, the lower part of it plunged many more hundreds of feet deep into the heart-rock and permanently fused there by the heat of his fall. The blast of his impact burned the trees flat for miles around, but new trees are growing through the ashes. Fresh snowfall carpets the floor of the shallow crater ten miles wide whose centre is him.

Call him Archangel, though it's not his name, he has none. He is what he is. But call him Archangel. It is ... appropriate. The duration of his existence unfolds from everlasting to everlasting, measured by the lifespan of all the stars.

At least, that was how it seemed, until, in one impossible moment, the shadow fell across him. Now he's as you see him, caught, unable to escape, stuck hard in the planetary crust, at the bottom of the uncertainty well. He cannot adjust his density. He cannot extrude any part of himself by even a few inches. He cannot move at all. Only his perceptions can travel, and even that only within the limits of this one trivial, cramped, poisoned and shadowed planet. He is bound in a straitened prison, scarcely larger than his own self.

And he's afraid of dying.

He examines his fear carefully. Pain and surprise are its flanking attendants, but it is the fear that intrigues him. So this is what fear is like. It could be useful. If he is to live.

His attentive gaze, vast and cool and inhuman, moves restlessly across the surface of the planet, sifting through the teeming profusion of minds that populates it. So many minds. He opens them up, first one and then another, looking for what he needs. And he draws his plans.

6

Lom took the overnight steamer down the Yannis and reached the rail terminus at Yislovsk just after dawn the next day. There was an hour to wait for the Mirgorod train. The waiting room was crammed with fresh conscripts for the southern front, crop-haired and boisterous, so he bought a bag of pirogi and settled on a bench outside, sheltered from the blustering sleet. He shivered inside his heavy black woollen cloak, his feet numb, the pirogi warm in his hands. Stevedores, sacking tied round their shoulders against the rain, were unloading barges. Passengers wandered across the wet quay, picking their way across the rails, squeezing between trucks and wagons. A crane arm swept the sky, the grind of its winch engine competing against the sound of the rain and the wash of the river against the quayside. The first warning bell rang. Fifteen minutes to departure. On a whim, Lom went across to the telegraph office and wired ahead to Raku Vishnik, hoping to save himself the cost of a room in Mirgorod.

The train was a twelve-foot-gauge monster, the locomotive as high as a house. The *Admiral Grebencho*, in the purple livery of the Edelfeld Sparre line. Three cylinders, double Chapkyl blastpipe, sleek, rounded, backswept prow, pulling thirty carriages. The *Admiral* could make a hundred and fifty versts an hour on the straight, but they travelled with meticulous slowness, stopping at every halt and crossing place, sliding across vast flat country.

Krasnoyarsk. Novorossiysk. Volynovsk. Elgen. Magaden.

Lom had spent an entire week's salary on a first-class compartment. He travelled in solitude, in a slow blur of daylight and darkness. His only company was a framed photograph of the Novozhd and two posters: CITIZEN! WHOM ARE YOU WITH? and COME TO LAKE TSYRKHAL! THE WATER IS WARM!

The unchanging landscape of birch forest made all movement seem an illusion. Time grew thickened and lazy, measured out in the glasses of tea the provodnik brought from the samovar at the end of the corridor. Lom watched the trees and slept, stretched out on the green leather upholstery. Five days of enforced inactivity ... the trundling of iron wheels and the slow passage of trees and earth and sky ... rest in motion ...

The birches bored him. They were unimpressive: widely-spaced chalk marks. Nothing like the forest east of Podchornok. That was proper forest. Dark. Mossy. Thick. He'd lived all his life in its shadow. Podchornok was the last town before the forest began: from Durnovo-Burliuk Street you could see the low hills of the tree edge. The measureless forest. No one knew how big it was, or what – if anything – lay beyond it. Normally, Lom tried not to think about the forest too much – it was addictive, it consumed the hours – but now, with nothing else to do, he imagined what it would be like to walk there, smelling the damp earth, digging his fingers into layers of mouldering leaves and rotting, mushroomy fallen wood. Swimming in the white lakes. Great wolves and giant elk moving through splashes of sunlight.

The Vlast mounted periodic incursions into the trees. Artel followed artel into the woods, only to find themselves caught in impenetrable thickets of thorn, their horses floundering up to their bellies in mud. River expeditions drifted through tangled shadow, feeling themselves shrinking, diminishing, losing significance as the world grew silent and strange. Aircraft flew over an illimitable carpet of trees flecked with the glint of rivers and lakes. The silence of the forest remained undisturbed.

Karka. Lapotev. Narymsk. Kaunats. Vorkutagorsk.

Having no money for the restaurant car, Lom carried with him a supply of bread and white crumbly cheese. Bored of this eventually, he got off the train at Chelyagorsk, where they had a two-hour stop, and spent a few kopeks on some mushrooms and dried fish and a newspaper. There was a wooden hut at the end of the platform. A sign said EXHIBITION OF PRESERVED ZOOMORPHS – 5 KOPEKS. A pale girl in a knitted headscarf was sitting on a flimsy chair by the door. She was shivering. Her eyes watery with the cold.

'Is it good?' he said. 'The exhibition. Is it worth seeing?'

The girl shrugged. 'I guess. It's five kopeks.'

'Do you get many visitors?'

'No. Do you want to go in? It's five kopeks.'

He gave her the money. She put it in her pocket carefully.

The hut was unheated and dim and filled with dusty stuffed animals: some drab wildfowl, a pair of scrawny wolves, a cringing bear. Feeble specimens compared to the forest beasts of his imagination. And there was a female mammoth, extracted from permafrost to the north. She had been mounted exactly as she was found, sitting back on her haunches, one forefoot set on the ground, as if she had fallen into a bog and was trying to climb out. Her hair was reddish, rough, worn thin in patches, and she squinted at Lom with mean, resentful eyes, small and black and glittering like sloes. Yellowing tusks arched up in supplication towards the pitch ceiling. For the rest of the journey she came to him in his dreams.

One incident broke the limpid surface of the long, slow journey. In the next compartment to Lom's an old man – clouded eyes, a thick spade of a beard combed with a central parting – was travelling with his wife and a dark-haired girl of six or so. Lom heard him through the partition, coughing, grumbling, swearing at his wife for letting the cold air in.

There was a commotion as the train was coming into Tuga. Lom found the wife in the corridor, wailing in dry-eyed distress, surrounded by guards and curious passengers. The girl was watching, silent and wary in the background. It turned out the old man had run from the compartment in his slippers, rushed down the length of the carriage and pushed open the door onto the small ledge at the end, just as the train was slowing. He'd fallen between the cars, and was dead.

Lom watched them bring a stretcher to carry off his shrunken old body. Blood was leaking from his mouth. The wife and child and all their baggage followed him off the train.

As Lom turned to go back to his compartment, a gendarme grabbed him by the arm.

'You,' he said. 'You.'

'What do you want?'

'What do you know about the man who died?'

'Nothing. Why?'

'You were watching.'

'So was everyone.'

'But not like you. Where are you from?'

'Podchornok. I joined the train at Yislovsk. But—'

The gendarme was standing too close, looking up into Lom's face. He thrust his hand forward, almost jabbing it into Lom's midriff.

'Papers. Your papers.'

'What papers?'

'Papers. Passport. Permission to travel. Certification of funds. Certification of sound health and freedom from infestation. *Papers.*'

'There was no time,' said Lom. 'And I don't need papers.'

'Everyone needs papers. If you've got no papers, you're coming with me. Unless—' The gendarme pushed his face up closer to Lom's. 'Unless you've got a big fat purse.'

'Fuck you,' said Lom quietly, and turned away.

The gendarme grabbed his shoulder and spun him round. 'You're coming with me. Now. Bastard.'

'You're talking to a senior investigator in the third department of the political police. You don't call me bastard. You call me sir.'

For a moment the gendarme hesitated; but only for a moment.

'I don't care if you're the fucking Novozhd himself. If you've got no papers, you're mine.'

'Like I said, I don't need papers.' Lom took off his cap to let the man see the irremovable seal, the small dark coin of angel flesh embedded in the bone of his forehead like a blank third eye. 'I have this. This is better.'

On the fifth day the birch trees thinned out, separated now by long tracts of flat and treeless waste, black mud under dirty melting snow, and on the sixth morning the train emerged abruptly into a flat watery landscape. Lakes. Rivers. Marshland. Low, misty cloud. And sometimes a glint of harder grey on the skyline that was the sea. Stops became more frequent, though the towns were still small. Rain trickled down the windowpane in small droplets. A large, stumpy, dark red mass appeared on the horizon. It looked like an enormous rock. The Ouspenskaya Torso.

Then, suddenly, without warning, the train was high above the landscape and he was looking down on houses: ramshackle wooden structures with pig yards and cabbage rows; yellow tenements; streets and traffic; the pewter glint of canals and basins. They were on the Bivorg Viaduct, hopping from island to island, closing on the Litenskaya. The rain gave everything a vivid, polished sheen of wetness. Lom felt a nameless stirring of excitement. Arrival. New things coming. The capital. Mirgorod.

7

Josef Kantor had a tiny office on the Ring Wharf, an unmarked doorway at the top of an iron staircase among mazy yards and warehouses, tucked away behind bales, vats, crates, barrels and carboys. It reeked of coal and tar and the spice and citrus smells of imported foodstuffs. There was room for a desk, a shelf for books and a small grate for a fire. Kantor had a portable printing press hidden under a blanket, and here he produced the leaflets he distributed along the wharves.

Every day, he walked among the steam-cranes and the rail trucks, the hammering, the waves of heat and showers of sparks, the supervising engineers with their oilskin notebooks, the collective industry of men. He watched them work on the naked, propped bodies of ships in dry dock and the towering frames of new ships rising. Day by day, immense steel vessels took shape out of chaos, bigger and stronger and more numerous than any before them. *Speed. Power. Control. This is a new thing*, thought Kantor, and wrote it in his leaflets. *This is the future. It requires new ways of thinking: new philosophy, new morality, a new kind of person. All that is old and useless must be destroyed to make way.*

Kantor slept on his desk, and on cold nights he built a wall of books around himself to keep out draughts. He'd learned the books trick at Vig, in a moss-caulked hut he shared with three families and the psychopath Vereschak. On winter nights in Vig, your breath iced on your beard while you slept. Vig had taught Kantor the luxury of being alone. He had learned the prisoner's way of withdrawing inside himself and entering a private inner space the persecutors couldn't reach.

Kantor's life had been shaped by the dialectic of fear and killing:

if you feared something, you studied it, learned all you could from it, and then you killed it. And when you encountered a stronger thing to fear, you did it again. And again. And so you grew stronger, until the fear you caused was greater than the fear you felt. It was his secret satisfaction that he had begun to learn this great lesson even before he was born. He was an aphex twin: a shrivelled, dead little brother had flushed out after him with the placenta and spilled across his mother's childbed sheet. Before he even saw the light of day, he had killed and consumed his rival.

His father, the great Avril, hero of the Birzel Rebellion, had made his living packing herrings in ice. Avril Kantor loathed his work and himself for doing it. He came home stinking of brandy and fish. Josef heard the crude voice and saw his mother kicked across the floor. Felt the ice-hardened fist in his own face. He didn't hate his father. He admired his power to hurt and the fear he caused. Only later, when he understood more, did he come to despise him for hurting only weakness, and sacrificing his own life in a grand futile gesture of revolt.

The Kantor family name earned Josef a place at the Bergh Academy. He was safe then from the fish wharves that ruined his father, but Bergh's was a dull and vicious place. The masters spied on the students, searched their possessions, encouraged them to inform on each other. They beat him for reading prohibited books and lending them to the other boys. He studied the masters' methods and hated the unimaginative, unproductive purposes to which they put their dominance. On the day he'd grown strong enough, he went to find the mathematics master alone, gripped him by the hair and cracked his face down onto his desk.

'If I'm beaten again, I will come back and kill you,' he whispered.

The teacher wore the bruise for a week. Josef was left alone at Bergh's after that. He grew tall and lean and hard and full of energy. The first work the Lezarye Committee gave him was distributing leaflets to the railway workers. He was caught and badly beaten, while Anastas Bragin, Director of Railways, looked on, his face flushed rosy pink. Three nights later Josef Kantor climbed into Bragin's garden with a revolver. It was late spring, and the sun was still in the sky though it was after eleven at night. The air in the garden was heavy with warmth and bees and lime blossom perfume. Bragin was working by lamplight at a desk in a downstairs room with the window open. Kantor trampled fragrant earth to get to the casement. He leaned in.

'Remember me?'

He waited a moment before he shot Bragin in the head. He was seventeen then.

The police picked him up after the Birzel Rebellion. They wanted to know where his father was hiding. They broke his hands and burned his feet and kicked his balls until they swelled like lemons, but he didn't tell them. They gave up in the end, and left him alone, and then he told them where his father was. The police forced him to watch his father's execution. That was a pleasure. The icing on the cake. He was stronger than them all.

There was a rapping at the door of the office. Kantor swore under his breath. It would be Vitt. Vitt and the others. Vitt had said they would come, though Kantor had forbidden it. He hated people coming here. It compromised his security and invaded his private space. But they'd insisted. Vitt had insisted.

The knocking came again, louder. Determined. They were early.

'Come in then, Vitt,' he called. 'Come in if you must. This had better be good.'

They crowded into the room. Kantor surveyed their faces. So many useless, vapid, calf-like faces. He'd told them to lie low, that was the proper way, but after a few days they'd got restless and suspicious. Too frightened of the police, not frightened enough of him. Vitt had dragged them along.

'The banknotes are marked,' Vitt was saying. 'They've published the serial numbers in the *Gazetta*.'

'The roubles go to the Government of Exile Within,' said Kantor. 'You know that. Their problem, not ours.'

'They were waiting for us,' said Lidia. 'They knew we were coming. They knew when and where.'

'And we lost Akaki,' said Vitt. 'Akaki was a good comrade.'

'Deaths are inevitable,' said Kantor. 'Nothing worth having is got without great price. Be under no illusion, there is worse to come. Storms and torrents of blood will mark the struggle to end oppression. Are you ready for that?'

They stared at him sourly.

'But—'

'Is this a challenge, Vitt?'

Vitt stopped dead, his mouth open, the colour draining from his face.

'No. No, Josef. I'm only trying to …'

Kantor looked around the room, fixing every one of them, one by one, with hard eyes. It was time.

'Yes,' he said. 'They were waiting for us, and you know what that means, but none of you has the courage to say it. One of us is an informer.'

'Maybe it was—' Stefania began.

"Let's go over it again,' said Kantor. 'You, Vitt, threw a bomb that did not explode, and then you, Vitt, ran like a hare.'

'I—'

'I smell you, Vitt. I smell treachery and lies. I smell the policeman's coin in your pocket.'

'No, Josef! Maybe it was Petrov? Where is he today? Has anyone seen him? It was *Petrov*!'

'I smell you Vitt, and I'm never wrong. See how you crumble? This is how you crawled and squealed when the police took you. This is the traitor's courage. This is the disease within.'

Kantor took the revolver from his pocket and held it out in the palm of his hand.

'Who will do what must be done? Must I do it myself?'

'Let me,' said Lidia. 'Please, Josef.'

Kantor gave her the revolver. Vitt upped from his seat and made for the door, but Stefania stuck out her foot. He fell on his face with a sickening slap.

'Oh, no,' he murmured. 'No.'

Lidia put the muzzle to the back of his head.

'Bye, fat boy.'

She fired.

'I wish,' said Kantor, wiping a splash of something warm from his face, 'I wish you'd done that outside.'

No sooner had Kantor closed the door behind them than he felt the attention of Archangel enter the room. The furniture crackled with fear.

'No,' said Kantor quietly. 'No. I don't want this. Not again.'

Archangel opened him up and came into him. Ripping his way

inside his head. Occupying everything. Taking everything. Leaving nowhere private. His voice was a roaring whisper.

They fear you, it said. *But whom do you fear?*

Kantor lay on his back on the floor, his limbs in rigid spasm, his eyes fixed open, staring at nothing. Archangel's alien voice in his mind was a voice of shining darkness, absolutely intelligent, absolutely cold, like a midnight polar sky, clean of cloud and shot through with veins of starlight.

Whom do you fear?

Archangel allowed him a little room, in which to formulate his response.

'You,' whispered Kantor. 'I fear you.'

You are wasting time. Think like a master, not like a slave. Are you listening to me?

Kantor tried to speak but the muscles of his face were stuck and his throat was blocked with the inert flesh of his tongue. He tried to drive out the thing that had torn open his mind and come inside. It was like trying to push his face through raw and solid rock.

There must be fear. There must be war. There must be death. Everything is weak. Everything will shake. I will put this world in your hands. And others. Many many others. And you will do one thing for me. One small thing.

Destroy the Pollandore.

8

The platforms of the Wieland Station, enclosed under a wide, arching canopy of girders and glass, roared. Shrill whistles, shouts, venting steam, the clank of shunting iron. The smell of hot oil, hot metal, stale air, dust. The roof glass, smeared with sooty rain, cast a dull grey light. Train lamps burned yellow. Raucous announcements of arrivals and departures punctuated the 'Tarsis Overture' on the tannoy.

Lom collected his valise from the luggage car himself. It was heavy and awkward, a hefty oblong box of brown leather, three brass-buckled belts and a brass clasp. He'd dressed for the cold, his cap pulled down tight down over his forehead, but the station was hot and close. By the time he'd hauled his baggage down the wide, shallow marble staircase into the concourse, he was hot with sweat and the din was ringing in his ears.

He let the crowds part around him. Guards and porters shouted destinations. Droshki and kareta drivers called for business. A giant lumbered past, hauling a trolley. Everyone was in uniform, not just the railway workers, drivers, policemen and militia, but students and door-keepers and concierges and clerks, wet nurses and governesses, messengers and mail carriers. The only ones not in uniform were the wealthy travelling families, the labourers in their greasy jackets and the civil servants in their dark woollen coats. Lom scanned the passing faces for Raku Vishnik. There was no sign of him. Maybe the telegram hadn't reached him. Maybe, after fourteen – no, fifteen – years, Vishnik had read it and thrown it away.

'Clear the way there!'

Lom stepped aside. A ragged column of soldiers was shuffling through the central hall and up the shallow stairs to the platforms. The smell of the front came with them: they stank of herring, tobacco, wet earth, mildew, lice and rust. The wounded came at the rear. The *broken-faced,* they were called. It was a literal term. Men with pieces of their heads missing. One had lost a chunk out of the side of his skull, taking the ear with it. Another had no jaw: nothing but a raw mess between his upper teeth and his neck.

At the end of the column two privates were struggling to support a third, walking between them, or not walking but continually falling forward. Trembling violently from head to foot, as if he was doing some kind of mad dance, as if his clothes were infested with foul biting bugs. He had a gentle face, bookish, the face of a librarian or a schoolteacher. Apart from his eyes. He was staring at something. Staring backwards in time to a fixed, permanent event, an endless loop of repetition beyond which he could neither see nor move.

Lom felt his stomach tighten. The war was far away. You tried not to think about it.

The veterans went on and up, absorbed back into the crowd. Lom looked at his watch. It had stopped. He'd forgotten to wind it on the train. The station clock stood on a pillar in the centre of the concourse, its minute hand five feet long and creeping with perceptible jolts around its huge yellowed face. Ten past six. He was late for Krogh.

9

It took Lom an hour to get across the city to the Lodka. When he got there, he leaned on the balustrade of the Yekaterinsky Bridge, looking up at it. The momentous building, a great dark slab, rose and bellied outwards like the prow of a vast stationary ship against the dark purple sky, the swollen, luminous stars, the windblown accumulating rags of cloud. Rain was in the air. Nightfall smelled of the city and sea, obscuring colour and detail, simplifying form. He felt the presence of the angel stone embedded in the walls. It called to the seal in his head, and the seal stirred in response.

The Lodka stood on an island, the Yekatarina Canal passing along one side, the Mir on the other. Six hundred yards long, a hundred and twenty yards high, it enclosed ten million cubic yards of air and a thousand miles of intricately interlocking offices, corridors and stairways, the cerebral cortex of a stone brain. It was said the Lodka had been built so huge and so hastily that when it was finished, many of the rooms could not be reached at all. Passageways ran from nowhere to nowhere. Stairwells without stairs. Exitless labyrinths. From high windows you could look down on entrance-less vacant courtyards, the innermost secrets of the Vlast. Amber lights burned in a thousand windows. Behind each window, ministers and civil servants, clerks and archivists and secret policemen were working late. In one of those rooms Under Secretary Krogh of the Ministry of Vlast Security was waiting for him. Lom crossed the bridge and went up the steps to the entrance.

Krogh's private secretary was sitting in the outer office. Files were stacked in deep neat piles on his desk, each one tagged with handwritten slips of paper and coloured labels. He looked up without interest when Lom came in.

'You're late, Investigator. The Under Secretary is a busy man.'

'Then you'd better get me in there straight away.'

'Your appointment was for six.'

'I was sent for. I've come.'

'Pavel?' A voice called from the inner office. 'Is that Lom? Bring the man in here.'

Krogh's office was large and empty. Krogh himself was sitting at the far end, behind a plain wooden table in an eight-sided bay with uncurtained windows on every side. In daylight he would have had an almost circular view across the city, but now the windows were black and only reflected Krogh from eight different angles. The flesh of his face was soft and pouched, but his eyes under heavy half-closed lids were bright with calculation.

Lom waited while Krogh examined him. His head hurt where the angel seal was set into it. A dull, thudding ache: the tympanation of an inward drum.

'You're either an idiot or a courageous man, Lom. Which is it?'

'You didn't bring me all the way to Mirgorod so you could call me an idiot.'

'Yough!' Krogh made an extraordinary, high-pitched sound. It was laughter. He picked up a folder that lay in front of him on the desk.

'This is the file on you, Lom. I've been reading it. You were one of Savinkov's. One doesn't meet many. And you have talent. But still only an Investigator. No promotion for, what is it, ten years?'

'Eleven.'

'And three applications for transfer to Mirgorod. All rejected.'

'No reason was given. Not to me.'

'Your superiors in Podchornok refer to attitudinal problems. Is that right?'

Lom shrugged.

'There's room for men like you, Investigator. Opportunities. That's why you're here. Would you do something for me? A very particular task?'

'I'd need to know what it was.'

The ache in Lom's head was stronger now. Shafts of pain at the place where the angel stone was cut in. Patches of brightness and colour disturbed his vision. None of the angles in the room was right.

'You're cautious,' said Krogh. 'Good. Caution is a good quality. In some circumstances. But we have reached an impasse, Investigator. I can't tell you anything until I know that you're on my side. And mine only. Only mine, Lom.' Krogh spread his hands. Slender hands, slender fingers, pale soft dry skin. 'So. Where do we go from here? How should we proceed?'

'I've had a long journey, Under Secretary. I've been on a train for the last six days. I'm tired and my head hurts. Unless you brought me all this way just so you could not tell me anything, you'd better say what this is all about.'

Krogh exhaled. A faint subsiding sigh.

'I'm beginning to see why your people find you difficult. Nevertheless, you have a point. Does the name Josef Kantor mean anything to you?'

'No.'

Krogh sank back, his head resting against the red leather chair-back.

'Josef Kantor,' he began, 'was nineteen at the time of the Birzel Rebellion. His father was a ringleader: he was executed by firing squad. Here at the Lodka. Josef Kantor himself was also involved. He spoke at the siege of the Armoury, and drafted the so-called Birzel Declaration. Do you know the Declaration, Lom?'

'I've heard of it.'

'It's fine work. Very fine. You should know it by heart. One should know one's adversary.'

Krogh leaned forward in his chair.

'*We believe,*' he began in a louder, clearer voice. '*We believe that the Vlast of One Truth has no right in Lezarye, never had any right in Lezarye, and never can have any right in Lezarye. The rule of the Vlast is forever condemned as a usurpation of the justified government of the people of Lezarye, and a crime against human progress of the Other Rational Peoples. We stand ready to die in the affirmation of this truth. We hereby proclaim the Nation of Lezarye as a sovereign independent people, and we pledge our lives and the lives of our comrades-in-arms to the cause of its freedom, its continued development, and its proper exaltation among the free nations of the continent.*'

Krogh paused. Lom said nothing.

'Fine words, Lom. Fine words. Kantor was arrested, of course, but – and I cannot explain this, the file is obscure – his sentence was limited to three years' internal exile. To your province, Investigator. And there he might have sat out his sentence in relative comfort and returned to the city, but he did not. He made persistent attempts to escape. He killed a guard. So. For this he got twenty years at the penal colony of Vig. Such a sentence is rarely completed, but Kantor survived. And then, a year ago, for reasons again obscure, he was simply released. He came back to Mirgorod and disappeared from our view. And also about a year ago,' Krogh continued, 'we began to notice a new kind of terror in Mirgorod. Of course we have our share of anarchists. Nihilists. Nationalists. There is always a certain irreducible level of outrage. But this was a new sense of purpose. Daring. Destructiveness. Cruelty. There was a new leader, that was obvious. There were names, many names: eventually we discovered they all led to one person.'

'Kantor.'

'Indeed. This month alone he has been responsible for the assassination of Commissioner Halonen, a mutiny at the Goll Dockyard and only last week an attack on the Bank of Foreign Commerce. They got thirty million roubles. Can you imagine what a man like Kantor is capable of, with thirty million roubles?'

'I read about the bank raid in the papers,' said Lom. 'But why are you telling me this?'

Krogh waved the question away.

'I've been after Kantor for a year,' he continued. 'A year, Lom! But I never get anywhere near him. Why?'

'I guess he has friends,' said Lom.

Krogh looked at him narrowly. A glint of appreciation.

'Exactly. Yes. You are sharp. Good. I cannot get near Kantor because he is protected. By people in the Vlast – people here, in the Lodka itself.'

'OK,' said Lom. 'But why? Why would they do that?'

'I guess,' said Krogh, 'that some understanding of the international situation percolates even as far as Podchornok? You realise, for instance, that we are losing the war with the Archipelago?'

'I only know what's in the newspapers. Seva was retaken last week.'

'And lost again the next day. The Vlast cannot sustain this war for another year. Our financial position is weak. The troops are refusing to fight. The Archipelago has proposed terms for a negotiated peace, and ...' Krogh broke off. 'This is confidential, Lom, you understand that?'

'Of course.'

'The Novozhd is preparing to open negotiations. Peace with honour, Lom. An end to the war.'

'I see.'

'Yet there are … elements in Mirgorod – in the Vlast – elements who find the concept of negotiation unacceptable. There are those who say there should be no end to the war at all. Ever. Warfare waged for unlimited ends! A battle waged not against people like ourselves but against the contrary principle. The great enemy.'

'But—'

'These people are mad, Lom. Their aims are absurd. Absolute and total war is an absurd aim. Exhaustion and death. Ruin for the winners as much as the losers. You see this, you're an intelligent man. The Novozhd understands it, though many around him do not. The negotiations must not fail. There will not be a second chance.'

'Surely these are matters for diplomats. I don't see—'

'The Novozhd's enemies are determined to bring him down. They will use any means possible, and they will work with anyone – anyone – who can further their cause.'

'Including Josef Kantor?'

'Precisely. Kantor is a one-man war zone, Lom. His campaigns cause chaos. He sows fear and distrust. People lose faith. The Novozhd is failing to control him. I am failing. We are all failing. The security services grow restless. People are already whispering against us. Against the Novozhd. Which of course means opportunity for those who wish to replace him. The time is ripening for a coup. This is not accidental. There is a plan. There is a plot.'

'I see.'

'Kantor is the lynchpin, Lom. Kantor is king terrorist. The main man. Bring him down and it all comes down. Bring him down and the Novozhd is safe.'

'I understand. But … why are you telling me all this? What's it got to do with me?'

'I want you to find Kantor, Lom. Find him for me.'

'But … why me? I know nothing of Mirgorod, I know nobody here. You have the whole police department … the gendarmerie … the third section … the militia …'

'These disqualifications are what make you the one I need. The only one I must have. Why have I got your file, Lom? What brought you to my notice?'

'I have no idea.'

Krogh picked up the folder again.

'There are enough complaints against you in here,' he said, 'to have you exiled to Vig yourself tomorrow. Serious charges. I see through all that, of course. Innuendo and fabrication. I see what motivates them. You're not afraid to make enemies, and they hate that. That's why I need you, Lom. The Novozhd's enemies are all around me. I know they are there, but I don't know who they are. I can trust nobody. *Nobody*. But *you*, Investigator. Consider ...' Krogh ticked off the points on his fingers. 'A good detective. Loyal to the Vlast. Incorrupt. Independent. Courageous. Probably not stupid. You know nobody in the city. Nobody knows you. You see where I'm going?'

'Well, yes but—'

'You will probably fail, of course,' said Krogh. 'But you might just succeed. You find Kantor, Lom, and you stop him. By any means possible. Any at all. And more – you find out who's running him. Somebody here is pulling Kantor's strings. Find out who it is. You find out what the bastards are up to, Lom, and when you do, you tell *me*. *Only* me. Got that?'

'Yes.'

'You'll be on your own,' said Krogh. 'You'll have no help. No help at all. This is your chance, Lom, if you can take it.'

10

Josef Kantor was reading at his desk. The window of his room stood open. He liked how night sharpened the sounds and perfumes of the wharf. He liked to let it into his room. There was no need for the lamp: arc lights and glare and spark-showers flickered across the pages of his book. There was no better light to read by. The light of men working. The light of the future.

He heard the quiet footfall on wet paving, the footsteps climbing the iron staircase. One person alone. A woman, probably. He was waiting in the shadow just outside his door when she reached the top, his hand in his jacket pocket nursing his revolver. He made sure she was in the light and he was not.

'Who are you?' he said.

'I'm sorry,' she said. 'I meant never to come here, but I had no choice.'

A group of men just off their shift were coming up the alleyway, talking loudly. Curious glances at the woman on the staircase. She wasn't the kind you saw in the yard at night. They would remember. Kantor didn't need that sort of attention.

'Go in,' said Kantor.

He followed her into the room and lit the lamp. He saw that she was young – early twenties, maybe – and thin. Her hands were rough and red from manual work, her wrists bony against the dark fabric of her sleeves, but her face was filled with life and intelligence. Thick black hair, cut short around her neck, fell across her brow, curled and wet. It had been raining earlier, though now it was not. Her coat was made of thin, poor stuff, little use against the weather, but, fresh and flushed from the cold, she brought an outside air into the room, not the industry and commerce of the shipyards but fresh earth and wet leaves. She met his gaze without hesitation: her eyes looking into his were bright and dark.

There was something about her. It unsettled him. She was not familiar, exactly, but there was a quality in her that he almost recognised, though he couldn't place it.

'You've made a mistake,' he said. 'Wrong person. Wrong place.'

'No. You're Josef Kantor.'

Kantor didn't like his name spoken by strangers.

'I've told you. You're mistaken,' he said. 'You're confusing me with someone else.'

'Please,' she said. 'This is important. I'm not going until we've talked. You owe me that.'

She took off her coat, draped it over the back of a chair and sat down. Underneath the coat she was wearing a knitted cardigan of dark green wool. Severe simplicity. Her throat was bare and her breasts were small inside the cardigan. Kantor was curious.

'Since you refuse to leave,' he said, 'you'd better tell me who you are.'

'I'm your daughter.'

Kantor looked at her blankly. He was, for once, surprised. Genuinely surprised.

'I have no daughter,' he said.

'Yes, you do. It's me. I am Maroussia Shaumian.'

It took Kantor a moment to adjust. He had not expected this, but he should have: of course he should. He had known there was a child, the Shaumian woman's child, the child of the frightened woman he'd married all those years ago, before Vig, before everything. That affair had been a young man's mistake: but, he realised now, it had been a far worse mistake to let them live. He studied the young woman more carefully.

'So,' he said at last. 'You are that girl. How did you find me?'

'Lakoba Petrov told me where you were.'

'Petrov? The painter? You should choose better friends than Petrov.'

'I haven't come here to talk about my friends.'

'No?' said Kantor. 'So what is this? A family talk? I am not interested in families.'

Maroussia put her hand in the pocket of her cardigan and brought out a small object cupped in her hand. She held it out to him. It was a

36

thing like a nest, a rough ball made of twigs and leaves, fine bones and dried berries held together with blobs of yellowish wax and knotted grass. 'I want you to tell me what this is,' she said.

Kantor took it from her. As soon as he held it, everything in the room was the wrong size, too big and too small at the same time, the angles dizzy, the floor dropping away precipitously at his feet. The smell of resinous trees and damp earth was strong in the air. The forest presence. Kantor hadn't felt it for more than twenty years. He had forgotten how much he hated it. He swallowed back the feeling of sickness that rose in his throat and moved to throw the disgusting thing onto the fire.

'Don't!' Maroussia snatched it back from him. 'Do you know what it is?' she said. 'Do you know what it means?'

'No,' he said. 'No. Where did you get it?'

'Mother has them. I stole this one from her. I don't know where she gets them from, but I think they come from the forest, or have something to do with it.'

'Nothing useful ever came from that muddy rainy chaos world under the trees. That's all just shit. So much shit.'

'I think these things are important.'

'Then ask your mother what they are.'

'She can't tell me.'

'Why not?'

'Do you really not know? Don't you know anything about us at all? You could have found out, if you wanted to.'

It was true. He could have taken steps. He had considered it while he was at Vig, after the Shaumian woman had left him, and later. But it would have meant asking questions. He had told himself it was better to share with no one the knowledge of their existence. That had been stupid. He could see that, now. Now, it was obvious.

'My mother isn't well,' the girl was saying. 'She hasn't been well for years. In her mind, I mean. She's always frightened. She thinks bad things are happening and she is being watched. Followed. She never goes out, and she's always muttering about the trees. For months now these things have been appearing in our room. I've seen three or four, but I think there have been more. She pulls them apart and throws them away. She won't say anything about them, but she keeps talking about something that happened in Vig. Something that happened when she went into the trees.'

'You should forget about all that,' said Kantor. 'Forget the past. Detach yourself. Forget this nostalgia for the old muddy places. Trolls and witches in the woods. These stories aren't meant to be believed. Their time is finished.'

'They're not stories. They're real. And they're here. They're in the city. The city was built on top of it, but the old world is still here.' She held up the little ball of twigs and stuff. 'These are real. These are important. They're from the forest, and my mother is meant to understand something, but she doesn't. Something happened to her in the forest long ago. And ...' She hesitated. 'She keeps talking about the Pollandore. I need you to tell me what happened then. I need you to tell me about the Pollandore.'

For the second time, Kantor was genuinely startled. Whatever he had expected her to say, it was not that.

'The Pollandore?' he said. 'It doesn't exist.'

'I don't believe that. I need you to tell me about it. And tell me about my mother. What happened to her in the forest? It's all connected. I need to understand it. I have a right to know. You're my father. You have to tell me.'

Kantor was tired of playing games. It was time to end this. End the pretence. Open her eyes. Peel back the lids. Make the child stare at some truth.

'I'm not your father,' he said.

She stared at him.

'What?' she said. 'What do you mean? Yes you are.'

'That's what your mother told you, apparently, but she lied. Of course she lied. She always lied. How could I be your father? She would not ... your mother would not ... She refused me ... For months. Before she became pregnant. She went into the trees. She kept going there. And then she abandoned me and ran back home to Mirgorod. You're not my child. I'm not your father. I couldn't be.'

There was raw shock in her face.

'I don't believe you,' she said. 'You're lying.'

But he saw that she did believe him.

'What does it matter, anyway?' he said. 'What difference does it make?'

'It matters,' she said. 'It matters to me.'

'Hoping for a cuddle from Daddy? Then ask your mother who he is. If you can get any sense out of the old bitch.'

The girl was staring at him. Her face was white and set hard. Blank like a mask. So be it. She would not look to him for help again.

'You bastard,' she said quietly. 'You bastard.'

'Technically, that's you. The forest whore's bastard daughter.'

'Fuck you.'

After she had gone Kantor extinguished the lamp again and sat for a long time, considering carefully. The girl's visit had stirred old memories. Vig. The forest edge. The Pollandore. He'd thought he had eradicated such things. Killed and forgotten them. But they were only repressed. And the repressed always returns. The girl had said that.

He should have done something about the Shaumian women long ago: that he had not done so revealed a weakness he hadn't known was in him, and such weakness was dangerous. More than that, the girl was a threat in her own right. She was rank with the forest, and surprisingly strong. She had caused him to show his weakness to her. He would have to do something: the necessity of that was clear at last. He must end it now. He was glad she had come. Laying bare weakness was the first step to becoming stronger. In the familiar dialectic of fear and killing, only the future mattered. Only the future was at stake.

11

Maroussia Shaumian walked out through the night din and confusion of the dockyard and on into nondescript streets of tenements and small warehouses. She was trembling. She needed to think, but she could not. There was too much. She walked. Wanting to be tired. Not wanting to go home. Scarcely noticing where she went.

There was rain in the air and more rain coming, a mass of dark low cloud building towards the east, but overhead there were gaps of clear blackness and stars. She didn't know what time it was. Late.

She came at last to the Stolypin Embankment: a row of globe lamps along the parapet, held up by bronze porpoises. Glistening cobbles under lamplight. Beyond the parapet, she felt more than saw the slow-moving Mir, sliding out into the Reach, barges and late water taxis still pushing against the black river. The long, punctuated reflections of their navigation lights trickled towards her, and the talk of the boat-men carried across the water, intimate and quiet. She couldn't make out the words: it felt like language from another country. A gendarme was observing her from his kiosk, but she ignored him and went to sit on a bench, watching the wide dark river, its flow, its weight, its still-ness in movement. She took the knotted nest of forest stuff out of her pocket and held it to her face, breathing in its strange earthy perfume. Filling her lungs.

And then it happened, as it sometimes did.

A tremble of movement crossed the black underside of the clouds, like wind across a pool, and the buildings of the night city prickled; the nap of the city rising, uneasy, anxious. Maroussia waited, listen-ing. Nothing more came. Nothing changed. The rain-freighted clouds settled into a new shape. And then, suddenly, the solidity of Mirgorod stone and iron broke open and slid away, vertiginously. The blackness and ripple of the water detached itself from the river and slipped upwards, filling the air, and everything changed. The night was thick with leaking possibilities. Soft evaporations. Fragments and intimations of other possible lives, drifting off the river and across the dirty pavements. Hopes, like moon-ghosts, leaking out of the streets.

The barges, swollen and heavy-perfumed, dipped their sterns and raised their bows, opening their mouths as if to speak, exhaling shining yellow. The porpoises threw their mist-swollen, corn-gold lamp-globes against the sky. The cobbles of the wharf opened their petals like peals of blue thunder. The stars were large and luminous night-blue fruit. And the gendarme in his kiosk was ten feet tall, spilling streams of perfume and darkshine from his face and skin and hair.

Everything dark shone with its own quiet radiance and nothing was anything except what it was. Maroussia felt the living profusion of it all, woven into bright constellations of awareness, spreading out across the city. She looked at her own hands. They were made of dark wet leaves. And then the clouds closed over the stars and it started to rain in big slow single drops, and Mirgorod settled in about her again, as it always did.

12

It was late when Lom got out of Krogh's office. The streets about the Lodka were deserted. Shuttered and lightless offices. The wind threw pellets of rain in his face. Water spurted from downpipes and spouts and overflowing gutters, splashing on the pavements. Occasionally a private kareta passed him, windows up, blinds drawn.

In his valise he had a folder of newspaper clippings – accounts of attacks and atrocities attributed to Kantor and his people, Krogh had said – and one photograph, old and poorly developed, of Kantor himself, taken almost twenty years ago, at the time of his transfer to Vig. And he had a mission. A real job to do. At last. Mirgorod spread out around him, rumbling quietly in the dark of rain and night. A million people, and somewhere among them Josef Kantor. And behind him, shadow people. Poison in the system. The ache in Lom's head had gone, but it had left him hungry. He needed something to eat. He needed a place to stay. He needed a way in. A starting point. He wished he'd asked Krogh about money.

In his pocket he had Raku Vishnik's address: an apartment somewhere on Big Side. He had a vague idea of where it was, somewhere to the north, beyond the curve of the River Mir. Not more than a couple of miles. He had no money for a hotel, and he didn't want to pay for a droshki ride, even if he could find one. He would go to Raku. Assuming he was still there. Lom buttoned his cloak to the neck and started to walk. A fresh deluge dashed against his face and trickled down his neck. A long black ZorKi Zavod armoured sedan purred past him, chauffeur-driven, darkened black windows, the rain glittering in its headlamp beams. White-walled tyres splashing through pools in the road. Lom hunched his shoulders and kept moving.

The hypnotic rhythm of walking. The sound of water against stone. As he walked, Lom thought about the city. Mirgorod. He'd never seen it before, but all his life he had lived with the idea of it. The great capital, the Founder's city, the heart of the Vlast. Even as a child, long before the idea of joining the police had taken shape, the dream of Mirgorod had taken root in his imagination. He remembered the moment. Memories rose out of the wet streets. He was back in Podchornok, at the Institute of Truth. Seven years old. Eight. It was another day of rain, but he was in the library, looking out. He liked the library: there were deep, tall windows, their sills wide enough to climb up onto and crouch there. Although it was grey daylight, he pulled the curtain shut and he was alone: on one side the heavy curtain, and on the other the windowpane, rain splattering against it and running in little floods down the outside of the glass. Beyond the window, the edge of the wood – not the forest, just an ordinary wood, rain-darkened, leafless under a low grey sky. And him, reading by rainlight.

He even remembered the book he had been reading. *The Life of our Founder: A Version for Children.* The chapter on the founding of Mirgorod. There was an illustration of the Founder on horseback, accompanied by his retinue on lesser horses. They had drawn to a halt on a low hummock surrounded by flat empty marshland, and the Founder had thrust his great sword upright into the bog.

'Here!' he said. 'Here shall our city stand.'

It was a famously preposterous location for a city. The ground was soft and marshy, scattered with low outcrops of rock like islands among the rough grass and reedy pools and soft, silken mud. No human settlement within two hundred versts. No road. No safe harbour. Nothing. Yet *here* the Founder had said, because he could see what all his counsellors and diplomats and soldiers could not. He could see the great River Mir reaching the ocean. He could see that the river was linked by deep inland lakes and other rivers and easy portages to the whole continent to the east. He could see that to the west lay great oceans. Only the Founder could see that this lonely place was not the back end of nowhere but a window on the world.

'We can't build a city in this awful place!' the Founder's retinue cried, splashing knee-deep in the mud, their horses struggling and stumbling.

'Yes,' the Founder had said. 'We can. We will.'

'Hey, you!'

Lom was passing a small shop of some kind, still open. A man came lurching out.

'Hey, come on. Drink with us.'

Lom ignored him.

'Wait. That's my cloak. Give it me, you bastard. You stole my cloak.'

Lom fingered his cosh. The length of hard rubber, sheathed with silk, rested in a specially tailored pocket in the sleeve of his shirt, near the wrist. He undid the small button that let it slip into his hand and turned.

'You'd better go back inside,' he said.

The man saw the weapon in his hand. Stared at him, swaying slightly.

'Ah, fuck you,' he said, and turned away.

Lom walked on, deeper into the city. Kantor's city. But his city too: he would make it so. He was the hunter, the good policeman, the unafraid. He passed a bar, but it was closed and dark. Its name written on the window in flaking gold paint. The Ouspensky Angel. When, in the last years of the Founder's reign, the first dying angel had fallen from the sky and crashed into the Ouspenskaya Marsh, it had been taken as a sign of acknowledgement and consecration. Over the centuries the stone of the angel's limbs had been used to furnish protection for the Lodka and other great buildings, and to make mudjhiks to garrison the city, but its torso had been left to lie where it still was, visible to all newcomers as they arrived in the city. The *Life of our Founder* had a picture of the falling angel and a simple sketch map of 'Mirgorod Today' showing the cobweb of streets and canals, the city like a dark spreading net. Lom remembered how he had stared at that map, and the picture of the falling angel, that time in the library. The strange, nameless longing the pictures had stirred in him. The sense of possibilities. Purposes. The adventures that life could hold.

And then Lom remembered...

... now, for the first time...

He had forgotten ... for a quarter of a century...

... when he was reading that book, looking at that picture, imagination stirring ... he remembered...

... the hand ripping aside the curtain from the library window

44

and the hate-filled face stuck into his, the sour breath, the cruel hand snatching the book from his hand, the voice screeching at him.

'Here you are, you vicious little bastard! Now you're caught, you evil piece of shit!'

The claw-hand grabbed him by the neck, fingernails gouging his skin, and hauled him out of the window seat. He fell hard, down onto the library floor.

Lom stopped in the middle of the street, pausing for breath, letting the rain run down his face. The memory of that moment had shocked him. He had put it away so deep. Forgotten it. A hurt from a different world, it meant nothing to the policeman he had become. Put it aside again, he told himself, think about it later. Maybe. Now, immediately, he needed to get out of this rain and night. He wondered if he was lost. There were no signs. No sense of direction in the empty streets. He had been stupid not to take a ride.

Rain skittered down alleyways, riding curls of wind. Rain slid across roof-slates and tumbled down sluices and drainpipes and slipped through grilles into storm drains. Rain assembled itself in ropes in gutters and drains, and collected itself in watchful, waiting puddles and cisterns. Rain saturated old wood and porous stone and bare earth. Rain-mirrors on the ground looked up into the face of the falling rain. The wind-twisted air was crowded with flocks of rain: rain-sparrows and rain-pigeons, crows of rain. Rain-rats ran across the pavement and rain-dogs lurked in the shadows. Every column and droplet, every pool and puddle and sluice and splash, every slick, every windblown spillage of water and air, was alive. The rain was watching him.

Ever since the builders first came, the rain had been trickling through the cracks and gaps in the carapace of the chitinous city, sliding under the tiles and lead of the roofs, slipping through the cracks between paving slabs and cobbles, pooling on the floors of cellars, insinuating itself into the foundations, soaking through to the earth beneath the streets. Every rainfall dissolved away an infinitesimal layer of Mirgorod stone, leached a trace of mineral salts from the mortar, wore the sharp edges imperceptibly smoother, rounded off the hard corners a little bit more, abraded fine grooves down the walls and buttresses. Fine jemmies and levers of rain slid between ashlar and coping. Little by little, century by century, the rain was washing the city away.

The rain trickled down Lom's face, tasting him. The rain traced the folds of his skin and huddled in the whorls of his ears. The rain splashed against the angel-stone tablet in his skull. The rain tasted angel, the rain smelled policeman, the rain trickled over the hard certainties of the Vlast and the law, stoppered up with angel meat. While Lom walked on, oblivious, absorbed in memories, the rain was nudging him ever further away from the peopled streets, towards the older, softer, rainier places.

Memory hit him like a fist in the belly.

How was it he'd forgotten her? Buried her so deep? Never thought of her? Never. Never. Not till now.

She had dragged him down corridors and up stairways to the Provost's room.

'Here you are!' she shrieked at the Provost. 'I told you! He is corrupted. He is foul. He should never have been admitted. I said so.'

There was a fire of logs burning in the room. She had taken something of his, something important, and gone across to the fire and put it carefully in.

'*No!*' he'd cried. '*No!*'

He'd thrown himself across the room and scrabbled at the burning logs. He remembered her, screeching like an animal, punching him across the back of the head, and … Something had happened. What? He couldn't remember There was a door he couldn't open, and something terrible was behind it. What had he done? He felt the shame and guilt, the permanent stain it had left, but he didn't … he couldn't … he had no recollection of what it was.

But he did know that the next day they had cut into the front of his head and placed the sliver of angel stone there, and that had made him good.

Lom rested his valise and wiped the rain from his face. He was passing through narrow defiles between once-grand buildings that were tenements now, propped up with flimsy accretions and lean-tos. Gulfs of night and rain opened between the few street lamps. Mirgorod had withdrawn indoors for the night, and his sodden clothes had tightened around him, becoming a warm mould, wrapping him in his own body heat. The sound of the rain seemed to seal him in. Dark alley-mouths gaped. Broken wooden fences barricaded gaps of waste ground. Small doorways cut into high brick walls.

He might have seen something, some shape slipping back out of the lamplight. He felt again for the smooth weight of the cosh in his sleeve.

He came to the margin of an endless cobbled square, the far side all but invisible behind the night rain. There was a lamp in the middle of the square, and some kind of kiosk beneath it. Two horses standing against the rain, their heads turned to watch him. And a covered droshki waiting. He walked fast towards it, but he hadn't crossed half the wide open space when the driver appeared from the kiosk and climbed up into the seat.

'Hey!' shouted Lom. 'Hey! Wait!'

Lom started to run, awkwardly, hampered by a horizontal gust of sleet in his face, and his rain-heavy cloak, and his luggage. It was hopeless. The droshki drove away into the dark on the farther side.

'Shit.'

The rain fell harder and colder. It stung his face and pressed down on him like a heavy weight. Wind-spun rain gathered itself in front of him and resolved itself into a thing of rain, a man of rain – no – a woman of rain – taller than human, a hardened column of rain and air.

And then the rain attacked him.

Lom spun around and tried to hide from it, but when he turned it was in front of him still. It lashed out and struck him. A fist of rain. A hard smash of wind off the sea, filled with rain. A stinging punch of rain in his face. He fell to the ground, tasting rain and blood in his mouth. The rain became a great foot and stamped on him, driving him face-down into the stone, driving the breath from him.

He was going to die.

He hauled himself to his feet and tried to run, slipping and stumbling across the cobbles. But he was running towards his enemy, not away. The rain surrounded him, and met him wherever he turned, dashing pebbles and nails of rain into his face. He held up his hand to protect his eyes. The droshki kiosk was in front of him. He stumbled towards it and pulled at the door. It wouldn't open. He tried to barge into it with his shoulder, but the rain kicked his legs out from under him and he fell on his back, cracking his head. When the world came back into focus he was looking up into the face of the rain. His nose and mouth began to fill. He gasped for air and his throat filled with rain and blood. Rain kneeled on his ribs, driving the breath out of him. He was drowning in rain.

Something broke open inside him then. He felt it burst, as if a chain-link had snapped apart. A lock broken open. Some containment that had been placed inside him long ago had come undone.

He remembered.

He remembered what he had done that afternoon in the Provost's room.

He remembered how he had gathered up all the air in the room and thrown it at her, and she had screamed and fallen. He remembered the pop that had followed when the air recoiled, refilling the temporary vacuum. He remembered the Provost's papers flying about the room, the air filled with a cloud of hot embers and ash and smoke from the fire, the chair falling sideways, the picture crashing down from the wall. He remembered what he had done, and he remembered what it had felt like, and he remembered how he hadn't known, not then and not later, how he had done it.

He tried to do it again. *Now!*

He reached out into the squalling, churning air and gathered up a ball of wind and rain. He tried to compact it as hard as he could. And he flung it at the figure of rain.

It was a feeble effort. It made no difference. Nothing could. He was going to die.

The thing of rain was standing over him, suddenly gentler now. Lom felt the attention of its regard, appraising him, wondering. A hand of rain reached down and touched his forehead gently. Fingertips of rain stroked the shard of angel stone cut into his head. He seemed to feel a brush of kindness. Pity.

Poor boy, it seemed to say. *Poor boy.*

The thing of rain dissolved into rain, and he was alone.

He picked himself up off the ground, bruised, exhausted, soaked. He needed to get inside. Out of the rain. And quickly.

13

It was almost midnight when Lom arrived, bruised, soaked and chilled to the core, at Vishnik's address. Pelican Quay turned out to be a canal-side row of houses, one among many such streets on Big Side, north of the river. The rain had paused. A damp and cave-like smell on the air and the heavy iron bollards and railings on the far side of the road betrayed the invisible night presence of the canal. Number 231 was a tall flat-fronted tenement squeezed between neighbouring buildings, the kind of house once built for grander families but partitioned now into many smaller, boxy apartments for the accommodation of tailors, locksmiths, cooks, civil servants of the lower ranks. Many pairs of eyes were observing him: although it was late, the dvorniks were out, each hunched in a folding chair under his own dim lamp in the lea of his domain. The dvornik of number 231 was drinking from a tin mug. His face gleamed moonily. His cheeks had collapsed to form loose jowls at the level of his chin.

'Raku Vishnik,' said Lom. 'Apartment 4.'

'No visitors after nine.'

'He's expecting me. He keeps late hours.'

The dvornik looked at Lom's scruffy valise. His sodden clothes. His dripping hair.

'No overnights.'

Lom fumbled in his pocket. 'I appreciate the inconvenience. Twenty kopeks should cover it'

'A hundred.'

'Fifty.'

The dvornik grunted and held out a hand. He wore thick fingerless woollen gloves: even in the sparse lamplight they looked in need of a wash.

'Second floor. Don't use the lift and don't turn on the lights.'

The stairs were dark and narrow, lit by street light falling through high small windows. Stale cooking smells. A thin carpet in the corridor. The bell of Number 4 sounded faint and toy-like, like it was made of tin.

Lom waited. Nobody came. He stood there, dripping, in the dark passageway. He realised that he was shaking, and not just with cold and hunger and the fatigue of carrying his case through the empty streets. The taste of the living rain was in his mouth. The smell of it on his face and his clothes. He had heard of such things, the possibilities of them. You didn't live at the edge of the forest without being sometimes aware of the wakefulness of the wilder things: the life of the wind, the sentience of the watchful trees. The memory of the damp, living earth. But not in Mirgorod. He had not expected to find such things here: Mirgorod was the capital of solidity, the Founder's Strength, the Vlast of the One Truth.

He needed Vishnik to open up. He rang the bell again. Nothing happened. Maybe Vishnik was already in bed. He rang twice more and banged on the door. There was a muffled sound of movement within, and it opened slowly. A pale, drawn face appeared. Dark eyes, blank and unfocused, looked into his own.

'Yes?'

'Raku?'

The dark eyes looked past him to see if someone else was in the corridor. Vishnik was dressed to go out: an unbuttoned gabardine draped from his shoulders, a small overnight bag in his hand. He was taller than Lom remembered, but the same glossy fringe of black hair flopped across his forehead. The same dark brown eyes behind rimless circular lenses. But the eyes were glassy with fear.

'Raku. It's me. Vissarion.'

Vishnik's hands were balled in tight fists. He was shaking with anger. 'Fuck,' he said. 'Fuck. What the fuck are you doing.'

'Raku? Didn't you get my telegram?'

'No I didn't get any fucking telegram. Shit. What are you doing? I don't see you for half a lifetime and then you're hammering on my door in the middle of the night.'

'I wired. Five, six days ago. I said I would be coming. I said it would be late.'

Vishnik held up his bag. Shoved it at Lom. 'See this? What's this? Clothes. Bread. So I don't have to go in my pyjamas when they come. How did you get in here anyway? The dvornik shouldn't have—'

'I gave him fifty kopeks.'

'Fifty? That's not enough. He has to report visitors to the police.'

'What's he going to report? I am the police.'

'Some fucking policeman. Look at you. Dripping on the carpet.' He looked at Lom's valise. 'You got dry things in there?'

'Yes.'

'Wait.'

Vishnik disappeared. Rain seeped out of Lom's hair and down his face. Rain dripped from the hem of his cloak and spilled from his trouser cuffs.

Vishnik came back carrying a towel.

'There's a bathroom at the end of the corridor.'

'Thanks.'

'Yeah. Shit. Well, get dry.'

Lom tucked the towel under his arm, picked up the valise and started down the corridor.

'Oh, and Vissarion.'

'Yes?'

'It's good to see you. I thought I never would.'

Fifteen minutes later Lom was sitting on Vishnik's couch with a glass of aquavit. There was food on the table. Solyanka with cabbage and lamb. Thick black bread. He leaned back and let the room wrap itself around him. Heavy velvet curtains of a faded brick colour hung across the window. Electric table lamps cast warm shadows. A paraffin heater burned in the corner. Bookshelves everywhere. More books piled on the floor and stacked on the desk. And on a side table, carefully arranged, a strange assemblage of objects: a broken red lacquer tea caddy; a grey and blue mocha mug with no handle; a china dog; a piece of stained wood, stuck through with bent and rusting nails; broken shards of ceramic and glass; a feather; a bowl of damp black earth. Odd things that could have been picked up in the street. Set out like the ritual items of a shaman of the city.

But it was the collection of art that made the room extraordinary. In plain dark frames, squeezed in between the bookshelves, hung in corners and high up near the ceiling, the paintings were like none Lom had seen before. They were of shapes and colours only. Sharp angular quadrilaterals of red and blue and green, smashed against a background of dark grey that reminded him of city buildings at twilight, but falling. Collapsing. Black lines slashed across jumbled boxes of faded terracotta. Thick, unfinished scrapes of paint – midnight blue – burnt earth – colours of rain and steel. Mad, childish clouds and curlicues and watery rivers of purple and gold and acidic, medicinal green. As Lom looked he began to see that there were objects in them – sometimes – or at least suggestions of objects. Bits and pieces of objects. A bicycle wheel. A bottle-cork. A bridge reflected in a river, exploded by sunset. A horse. The spout of a jug. Sometimes there was writing – typographic fragments, scrawled vowels, tumbled alphabets, but never a whole word.

Vishnik was sitting at the desk nursing a glass. He looked thin, almost gaunt. His hands were still trembling, but his eyes were warmer now, filled with the dark familiar ardour, missing nothing. It was the same clear serious face, illuminated with an intense intelligence. There was something wild and sad there, which hadn't been there when they were young. But this was Raku Vishnik still.

'You gave me a fright, my friend,' Vishnik was saying. 'I was ungracious. I apologise. I spend too much time alone these days. One becomes a little strung out, shall we say.'

'What about your work?' said Lom. 'The university.'

Lom had gone with Vishnik to see him onto the boat, the day he left Podchornok for Mirgorod. Vishnik was going to study history at the university, while Lom was to stay in Podchornok and join the police. Vishnik had dressed flamboyantly then. Wide-brimmed hats and bright bow ties. The fringe longer and floppier. They'd exchanged letters full of cleverness and joking and the futures that awaited them both in their chosen professions. Vishnik was going to become a professor, and he had. But the correspondence dwindled over the years and finally stopped. Lom had settled into the routine of the Provinciate Investigations Department.

'The university?' said Vishnik. 'Ah. Now they, they are fuckers. They don't let me teach any more. My background became known.

My family. Someone let the bloody secret out. Aristocrats. Nobility. *Former persons*. Some of the darling students complained. And then of course there was the matter of my connections with the artists. The poets. The cabaret clubs. I used to write about all that. Did you know? Of course not. Criticism. Essays. Journalism. The magazines could never afford to pay me, but sometimes they gave me a painting.' He waved clumsily at the walls. 'But that's all over. It appears I became an embarrassment to the authorities. The hardliners run the show now, on matters of aesthetics like everything else. These pictures are degenerate. Fuck. They closed the galleries and the magazines. The painters are forbidden to paint. They still do, of course. But it's dangerous now. And I am silenced. Forbidden to publish. Forbidden to teach.'

He emptied his glass and filled it again. Poured one for Lom.

'That's tough,' said Lom. 'I'm sorry.'

'I was lucky. Not completely cast into the outermost darkness. I think some of my fucker colleagues did have the grace to feel a little ashamed. They have made me the official historian of Mirgorod, no less. In that august capacity I sit here before you now. There's even a small stipend. I can afford to eat. Not that anyone wants a history of Mirgorod. I doubt it will ever be published. I'm not spoken to, Vissarion, not any more. And I'm watched. I'm on the list. My time will come. I thought it had, when you came banging at the fucking door. They always come in the night. Never the fucking morning. Never fucking lunchtime. Always the fucking middle of the fucking night.'

'I'm sorry. I didn't think—'

'Fuck it. Fuck them, Vissarion. Tell me that you haven't changed.'

'I haven't changed.'

Vishnik raised his glass.

'To friendship, then. Welcome to Mirgorod.'

Archangel studies his planet, his prison, his cage. He assembles the fragments, the minds he has sifted and collected, and comes to understand it better. The planet has a history, and history is a voice. The people of the planet serve their history as photons serve light, as agglomerations of massiveness serve gravity. The voice of history is a dark force.

And Archangel comes to understand that the voice of this planet's history is broken. In the future that is coming and has already been, the future that re-imagines its own antecedence, a catastrophic mistake is made.

53

And he learns something else, which is a danger to him. Cruel and immediate danger. Somewhere nearby there still exists a well of old possibility. The vestige of an older voice. The lost story that can no longer speak is tucked away somewhere in silent obscurity. It does not exist in the world but it is there. Beside it. In potential. A seed dormant. A storage cell untapped.

And this encapsulation of failed futurity is ripening, and breaking, and beginning to leak. It is beginning to wonder: maybe what is done will yet be undone?

Archangel roars.

'THAT CANNOT BE ALLOWED TO HAPPEN!'

Archangel must return to the space between the stars, which is his birthright and his stolen domain. Not merely return to it, but seize it, consume it, become it. Become the stars. Become the galaxies. Better than before. He sees how it can be done. This planet can do it for him.

'Let the voice of the planet be my voice. Let the voice of its history be mine. A fear voice. A power voice. Make the voice of history be my larynx. Retell the broken story in a new way. Make the expression of the world unfolding be the planning, cunning, conscious, necessary, unequivocal expression of me, Archangel, voice of the future, voice of the world, speaking through all people always everywhere.

'Let the people take flight from this one planet to all the stars, all the galaxies, all the intergalactic immensities everywhere always – and let them speak me! A billion billion billion people always everywhere in glittering crimson ships across the black-red-gold recurving energy-mass-time seething scattered shouting me. The perpetual unfolding flowering of the voice of me. All filled with the angelness of me.

'So it will be.

'But first, for this to happen, that fatal other source – the fracturing egg of other possibilities that impossibly continues – must be destroyed.'

This then is the first syllable of the first word of the first phrase of the first sentence of the voice of Archangel.

'DESTROY THE POLLANDORE!'

14

L om woke early the next morning. As the first greying of the dawn filtered through the gaps in the curtains in Vishnik's study, he lay on his back on the couch, turning the question of Kantor over in his mind. How to find him. How to even begin. Krogh had told him he would have no help, no resources, no official support from the immense intelligence machine of the Vlast. Krogh's private secretary would fix him an access pass for the Lodka, and an office there, under cover of some suitably bland pretext to account for his presence, but that was all.

He had read Krogh's file of clippings on Kantor late into the night. It was an accumulation of robberies, bombings, assassinations. There was no pattern that he could find. The targets were indiscriminate, the victims seemingly random: for every senior official of the Vlast or prominent soldier or policeman killed, there were dozens of innocent passers-by caught in appalling eruptions of destructive violence. There was no clear purpose: responsibility for each attack was claimed by a different obscure and transient dissident grouping, or by none, and none of the perpetrators had ever been taken alive.

He had spent a long time staring at the photograph of the young Josef Kantor that Krogh had given him. He tried to find in that face the lineaments of calculating cruelty that could drive such a murderous campaign. But it was just a face: long and narrow, scarred by the pockmarks of some childhood illness, but handsome. Kantor looked into the camera with dark, interested eyes from under a thick mop of dark hair, uncombed. Although the picture must have been taken in an interrogation cell, there was the hint of a smile in the turn of his wide mouth. This was a confident, intelligent young man, a man you could like, even admire. A man you would want to like you.

Of course, the photograph had been taken two decades ago. Twenty years at Vig would change anyone. Because of this man, an atmosphere of anxiety and distrust and lurking incipient panic had settled on Mirgorod. Lom felt it in the newspaper accounts. He noticed also how in recent months, alongside the official condemnation of the atrocities, there was a growing tendency to criticise the authorities for failing to stem the tide of fear. And this criticism, though it was couched in carefully imprecise language, was increasingly directed towards the Novozhd himself. The hints were there: the Novozhd was old, he was weak, he was indecisive. Was he not, perhaps, even deliberately letting the terror campaign continue, as a means to shore up his own failing authority? These attacks on the Novozhd were always anonymous, but – in the light of Krogh's accusations – Lom felt he could sense the presence of an organising, directing hand behind them.

One thing was certain. Lying on the couch thinking about it would get him nowhere. He pushed his blanket aside. He needed to move. He needed to start.

In Vishnik's bathroom the plumbing groaned and and clanked and delivered a trickle of cold brown water into the basin. Lom shaved with his old cut-throat razor. Through a small high casement came the sounds of Mirgorod beginning its day: the rumble of an early tramcar, the klaxon of a canal boat, the clatter of grilles and shutters opening. He breathed the city air seeping in through the window, mingling diesel fumes, coal-smoke, canal water and wet pavements with the scent of his shaving soap. The city prickled and trembled with energy, humming at a frequency just too low to be audible, but tangible enough to put him on edge.

He dried his face on the threadbare corner of a towel and went back down the corridor to Vishnik's room. Vishnik was sitting at his desk. He had the newspaper spread open – the *Mirgorod Lamp* – but he was looking out of the window, sipping from the blue and white mug, his left hand fidgeting restlessly, tapping a jumpy rhythm with slender fingers.

Lom had laid his uniform out ready on the couch: black serge, silver epaulettes, buttons of polished antler. He pulled on his boots, also black, shined, smelling richly of leather. He stripped and cleaned his gun. It was a beautiful thing, a black-handled top-break Zorn service side-arm: .455 black powder cartridges in half-moon clips; overall length, 11.25 inches; weight 2.5 pounds unloaded; muzzle velocity, 620 feet per second; effective range, fifty yards. Like most things in Podchornok, it was thirty years out of date, but he liked it. He worked carefully and with a certain simple pleasure. Vishnik watched him.

'Vissarion?' he said at last. 'Just what the fuck is it that you are doing here, my friend?'

'Ever hear of Josef Kantor?'

'Kantor? Of course. That was a name to remember, once. A Lezarye intellectual, a polemicist, young, but he had a following. He knew how to please a crowd. A fine way with words. But he was silenced decades ago. Exiled. I assume he's dead now.'

'He isn't dead. He's in Mirgorod.' Lom told Vishnik what Krogh had said.

'There've always been sects and cabals in the Lodka,' said Vishnik. 'The White Sea Group. Opus Omnium Consummationis. The Iron Guard. Bagrationites. Gruodists. Some wanting to liberalise, some to purify. But why are you telling me this?'

'You asked.'

'Sure, but—'

'I need help, Raku. Someone who knows the city, because I don't. And I need somewhere to stay.'

'That's a lot to ask. A very fuck of a lot to ask, if I may say so.'

Lom reassembled the gun, put it in the shoulder holster and strapped it on.

'I know.'

'So,' said Vishnik eventually. 'OK. Sure. You are my friend. So why not. Where do you start?'

'I don't know. Somewhere. Anywhere. Find a thread and pull on it. See where it takes me.'

He picked up Vishnik's paper. It was that morning's edition. Idly he turned the pages, skimming the headlines.

GUNBOATS POUND SUMBER. ARCHIPELAGO ADVANCE STALLED OUTSIDE HANSIG. BACKGAMMON CHAMPION ASSASSINATED: LEZARYE SEPARATISTS CLAIM RESPONSIBILITY: LODKA PROMISES REPRISALS.

TRAITORS MUST BE SMASHED BY FORCE! the editorial thundered.

> The verminous souks and ghettos where these vile criminals are nurtured must be cleaned up once and for all. Our leaders have been too soft for too long. Yes, we are a civilised folk, but these evil elements trample on our forbearance and spit on our decency. They are a disease, but we know the cure. We applaud the recent speech by Commander Lavrentina Chazia at the Armoury Parade Ground. Hers is the attitude our capital needs more of. We urge …

Like Krogh's file of clippings, the paper was filled with traces of terror, of war, of Kantor and the nameless forces working against the Novozhd. But there was other stuff as well. Other voices, other threads, omitted from Krogh's selective collection.

An inside spread described new plans for massive monumental ossuaries to hold the corpses of the fallen soldiers, sailors and airmen of the Archipelago War: 'On the rocky coast of the Cetic Ocean there will grow up grandiose structures … Massive towers stretching high in the eastern plains will rise as symbols of the subduing of the chaotic forces of the outcast islands through the disciplined might of the Vlast.' They were to be called Castles of the Dead. There were artist's impressions, with tiny, lost-looking stick families wandering in the grounds, inserted for scale.

MOTHER MURDERS LITTLE ONES. A lawyer, Afonka Voscovec, had suffocated her three children with a pillow and hanged herself. She'd left a note. 'The floors keep opening,' she'd written. 'Will no one stop it?'

Lom was about to throw the paper aside when he noticed a small piece in the social columns. A photograph of an officer of the militia shaking hands with the Commissioner of the Mirgorod Bank of Foreign Commerce. 'Major Artyom Safran, whose brave action defended the bank in Levrovskaya Square against a frontal terrorist assault, receives the congratulations of a grateful Olland Nett. Major Safran is a mudjhik handler.' Levrovskaya Square was, according to Krogh, Kantor's most recent atrocity. If this Major Safran had been there, that meant he had seen Kantor or at least his people. It was a connection.

Lom studied the photograph carefully. The legs and belly of the mudjhik could just be made out in shadow behind the Major's head. And in his head, in the middle of his brow, was a seal of angel flesh, the twin of Lom's own.

He stood up. It was time to go.

He took the lift down to the exit. The dvornik was in his cubbyhole. If the uniform impressed him, he didn't let it show. There was a cork board behind his head, with notices pinned to it: the address of the local advice bureau, details of winter relief collections, blackout exercises, changes to social insurance, a soap rationing scheme.

'Yes? What?'

'I'm going to be staying here for a few days. With Professor Vishnik.' Lom showed his warrant card. The dvornik glanced at it. Still not impressed. 'My presence here is authorised. By me. The Professor is under my protection. You are to report nothing. To no one. The fact that I am here – when I come – when I go – that's up to me. You notice nothing. You say nothing. You remember nothing.'

The dvornik had his tin cup in his hand. He took a sip from it and shrugged. Barely. Perhaps.

'Understand?'

'Whatever you say, General.'

15

Lom found the office Krogh's private secretary had fixed for him at the Lodka. One office among thousands, a windowless box on an upper floor among storerooms, filing rooms, cleaning cupboards, boilers. It took him half an hour wandering corridors and stairways to track it down. There was a freshly typed card in the slot by the door handle: INVESTIGATOR V Y LOM. PODCHORNOK OBLAST. PROVINCIAL LIAISON REVIEW SECRETARIAT.

In the office there was a chair, a coat rack, a desk. Lom went through the drawers: stationery lint; a lidless, dried-up bottle of ink. Somebody had hung a placard on the wall.

Citizens! Let us all march faster
Through what remains of our days!
You might forget the fruitful summers
When the wombs of the mothers swelled
But you'll never forget the Vlast you hungered and bled for
When enemies gathered and winter came.

He laid out his notepad and sharpened his pencils. He gave the room two more minutes. It felt about a minute and a half too long. *Do something. Do anything. Make a start.*

Lom left the office behind and set himself adrift in the mazy corridors of the Lodka. There were floor plans posted at intersections, but they were no help: the room numbers and abbreviations in small print, amended in manuscript, bore little relationship to the labels on doors and stairwells. He knew that the place he wanted would be *down*. Such places were always near the root of things. Tucked away. Like death always was.

He came into a more crowded part of the building: secretaries in groups, carrying folders of letters, talking; porters wheeling trolleys of files and loose papers; policemen, uniformed and not; civil servants arguing quota and precedent, trading the currency of acronyms. The placards on committee room doors were syllables in a mysterious language. Hints and signs.

CENTGEN.

COMPOLIT.

GENCOM.

INTPOP.

POLITCENT.

He half expected someone to stop him and ask him what he was doing there, so he prepared a line about the urgent need to improve liaison with the Eastern Provinciates. He found he had a lot to say on the subject: it was an issue that actually did need attention. He began to think of improvements that could be made to the committee structure and lines of command. Perhaps he should write a memo for Krogh? He started to take out his notebook to write some thoughts down.

What the fuck am I doing?

He put the notebook back in his pocket. The Lodka was getting under his skin already, releasing the inner bureaucrat. Doors, wedged open, showed glimpses of desks, bowed concentrating heads, pencils poised over lists. Empty conference tables, waiting. The quiet music of distant telephone bells and typewriter clatter. The smell of polished linoleum and paper dust. Stairs and corridors without end. The Lodka cruised on the surface of the city like an immense ship, and like a ship it had no relationship with the depths over which it sailed, except to trawl for what lived there.

He let these thoughts drift on, preoccupying the surface layers of his mind, while the Lodka carried him forward, floating him through its labyrinths on a current you could only perceive if you didn't look for it too hard. This was a technique that always worked for him in office buildings: they were alive and efficient, and knew where you needed to go; if you trusted them and kept an open mind, they took you there.

On the ground floor he followed his nose, tracing the faint scent of sweetness and corruption down a narrow stairwell to its source. A sign on the swing doors said MORTUARY. And beyond the door, a corridor floored with linoleum, brick-red to hide the stains. The attendant led him to an elevator and closed the metal grille with a crash. They descended.

'You're in luck. We burn them after a week. You're just in time. They'll be a bit ripe though, your friends.'

The attendant gave him a cigarette. It wasn't because of the dead – they weren't so bad – it was the sickly sweetness of the formaldehyde, the sting of disinfectant in your lungs. That was worse. The harshness of the smoke took Lom by surprise: it scoured his throat and clenched his lungs. He coughed.

'You going to puke?'

'Let's get on with it.'

The Cold Room was tiled in white and lit to a bright, gleaming harshness. Their breath flowered ghosts on the stark air.

'Anyone else been to see them?'

The attendant ran his finger down a column in a book on the desk by the door.

'Nope. Wait here.'

Lom dragged hard on the cigarette. Two, three, four times. It burned too quickly. A precarious length of ash built up, its core still burning. The cardboard was too thick.

The attendant came back pushing a steel trolley. A mounded shape lay on it, muffled by a thin, stained sheet.

'You'll have to help me with the giant,' he said. 'They're heavy bastards.'

Lom let his cigarette drop half-finished on the white-tiled floor, ground it out with his boot, and followed the attendant between heavy rubber curtains into the refrigerator room. Many bodies on trolleys were parked along the walls, but there was no mistaking the bulk of the giant on its flatbed truck. Lom took the head end and pushed.

'You can leave me,' he said when they were done. 'I'll let you know when I'm finished.'

Sheets pulled back, the two cadavers lay side by side, like father and son. What was he hoping to find? A clue. That's what detectives did. Dead bodies told you things. But these bodies were simply dead. Very.

He checked the record sheets. The man had been identified as Akaki

Serov. 'Male. Hair red. Dyed brown. Age app. 30–35.' The face had matched a photograph on a file somewhere: there was a serial number, a reference to the Gaukh Archive. The face on the trolley was unmarked apart from a few small cuts and puncture wounds, but nobody would recognise it now. The flesh was discoloured and collapsed, the lips withdrawn from the teeth in the speechless grin of death. The torso was swollen tight like a balloon. The blood had drained down to settle in his back and his buttocks. A wound in his neck was lipped with darkened, crusted ooze – a nether mouth, also speechless. There were no legs.

Lom hesitated. He should take fingerprints. He should prise the jaws open to check for secreted ... what? ... secrets. In life, he could have worked with him. Serov dyed his hair: he was vain, then. Or try-ing to change his appearance. Human things. Things Lom could use. Serov might have felt a grudge against someone. Taken a bribe. Feared pain. Something. That was how Lom interrogated people: seducing, cajoling, threatening, building a relationship, coming to a conclusion. But the dead told you nothing. It was their defining characteristic, the only thing that remained to them: being dead.

He turned to the other corpse.

The giant had been found by the empty strong-car. There was no name for this one, no photograph to match his face on a file, not much face left to match. His flesh was hard and waxy white. Bloodless. Between his legs, where his lower belly and genitals and thighs should have been, there was nothing. A gouged-out hollow. Ragged. Burned. Vacant. The front of his body was seared and puckered. Flash burns. And there was a gunshot wound in his face that had exploded the back of his skull.

The bullet was a puzzle. He must have been dying already – the en-tire middle part of his body blown to mush – but someone had taken the trouble to shoot him anyway. Why? A kindness? A silencing? A message for others to read? There were too many stories here. Too many possibilities were the same as none. They took you nowhere. The dead, being dead, were of no help.

Lom put his hands in his pockets, trying to warm them. The cold of the room was beginning to numb his face. He needed to get out of there.

Do something else. Pull on another thread.

16

Maroussia Shaumian climbed the familiar stairs to Lakoba Petrov's studio and pushed open the door. Grey daylight flooded the sparse, airy room. Gusts of rain clattered against the high north-facing windows. She knew the room well: its wide bleak intensity, its smell of paint and turpentine, uneaten food and stale clothing. She used to come here often.

Petrov had been working on Maroussia's portrait, on and off, for months. He was painting her nude, in reds and purples and shadowed blacks of savage energy, her body twisted away from the viewer in a violent torsion that revealed the side of one breast under the angle of her arm. A vase of flowers was falling across a tablecloth behind her, as if she had kicked the table in the violence of the movement that hid her face. Petrov had said it was an important work: he was using it to feel his way out of conventional, scholastic painting of the female form, searching for a way to express directly his dispassionate desire and his indifference to the suffocating conventions of love and beauty. But he had lost interest in painting her since he'd got involved with Kantor. He had changed, becoming distant and distracted. Maroussia had come there less and less, and finally not at all.

She had met Petrov at the Crimson Marmot Club, where she had started going in the evenings after work. She had gravitated towards the place because she felt obscurely hungry for new things. New ways of looking at the world. But the Marmot's had been disappointing: a refuge where artists and intellectuals gathered to drink and boast instead of work. Everyone there had tried to get inside her skirts. Everyone except Petrov.

'What do you want from this place?' he had asked her.

'I don't know,' she'd said seriously. 'Something. Anything. So long as it's new.'

'Is anything ever really new?' Petrov had said. 'The present only exists by reference to the past.' That was the kind of thing you said at the Marmot's.

Maroussia had frowned. 'The past is a better place than the present,' she said. 'The present is a bad place, and the future will be bad too. Unless we can start again. Unless we can find a new way.'

Petrov had laughed. 'You won't find anything new at the Marmot's. Look at them. Every one a poser, every one a hypocrite, every one a mountebank. They talk about the revolution of the modern, but all they're after is fame and money.'

'Are you like that?'

'Not me, no,' Petrov had said. 'I mean what I say. One must begin the revolution with oneself. One must remove all barriers and inhibitions within oneself first, before one can do work that is truly new. One must do all the things it is possible to do. Experience the extremes of life. I don't care what other people think about me: I want to shock *myself*.'

She had liked him then. She hadn't seen then the danger of his words, the literal seriousness of his desire to shock and destroy. They had met again at the Marmot's, several times, talking earnestly. Maroussia had wondered if they might become lovers, but it hadn't happened.

And now, he scarcely looked up when she came in. The studio was bitterly cold, but he was working regardless, in fingerless mittens and a woollen cap, the paint-spattered table at his side set out with jars and tubes and brushes. He painted hastily, with bold, rapid strokes, stabbing away at the immense canvas that towered above him.

'Lakoba?' said Maroussia. 'I wanted to ask you something.'

Petrov didn't look round.

'I will not paint you today,' he said. 'That picture is finished. They're all finished. This is the last.'

'What are you doing?' she said. 'Can I look?'

He shrugged indifferently and turned away to busy himself at the table. Maroussia stared up at the picture he had made. It was colossal, like nothing he had made before. At the centre of it was a giant, laid out on a black road, apparently dead, his head and feet bare, surrounded by six lighted candles, each set in a golden candlestick and burning with a circle of orange light. A woman in a white skirt – suffering humanity – threw up her arms in grief. Dark, crooked buildings, roofed with blood, loomed around them. Behind the roofs and taller than all the buildings a man walked past, playing a violin. He seemed to be dancing. The lurid yellow-green sky streamed with black clouds.

'This is good,' she said. 'Really good. It's different. Has it got a title?'

'It's Vaso,' he said. '*The Death of the Giant Vaso, Killed in a Bank Raid.*' But he didn't look round. Her presence seemed to irritate him.

'Lakoba?' she said. 'I want to ask you something. It's important. I want to find Raku Vishnik.'

Petrov didn't reply.

'Raku Vishnik,' she said again. 'I need to see him. He didn't come to the Marmot's last night.' She paused, but he didn't answer. 'Lakoba?'

'What?' he said at last. 'What did you say?'

'Raku Vishnik. I need to find him. Quickly. I need his address.'

'Vishnik?' said Petrov vaguely. 'You won't find him during the daytime. He wanders. He always wanders. He's on the streets somewhere. He walks.'

'Where then? He wasn't at the Marmot's.'

'No. I haven't seen him there. Not for weeks.'

'Where then?'

'You must go to his apartment. At night. Late at night. Very late.'

'What's his address?'

'What?'

'Vishnik's address? Where does he live?'

'Oh,' said Petrov vaguely. 'He's on Pelican Quay. I don't know the house. Ask the dvorniks.'

For the first time he turned to look at her. Maroussia was shocked by how different he looked. He had changed so much in the weeks that had passed. His hair was wild and matted, but his face was illuminated with a strange intense distracted clarity. His pupils were dilated, wide and dark. He was staring avidly at the world, and at her, but he wasn't seeing what was there: he was looking *through* her, beyond her, towards some future only he could see. And he stank. Now that he was close to her, she was aware that his breath was bad, his clothes smelled of sourness and sweat.

'Something's wrong, Lakoba,' she said. 'What is it?'

Petrov opened his mouth to speak again but did not. He looked as if his brain was fizzing with images … ideas … words … purpose – what he must do. But he could say nothing. He tried, but he could not.

'Lakoba?' Maroussia said again. 'What's wrong?'

'Go,' he said at last. 'You have to go now.'

'Why? What's happened?'

'You have to go.'

'Why?'

'I want you to go. I won't need you again. Don't come here again. Not any more.'

'What are you talking about? What have I done?'

'Everything is finished now. I am leaving it behind.'

'Where are you going?'

'There is no more to say. No more words. Words are finished now. Personal things don't matter any more: my personal life is dead, and soon my body will also die.'

'Lakoba—'

'Go. Just go.'

Maroussia left Petrov to his empty room and the immense dead giant. Once again, for the second time in as many days, she walked away from a door that had closed against her. She didn't want to go to work, and she didn't want to go home – not home to her mother, trapped in quiet shadow, waiting silently, too terrified to leave the room, too terrified to look out of the window, too terrified to open the cupboards, too terrified to move at all – she didn't want to go anywhere. But it was still early, not even afternoon: she would have to wait till night to go to Raku Vishnik's. Vishnik might tell her about the Pollandore. He was the historian. He might know.

17

That morning, after Lom left, Raku Vishnik went to the Apraksin Bazaar. He liked the Apraksin, with its garish din and aromatic confusion, its large arcades and sagging balconies of shopfronts and stalls, the central atrium of market sellers and coffee kiosks. Areas of the Apraksin were reserved for different trades: silver, spices, rugs, clothes, shoes, umbrellas, papers and inks, rope and cordage, parts for motors and appliances, tools, chairs, tobacco, marble slabs. Poppy. One distant corner for stolen goods. And at the very top, under a canopy of glass, was an indoor garden littered with unwanted broken statuary: a dog, a child on a bench, a stained sleeping polar bear. Katya's Alley.

Vishnik wandered from stall to stall, floor to floor, making lists, drawing sketches, taking photographs, picking up discarded bits of stuff – a tram ticket, a dropped theatre programme. He recorded it all.

Mirgorod, graveyard of dreams.

He had roamed back and forth like this across the city every day for more than a year, a satchel slung over his shoulder with a fat oilskin notebook, a mechanical pencil, a collection of maps and a camera. The official historian of Mirgorod. He took his duties seriously, even if no one else did. He was systematically mining the alleyways, the streets, the prospects. Blue–green verdigrised domes. Cupolas. Pinnacles. Towers. Statues of horsemen and angels. The Opera. The Sea Station. The Chesma. The Obovodniy Bridge. It all went into his notebooks and onto his maps. He noted the smell of linden trees in the spring and the smell of damp moss under the bridges in the autumn. He photographed chalk scrawlings on the walls, torn advertisements, drinking fountains, the patterns made by telephone wires against the sky. A wrought-iron clock tower with four faces under a dome.

What he found was strangeness. Vishnik had come to see that the whole city was like a work of fiction: a book of secrets, hints and signs. A city in a mirror. Every detail was a message, written in mirror writing.

A wrong turning has been taken. Everything is fucked.

As he worked through the city week by week and month by month, he found it shifting. Slippery. He would map an area, but when he returned to it, it would be different: doorways that had been bricked up were open now; shops and alleyways that he'd noted were no longer there, and others were in their place, with all the appearance of having been there for years. It was as if there was another city, present but mostly invisible, a city that showed itself and then hid. He was being teased – stalked – by the visible city's wilder, playful twin, which set him puzzles, clues and acrostics: manifestations which hinted at the meaning they obscured.

Tying myself in knots, that's what I'm doing. There must be cause and pattern somewhere. I'm a historian: finding cause and pattern is what I do. And it's here, but I can't see it. I just can't fucking see it.

Vishnik was hunting traces: the trail of vanished enterprise, the hint of occupations yet to come, the scent of possibilities haunting the present. Such as this jeweller and watchmaker, whose wooden sign of business (S. LARKOV) was fixed over – but didn't completely cover – the larger inscription in bottle green on purple tiling RUDOLF GOTMAN – BOOKSELLER – PERIODICALS – FINE BINDINGS. Vishnik noted Gotman's advertisement on his plan of the Apraksin and took out his camera to photograph the palimpsest vitrine.

'You. What do you want? What are you doing?'

Oh my fuck. Not again.

A small man – slick black hair, round face polished to a high sheen – had come out of the shop. S. Larkov. He wore gold half-moon glasses on his nose and a gold watch chain across his tight waistcoat. Expandable polished-steel sleeve suspenders gripped his narrow biceps, making the crisp white cotton of his shirtsleeves balloon.

'I said, what are you doing?'

'Taking pictures,' said Vishnik, and offered him a card.

Prof. Raku Andreievich Vishnik
Historian of Mirgorod
City Photographer
231 Pelican Quay, Apt. 4
Vandayanka
Big Side
Mirgorod

The jeweller brushed it aside. 'This means nothing. Who photographs such places? Who makes maps of them?'

'I do,' said Vishnik.

'I'll tell you who. Spies. Terrorists. Agents of the Archipelago. Here, give me that!' He grabbed for the camera. Vishnik snatched it back out of his grip.

'Listen, you fuck. I'm a historian—'

Larkov's face was stiff with hatred. His tiny eyes as tight and sharp and cramped as the cogwheels in the watches he picked over at his bench.

'What if you are? Your sort are disgusting. Parasites. Intelligentsia. Only looking after their own. The Novozhd will—'

People were coming out of the neighbouring shops. Larkov made another snatch at the camera and missed, but caught the strap of Vishnik's satchel.

'Stay where you are. I haven't finished with you. Intellectual!' The man propelled the word into Vishnik's face, spattering him with warm spittle.

'You piss off,' said Vishnik. 'Piss away off.'

He jerked the satchel away from Larkov.

'Gendarme! Gendarme! Stop the bastard!'

Vishnik saw a green uniform coming from the other direction. Time to go.

18

From the mortuary Lom found his way eventually, via many corridors and stairs, to the Central Registry of the Lodka. He had wanted to see this place for years, and when he found it he stopped a moment in the entrance, taking it in.

It was a vast circular hall, floored with flagstones, ringed by tiers of galleries, roofed with a dome of glass and iron. It had the airy stillness of a great library and the smell of wood polish and ageing paper that a library has. Rows of readers' desks radiated outwards from the hub of the room like the spokes of a wheel. Each desk had a blue-shaded electric lamp of brass, a blue blotter, a chair upholstered in blue leather. Three thousand readers could work there at once, though not more than a tenth of that number was present now, bent in quiet study.

At the centre of the vast hall, rising more than a hundred feet high, almost to the underside of the dome, was the Gaukh Engine. Lom had seen a photograph of it once. It had been beautiful in the picture, but nothing prepared him for the reality. It was immense. An elegant nested construction of interlinked vertical wheels of steel and polished wood carried, like fairground wheels, dozens of heavy gondolas. The whole machine was in constant motion, its wheels turning and stopping and turning. The murmuring of its electric motors gave the hall a quiet, restful air.

A woman – pink arms, a round red face, hair wound in braids about her head, a white sweater under her uniform tunic – was watching him.

'Yes?' she said. 'Can I help?'

'I'm looking for a file,' said Lom. 'Name of Kantor. I haven't been here before.'

The archivist came around from behind the desk. She was shorter and wider than he had thought. There were crumbs in the lap of her skirt.

'Follow me,' she said.

She led him to one of the control desks. There were two arrays of lettered keys, like the keyboards of two typewriters.

'This one is for surnames, and this is for code names. Enter the first three letters of the name you want, then press the button and the engine will bring the correct gondola. Gondolas contain index cards. When you find the one you're looking for, copy the reference number in the top right corner and bring it to me. The index is phonetic, not alphabetical – sometimes a name is only overheard, and the spelling is uncertain. Cards are colour coded: yellow for students, green for anarchists, purple for nationalists, and so on. It's all here.' She showed him a hand-coloured legend pinned to the desk.

'How many cards do you have here?'

'Thirty-five million. Approximately.'

Lom keyed in the letters. K A N. Pressed the button. The wheels turned slowly, until the right car stopped in front of him. He lifted the hinged lid to reveal tray after tray of cards suspended from racks on an axle. He spun through the racks. There was a half-tray of Kantors, generations of them, but only two Josefs with a birth date in the last half-century. One card was white, indicating a minor public official included for completeness, against whom nothing was known. The other was lavender, creased and dog-eared, cross-referenced to at least twenty separate code names. Lom noted the reference on a slip of paper from the pad provided and handed it in.

While the archivist was gone, Lom wandered around the hall. There were card index cabinets, rows of guard-book catalogues. Newspapers, periodicals, journals, directories, maps, atlases, gazetteers, timetables. The publications, proceedings and membership lists of every organis- ation and society. The records of universities, technical colleges and schools. Galleries rose up to the domed ceiling. Swing doors led to the specialised archives and collections: keys, said a notice, could be col- lected from the desk by the holder of appropriate authorisation.

The foundation of any security organisation is its archives. That was what Commander Chazia had said in her address to the assembled police and militia of the Podchornok Oblast the previous year. Lom and Ziller had arrived late to find the room over-filled and over-hot. They had to stand at the back, craning to get a decent view between the bullet heads of a pair of gendarmes from Siflosk. Deputy Laurits had made a long and unctuous speech of welcome. The visit of the great Lavrentina Chazia, head of Vlast Secret Police, in all her pomp, was a momentous occasion, a moment for the provincial service to feel close to the heart of the great machinery of the Vlast.

Chazia had dominated the room: a small woman but, standing on the simple stage at the front of the hall, a pillar of air and energy, pale and intense, neat and slender and upright, her voice carrying effortlessly to the back of the hall. She had drawn and held the attention of every man there. *We are hers*, they found themselves thinking. *We are her soldiers. We are working for her.*

The reports they provided *mattered*, that was Chazia's message to them: they were *used*; they had to be done *right*. Lom listened intently as she unfolded the process by which raw intelligence from across the Dominions of the Vlast was gathered and sifted. It was a huge undertaking, rigorous, elegant, thorough: beautifully simple in its conception, dizzying in its scale and reach.

The Vlast's information machine was in fact three machines, or rather it was a machine in three parts: that was how Chazia expounded it. First, there was the soft machine, the flesh machine, the machine of many humans. They were the Outer Agents: uniformed policemen, plain-clothes detectives, infiltrators and provocateurs – tens if not hundreds of thousands of them – watching and listening, collecting information about the political activities, opinions and social connections of the population. The Outer Agents used direct observation, and they also employed their own informants – dvorniks, tram drivers, schoolteachers, children. Their primary targets were the shifting and fissile groups of dissidents, separatists, anarchists, nationalists, democrats, nihilists, terrorists, insurgents and countless other dangerous sects and cults that sought to undermine the Vlast. Naturally they also collected an enormous amount of collateral intelligence on the families, neighbours and associates of such people, and on public servants and prominent citizens generally, for the purposes of cross-reference, elimination and potential future usefulness.

The soft machine fed the second machine, the paper machine: tons and tons of paper; miles of paper; paper stored in the dark cavernous stacks that ramified through the basements and inner recesses of the Lodka. Nothing was thrown away: nothing had ever been thrown away in the history of the centuries-long surveillance. The technicians of the paper machine were the archivists and code breakers and, at the pinnacle of the hierarchy, the analysts. It was they who, working from summary observation sheets, prepared the semi-magical *Circles of Contact*. Finding cadres, plots and secret cells in the teeming mass of the population was harder than finding needles in haystacks. *Circles of Contact* was how you did it. You began by writing a name – the Subject – at the centre of a large sheet of paper and drawing a circle around it. Then you drew spokes radiating from the circle, and at the end of each spoke you put the name of one of the Subject's contacts or associates. The more frequent or closer the contact, the thicker the connecting spoke. Each associated name then became the centre of its own circle, a new node in its own right, and the process was repeated. The idea was to find the patterns – connections – linked loops – that would crystallise out of seemingly inchoate lists of names and dates and demonstrate the presence of a tightly knit but secretive connection. Lom found it exhilarating. It was like focusing a microscope lens and seeing some tiny malignant creature swimming in a bath of fluid. This was why he had become a policeman. To understand the pattern, to find the alien cruelty at its heart, to cut it out.

And the third machine, Chazia had said, the heart and brain of the operation, was the machine of steel and electricity: the famous Gaukh Engine, right at the heart of the Lodka. And now Lom was standing in its shadow.

The archivist came back.

'The material you ordered is unavailable,' she said.

'What does that mean?'

'It means you can't have it. You don't have the appropriate authorisation.'

'Where do I get authorisation? I mean urgently. I mean now.'

'This material is stored in Commander Chazia's personal archive. They are her personal papers, and her personal permission is required. In writing. I'm sorry, Investigator. There's nothing I can do.'

'Thank you,' he said. 'Thank you. I'm grateful for your help.'

Shit.
I'm running out of threads.
Pull another one.

19

T he tattered pelmet of an awning fluttered in the wind. It was
the colour of leather. Florid script crawled across it. *Bakery.*
Galina Tropina. Confections. Coff—.

Vishnik went in.

The woman behind the counter frowned at him. She had arms the
colour and texture of uncooked pastry, and her hair was artificially
curled, sticky-looking, dyed a brash, desiccated copper. There were a
couple of empty tables at the back.

'I would like coffee,' said Vishnik. 'Strong, please. And aquavit. A
small glass of that. Plum. Thank you.'

His legs were trembling. He was getting sensitive: things were getting to him more than they should. *I've been spending too much time on
my own.* He used to like being alone, when he was young. But that was
a different kind of loneliness: the solitude of the only child who knows
that he is free and safe and loved. That was the rich, enchanted solitude
of *Before*. Before the purge of the last aristocrats, when the militia had
come winkling them out of the obscure burrows they had made for
themselves in their distant country estates.

*That was a different world. The storms smashed it long ago. All I am
now is fucking memories. I move through life facing backwards.*

He checked the camera. It was a precise, purposeful thing. A Kono.
When he was growing up in Vyra, a camera was a hefty contraption
of wood and brass and leather bellows, which required a solid and
man-high mahogany tripod to hold it steady. But the Kono was matte
black metal, about the size of his notebook, and sat comfortably in
the palm of his hand, satisfyingly solid and weighty. Vishnik had built
a darkroom in the kitchen of his apartment, where he developed his

own films and made his own prints, which he kept in boxes. Many, many boxes.

A girl came into the bakery and put a basket of provisions on the counter. Her black dress fell loosely from her narrow, bony shoulders. Her fine strengthless hair had parted at the back to show the pale nape of her neck. She wore thick grey stockings and scuffed, awkward shoes. The woman behind the counter smiled at her. The smile was a sunburst of love, extraordinary, generous and good, and in the moment of that smile it happened: the surface of the world split open, spilling potential, spilling possibility, spilling the hidden truth of things.

The sheen of the zinc counter top separated itself and slid upwards and sideways, a detached plane of reflective colour, splashed with the vivid blues and greens of the tourist posters on the opposite wall. The hot-water urn opened its eyes and grinned. The floorboards turned red–gold and began to curl and writhe. The woman's arms were flat, biscuity, her hands floated free, dancing with poppy-seed rolls to the tune of the gusting rain, and the girl in the black dress was floating in the air, face downwards, bumping against the ceiling, singing 'The Sailor's Sorrow' in a thin, clear voice.

O Mirgorod, O Mirgorod,
Sweet city of rain and dreams.
Wait for me, wait for me,
And I'll come back.

Cautiously, slowly, so as not to disturb the limpid surface of the moment, Vishnik raised his camera to his eye and released the shutter. He wound the film on slowly – cautiously – with his thumb and took another. And another. Then he opened his notebook and began to write, spilling words quickly and fluently across the page.

The Pollandore, buried beneath a great and populous upper cata-comb of stone in the heart of the city, waits, revolving.

In darkness, but having its own light, it turns on its axis slowly. Swelling and subsiding. Gently.

Like a heart.
Like a lung.
Like respiration.

Every so often – more frequently now, perhaps, but who could measure that? – somewhere inside it – deep within its diminutive immensity – a miniscule split fissures slightly wider – a cracking – barely audible, had there been anyone to hear it (there wasn't) – the faintest spill of light and earthy perfume.

Almost nothing, really.

The egg of time, ripening.

20

Lom stopped in front of the Armoury and looked up. Narrow and needle-sharp, the One Column on Spilled Blood speared a thousand feet high out of the roof. The militia was head-quartered at the Armoury, not the Lodka, a distinction they carefully maintained. Being both soldiers and police, yet not exactly either, the militia considered themselves an elite within the security service, the Novozhd's killers of choice.

He climbed the splay of shallow steps and pushed his way through heavy brass-furnished doors into a place of high ceilings; black and white tiled floors; cool, shadowed air; the echoes of footsteps; the smell of polish, sweat, uniforms and old paper. There were texts on the walls, not the exhortations and propaganda that encrusted the city, but the core tenets of the committed Vlast.

ALL THAT IS COMING IS HERE ALREADY.

HISTORY IS THE UNFOLDING OF THE CLOTH, BUT THE CLOTH HAS ALREADY BEEN CUT AND EVERY STITCH SEWN.

A clerk behind a high counter was watching him.

'I'm looking for Major Safran,' said Lom

'Just missed him. He left about ten minutes ago.'

'How do I find him?'

'Try the stables. He'll be with the mudjhik. Never goes home with-out saying goodbye.'

The stables, when he found them, were a separate block on the far side of the parade ground. The doors, fifteen feet high and made of solid heavy planks, stood open. Lom stepped inside and found himself in a high-ceilinged hall of stone: slit windows near the roof; unwarmed shadows and dustmotes in the air. It didn't smell like stables. No straw. No leather. No horse shit. The mudjhik was standing motionless at the far end of the hall, in shadow. A militia man was sitting at its feet, his back against the wall.

'I'm looking for Major Safran.'

'That's me.'

Lom took a step forward. The mudjhik stirred.

'Come on,' said Safran. 'He'll be still.'

The mudjhik was a dull red in the dim light, the colour of bricks and old meat. Taller than any giant Lom had seen, and solider, squarer: a statue of rust-coloured angel stone, except it wasn't a statue. Lom felt the dark energy of its presence. Its watchfulness. The mudjhik's intense, disinterested, eyeless gaze passed across him and the sliver of angel stuff in Lom's forehead tingled in response. It was like putting the tip of his tongue on the nub of a battery cell: the same unsettled sourness, the same metallic prickling. The same false implication of being alive.

Safran waited for Lom to come to him. He was about thirty years old, perhaps, smooth shaven, his hair clipped short and so fair it was almost colourless. His uniform was crisp and neat. A small, tight knot tied his necktie. Without the uniform he could have been anything: a teacher, a civil servant, an interrogator: the joylessly nutritious, right-thinking staple of the Vlast. And yet there was something else. Safran seemed ... *awakened*. The life-desire of the mudjhik glimmered in his wash-pale eyes. His slender hands moved restlessly at his side, and the mudjhik's own hands echoed the movement faintly. And there was the angel seal, the third blank eye, in the front of his head.

'Well? I've got five minutes.'

Lom took off his cap. Letting Safran see his own seal set in his brow.

Safran grunted. 'You can feel him then.'

'It's watching me?'

'Of course.'

Lom looked up into the mudjhik's face. Except it had no face, only a rough and eyeless approximation of one. It wasn't looking anywhere in particular, not with its head sockets, but it was looking at him.

'They call them dead,' Safran was saying, 'and they use them like pieces of meat and rock, but that's not right, is it? You'd know what I mean.'

'Would I?'

'We know, people like you and me. The angel stuff is in us. We know they're not dead.'

Lom stepped up to the mudjhik and placed his hand on its heavy thigh. It was smooth to the touch, and warm.

'Is it true,' he said, 'that it contains the brain and spinal cord of a dead animal?'

'You shouldn't touch him. He has his own mind. He acts quickly.'

'With a dead cat for a brain?'

Lom didn't remove his hand. He was probing the mudjhik, as it was probing him. He encountered the distant pulse of awareness. Like colours, but not.

'Not cat,' said Safran. 'Dog. It's in there somewhere, but it's not important. You really should step away.'

It was like being nudged by a shunting engine. Lom didn't see it move, but suddenly he was lying on his back, breath rasping, mouth gaping, hot shards of pain in his ribs. Safran was standing over him, looking down.

Lom rolled over and rose to his knees, head down, retching sour spittle onto the floor. No blood. That was something. He felt the mudjhik pushing fingers of awareness into his nose, his throat, his chest.

Stop!

Lom repelled the intrusion, slamming back at it hard. He wasn't sure how he knew what to do, but he did. He felt the mudjhik's surprise. And Safran's.

Lom hauled himself unsteadily to his feet, wiping his mouth with the back of his hand.

'You're a crazy man,' said Safran.

Lom was becoming aware of the link between Safran and the mudjhik. There was a flow between them, a cord of shared awareness.

'Did you make it do that?'

'That's not how it works.'

'But you could have stopped it.'

'I don't know. Maybe. I didn't try.'

'And if I hit you, what would it do?'

'Defend me.'

'I saw your picture in the paper.'

81

'What are you talking about?'

'Levrovskaya Square. You were getting a handshake from a bank. I wasn't sure what for.'

'Protecting the money.'

'But you didn't. Thirty million roubles disappeared from under your nose.'

Lom was rubbing his chest and pressing his ribs experimentally. The pain made him wince but nothing felt broken. The mudjhik had judged it just right.

'It might have been worse,' said Safran. 'They didn't get into the bank.'

'They weren't trying to. The strong-car was the target.'

'Maybe. Maybe not. The bank was happy. It wasn't their money. Hadn't been delivered.'

'You were waiting for them. You must have known they were coming.'

'So?'

'You could have stopped it. You were meant to let them get away.'

'You should be careful, making accusations like that.' The mudjhik took a step forward. 'People have been killed wandering about in here. Accidents. It's dangerous around mudjhiks if they don't know you.'

'Were you paid off?'

'What's your name, Investigator?'

'Lom. My name is Lom.'

'And who are you working for, Lom? Who are you with? Does anyone know you're here?'

'You could buy a lot of militia for thirty million roubles.'

'And you should piss off.'

'So how did you know they were coming?'

'Detective work.'

'You had an informant. Someone in the gang, maybe. Who was it?'

'Don't they teach you the rules where you come from, Lom? What's the rule of informants? The first rule?'

Never reveal the name. Not even to your own director. Even you, you yourself, must forget his name for ever. Remember only the cryptonym. One careless word will ruin both your lives for ever.

'You're in trouble, Major. Corruptly receiving bribes. Standing aside to let thirty million roubles go missing.'

'You couldn't prove that. Even if it was true, which it isn't.'

'You were following orders then. Whose? Tell me whose.'

'Shit. You're not joking are you.'

'You want to stay a major for ever?

'What?'

'Taking bribes is one thing. But nobody likes the ones that get caught. It's not competent. It's not commanding officer material.'

'I should kill you myself.'

The mudjhik's feet moved. A sound like millstones grinding.

'But you won't. You don't know who I'm working for. You don't know who sent me. You think I'm here for the hell of it?'

'Who?'

'No.'

Safran shrugged and looked at his watch.

'There was no informant.'

'Yes, there was.'

'No, there really wasn't. It was just some drunk. I have people who make it their business to be amenable in the bars where the artists go. They keep their ears open. It's not hard. Artists are always pissed. Neurotic. Boastful. Shutting them up is the hard thing. Anyway, there was this particular one, highly strung even in that company. Mild enough sober, but he likes a brandy and opium mix, and after a few of those he starts abusing anyone in range.'

'And?'

'So one evening this idiot starts broadcasting to the world that he's mixed up with some great nationalist hero, and he's got a sack full of bombs. You should all be shit scared of me, that was his line. One day soon there's going to be a rampage. He tells everyone how he and his new friends are going to rob a strong-car when it makes a delivery to a particular bank he mentions. Turned out it was true.'

'The name?'

'Curly-haired fellow. A woman's man. Studio somewhere in the quarter. I broke in to have a look. It stank. Obscene pictures too.'

'The name.'

'Petrov. Lakoba Petrov.'

21

Lom wanted to go back into the Registry to see if there was a file on Petrov, but when he got there he found the doors shut against him. The Gaukh Engine was closed to readers for the rest of the day. Shit. He looked at his watch. It was just past four. He considered going to his office, but what was the point? It occurred to him that he hadn't eaten since breakfast. To eat he needed money, and for that he needed Krogh.

Krogh's private secretary was in the outer office. He made a show of closing the file he was reading – *Not for your eyes, Lom* – and stood up. Making the most of his height advantage.

'Ah. Investigator Lom.'

'Nice office you got me,' said Lom. 'Thanks.'

'Thought you'd appreciate it. How's the Kantor case going? Anything to report?'

'Not to you.'

The private secretary picked up the desk diary.

'I can fit you in with the Under Secretary this evening. He's very busy. But I can find a space. As soon as you like, in fact. Soon as you're ready, Investigator. Just say the word.'

'I need money.'

The private secretary sat down and leaned back, hands behind his head.

'I see. Why?'

'Because I do this for a job. The idea is I get paid for it. Also, expenses.'

'Have you discussed an imprest with the Under Secretary? As I said, I can fit you in.'

'No. You do it. Sign something. Open the cash tin. I need two hundred roubles. Now.'

'What expenses, actually?'

'Rent.'

'But you're staying with your friend, aren't you. The good citizen Professor Vishnik at Pelican Quay. The dvornik there is a conscientious worker, not the type to be browbeaten, or bribed come to that. I have the Vishnik file with me now, as it happens.' He picked up a folder from his desk and made a show of leafing through it. 'His terms of employment at the university are rather irregular, I feel.'

Lom leaned forward and rested his hands on the desk.

'Vishnik's my friend. Something happens to him, I'll know who to come and see about it. Just give me some money, Secretary. I don't intend to live off my friends, or steal food, and I don't intend to pay bribes for informants out of my own pocket. Especially not unreliable ones.'

The private secretary gave him a friendly grin.

'Of course, Investigator. Anything for the Under Secretary's personal police force.'

'And who,' said a woman's voice behind Lom, 'is this fellow, to get special treatment?'

It was Lavrentina Chazia. Commander of the Secret Police.

'This is Investigator Lom, Commander,' the private secretary said. 'He is doing sterling work for the Under Secretary. On provincial liaison.'

Lom wondered whether he had imagined an ironic note in the private secretary's reply: some hidden meaning, some moment of understanding that had passed between him and Chazia. Whatever, Chazia was examining him shrewdly, and he returned the gaze. Indeed, it was hard not to stare. She was changed, much changed, since he had seen her last. The sharpness and predatory energy were the same, but there was something wrong with her skin. Dark patches mottled her face and neck. They were on her hands as well: smooth markings, hard and faintly bluish under the office light. He recognised the colour – it was in his own forehead – it was angel skin. But he had never seen anything quite like this. There had been rumours even in Podchornok that Chazia had been working with the angel-flesh technicians, experimenting, pushing at the boundaries. Lom hadn't paid them much attention, but it seemed they were true.

85

'So,' said Chazia, 'this is the notorious Lom. You're from Podchornok, aren't you?'

Lom was surprised.

'That's right,' he said. 'I'm flattered. I'd hardly have expected someone like you – I mean, in your position—'

'Oh I know everything, Investigator. Everything that happens in the service is my business.' Again Lom had the uneasy feeling that she meant more than she said. Her pale narrow eyes glittered with a strange energy that was more than confidence. Something almost like relish. Hunger. 'For example,' Chazia continued, 'I know that you were over at the Armoury this afternoon. Talking with Major Safran. No doubt you were … *liaising* with him.'

Lom felt his stomach lurch. The private secretary was watching him curiously. Lom felt … lost. Stupid. That was what he was supposed to feel, of course. Chazia was playing with him. It occurred to him that she hadn't turned up in Krogh's office by chance. She was showing herself to him. Letting him know who his enemies were. But why? What did it mean? Some political thing between her and Krogh that had nothing to do with him? Possibly.

'Safran and I are both products of Savinkov's,' he said, indicating the lozenge of angel stuff in his head. 'I don't get many chances to compare notes.'

He wondered whether Chazia had already talked to Safran herself, whether she knew of his interest in the Levrovskaya Square robbery, and Petrov. But there was no way to read her expression.

'Of course,' she said. 'I hope you got something out of it.' She smiled, showing sharp even teeth, and her pale eyes flashed again, but her face showed little expression, as if the patches of angel stuff had stiffened it somehow. The effect made Lom feel even more queasy. Out of his depth. He was relieved when she had gone.

22

Lom took a tram back to Vishnik's apartment.

The private secretary had signed him a chit. It took Lom more than an hour to find the office where he could get it cashed. It was only twenty roubles.

'I'd give you more, Investigator,' he had said. 'If I could. But this is the limit of my delegated expenditure authority.' He didn't even try to pretend this was true. 'Of course, if you'd prefer to see the Under Secretary...'

At least now he had cash in his pocket. He stopped off on the way back to Pelican Quay and bought some onions, lamb, a box of pastries and a couple of bottles of plum brandy. Vishnik wouldn't take rent, but it was something.

When he got to the apartment, Vishnik was waiting for him, full of energy, strangely exultant, dressed to go out. Lom sat on the couch and started to pull his boots off. He shoved the bag of shopping towards Vishnik with his foot.

'Here. Dinner.'

'This is no time for fucking eating, my friend,' said Vishnik. 'It's only six. We'll go out. I want to take you to the Dreksler-Kino.'

'Another day maybe. I've got to work.'

'What work, exactly?'

'Thinking.'

'Think at the Dreksler. You can't be in Mirgorod and not see the Dreksler. It's a wonder, a fucking wonder of the world. And today is Angelfall Day. '

Lom sighed. 'OK. Why not.'

Lom didn't wear his uniform. On the crowded tram he and Vishnik were the only passengers without one. The Dreksler-Kino was draped with fresh new flags and banners, red and gold. Its immense marble dome was awash with floodlight. Vertical searchlights turned the clouds overhead into a vast liquescent ceiling that swelled and shifted, shedding fine drifts of rain. Inside, twenty thousand seats, ranged in blocks and tiers and galleries, faced a great waterfall of dim red velvet curtain. The auditorium was crowded to capacity. A woman with a flashlight and a printed floor plan led them to their seats, and almost immediately the houselights dimmed. Twenty thousand people became an intimate private crowd, together in the dark.

There were cartoons, and then the newsreel opened with a mass rally at the Sports Palace, intercut with scenes from the southern front. The war was going well, said the calm, warm voice of the commentator. On the screen, artillery roared and kicked up churned mud. Columns of troops marched past the camera, waving, smoking cigarettes, grinning. *Citizen! Stand tall! The drum of war thunders and thunders!* The crowd cheered.

The commentator was reading a poem over scenes of wind moving across grassy plains; factories; columns of lorries and tanks.

In snow-covered lands – in fields of wheat –
In roaring factories –
Ecstatic and on fire with happy purpose –
With you in our hearts, dear Novozhd –
We work – we fight –
We march to Victory!

There was stomping, jeering and whistling when the screen showed aircraft of the Archipelago being shot down over the sea. Corkscrews of oil-black smoke followed the silver specks down to a final silent blossoming of spray.

A familiar avuncular face filled the screen. The face that watched daily from a hundred, a thousand posters, newspapers and books. The Novozhd, with his abundant moustache and the merry smile in his eye.

Citizens of the Vlast, prepare yourselves for an important statement.

He's looking older, thought Lom. Must be over sixty by now. Thirty years since he grabbed power in the Council and gave the Vlast his famous kick up the arse. *The Great Revitalisation*. Eight years since he re-opened the war with the Archipelago. Three decades of iron kindness. *I go the way the angels dictate with the confidence of a sleepwalker.*

In the Dreksler-Kino everyone rose to salute, and all across the Dominions of the Vlast people were doing the same.

'Citizens,' the Novozhd began, leaning confidingly towards the camera. 'My brothers and sisters, my friends. It is now three hundred and seventy-eight years exactly, to the hour, since the first of the angels fell to us. There and then, in the Ouspenskaya Marsh, our history began. From that event, all that we have and all that we are, our great and eternal Vlast itself, took root and grew. We all know the story. I remember my mother when she used to sit by my bed and tell it to me. I was a child then, eyes wide with wonderment.'

The auditorium was in absolute silence. The Novozhd had never spoken in such intimate and fraternal terms before.

'My mother told me how our Founder came to see for himself this marvellous being that had tumbled out of the night sky. And when he came, our Founder didn't only see the angel, he saw the future. Some say the angel spoke to him before he died. The Founder himself left no testimony on that count, so we must say we don't know if it's true, although ...' The Novozhd paused and looked the camera in the eye. 'I know what I believe.' A murmur of assent and a trickle of quiet applause brushed across the crowd. 'On that day,' the Novozhd was saying, 'the Founder saw the shape of the Vlast as it could be. From the ice in the north to the ice in the south, from eastern forest to western sea, one Truth. One Greatness. That's what the first angel gave us, my friends, and paid for with the price of his death.'

Lom had looked up synonyms of Vlast once. They filled almost half a column. Ascendancy. Domination. Rule. Lordship. Mastery. Grasp. Rod. Control. Command. Power. Authority. Governance. Arm. Hand. Grip. Hold. Government. Sway. Reign. Dominance. Dominion. Office. Nation.

'You know this, friends,' the Novozhd was saying. 'Your mothers told you, just as mine told me. And this isn't all. Something else came to us with the first angel, and it kept on coming as other angels tumbled down to us like ripened fruit falling out of the clear sky.'

'All of them dead,' whispered Vishnik. 'Every single fucking one of them dead.'

'Brave warrior heroes,' the Novozhd was saying, 'fallen in the battles that broke the moon. Giving their lives in the eternal justified war. A war that wasn't – and isn't – against flesh and blood enemies, but against powers, against hidden principalities, against the rulers of the present darkness that surrounds us.

'And what else did the angels bring us? Didn't they give us the Gift of Certain Truth? Try to imagine, my brothers and sisters, my friends. Imagine if you can what it must have been like to live in this world before the first angelfall, when people like us looked up at the night sky and wondered – only wondered! – what might be there. They knew nothing. They could only guess and dream. Speculation, ignorance and superstition. Dark, terrible times. Until we were freed from all that. The long cloudy Ages of Doubt were closed. We were given incontrovertible, imperishable, touchable EVIDENCE. Ever since the first angelfall, we have KNOWN.' The Novozhd half-stood in his chair and smacked his fist into this palm. 'KNOWN! On this day, three hundred and seventy-eight years ago, the first of the Years of the True and Certain Justified Vlast began! May we live for ever in the wing-shadow of the angels!'

Roars from the twenty thousand. Shouting. Crowds on their feet, stamping. On the screen the image of the Novozhd paused, anticipating the ovation now being shouted and sung across five time zones. After a suitable period he raised his hand. Acknowledging, calming, requiring silence.

'And today a new chapter is beginning.'

The audience fell quiet. This was something different.

'We have been fighting our own war, friends, which is part of the great war of the angels, and not different from it. We too have been fighting against hidden powers and unsanctified principalities. The Archipelago – the islands of the Outsiders – the Unacknowledged and Unaccepted Lands – where no angels have ever fallen. Where even their existence is not taken for certain and true.

'Many brave warriors of the Vlast have fallen in the struggle. I know them all, I have felt the anguish of each one, and I've cried your tears – you who are listening to me now and thinking of your own sons and daughters, brothers, sisters, fathers, mothers, comrades and friends. Let's remember the fallen today. We owe them an unpayable debt. Don't be ashamed to weep for them sometimes. I do. But praise them also.

'I know you all. I am your friend as you are mine. The angels know you too. Friends, I am here to tell you that the time of Victory is close! The Archipelago is sending an ambassador to Mirgorod to sue for peace with us. The enemy weakens and tires. The light of truth dawns in their eyes. Yes, my friends. Victory draws near. One last push! One last supreme effort! The great day is soon.

'I want you to hear this from my own lips. Pay close attention now and remember. On this very day of Truth and Light I want you to hear it and be sure. Your love is with me. Our victory will be absolute and total. With the Truth of the Angel clear in our minds it cannot be otherwise. Goodnight.'

The image of the Novozhd at his desk faded out, replaced by a full close-up of his face. He was outside now. The sunshine was in his face, making him crinkle the corners of his eyes in laughter lines. A breeze teased his hair. As the opening bars of the 'Friendship Song' began to play, the words started scrolling slowly up the screen and twenty thousand voices sang.

All join in our song about him –
About our beloved – our Novozhd!
And us his true friends –
The people – his friends!
Count us? You cannot!
No more could you count
The water in the sea!
All join in our song about him!

'Fuck,' said Vishnik as they filed out slowly into the rain. 'We need a drink.'

23

It was almost midnight. After the Dreksler-Kino, Vishnik had dragged Lom to a bar where they drank thin currant wine. He would have stayed there all night if Lom hadn't insisted on going back and getting some food. And now Lom was sitting on the couch in Vishnik's room with his legs stretched out along the seat. His chest was sore and bruised where the mudjhik had hit him, but the stove had heated the room to a warm fug and the bottle of plum brandy was nearly empty. The apartment smelled of lamb goulash and burning paraffin, and also of something else – the sweet tang of hydroquinone. Lom recognised it from the photographic laboratory at Podchornok.

'That smell. Is that developer?'

'What?' said Vishnik. 'Oh. Yes. I was printing.' His face was flushed. He had been drinking steadily all evening. 'Photographs. Have you ever made photographs, my friend? Marvellous. Very fucking so. You're completely absorbed, you see. In the moment. Immersed in your surroundings. Watching your subject. Observing. How does the light fall? What is the shutter speed? Aperture? Depth of field? It is an intimate thing. Very fucking intimate. It drives out all other thoughts. Your heart rate slows. Your blood pressure falls. You are in a waking dream. Time is nowhere. Nowhere.' Vishnik lurched unsteadily to his feet. 'Wait. Wait. I'll show you. Wait.'

He was going towards the kitchen when there was a loud rapping at the outer door. Vishnik froze and stared at Lom. The fear was in his face again. His eyes went to the bag waiting packed by the door.

'I'll get it,' said Lom. 'I'll deal with it. You wait here.'

Lom opened the door, half expecting uniforms. But there was only a woman, her wide dark eyes staring into his.

'Oh,' she said. 'I was looking for Raku Vishnik. I thought this was his place. I'm sorry. Would you know, I mean, which—?'

Vishnik had come up behind him.

'Maroussia?' he said. 'I thought it was your voice. This is a good surprise. Don't stand in the doorway. Come in. Please. Come in.'

She hesitated, glancing at Lom.

'I'm sorry, Raku. I wanted to ask you something. But it can wait. You're not alone. Now's not the time. I'll come back.'

'Ridiculous,' said Vishnik. 'Fucking so. You can speak in front of Vissarion, for sure. He is my oldest friend, and he is a good man. If there is trouble, perhaps he can help. At least come in now you're here. Warm yourself. Eat something. Have brandy with us. '

'No,' she said. 'There's no trouble. It doesn't matter.'

Lom had been watching her carefully. The yellow light from Vishnik's room splashed across her troubled, intelligent face. She looked worn out and alone. Like she needed friends. She would be worth helping, Lom found himself thinking. He wanted her to stay.

'Don't mind me,' he said. 'Please. You look tired.'

She hesitated.

'OK then,' she said. 'Just for a moment.'

Lom stood back to let her in. As she passed he caught her faint perfume: not perfume, but an open, outdoor scent. Rain on cool earth.

'Well,' said Vishnik. 'How can I help?' He was pacing the room, eager and animated. 'What is it that I can do for you? There must be something, for you to come so late. Tell me, please. I am eager for gallantry. For me, the chances are few. Ask me, and it is yours.' His eyes were alive with pleasure. He was more than a little drunk.

Maroussia looked at Lom again.

'I don't know that I should ...' she said.

'Oh for the sake of fuck, Maroussia,' said Vishnik. 'Tell us what you need.'

She took a breath. 'OK. I want you to tell me about the Pollandore, Raku. I want you to tell me anything you know about it. Anything and everything.'

Vishnik stopped pacing and stared at her.

'The Pollandore?'

'Yes.' Maroussia was looking at him earnestly. Determined. 'The Pollandore. Please. It's important.'

'But … fuck, this I was not expecting … of all things, this.' Vishnik fetched another bottle from the shelf and settled himself in a sprawl on the rug on floor. 'Why are you asking me this?'

'You know about it? You can tell me?'

'I've come across the story. It's an old Lezarye thing. Suppressed by the Vlast long ago. Nobody knows about the Pollandore any more.'

'I do,' said Maroussia. 'My mother used to talk about it. A lot. She still does.'

'Really?' said Vishnik. 'I thought … those stories are forgotten now.' He turned to Lom. 'Did you ever hear of the Pollandore, Vissarion?'

Lom shrugged. 'No. What is it?'

'Maroussia?' said Vishnik. 'Will you tell him?'

'No,' said Maroussia. 'I want to hear it from someone else.'

'OK,' said Vishnik. 'So then.' He poured himself another glass. 'Do you ever think about what the world was like before the Vlast, Vissarion?'

'No,' said Lom. 'Not much.'

'Four hundred years,' said Vishnik. 'But it might as well have been four thousand, no? Our civilisation, if we might even call it that, has lived for so long in the shadow of the angels' war, our history is so steeped in it, we live with its consequences in our very patterns of thought. Who can even fucking measure the damage it has done?' Vishnik paused. 'That's what the Pollandore is about. The time before the war of the angels.'

'The Lezarye walking the long homeland,' said Maroussia quietly. 'The single moon in the sky, not broken yet.'

'The world had gods of its own, then,' Vishnik was saying. 'That's how the story goes. Small gods. Gentle, subtle, local gods. But those gods are gone now. They withdrew when the angels began. They foresaw destruction and a terrible, unbearable future. They couldn't co-exist with that. Their time had to end.'

Vishnik emptied his glass and poured another. Lom wondered just how drunk he was. And how long since he'd had an audience like this.

'But before they went,' Vishnik continued, 'one of them, a forest god, made a copy of the world, the whole world, as it was at the moment before the first angel fell to earth. It was a pocket world, a world in stasis. Everything squeezed up into a tiny box. A packet of potential that would exist outside space and time, containing not things themselves but the potential for things. Possibilities. Do you see?'

'Yes,' said Lom. 'I guess so.'

'The idea was,' said Vishnik, 'that this other future, the future that could not now be, in our world, was to be kept safe. Waiting. A reserve. A fall-back. A cupboard. A seed. That's the Pollandore. That's the legend, anyway.'

'But what happened to it, Raku?' said Maroussia. 'Where did it go?'

'The people of Lezarye kept it safe for a while, but in the end the Vlast took it.'

'Yes,' said Maroussia. She was leaning forward. Looking at Vishnik intently. 'But what did they do with it? Where is it now?'

Vishnik shrugged.

'They tried to destroy it,' he said, 'but they could not. It was lost. Why are you asking me this, Maroussia? These are old forgotten things.'

'I want to find it.'

'Find it?' Vishnik looked startled. 'Fuck.'

'Yes. And please don't tell me it doesn't exist. I don't want to hear that again.'

'But ... It's a good story, yes. A symbol. Truth in a picture. But what makes you think this? That it actually exists?'

Maroussia hesitated. Lom tried to read her expression but couldn't. She was looking at Vishnik with a pale and troubled look.

'Things have been ... happening,' she said. 'Things have been coming ... to my mother. From the forest. She was there once, long ago, before I was born, and something happened. I don't know what. But she always used to talk about the Pollandore. And now ... Things happen in the city. I see ... stuff that isn't there ... only it's more real than what is there. It's like glimpses of a different version of the world. It's as if the Pollandore was trying to open. That's what it feels like. That's what it is.' She stopped. 'I'm sorry. I'm not saying this right.'

But Vishnik was hardly listening any more.

'Oh, my darling girl!' he said. 'You see these things too? I thought I was the only one. And you think it's the *Pollandore*? That's ... that's ... I hadn't seen that, but it could be. It could be so. What an idea *that* is. Fuck. Yes. But—'

'Raku? Do you mean you know what I'm talking about?' said

Maroussia. 'Fuck,' said Vishnik. 'I could hug you. I could fucking hug you.'

'Could somebody tell me, please,' said Lom, 'just what the hell you two are talking about?'

'Tell you?' said Vishnik. 'Fuck. Show you.' He stood up and lurched unsteadily in the direction of the kitchen.

'Raku?' said Lom. 'What are you—'

'Wait,' said Vishnik. 'This is what I was going to show you anyway. Wait.'

Lom and Maroussia sat for a moment in awkward silence while Vishnik rummaged in the other room and came back with a large round hatbox. He dumped it on the low table and took off the lid.

'Here,' he said. 'Look.'

The box contained photographs. Hundreds of them. Vishnik shuffled through them, picking out one after another.

'See?' said Vishnik. 'See?'

The photographs were odd and beautiful. A light in a window at dusk, shining from a derelict building. A penumbra of gleaming mist about a house. A great dark cloud in the sky. There was a sad magic in them all. It was in the sunlight on a street corner, in the ripples in a pool of rain on the pavement, in the way the light caught the moss on a tree. Gleams and glimpses. Tracks and traces. There was a purity of purpose in Vishnik's work that was strangely moving.

'I'll tell you something,' said Vishnik, pointing to one picture. 'That building there. See it. It does not exist. It never did. I photographed it, but it's not there. I have been back. Nothing.' He picked up another. His face was flushed. His breath ripe with brandy. 'See this burned-out store? There was no fire. See this alleyway? Its not on any map. See this island? There is no island in this water. And this couple has no children. I know them, Vissarion. They live here. But see … there … that child?'

Maroussia was looking through the photographs intently, staring at each one with a frown of concentration. She said nothing.

'And these,' Vishnik was saying, opening a small package and laying the contents out on the table. 'These are my specials. My very fucking absolutely specials.'

The first picture was a street scene, but the familiar world had been torn open and reconstructed all askew. The street skidded. It toppled and flowed. All the angles were wrong. The ground tilted forwards, tipping the people towards the camera. It wasn't an illusion of perspective, the people knew it was happening. A bearded man and an old woman threw up their arms and wailed. A baby flew out of its mother's arms.

Maroussia picked up the picture and stared at it for a long time.

'Oh Raku,' she whispered. 'This is it. Yes. This is it.'

Raku went to sit next to her.

'How often do you see this?' he said quietly.

'Not often,' said Maroussia. 'Sometimes. You?'

'All the fucking time. But then I look for it. Every day.'

'How long have you been doing this, Raku?'

'Two years,' said Vishnik. 'Maybe more. Other people are seeing it too, I'm sure of it. It's not the kind of thing you talk about though.'

Lom remembered the woman in the paper, the mother who had killed her children. *The floors keep opening,* that was what she'd said. *Will no one stop it?* He looked through the other pictures. Vishnik's specials. One showed an interior, a hotel bar, but the walls of the room were broken open to the elements and the ceiling was studded with stars. A woman's head was floating upside down in the corner of the picture, smiling. The barman, from the waist up, floated in mid-air, while his legs – were they his? – danced at the other end of the room. In another, a girl was descending like a messenger from the sky to milk a luminous cow. In her ecstasy at the lights blazing across the black night, she had left her head behind. The whole city was ripping open at the seams.

'You made these?' said Lom.

'All the time,' said Vishnik. 'Always.' He picked one out and showed it to Maroussia. 'This is today's. It's a good one.'

She looked at it and passed it to Lom. The print was still damp. It had been taken in a café or a bakery, something like that. There was a girl in a black dress floating in the air. Up near the ceiling. The top had come off the counter: it was up there with her.

'These are good,' said Lom. 'How do you do it?'

'What, you think these are fakes?' said Vishnik.

'Well—'

'Fuck off with fakes. Of course they're not fucking fakes. This is

what's happening. Out there. This is the city. Maroussia has seen this.'
He looked at her. 'No? Am I not right?'

'Yes,' said Maroussia. 'It's the Pollandore.'

'See?' said Vishnik. 'Shit. Why would I make such stuff up? Why do
fakes? Fuck, Vissarion. You've been a policeman too long.'

Maroussia stared at Lom.

'What?' she said. 'What did he say? You? You're the *police*?'

Lom didn't say anything.

'Well,' said Vishnik. The colour had drained from his face. 'Yes, I
suppose he is a policeman. Of a sort. But a good policeman. Not really
a policeman at all.'

'Raku?' said Maroussia quietly. 'What have you done?'

'It's OK,' said Lom. 'Don't worry, I won't—'

But Maroussia was on her feet, gathering her coat. Her face was
closed up tight. She looked ... alone. He wanted to reach out to her.
He didn't want her to go, not like this.

'Maroussia—' he said.

'Leave me alone. Don't say anything to me. I've made a mistake. I
have to go.'

Vishnik was aghast.

'No.' he said. 'Don't go. Not when we've just ... Fuck. Fuck. But it's
fine. Vissarion is a friend. Your friend.'

'Don't be an idiot, Raku,' said Maroussia. 'That could never be.'

Lom watched her walk out of the room, straight and taut and brave.
He felt something break open quietly inside him. A new rawness. An
empty fullness. An uncertainty that felt like sadness or hunger, but
wasn't.

24

In a train travelling west towards Mirgorod there is a first-class compartment with its window blinds drawn, which the guards think is empty and locked. The guards know – though they couldn't say how they know – that there's something wrong with it, something ill-defined which needs a mechanic, which makes it unsuitable for occupation, and which they themselves should keep clear of. That's fine. No inconvenience for them. It's the end compartment of the furthest carriage, and first class is barely a quarter full. When they arrive in Mirgorod there'll be the fuss of detraining, and by the time that's done the episode of the closed compartment will be forgotten. When the train's ready to leave again, the compartment will be fine, except – should anyone notice, which isn't likely – for a lingering trace of ozone and leaf-mould in the air.

Just at the moment there are two figures sitting opposite each other in the darkness of the closed and blinded compartment. They are making a long journey. Should anyone happen to see them – which nobody does – they would appear to be human: two women, not young, riding in composed, restful, silent patience, swaying slightly with the movement of the train. Both appear to be dressed in layers of thin cloth in muted woodland colours of bark and moss. Their heads are covered, their faces lost in shadow. Or they would be, if they had faces, which – strictly speaking – neither does.

One of them – the one facing the direction of travel, as if eager to reach her destination, for her purpose is to arrive – is a paluba. The word is complex: its possible meanings include old woman, witch, hag, female tramp, manikin, tailor's dummy, waxwork, puppet and doll, none of which is exactly accurate here, though all have some bearing on the true nature of the figure, which is an artefact carefully constructed of birch branches and earth and the bones of small birds and mammals. The paluba is a kind of vehicle, a conveyance, currently travelling inside another conveyance, artfully made to carry the awareness of its creator and act as a proxy body for her, while she herself remains in the endless forest, in the safety of the trees which she can never leave.

The paluba's maker has placed a little gobbet of herself, a ball of bees' wax nestled inside the paluba's chest cavity, approximately where the heart would be. The wax has been mixed with many intimate traces of its maker – her saliva, her blood, her hair, a paring of fingernail, smears of sweat and other fluids, a condensation of breath – and many intimate words have been whispered over it, as the maker kneaded it between her warm palms for many hours over many days, making it well, making it strong, so that she would remain connected with it as the paluba travelled ever further westward. The maker doesn't stay with the paluba all the time. That would be exhausting and unnecessary. She can find it when she needs to. She can guide its steps, perceive with its senses and speak with its tongue, which is the tongue of a hind deer. When she needs to. For now, the paluba is empty. It's waiting, endlessly patient, facing its direction of travel. Facing westwards. Facing Mirgorod.

The paluba's companion faces opposite, eastwards, back towards the border of the endless forest. And whereas the paluba has a hand-made body, a material caricature of the living human form, the companion is the opposite of this also. For while she is not an artifice but a living creature, she has no body at all. Inside her shrouds of cloth there is nothing but air, only air – collected, coherent, densely-tangible forest air. She is the breath of the forest, walking.

As the train edges slowly closer to Mirgorod, the paluba's companion feels the widening distance between herself and the forest as an ever-increasing pain. She wants to go home. She needs to go home. Nothing would be easier for her than to leave, but she cannot. It is only her presence close to the paluba that enables it to continue to hold together and function so far from the forest. If she were to abandon the paluba it would fall apart. It would become inert, nothing more than the heap of rags and stuff of which it is made. Without her, the paluba's mission would fail, and with it would fail the hope of the forest, the only hope of the world.

25

The next morning, Lom took the tram back to the Lodka. He had a lead from Safran – the name of the painter, Petrov, who was one of Kantor's gang and had betrayed the Levrovskaya raid – not much of a lead, but something. A link to Kantor. Lom tried to keep his focus on Kantor, but his thoughts kept sliding sideways. Chazia was a presence in the background, unsettling him. A dark, angel-stained presence. She had showed herself to him deliberately. Playing a game with him. He was sure of that, though he didn't understand why. Yet it wasn't her face he kept seeing in the street on the other side of the tram window, but Maroussia Shaumian's. She had got under his skin. He hadn't liked the way she looked at him as she left last night: the mixture of fear and scorn in her face had cut him raw. For the first time, it didn't feel so good, being a policeman.

The tram had come to a stop. The engine cut out. A murmuring broke out among the dulled morning passengers.

'We're going nowhere,' the driver called. 'They've cut the power. Traffic's all snarled up. I guess there's another march somewhere up ahead.'

Lom sighed and got out to walk. It wasn't far.

A few hesitant snowflakes twisted slowly down out of the grey sky and littered the streets. People kept their heads down. As he got nearer the Lodka, Lom noticed the crowds getting slower and thicker. There was a sound of distant music. Hymns. He turned a corner and was brought up short by a mass of people passing slowly down the street.

They were singing as they came, not marching but walking. There were old men in sheepskin hats and women in quilted coats. Students in threadbare cloaks. Workers from the Telephone and Telegraph

Office and the tramcar depot. Schoolchildren and wounded soldiers, bandaged and hobbling. There were giants, shuffling forward, struggling to match the slow pace. Faces in uncountable passing thousands, following a hundred banners, shouting the slogans of a dozen causes. STOP THE WAR! PAY THE SOLDIERS! FREE TRADE UNIONS! LIBERATE THE PEOPLE OF LEZARYE! The finest banners belonged to the unions and free councils. They were made of silk, embroidered in beautiful reds and golds and blacks and hung with tassels. Each took three men to hold the poles and three more to go in front, pulling the tassels down to keep the banner taut and straight against the wind. The banner men wore long coats and bowler hats.

They were going his way, so Lom stepped into the road and walked along beside them. These people weren't terrorists or even dissidents. They were ordinary people, most of them, ordinary faces filled now with energy and purpose and an unfamiliar sort of joy. Lom felt the warmth of their fellowship. It was a kind of bravery. He almost wished he was part of it. A few people in the crowd looked at him oddly because of his uniform, but they said nothing. The traffic halted to let them pass. People on the pavement watched, curious or indifferent. Some jeered, but others offered words of encouragement and a few stepped off the kerb to join them. Gendarmes in their plywood street-corner kiosks fingered their batons uncertainly and avoided eye contact. They had no instructions.

Lom scanned the faces in the crowd automatically, the way he always did. Looking for nothing in particular, waiting for something to grab his attention. There was a man striding with the crowd, not keeping his place but weaving through them, working his way slowly forward towards the front, handing out leaflets as he went. He was wearing a striking grey fedora. His overcoat flapped open and his pink silk shirt was a splash of colour in the crowd. He came within a few feet of Lom, singing the chorus from *Nina* in a fine tenor voice.

Lom felt a lurch of recognition. The man's face meant something to him, though at first he couldn't make a connection. Then it came to him. Long and narrow and pockmarked, with those wide brown eyes, it could have been Josef Kantor. This man was older – of course he would be – and his face was filled out compared to the lean features in Krogh's old photograph. But it could have been Kantor. Lom was almost certain it was.

Lom's heart was pounding. He could hardly go up and seize him. Apart from any doubts about the man's identity, if he – in his uniform, with few other police around – tried to seize someone by force out of this crowd, things would get nasty. He'd be lucky to get out of it with his life. Certainly, he wouldn't get out of it with Kantor. Lom walked on, watching the man who might have been Kantor make his way expertly through the crowd.

For a while Lom tried to keep up with him. The man was tall, and in his fedora he was hard to lose sight of. But he was working his way steadily deeper into the crowd. As Lom went after him, his uniform began to attract attention. People jostled him and swore. Twice he was almost tripped. If he fell, he would have been kicked and trampled. He was sure of it.

A strong hand gripped his arm and squeezed, dragging him roughly round. A fat, creased face was shoved close to his.

'Idiot. Get the fuck out of here. What are you trying to do? Start a fucking riot?'

The man shoved him towards the edge of the crowd. Lom bumped hard against someone's back. Something sharp hit him on the back of the head, momentarily dizzying him.

'Hey,' said another voice behind him. A quiet voice, almost a whisper. 'Hey. Look at me. Arsehole.'

Lom turned in time to see the glint of a short blade held low, at waist level, in someone's hand. He lurched sideways, trying to get out of range. He couldn't even tell, in the crowd, who had the knife. Most of the walkers were still ignoring him, still walking on, ordinary faces wanting to do a good thing. Kantor, if it had been Kantor, had disappeared from view.

Shit. He needed to get out of there. Warily, watchfully, trying not to be jostled again, he edged himself sideways until he could step out of the slow tide of people, back onto the pavement. Lom realised he was sweating. He paused for a moment to catch his breath and tried to find his bearings, looking for a side street or alley that would let him get to the Lodka without getting caught up in the march again.

26

Unaware of Lom's abortive pursuit of him, Josef Kantor continued to weave his way through the moving crowd. Kantor wasn't the leader of the march. Nobody was. A dozen separate organisations had called for the demonstration and claimed it as theirs. There was a vague plan of sorts: to march up Founder's Prospect to the Lodka and hold a vigil there, with speeches from the steps, then on to the Novozhd's official residence in the Yekaterinsky Park to present a petition at the gates.

The chiefs of each marching organisation walked apart from the others, following their own colours, suspicious of spies and provocateurs. Kantor moved from coterie to coterie with a word of encouragement and support. He was everyone's friend. Some of them wondered who he was. Some thought they knew him, though each one knew him by a different name – Pato, or Lura, or David, or Per, or simply the Singer. Some knew him as the go-between and negotiator who had drafted their petition, a masterpiece of inspiring words and lofty demands that meant different things to different people.

The size of the crowd grew as it went, exceeding all expectation, even of Kantor himself. Runners moved through it, passing back instructions and bringing forward news of the swelling numbers, until those at the front began to wonder what they had unleashed, and felt nervous. They were beginning to sense that something more momentous than they had intended was preparing to happen.

The song changed from *Nina* to the Lemke Hymn. Their breath flickered on the air, but their hearts were warm. They were no longer a hundred thousand separate, accidental people but one large animal moving forward with a strength and purpose of its own. A newly-formed being whose moment had come.

And then a hesitation began somewhere in the crowd, no one knew where, and spread, a gathering wave of silence and concern. The singing died away but the crowd kept on walking.

Kantor shoved his way to the front.

'What is it?' he said. 'What's happening?'

'Dragoons are gathering at the Lodka. They have mudjhiks, and orders to fire.'

'Rumours. There are always rumours.'

'Maybe.'

Kantor moved on to another group. The Union of Dockers and Tracklayers was always up for a fight. He grabbed their Steward, Lopukhin, by his sleeve.

'It's only a rumour,' said Kantor. 'Keep them going. Get them singing again.'

'Who cares if the dragoons are waiting for us?' said Lopukhin. 'They won't attack us. We are fellow citizens. What a moment for us! Imagine. The dragoons refusing a direct order!'

But Lopukhin's was only one voice among the leaders. Others were for turning aside and making straight for the Park. The argument continued all the way up Founder's Prospect, and they were still arguing when they found themselves at the edge of the Square of the Piteous Angel.

The square was empty. On the far side, the huge prow of the Lodka rose against the sky. And between the marchers and the Lodka were two lines of mounted dragoons. A mudjhik stood at each end and another in the middle.

Those at the head of the march tried to halt and turn back, but the great mass of the crowd had a momentum of its own, and those behind, unaware of what was happening, kept on coming. The shoving and jostling started. Kantor found Lopukhin again and seized him by the shoulder.

'Come on!' he shouted. 'This is your moment! Lead them, Lopukhin! Face the soldiers down!'

'Damn, yes!' cried Lopukhin. His face was flushed, his eyes bright and unfocused. 'I will!'

Lopukhin shoved his lieutenants in the back, making them stumble forward into the empty square. He grabbed the colours of the Union and jogged forward, yelling and waving it over his head.

'Come on, lads! Come on! They won't shoot us!'

Some of the men followed Lopukhin willingly and others were pushed forward by pressure from behind. Kantor slipped away to the edge of the crowd and took up a position in the doorway of a boot shop. At first nothing happened. The dragoons didn't respond, and the demonstrators grew confident. More and more spilled into the square. Then Kantor heard what he had been waiting for. From the back of the crowd a swelling noise rolled forward. At first it sounded like they were cheering. Then the screams grew clearer, and the crack of shots.

All was as it should be. The troops that had been waiting out of sight in the side streets, letting the crowd pass by, were attacking the flank and rear. The killing had begun.

27

Threading through back streets and alleys, Lom made his way round to a side entrance of the Lodka and back into the great Archive. He called up the file on Lakoba Petrov without difficulty – unlike the Kantor file, it was there, and there was no sign that it had been tampered with. He sat reading it at one of the long tables under the dome while the Gaukh Engine rumbled and turned quietly behind him. He'd switched on the desk lamp. It pooled buttery yellow light on the blue leather desktop. But he found it hard to concentrate on the file. His head was hurting, as it had done in Krogh's office. Patches of faint flickering colour disturbed his vision.

Lom rubbed at his forehead, feeling the seal of angel skin smooth and cool under his fingers, tracing the slight puckering of the skin around it. He was keyed up and unsettled after his dangerous encounter with the marching crowd. The glimpse of Kantor – it was him, he was sure of it – haunted him: the sureness with which he had moved through the jostling people, the easy confidence on his face. He hadn't looked like a hunted man.

But there was something else that troubled Lom, something deeper: watching the crowd marching, he had been drawn towards them. He had launched himself unthinkingly among them to follow Kantor. He had, he now realised, wanted to be one of them. He was, at some instinctive level, on their side. And yet ... the hostility, the contempt, even the hatred they had turned on him when they noticed him. Not him, the uniform. For the second time, it didn't feel so good, being a policeman.

Lom turned his attention to the papers on Petrov. It was a thin file. Petrov was a painter, one of the modern type, not approved by the

Vlast. Petrov wasn't popular, it appeared, not even among his fellow artists. He was a marginal figure: there was only a file on him at all because he came into contact with bigger figures. Artists. Composers. Writers. *Intelligentsia*. They gathered at a place called the Crimson Marmot Club, where Petrov seemed to be a fixture. He had a temper: the file contained accounts of arguments at the Crimson Marmot, scuffles he was involved in. And there had been a dispute with a picture framer. Petrov claimed he'd left a dozen of his works to be framed, the man denied all knowledge of them, and Petrov accused him of having stolen and sold them. He'd made a formal complaint. The framer said Petrov owed him for previous work, and there were no documents on either side. The investigating officer could resolve nothing. He'd filed a report, though. Must have been a quiet day.

Petrov appeared to have few friends of any kind, the report noted, apart from one woman, a life model who worked in a uniform factory near the Wieland Station. Her name was noted for thoroughness, though there was no address and no file reference. The name was Shaumian. *Maroussia Shaumian.*

Lom sat back in his chair and drew a deep breath. *Circles of Contact.*

He tried to imagine Petrov. The registry file gave only a vague outline, a man seen only through the lens of surveillance. He wondered what Petrov's pictures were like. There was one scrap of newsprint pinned inside the cover, clipped, said a manuscript note, from *The Mirgorod Honey Bee*, dated early that spring: a review of an exhibition at the Crimson Marmot Club. He'd ignored it before, but he looked at it now.

'It would be remiss,' the reviewer said,

> to overlook the work of Lakoba Petrov, though most do. This young painter is developing a fine individualism. His prickly personality, which is perhaps better known than his canvases in the city's advanced artistic circles, manifests itself in the three likenesses shown here as a reckless energy. He is impatient with the niceties of style – surely a trait to be admired – and he is not a tactful portraitist, but his use of colour is original and his brush strokes have a fierce movement. He captures through his sitters something of the essence of the modern Mirgorod man. A troubled anxiety lurks in the eyes of his subjects, and their surroundings seem jagged, uncertain, about

to fall away. A young man's work, certainly, but there is bravery and promise here. *The Honey Bee* hopes for good things from Lakoba Petrov in the future.

The review was by-lined Raku Vishnik.
Circles of Contact.

There was a high-pitched frightened shout from somewhere above him.

'Soldiers! There are soldiers in the square!' All across the immense reading room, readers looked up from their work. Lom searched for the cause of the commotion.

'They're charging!' the voice called again. And then Lom saw where it was coming from: somebody was leaning over the balustrade of the upper gallery, where the high arched windows were. He was waving frantically. 'The dragoons are charging!' he was shouting. 'They're going to kill them all!'

Lom ran up the gallery stairs. The upper windows of the Archive, under the dome, were crowded with people watching the demonstration. He squeezed in among them and looked out across the rooftops, through grey air filled with scrappy lumps of snow.

A line of dragoons was moving out across the square, the mudjhiks loping forward, drawing ahead of the riders. Some of the demonstrators broke away from the crowd and started to run for the side streets but stopped in confusion, seeing more troops emerging from there. The dragoons had them bottled up tight. A strange collective tremor passed through the demonstrators as the horsemen picked up speed and raised their blades and whips. Then the heads of riders and horses were moving among the crowd, arms high and slashing downwards. The mudjhiks, moving with surprising speed, waded into the thick of it, striking with their fists and stamping on the fallen.

The dragoons withdrew, circled around and attacked again. And again. Lom saw a group of men grab hold of one of the riders and pull him down until his horse was forced to stumble. Once they had him on the ground, they kicked him and stamped on him and hacked at him with his own sword.

And something else was happening, though nobody but Lom seemed to see it. *There were too many people in the square.* Among the demonstrators and the dragoons, Lom could see others walking there: a sifting crowd, soft-edged, translucent, tired and unaware of the killing all around them. They were not old, but their hair was already turning grey. Their shoulders were frail, their faces drawn unnaturally thin and their skin was as dry and lifeless as newsprint. If they spoke at all, they spoke only when necessary; their voices had no strength, and didn't carry more than a few paces. Whisperers. The dragoons rode through them as if they weren't there at all. Because they weren't.

Above the massacre the sky tipped crazily. Out of the low leaden cloud another sky was breaking through, bruised and purple. An orange sun was tumbling across it like a severed head, its radiance burning in the cloud canyons. Behind the muted grey and yellow facades of the familiar buildings in the square there was another city now. High, featureless buildings rising against the livid sky. One immense white column of a building dwarfed all the other blocks and towers. Ten times taller than the tallest of them, fifty times taller than the real sky-line of Mirgorod, it climbed upwards, tier upon tier, half a mile high, its lower flanks strengthened by fluted buttresses that were themselves many-windowed buildings. The top quarter of it was not a building at all, but an enormous stone statue of a man five hundred feet tall. He was standing, his left foot forward towards the city, his right arm raised and outstretched to greet and possess. He was bare-headed, and his long coat lifted slightly in the suggestion of wind. Although the statue was at least a mile away across the city, Lom could make out every detail of the man's lean, pockmarked face. His eyes were fixed on the visionary distance yet saw every detail of the millions of insect-small lives unfolding beneath his feet. He would be visible from every street in Mirgorod. He would rise out of the horizon to lead incoming ships. He was uncle, father, god. The city, the future, was his.

The statue was the man he had seen weaving his way through the demonstration that morning. The man whose more youthful face gazed confidently into the camera in the photograph in Krogh's file. Josef Kantor.

Tucked in its pocket of no-time and no-space, the Pollandore feels the nearness of the deaths in the Square of the Piteous Angel. Feels the footfall of mudjhiks, the spillage of blood. The panic.

To the Pollandore it is a hardening, a sclerosis ... and a loosening of grip. Something slipping away. Its surface growing milky and opaque. The silence that surrounds it darkening into distance.

From its well of silence the Pollandore reaches out.

Lom stood for a long time at the window, staring at the immense white statue of Kantor half a mile above the blocky, featureless city. What he was seeing, he knew, wasn't there. Not yet. It was a city that wasn't there, but could be. Would be. He could feel it taking shape and solidifying. He was seeing for himself one of the glimpses that Maroussia and Vishnik had talked about last night. A scene from one of Vishnik's photographs. But this was different: Vishnik's was a city of soft possibilities, sudden moments of opening into inwardness and truth; this city was hard and cruel and silent. Closed up. Uniform. A city of triumphal fear. The city of the whisperers and dominion of Kantor, imperial and immense. Mirgorod was a battleground, a contention zone: two future cities both trying to become. The hard city was winning.

And which side was he on?

But that wasn't the question, not yet. The question was, what were the sides? Kantor was an enemy of the Vlast, yet his statue presided over the dragoons at their murderous business in the Square of the Piteous Angel. Vishnik and Maroussia were feeling their way towards the softer city under the iron and stone of Mirgorod, and went in fear of the Vlast's police. Fear of him. The feel of his uniform against his skin disgusted him. What kind of policeman was he? He pushed the question aside. Of one thing he was sure. Kantor had to be stopped, and that was his job. Lom turned away from the window. He had made a decision. He had something to do.

When he came back down the stairs from the gallery window, the great reading room was almost empty. Only a few had stayed at their desks, head in hands, or staring into space, or pretending to work, trying to ignore the sounds of killing. Shutting it out. None of them was going to take any notice of him.

Instead of turning left at the bottom of the staircase and going back to his own desk, Lom went right, following the perimeter of the reading room until he reached a door of varnished wood. It was inset at face height with small square windows of rippled glass.

CLOSED ARCHIVE! AUTHORISED ACCESS ONLY!

He pushed through the door and let it close quietly behind him. His hands were sweating.

The corridor beyond was empty. Lit with dim electric bulbs in globes suspended from the high ceiling, it was lined with more doors, each with a small square of card in a brass holder with a hand-written number. Occasionally a name. Lom went slowly down the corridor reading them. It took for ever.

CMDR L Y CHAZIA.

Lom gripped the brass doorknob, turned and pushed. It was locked. He shoved, but it didn't shift. He thought of trying to kick it down, but the door was solid and heavy. The noise would bring someone. In his pocket he had a bunch of thin metal slivers. His hands were clumsy, slick with sweat. It took him three, four attempts to pick out the right tool. He had to bend down and put his ear close to the door so he could hear what he was doing above the sound of blood in his own ears.

At last the tumblers slipped into place.

He closed the door before he flicked the light switch. Illumination flared dimly. Green-painted walls, an empty desk, rows of steel-framed racks holding files and boxes of papers. Lom forced himself to move slowly down the aisles between the racks, reading the file cards. It wasn't hard to find what he was looking for. Chazia had been methodical. The lavender folder for Josef Kantor was in its place on the K shelf. It was fat and full. He took it and pushed it inside his tunic.

As he was leaving, something made him turn back and go round to the L shelf. It was there. A much slimmer folder, pale pink. LOM, VISSARION Y, INVESTIGATOR OF POLICE. He stuffed it inside his tunic next to Kantor's.

He was halfway across the still-deserted floor of the reading room, almost at the exit, before he realised he hadn't switched off the light inside the room. An archivist was watching him curiously. No way to go back.

Lom stepped out into the square. The snow had stopped falling, leaving the air damp with impending rain. The smell of burned cordite and the dead.

People were moving across the square, alone or in small groups, pausing to look at each body, searching for a familiar face, hoping not to find it. Their feet splashed and slipped across cobbles wet with slush and blood. The dragoons had gone, and the militia, uncertain what to do, were ignoring the searchers. Nobody seemed to be in charge. The grey whisperers were there still. Walking by on their own withdrawn, secretive purposes.

But a couple of blocks away everything was normal. People pursued their business. Trams came and went. Lom boarded one, taking the Vandayanka route, heading for Pelican Quay. When he got there, he stopped at a chandlery to buy a small rubberised canvas sack with a waterproof closure. Then he wandered over to a bench and sat watching the boats at their moorings, idly kicking at the pavement. When he'd managed to loosen a cobble stone, he bent down casually to prise it out of the ground. And slipped it into his pocket.

28

Half the city away, in a room in the House on the Purfas, the paluba sat at the end of the table under the gaze of the Inner Committee of the Secret Government of Lezarye in Exile Within. The windwalker stood behind her, filling the air with woodland scents, ozone and leaf mould and cold forest air.

The five men of the Committee were drinking clear amber tea from glasses in delicate tin holders, waiting for her to begin. They waited patiently, taking the long view, as their fathers had, and their fathers' fathers' fathers. Their room, their rules. They were the ones who carried the weight of the past. Theirs, the great duty to keep the traditions. One day they would overturn the Vlast and bring back the good ways. The rebellions of Lezarye, the Birzel among them, were theirs. They worked and thought in centuries, but their day would come, and they would be ready.

'Madam,' said the man at the far end of the table. Elderly, white hair clipped short and thick, a gold pin in the lapel of his thick dark suit. 'Please. It's been many years since we were honoured by an emissary from the forest. We are anxious to hear your news.'

'Stasis,' said the paluba. 'Balance. Archipelago. Continent. Forest.'

Her voice was quiet, leaves stirring in the wind. The men leaned forward slightly to catch her words.

'For centuries,' she continued, 'balance has prevailed.'

White hair nodded. 'This Novozhd is weak,' he said. 'His position is attacked from without and from within. He is losing his war with the Archipelago. Our moment is coming.'

She knew he was a liar. *Stasis is good*, that was what he meant. *Balance is satisfactory.*

The paluba rested her hand of twigs and earth and wax on the table. It settled like a moth on the pale surface of polished ash and drew their eyes.

Take it away, she felt these men thinking. *This is a foul and horrible thing. Get it off our table.*

Pay attention to me! That was what she wanted the hand to say. *I am the Other, the Unlike You. But I am here. Listen to me. Your world is not what you think.*

'Everything is different now,' she said aloud, looking around the table and fixing each man in turn with the sockets where her eyes would have been. 'Your stasis is broken. An angel has fallen in the forest, and lives. It is alive.'

'Impossible.'

'It is injured. It cannot move, though it struggles to free itself and may yet succeed. It is the strongest there has ever been. By far.'

'There hasn't been an angelfall for eighty years,' said the man on White Hair's right. 'And none has ever survived the impact. The war in heaven is over. Even some in the Vlast's own council say so.'

'Wait, Efim,' said White Hair. 'Let her speak.'

'The angel's power flows from it into the rock that holds it. It is killing the forest. The greater trees are failing.'

'Even if this is true—' said Efim.

The paluba ignored him. 'But the angel is frightened,' she said. 'It feels itself weakening. Failing. It has been looking for a way to defend itself. Or escape.'

'Peder! Surely we're not going to listen to this?'

'And now the angel has found a way,' said the paluba. 'It is building an alliance. Here in Mirgorod.'

Another man leaned over to speak in White Hair's ear. 'Can't we get rid of these awful creatures? The smell ...'

The paluba could hear the whisper of a moth's wing.

'Efim's right,' said a small man in a waistcoat. 'We don't have time for this. Tomorrow we'll have thirty million in our hands.'

'I've already said we shouldn't touch that money,' said another, a soft, round, moon-faced man in spectacles. 'Kantor's Fighting Organisation is too vicious, too wild. Our reputation suffers by association.'

'Ridiculous!' said the man in the waistcoat. 'This is war! We can't afford to be fastidious. While we do nothing our people are dying.

Pogroms are growing worse. Show trials. Executions. Whole streets are being cleansed while we sit here and talk and do nothing.'

They were voices, just voices, so many useless, chattering, indistinguishable, male, redundant, broken voices. The paluba hardly troubled to hear them. She already knew that she had failed here. She had known it when she saw the little glass of amber tea and smelled the fear in the room. Nonetheless, she must not give up. Everything must be attempted.

'There is no time!' said the paluba. 'None at all. We can stop what is coming. But we must move now. Now! The alliance of Lezarye and the forest—'

'And what are we to do, exactly?' said Efim. 'Send in the Fighting Organisation? Could they blow this angel up with their grenades?'

'The answer lies in the Pollandore.'

Efim stood up. 'I've had enough of these fairy tales. And of these disgusting … things. Call me when this rubbish is over.'

The paluba felt the finality of the room turning against her.

'The Pollandore is stirring,' she said. 'It is beginning to have effects. It is beginning to spill, perhaps even to break apart. Even in the forest we have felt it.'

'The Pollandore is nothing. More stories. More nonsense.'

'The time has come.' The paluba was whisper-roaring at them. 'Open the Pollandore. This is the message from the forest. The time is now. You have to open it.'

'What you ask is impossible. Even if we knew how to open it – whatever it is.'

'Even if it existed, even if this wasn't all absolute rubbish …'

'I bring you the key,' said the paluba. 'I offer it to you now. This is my message to you, the gift I bring you from the one who sleeps.'

'The Pollandore is in the keeping of the Vlast,' said Peder. 'Unless they have already destroyed it. I'm sorry, madam. We cannot help you in this. Not at all.'

She had failed. She had known it as soon as she came in, and it had proved to be so. But there was another way. The Shaumian women. She had hoped it wouldn't be necessary. It was not … reliable. That had been shown already, many times. But she would have to try. If there was time.

29

When Lom got back to the apartment, Vishnik was out. Lom turned on the lamp, poured a glass of aquavit and opened the dossier on Kantor. The early stuff was standard: student records, informants' reports of domestic life, associates and contacts. There was an extracted account of the Birzel Rebellion court proceedings and the Executive Order of Internal Exile. Notes on the subject's conduct in the camps. Something about a wife. She had followed him to the camp, but once there she had become pregnant by another man, abandoned Kantor and come back to the city.

Lom read the whole file through from cover to cover, but the papers only filled out what Krogh had told him without adding much, until he got to the end. In a separate pouch at the back, attached with a string tag, were some loose pages with manuscript notes on them in a tight, spidery hand. Some of the notes were initialled. *LYC.*

Lavrentina Chazia.

Lom sat up and began to read more carefully. This was something else. There was an account of Kantor's repeated escape attempts. Violent attacks on other inmates. He had crushed an informant's hand in a vice. '*A resourceful man,*' Chazia had scribbled across it. '*He dominates the camp. The guards fear him. Commandant reluctant to discuss the case.*'

On another page, in a different ink, were the words '*Spoke to Kantor today. He has agreed.*' Attached to the same report with a paper clip was a single sheet of lined paper torn from a bound notebook. It was covered in Chazia's scrawl, apparently written in haste, in pencil, and in parts illegible. It took him a long time to puzzle out the words, and some whole passages defeated him. '*It spoke to me at Vig! It is an angel, a living angel! There can be no doubt of it. We are acknowledged, we are acceptable. The power of it! The power is ...'* The next few lines were not readable. *'... hands trembling. I can't hold it all ...'* Illegible. *'... write before it fades. Not words – ideas, impressions, understandings – roaring floods of light. Much lost ...'* Illegible. *'... magnificent. This is the day! The new Vlast begins here. It speaks to Kantor also. It does.'*

There were a few more notes in Chazia's scrawl. They seemed to record further meetings with Kantor, but they were undated. Only a few unconnected words and figures. Lom could make nothing of them. Chazia had written across the bottom of one, *'It speaks to him. Always to him. Never to me.'*

30

There was a way to enter the Lodka revealed only to the most secret and trusted servants of the Vlast. It was a small shop, occupying the ground floor of a grimy brick house. The shop window, glazed with small square panes of dirty glass and lit by dim electric bulbs, displayed photographs of naked dancing girls. Books in plain yellow covers. Packets in flimsy paper wrappers marked with prices in spidery brown manuscript. The dried-out carcases of flies and moths.

The proprietor was a fat bearded man in gloves and striped shirt-sleeves, known only as Clover. If you spoke certain words to this Clover, he would nod, lift the partition in the counter and show you through a dusty glass door into the back parlour. From there you went through a curtained back exit, across an interior courtyard and down a narrow stairway into a mazy network of tunnels and cellars. It was easy to lose yourself in that subterranean labyrinth, but Josef Kantor knew the way well.

It was an unpleasant route. Kantor disliked it and used it as rarely as he could. The way was damp and dark, and stank of stale river-water. The tunnels and passageways were faced sometimes with stone, more often with rotten planks, and always with slime and streaks of mud. The floor was treacherous with dirty puddles and scattered rubbish. These underground passageways extended under much of inner Mirgorod. They were remnants of the original building work, if not – as some said – remains of some much more ancient settlement that pre-dated the coming of the Founder. Kantor tended to believe the latter. Sometimes he heard things – the shuffle of slow footsteps, mutterings and echoes of shouting – and saw the trails of heavy objects dragged through the mud. Not all the original inhabitants of the marshlands had been driven away by the coming of the city, and some that had left had returned. He wasn't nervous, threading his way through the maze, but he found it ... distasteful.

He came eventually to a locked metal gate that barred the way. He had a key, and let himself through onto an enclosed walkway slung beneath one of the bridges that crossed to the Lodka. Out of sight of the embankment and the windows of the building, it led into the upper basements of the vast stone building. Once inside, Kantor traced a circuitous route that led him gradually upwards, through unused corridors and by way of service elevators and blank stairwells, to the office of Lavrentina Chazia.

Kantor picked up a chair, placed it in front of her desk and sat down. Chazia ignored him and carried on working. Her face had always reminded Kantor of something reddish and cruel. A vixen. And the dark, smooth blemishes where her skin was turning to stone. They were spreading. It was getting worse. He watched her unconsciously scratching at the angel mark on the back of one hand. *She dabbles too much.*

'It was a complete success,' he said.

'What?' She didn't look up.

'The march. On the Lodka.'

'Oh. That. But we must talk about something else, Josef. Your position is compromised. Krogh knows who you are. He has the name. Josef Kantor.'

'Krogh is old and tired.'

'Krogh is clever,' said Chazia. 'He knows we're working against him and he knows he can't trust his own people. He's taken steps against you. An investigator. From the east. Someone with no connections here. He's set him to track you down.'

Kantor grunted. 'One investigator? That can be taken care of. You'll do that?'

'Of course.'

'We can't afford distractions.'

She looked up from her papers at last.

'You and I cannot meet again, Josef. Our plans must change. At least in so far as they involve you.'

'I'm not *dispensable,* Lavrentina. The angel speaks to me. Not you.'

Kantor saw Chazia's vixen head lean forward, her eyes widen a fraction. She scratched at the stone-coloured back of her hand again. Delicately wet her lips with the tip of her tongue. *How transparent she is. She gives herself away. She doesn't know she's doing it. How she wants to be close to power! How she desires it! She longs to feel power's hot breath on her skin, and open her legs for power. She is jealous of me, because the angel comes inside me, not her. She felt it once and she wants it again. She's hooked like a fish.*

'What does it say?' said Chazia. 'What does the angel say to you?'

He saw how weak she was. *Desiring to be near power is not the same as desiring power. It is the opposite.*

'It is impatient,' he said. 'It urges haste. It makes promises.'

'Promises?'

'To me, Lavrentina. Not to you. To me.'

'Of course you would say that. To save yourself.'

'One cannot lie about the angel. One cannot deceive it.'

Chazia showed the tip of her tongue again, pink between pale thin lips.

'Is it here? Is it with you … now?'

'Of course not. I couldn't speak to you if it was.'

'Why does it choose you, Josef? Why doesn't it come to me again?'

Kantor said nothing.

'Do you know why not?'

'No.'

'You could ask it.'

'No.'

Chazia sighed and leaned back in her chair.

'So. What does it promise you, Josef?'

'Stars. Galaxies. Universes. The red sun rising.'

'Meaning? Meaning what?'

Kantor looked at her and said nothing.

'Meaning nothing,' said Chazia.

'It has given me an instruction. The Pollandore must be destroyed.'

'It knows about that?'

'It knows everything.'

'Then it knows we cannot destroy the Pollandore. We have tried and failed.'

'It must be done'

121

'This doesn't change your position, of course,' she continued. 'The logic is inescapable.'

'I do not see it.'

'Think, Josef. See it from my perspective. Soon the Iron Guard will step in and put things right. This weak and backsliding regime will fall. The One Righteous War will recommence with renewed vigour.'

'With me alongside you, Lavrentina. That is the agreement. It must stand.'

'But consider this, Josef. How would it be if Krogh makes the connection between you and me? If he can *prove* it? If he takes this to the *Novozhd* before we are ready? Surely you see the impossibility of this?'

Kantor watched her steadily. He said nothing.

'What would you do, Josef?' she said. 'In my position?'

He shrugged. 'It is not complex,' he said. 'Krogh must be killed.'

Her eye flickered.

You are transparent to me. You garrulous intoxicated mad old fox-bitch.

'Nothing is easier than death,' he said. 'The more deaths there are, the better for our purpose.'

'But—'

'The solution is clear,' Kantor continued. 'Krogh must be killed. Of course …' He looked her in the eye. Held her gaze. 'If you don't have the stomach for that, I will do it myself. It doesn't matter so long as it is done.'

Chazia glared at him.

'It will be done,' she said. 'It's not a problem.'

'Thank you,' said Kantor. 'Good. Of course, that isn't why I came to see you.'

'So why did you come?'

'I have a couple of requests.' He smiled. 'No doubt these also will be no problem.'

Chazia bridled.

'Be careful, Josef. Don't go too far. You are not … safe.'

'No one is safe, Lavrentina. Such is the world. But there are some favours you could do for me.'

'What?'

'My former wife, the slut Feiga-Ita.'

Chazia looked at him in surprise. 'What about her?'

'Kill her. Kill that bastard daughter of hers too.'

'I see,' said Chazia. 'But ... surely you could do this yourself? You have people.'

'They would want to know why. That would not be helpful.'

Chazia sat back and considered.

'I see no objection,' she said eventually. 'But you will owe me, Josef. The service is not your personal execution squad. Is that all?'

'No. I want you to take me to the Pollandore. I want to see it.'

31

In Vishnik's apartment, Lom poured another glass and reached for the file with his own name on it. It was a standard personnel file, tied with ribbon. The registry slip on the front showed it had been referred to Commander Chazia only the day before. The day he had arrived in Mirgorod and seen Krogh. The referring signature was Krogh's own private secretary.

The file itself contained all the paperwork of an unexceptional career. Good but not brilliant academic achievement. Stalled promotions and rejected applications. The criticisms, complaints and accusations. And one other thing. The earliest document. A letter. Lom read it over and over again until he had it by heart. It was addressed to the Provost of the Podchornok Institute of Truth.

Righteous and Excellent Provost Savinkov

I bow to you deeply from the white of my face to the damp earth, and I commit to your care this boy, gathered in by my artel when, in pursuance of the Forest Extirpation Order, we removed the village and nemeton of Salakhard. The boy does not speak to us, but is believed to be a child of uncouth persons, and consequently now parentless. He is apparently not above six years old, and in all conscience we hesitate to end the life of one so young. But his remaining with us is not by any means practicable. Our orders take us further eastwards, under the trees. Perhaps he may be closed up, in the way you know how, and enfolded in the One Truth? He is yet young.

Your servant,

S V Labin, Captain

Lom leaned back on Vishnik's couch. Deeply buried memories: first memories, beginnings. He was lying under a tree, a thickened old beech that thrust torsos of root deep into the earth and rose high over his head, spreading its leafhead, casting a pool of blue shade on the spring-green grass. The sun hung above the tree, a moored fiery vessel, and small things moved in the thickets. The air was filled with strong, sour, earthy smells, and he could feel the ground beneath his back. He heard the leaves of trees and bushes moving as if in a wind. He was looking upwards, tracing the boughs of the tree where the trunk bifurcated and reached high into the mass of foliage, the million leaves, fresh and thick, bright with the green liquid fire of sunlight that was pouring through them. The tree was eating light and breathing clouds of perfume.

The perfumed tree-breath was its voice, its chemical tongue. It was speaking to the insect population in its bark and branches, warning and soothing them. It was speaking to its neighbour trees, who answered: tree spoke to tree, out across the endless forest. And it was speaking to him. Psychoactive pheromones drifted through the alveolar forests of his human lungs and the whorled synaptical pathways of his cerebral cortex.

At the institute at Podchornok they'd given the silent boy a name, Vissarion Lom, and all this they had taken from him.

Memory left him. For a while Lom simply sat, tired and empty, thinking of nothing, listening to the evening call of the gulls in the sea-coloured sky. Surfacing. It was almost dark when he finally moved. Lom gathered up the files and his notes, put them in the waterproof bag, weighted it with the quayside cobblestone and slipped it into the cistern in the bathroom. He settled down to wait for Vishnik to return. That night they would go to the Crimson Marmot Club. To see Lakoba Petrov.

32

The music got louder with each step down the alleyway. Letters in electric red flickered on and off above a door shut tight against the blowing rain and cold. *The Crimson Marmot*. Lom pushed the door open. A blast of thick, heated air, tobacco smoke and noise hit his face. Inside was a hot, boiling cauldron of red. Red, the colour of the Vlast, the colour of propaganda, the colour of blood, but also the colour of intimacy and desire. Loud voices shouting into excited faces.

Vishnik led the way through the crowd to a table. A young man was dancing nearby, an absorbed, solitary dance with unseeing eyes. His face was powdered chalky white. As his face caught the light Lom saw a ragged wound scar down his cheek. At the next table a snaggle-bearded man was smoking with his eyes closed. The woman with him looked bored. Her jacket shimmered as if it was silk. She was naked from the waist down. She laughed and drained her glass and got up to dance with the young man with the powdered face, swaying her hips and moving her hands in complicated knots. The young man didn't notice her. On a bench in the corner a couple were making love.

Lom leaned across to shout in Vishnik's ear: 'Who are these people?'

Vishnik shrugged.

'That doesn't matter here. They come to leave all that behind. Outside, in the daytime, they are clerks. Waiters. Former persons who used to be lawyers or the wives of generals. But this is the night side, a place without history. They come here for the now of it. Keep raising the level. Another notch. Another glass. Another powder. Here you make the most of your body and anyone else's you can. Does that shock you?'

126

'No,' said Lom. 'No. It doesn't.' He'd been to places in Podchornok where fat rich men went to get drunk and touch young bodies, but this was different. There was a version of himself that could be comfortable here. He looked around again. Searching the faces. 'Can you see Petrov? Is he here yet?'

'No, but it's still early.'

A waiter brought a bottle of champagne and two glasses. Lom watched him uncork and pour.

'Relax,' said Vishnik. 'Enjoy the evening.'

Lom's eyes were adjusting to the rich, dim redness of the Marmot's. The walls were crimson plush and hung with vast gilded mirrors that made the room seem larger than it was. Tables crowded one another in a horseshoe around a central space where dancers moved between people standing in noisy, excitable groups. At the back of the room was a small stage, its heavy curtains closed, and in one corner, musicians played instruments of the new music. Lom recognised some of them: a heckelphone, a lupophone, a bandonion, a glasschord. Others he couldn't identify. He sipped at the champagne and winced. It was thick, with a metallic perfume.

He'd expected something different of the Crimson Marmot: an art gallery, perhaps, with intense talk and samovars. There was art here, though. Wild, angular sketches on the walls. A larger-than-life humanesque manikin hanging from the ceiling, dressed as a soldier with the head of a bear. A figure, crouched high in the corner, with eight limbs and six pairs of woman's breasts. Lom realised it was meant to be an angel. It was made out of animal bones, old shoes, leather straps and rubbish. Candles burned in its eyes and a scrawled placard hung from its neck. *Motherland*. Beneath it, someone had pinned a notice to the wall.

ART IS DEBT! LONG LIFE TO THE MEAT MACHINE ART OF THE FORBAT!

With a crash of drums, the musicians fell silent and the curtain was drawn aside to reveal the small stage. A red banner unfurled. *The Neo-emotional Cabaret*. An ironic cheer went around the room, and a smattering of applause. Vishnik leaned across to Lom.

'You'll like this. This is different. This is new. This is fucking good.'

On the stage a man was crouching inside a large wooden crate, shouting nonsense words into a tube connected to a megaphone on top of the crate. 'Zaum! Zaum! Baba-zaum!' he chanted. The musicians hacked away with atonal enthusiasm. Lom caught some longer phrases of almost-coherent verse.

Wake up, you scoundrel self-abusers!
Materialists! Bread eaters! Mirgorod is a cliff –
bare snow in banked-up drifts – daybreak.
Winter's late dawn – worn out – shivering –
descends the river like smallpox.

Lom was relieved when it finished. The curtain closed and the band struck up again. Pink spotlights lit the dance floor. Lom hadn't noticed the dancer enter, but she was there. Her breasts were bare and she wore a long flickering skirt, divided to give her legs room for movement. The dancer's body was thin and muscular, her breasts small and narrow, her black hair cut short, and she danced fast and thoughtlessly, shouting and jerking to the music, advancing towards the audience and then retreating with a shrug. Pleasing herself. Not trying. Just doing.

And then, to cheers and applause, she was gone. Most of the band stood up and went to the bar, leaving the glasschord player alone to unwind some kind of drifting, song-like melody.

Vishnik took him by the arm and whispered in his ear, 'Petrov's come. At the table by the bar. The green shirt.'

Lom looked across to where a group of men were listening to a large bearded fellow talking loudly, his wet red mouth working, banging the table with his fist to punctuate his periods. Petrov was a silent bundle of energy in a corner seat, staring with obvious resentment at the talker. Lom studied him carefully. He was all wild, dark curly hair, a long sharp nose and dark eyes, wide and round, full of passionate need and intelligence and a crazed, intent sort of anger. His lips, pressed tight together, were full and almost bruised-looking. He looked as if someone had punched him and he was trying not to cry. When he leaned back in his chair, as if he was trying to get further away from the bearded shouter, his loose green shirt gaped open halfway to his waist, revealing the white, almost skeletal bone structure of his upper chest.

'Take me over, can you?' said Lom. 'I want to talk to him.'

Vishnik picked up the half-empty champagne bottle and the glasses and went across. Lom followed. Some of the men at the table nodded. The beard ignored them. So did Petrov.

'The city as a whole,' Beard was saying in a deep, resonant voice, 'is instinct with energising power. It inspires me. The more marches and strikes and riots – the more confrontation – the better it is for art. The agitation in the squares and factories is like the revving of the engines of the vehicles in the street. It provides heart. It is marvellous. Wonderful. I must have it, at all times, in order to work. It's the fuel my motor burns.'

Beard paused to take a drink.

'Did you hear?' said the young man with the powdered face. 'The Novozhd has said that from now on all his rallies will be held after dark. Isn't that perfect? It is already evening across the Vlast. Midnight! The Novozhd is an artist himself, though he won't admit it.'

Beard spluttered.

'The Novozhd! Do you know what he said about my picture of Lake Tsyrkhal?' He stared around the table, daring them to speak. 'I made the water yellow and black, and this is what the Novozhd said: *As a hunter, I know that Lake Tsyrkhal is not like that.* So now he forbids us to use colours which are different from those perceived by the normal eye. What is the point, I ask you, of a painter with a normal eye? Any idiot can see what's normal. But do I fear this Novozhd? No!'

'Does he fear you, Briakh?' said Petrov fiercely, uncoiling from the tense crouch he'd wound himself into. He was nursing a small glass of something thick and dark. 'Does the Novozhd fear you? Isn't that the question? I think he does not.'

Briakh glared at him.

'Meaning?'

'Meaning your paintings are nothing. All our paintings are nothing. This club is nothing. It's not even so much shit on his boots, so far as the Novozhd cares. We're only still here because he hasn't noticed us yet.'

'He put three of my pictures in his Exhibition of Degenerate Art. Three.'

'They get people to laugh at us, that's all. It's a distraction. Do you think the Novozhd lies awake at night because you made Lake Tsyrkhal black and yellow?'

Powdered Face giggled. '*The most perfect shape,*' he quoted, '*the*

sublimest image that has ever been created didn't come out of any artist's
studio: it is the infantryman's steel helmet. The artists ought to be tied up
next to their pictures so every citizen can spit in their faces.'

Briakh ignored him. He was staring at Petrov.

'And you, Petrov?' he said. 'Is the Novozhd scared of you? How many of your pictures does he have in his exhibition?'

'Painting's finished,' said Petrov quietly. 'I told you. There will be a new art. And he will know my name soon enough. He will know Petrov by his works. You all will. Yes, he should fear me.'

'Why?' said Lom into the silence. 'What are you going to do? Rob a bank?'

Petrov stared at him.

'Who are you?'

'He's my friend, Lakoba,' said Vishnik. 'He's from out of town.'

'Anyone can see that,' said Petrov. He turned to Lom. 'And do you like this place? It is our laboratory. We are all scientists here. We are studying the coming apocalypse.'

'Sounds to me you're planning to start it.'

'You shouldn't laugh at me.'

'As long as you bring us champagne,' said Briakh, 'you can laugh as much as you like.' He reached a heavy paw across to Vishnik's bottle, took a pull from the neck, emptied it and waved it at the bar. 'Another!' he boomed. 'Two more! Dry men are desperate here! Friend Vishnik's paying.'

Petrov stood up.

'Drink till you vomit,' he said. 'The crisis is now, but you wouldn't know it if it bit your arse.' He went unsteadily towards the exit.

'You're crazy drunk yourself, man!' Briakh shouted after him. 'Crazy drunk on that crazy-man syrup you drink.'

Lom got up and followed Petrov. He got entangled with a boy in a spangled crinoline and jewelled breast-caps who wanted to dance with him. By the time he got free and caught up with him, Petrov was halfway down the street.

'Can I walk with you a while?' said Lom.

'Why?'

'Curiosity. I agree with what you were saying in there. I wanted to hear more.'

'I don't believe you understood a word of it.'

'Maybe I don't know about painting. But I do know about blowing things up.'

'What's that got to do with anything?'

'That was fighting talk in there.' The rain was heavier now, whipped along on a bitter wind. Petrov, wearing only his half-buttoned green shirt, seemed oblivious to it. Lom wished he had brought his cloak out with him. His head was ringing with the noise and heat of the club. 'Unless it was just bluster,' he added. 'Like Briakh.'

'You're right about Briakh. Ha! Blusterer Briakh.'

'What about you?'

Petrov's face was close to his. His eyes were wide and black and shiny. Lom smelled the fumes of sweetness and alcohol on his breath.

'*I* have an *idea*,' said Petrov. '*I* have an *intention*. *I* have a *purpose*.'

'I'd like to hear about it.'

'You will. When it's done.'

'Why not tell me now? Perhaps I can help you. Let me buy you a drink somewhere out of the rain.'

'Help doesn't come into it. Help isn't necessary. And neither is talk. One can either talk or do, but not both, never both. You should tell that to Briakh. Tell all of them back there. They can't tell talk from do, any of them. That's their problem.'

Petrov walked on. Lom followed.

'We should talk though. We have a friend in common, I think.'

Petrov didn't stop walking. 'Who?' he said.

'Josef Kantor.'

'Kantor?'

'You know him then?'

'You said I did.'

'I guessed.'

'Kantor the Crab. Josef Krebs. Josef Cancer. The smell of the camps is in his skin. He can't wash it off. I think he made himself a shell when he was there and climbed inside it, and he has sat inside it for so long that now he's all shell. Nothing but shell, shell, and lidless eyes on little stalks staring out of it, like a crab. But people *like* him. Do you know that, Vishnik's friend? They think he has *charm*. They say those crab eyes of his twinkle like Uncle Novozhd. But they're idiots. There's no man left in there at all. He's all crab. Turtle. Cockroach. And shall I tell you something else about him?' Petrov stopped and turned to

131

Lom, swaying slightly, oblivious of the rain in his face. He began to speak very slowly and clearly. 'He has some other purpose which is not apparent.' He began to tap Lom on the chest with a straight forefinger. 'And. So. Do. You.'

'Me?'

'I don't like you, Vishnik's friend. I don't like you at all. Your hair is too short. You look around too much. You keep too many secrets and you play too many games. Vishnik should choose his friends better. You wear him. Like a coat. No, like a beard.'

'I—'

'He knows it, and he lets you. *That's* a friend. And you'll kill him because of it. You think I don't know a policeman when I see one?'

33

It was long after midnight, but not yet morning. Lom lay on the couch in Vishnik's apartment under a thin blanket, trying to force sleep to come, but it would not. The couch was too small and the stove had gone out long ago. All heat had seeped from the room, along with the illusion of warmth from the Crimson Marmot's champagne and brandy, leaving him cold and wakeful. Moonlight flooded in through a gap in the curtains: the glare of the two broken moons, wide-eyed and binocular, searchlighting out of a glassy, starless, vapourless sky. The room was drenched in it. The effect was remorseless: every detail was whited, brittle, monochrome. Petrov's drunken accusation cut at him again and again.

You think I don't know a policeman when I see one?

One day when he was about fourteen he'd been sent out on some errand, and there was a girl in a green dress in the alleyway by Alter's. Town boys were gathered around her. Shoving. Tripping. Touching. *What's in your bag? Show us your bag.*

Lom could have walked away, but he didn't.

'Hey!' he shouted. 'Leave her alone!'

They'd beaten him. Badly. The big one kept punching him in the face: a boy with a pelt of cropped hair across his skull. Every time the boy punched him in the face Lom fell over. And every time that happened, he shook his head and stumbled back to his feet. And the big one punched him again. And he fell. And got up. At first Lom had shouted at them. Yelled.

'Fuck off! Leave me alone! I haven't done anything to you!'

But that soon passed. He'd fallen silent. Fallen into the rhythm of it. Punch. Fall. Stand up. Punch. Fall. Stand up. There was no room for yelling. No breath for it either.

'I love this,' one of the boys was saying. 'Do it again, Savva. Hit him more. Go on. Yes. I love it.'

There was blood on Lom's face and he hardly knew what was happening. Everything was weightless and distant. The punches hardly hurt now. Every time he fell, he stood back up. It was mute, pointless resistance. His face was numb. He'd been beaten beyond the capacity for thought. There was nothing left but the automatic determination to get back up on his feet.

Eventually there would have come a time when he could not have got up again, but before he reached it Savva stopped. He was looking at Lom with something like fellowship in his eyes. And then one of the smaller ones, one of Savva's shoal, stepped in and punched at Lom's chin himself, but he didn't have Savva's power and Lom was numb to anything less. He didn't stumble or fall this time, but turned to look in the little one's feral, weasel eye, disinterestedly.

'Leave him,' said Savva. 'That's enough.'

Lom had felt something like friendship for Savva then, a feeling which had shamed him secretly ever since. That moment of instinctive friendship, he thought afterwards, had taught him something. The victim's gratitude toward his persecutor. How it felt so much like love.

Savva had taken his money. The Provost's money. Lom had been made to clean the lavatories every morning for a month. But a letter had come from the girl's father to thank the unknown boy in the uniform of the Institute who had come to his daughter's help. The father was Dr Arensberg the magistrate, and the Provost had given him Lom's name. An invitation arrived, addressed to Vissarion Lom himself. He was asked to the Arensbergs' house for tea, and the Provost had made him go. After the first time he'd become a regular visitor on weekend afternoons.

The Arensbergs' house was well known in Podchornok. It was large, steep-gabled, wooden, with clustered chimneys of warm red brick, set in its own orchard. The rooms were full of dogs and flowers, the smell of baking, and the Arensberg children at music practice. The family taught him to play euchre and svoy kozyri: Dr and Mrs Arensberg, the girl, Thea, and her brother Stepan, who was seventeen and going to be an officer in the hussars, sitting together, playing cards in the dusty sunlight. The smell of beeswax and amber tea.

Lom's visits to the Arensbergs were his first and only encounter with family domesticity. A private life. The warmth and decency that came with secure money. He'd known nothing of such houses before, or the families that lived in them, except what he saw through town-house windows at dusk, when the lights were lit and the curtains not yet drawn.

One day in summer Dr Arensberg called him into his study.

'What will you do, Vissarion? With your life, I mean? Your career?'

'Career? I don't know. I expect I will become a teacher.'

'Do you want to do that?'

'I've never considered it from that angle. It's what boys in my position do.'

'What would you say about joining the police? It's a good life, solid, a decent salary, a career in which talent can rise. One of the few. You could hope for a good position. In society I mean.'

And so Lom's future had been settled. He would be a policeman. The private decency of houses like the Arensbergs' was worth protecting. He was a fighter and he could keep it safe, and one day perhaps he would rise high enough in the service to have such a house himself, like the Deputy's on Sytin Prospect.

He passed the entrance examination without difficulty. It was in the very same week that he took the oath of commitment to the Vlast that the terrible dark blade fell. The knife went in.

Gendarmes came from Magadlovosk to the Arensbergs' house and took the doctor away. He was denounced. A profiteer. An enemy of the people. A spy for the Archipelago. They took him down the Yannis and he never returned. The house was seized, declared forfeit to the Vlast and granted to the new Commissar for Timber Yards. Stepan's commission was revoked. Mrs Arensberg, Stepan and Thea moved into a single room above a stationer's shop off Ansky Prospect.

Lom couldn't believe in Arensberg's guilt. It was a mistake. It would be cleared up. Someone had lied. A magistrate made his share of enemies. Lom would prove Arensberg's innocence one day, when he'd finished his training. He said as much to Thea when he went to see her, wearing his new cadet uniform, in the room off Ansky Prospect, with its yellow furniture and thin muslin curtains. She had tied a scarf around her hair and she was scrubbing layers of fat and dust off the kitchen shelves when he arrived.

Thea had thrown him out.

'Get out of here, policeman,' she said bitterly.

'Thea – I want to help you – all of you.'

'Don't you see you're one of them?'

'But only for you … for him …'

'That uniform makes me sick,' she said. 'Don't come here again.'

He stayed away for a few days to let her calm down, but when he went back, Mrs Arensberg – distant, polite, formal – told him Thea had left Podchornok. She was going to live in Yagda. She had cousins there, or aunts, or something. She planned to study and become a doctor like her father.

That same week Lom saw Raku Vishnik off to the University. In one week he'd lost them both, and the Arensbergs' house was gone for ever.

Lom had immersed himself in police work. As soon as he could, he called up the magistrate Arensberg's file. The evidence against him was overwhelming. He'd been sent to Vig, and died there. No cause of death was recorded. There was nothing to be done.

Fifteen years.

It hadn't been difficult. There was always someone to tell you what to do. Someone like Krogh. Krogh wasn't a bad man. But he wasn't a good man either. He wasn't any sort of man.

Detectives make nothing happen. They do the opposite, repairing the damage done by events: desire, anger, accident and change. Stitching the surface of things back together. But events break the surface open anyway. Inside you. Transforming the way you feel and see things. Taking an axe to the frozen sea inside us. Detectives can't clear up after that.

Sleep would not come. Lom lay there and listened to the rumble of the darkened city.

And then there was something else in the room. There had not been and now there was.

It was a dark and sour presence, a thing of blood and earth. No door had opened. No curtain had stirred. It had arrived. Somehow.

It was coming closer. Lom could see it now, at the edge of vision, soaked in the light of the moons. Standing, looking at him, sniffing the air. Lom dared not move his head to see it more clearly, but he knew what it was. He had seen such a thing before, once, laid out dead on the earth under a stand of silver birch. That one had been shaped like a man, or rather a child, short and slender, with a small head and a lean, wiry strength. But this one was different, and not only because it was alive, and stalking him. The body he had seen was naked and entirely white, with the whiteness of a thing that had never felt the light of the sun. This one wore clothes of a kind and the skin of its face and hands was oddly piebald. Large irregular blotches of blackness marked the pallor. It was a killer, an eater of blood.

Suddenly the thing was not where it had been, ten feet away between the window and the door. It was standing over him, leaning forward, opening its black mouth. Lom had not seen it cover the intervening space. He was certain it had not done so. It had simply … moved.

Such creatures cannot bear to be looked at. They hate the touch of the human gaze. When it saw that Lom was awake and staring into its eyes it flinched and staggered a step backwards. It recovered almost immediately, but it had given Lom the moment he needed to screw up all his fear and revulsion into a ball and cast it at the thing. In the same instant he threw off the blanket, leapt to his feet and lunged forward. But the thing was no longer where it had been. It was to his left, at his side, jumping up and gripping his shoulder, scrabbling at his neck. He felt the heat of its breath on his face. Smelled the cold wet smell of earth. In desperation Lom threw at his attacker all the air in the room. The creature staggered back and fell. Photographs scattered and a chair fell loudly sideways. A lamp crashed to the floor.

It was the surprise as much as the force of the attack that was effective. The piebald thing fell awkwardly. As it struggled to its feet, the back of its head was exposed. Wisps of thin hair across its surprisingly slender, conical skull. Lom stepped forward, the cosh from his sleeve gripped firmly. He wouldn't get another chance.

But it was not there. It was gone. Lom whipped round, braced for an attack from behind that he was unlikely to survive, but the moonlit room was empty.

The door from the bedroom opened.

'Vissarion? What the fuck are you doing?'

Vishnik lit the lamp. The study was in chaos. Heaps of books scattered everywhere. A picture fallen from the wall, its glass shattered.

'What happened? What have you done?' He saw the rips in Lom's shirt, the smears of blood from deep scratches on his face and neck, the delicate nastiness of the small cosh in his fist.

'It was a vyrdalak,' said Lom. 'A strange one.' He sat down heavily on the couch. Now that it was over, his legs were trembling and he felt emptily sick. He knew what the bite of such a creature could do. 'I guess the Commander wants her files back.'

34

Lakoba Petrov didn't go home after leaving the Marmot's. He no longer needed a place of his own. He hadn't eaten for so long, he no longer felt hungry. He threw away what remained of his money and walked through the night, drinking sweet water copiously wherever he could find it. The clear coldness of it made his soul also clear and cold. His Mirgorod burned. It was awash with cool, glorious rain and the rain washed him clean.

Again and again the night city detonated for him, bursting into roses of truth. He was walking through paintings, truer and better than any he had painted. He could have painted them if had chosen to do it. But why should he? There was no need. He had a better idea. As he walked the streets in a pyrotechnical excitement of fizzing synapses, he developed in words his new principle of art. An art that would leave painting behind altogether and become something new and pure and clean. The art of the coming destruction.

He did carry one tube of paint with him, though, in his pocket. A beautiful lilac–turquoise. In the lamplight, looking at his reflection in the mirror in a barber's shop window, he squeezed the paint onto his finger and wrote on his forehead. '*I, Petrov.*' It wasn't easy, mirror writing. He had to concentrate.

When he grew tired he lay down to sleep, and in the dawn when he woke his clothes crackled with the snapping of ice.

35

Maroussia Shaumian got out of bed in the chill grey of dawn. She lived in a one-room apartment with her mother out near the Oyster Bridge. There wasn't much: a bed to share, some yellow furniture, a thin and faded rug on bare boards. Her mother was sitting upright on a chair in the centre of the carpet, wearing only her dressing gown. Her thin hair, unbrushed, stood up round her head in a scrappy, pathetic halo. It was icy cold in the room, though the windows were closed tight. Her small breaths and Maroussia's own were tiny visible ghosts in the chill air.

'Come on,' said Maroussia, holding out her hand. 'I'll get the stove lit. Come and get dressed.'

Her mother flapped at her to be silent. Her hands were as soft and pale and strengthless as the empty eggshells of a small bird.

'What is it?' said Maroussia. 'What's the matter?'

'Come away from the window. They'll see you. They're watching.'

'There's nobody there. Just people in the street.'

'They're there, only you can't see them.'

'Where then? Show me.'

Her mother shook her head. Stubbornness was the only strong thing left in her. 'I'm not coming over there.'

'Get dressed at least.' Maroussia went towards the wardrobe.

Her mother whimpered quietly. 'Don't open it,' she breathed. 'Maroussia. Please. Don't.'

Maroussia began to set out food on the table for their breakfast. There'd been a time when she would have dragged her mother across to the window or even out into the street, to show her that what she feared wasn't there. Hoping to shake her out of it. Sometimes she had literally grabbed her and shaken her by the shoulders, hard, until it must have hurt, and shouted into her face. *It's all right. It's all right. There's nothing there. Please, just be normal.* But it made no difference. Nothing did. The nights were the worst. Maroussia would wake to find her mother piling up their few bits of furniture against the door. 'They're coming back,' she would be muttering. 'The trees are coming back.'

She still called her 'mother', though the word had long ago stopped being even the empty shell of an exhausted, bitter joke. 'Mother' was the faded inscription on an empty box.

Maroussia touched her mother on the shoulder.

'Come over to the table,' she said. 'You must be hungry.'

There was bread, sausage, a potato. Her mother looked at it. 'Where's it from?'

'Issy and Zena's'

'Oh no, I couldn't touch anything from there.'

Maroussia couldn't say that the falling of the shadow across her mother's life had come as a surprise. Although she had never been sat down and told the story of their lives, she had pieced it together over the years.

Her mother had been Feiga-Ita Shaumian, and then Feiga-Ita Kantor, and then Feiga-Ita Shaumian again. The Shaumians had been one of the great families of Lezarye, and Feiga-Ita's marriage to Josef Kantor was a grand occasion: he the firebrand orator and Hope of the Future, she his loving and industrious amanuensis. When Josef was sent into internal exile in the aftermath of the Birzel Rebellion, Feiga-Ita had gone with him, though she didn't have to. But then, suddenly, she'd abandoned her husband, even though she was pregnant, and gone back to the city. She endured the long journey to Mirgorod alone and ill. It had been a difficult pregnancy. In Mirgorod she had reverted to her former name, borne the child, called her Maroussia, cut off all contact with her old life, her family, the dreamers of Lezarye, brought up the daughter in a succession of obscure and shabby attics.

At first there had been good times. Maroussia remembered the games and stories, the small adventures out into the city and beyond, to the sea and to the suburban parks that ringed the city, but Feiga-Ita had lapsed at last into this permanent darkness of the heart. Maroussia had got used to sharing their room with the dark predatory walking shadows of trees and the spies and accusers that followed her mother down the street and waited in the darkness of alleyways, stairwells and wardrobes.

She cut a slice of hard black bread and some sausage and ate it herself.

Her mother, feeling herself watched, looked across at her with wide, watery eyes.

'Maroussia?' she said.

'Yes?'

You won't tell them, will you?'

'What?'

'Don't ever tell them what I did.'

'I have to go now,' said Maroussia. 'I have to go.'

36

Lom sat at the desk in Vishnik's apartment, turning over the
pages of the Kantor folder again. Wondering where to go
from here. Chazia wanted her file back. She was a dangerous
enemy: she had tried to kill him once, and she would try again. Kantor
was Chazia's agent. So much was obvious from the file. It was proof
– enough to take to Krogh and let him deal with Chazia. But it was
unsatisfactory. Would Krogh deal with Chazia? Could he? And Lom
wanted more. He wanted Kantor.

He was about to close the folder when he noticed a paper he had
overlooked before, because it was out of date order, torn loose and
tucked inside the flap at the back of the file. It was just a routine official
instruction, concerned with Kantor's removal to Vig. The accompany-
ing report said that his wife had already returned to Mirgorod. Wife's
name: Shaumian, Feiga-Ita. Chazia had added a note in pencil: '*There
is a daughter. Not his. KEEP IN VIEW.*' The last three words triple
underlined. Pinned to the back of the instruction sheet was a typed
half-sheet with an address:

> Shaumian, Feiga-Ita & Shaumian, Maroussia
> 387 Velazhin, Apt. 23
> Oyster Bridge
> White Side

Chazia had written against each name a series of letters and numer-
als. Lom recognised them as file references for the Gaukh Engine.
Kantor had a wife, and Maroussia Shaumian was her *daughter*?
Circles of contact.
Shit.

37

The paluba and her companion of forest air stood in the doorway of an empty building, watching the entrance to the Shaumians' apartment block across the street. They were waiting for the daughter to leave. They wanted to find the mother alone. It was the mother they knew. From many years before. She was their better hope.

When they saw the daughter go, they crossed the road and climbed the stairs. No one saw them. There were people there, in the street, but they were not seen.

The paluba paused outside the apartment door, on the tiny landing at a bend in the stairs. She could feel the Pollandore as a strong presence in the room and seeping out of it. She could feel its thrilling touch. New things were possible here. She scratched and tapped at the door with her fingers of birch twig and squirrel's tendon.

'Feiga-Ita Shaumian, let me in.' Her voice buzzed and rattled like gusts of air in the strings of a wind harp. There was no answer. Nothing moved behind the door, but the paluba sensed a listener in the dark.

'Feiga-Ita Shaumian, open the door.'

Silence.

'Feiga-Ita Shaumian. You know me. Let me in. I have a message. From him.'

Silence.

'Feiga-Ita Shaumian!'

'He's dead.'

It was quieter than a whisper. The old woman was talking to herself, her words drained of energy by a fear so old and heavy it was like listening for the trickle of dust under stones. But the paluba heard.

'No,' she said. 'He is alive.'

'He is dead.'

'No. He sent you letters, but you never replied.'

'There were no letters.'

'He is your daughter's father.'

Silence.

'Feiga-Ita Shaumian, open the door.'

Silence. No, not silence. Short, harsh breathing. The scraping of furniture across a wooden floor. Bumping against the other side of the door. Being piled up.

'Feiga-Ita Shaumian, I have a message for you.'

'There are trees in my room. Get them out of my room. Leave me alone.'

'He needs you now. He needs his daughter. You must hear his message. Let me in.'

'I am standing by the window. If you try to come in I'll jump.'

The paluba heard the casement opening. Heard the faint sounds from the street become louder. Felt the stir of air from outside.

'You could come with us. We will take you with us. Back to the woods.'

Silence. Quiet, ragged gulps of breath.

'We will take you both, the daughter too, when what must be done is done.'

Silence.

The figure of air made a slight motion and the door blew inwards, splintering off its hinges, but the furniture piled behind it budged only a few inches. Inside, Maroussia's mother moaned.

'Please don't make me jump,' she said. 'Make the trees go away. Please.'

'The Pollandore must be opened, Feiga-Ita. The time has come. You or she must do it. There is no one else now. It needs to be done.'

Inside the room there was only breathing.

Silence.

The paluba laid her dry simulacrum of a hand against the door as if she were going to push it aside. But she didn't.

'Do this thing, Feiga-Ita Shaumian. Or tell the daughter. The daughter can do it. Will you tell her?'

Silence.

The paluba brought a small object out from under her garment. It was an intricate hollow knot of tiny twigs, feathers and twine, somewhat larger than a chicken's egg, with a handful of dried reddish berries rattling around inside it. Globules of a yellowish waxy substance adhered to the outside. She put it to her mouth and breathed on it, then laid it on the floor in front of the broken door.

'When you see your daughter, Feiga-Ita, give her this. It is a gift from him. It is the key to the world.'

She waited a moment longer, but there was only silence. The paluba turned away. Her time was ebbing. And so was hope. She and her companion descended the stairs.

Some time later – an hour – two hours – there came the sound of furniture scraping across the floor inside the room. Slowly. Hesitantly. Then nothing.

Then the broken door was pulled aside and Feiga-Ita Shaumian came out.

She saw the small object left for her on the landing, picked it up gingerly with her fingertips and slipped it into a small, flimsy bag. Holding the bag carefully in both hands she went slowly down the stairs and out into the street.

38

An hour later Lom arrived at the Shaumians' apartment and found the door broken off its hinges and thrown to one side. He went in and looked around. Furniture was overturned and the window stood wide open: thin unlined curtains stirred in the cold breeze. He pulled open a drawer in the table. There was nothing inside but a few pieces of cheap and ill-matched cutlery. What had he expected?

'You've missed them. They just left.'

The woman was standing behind him in the doorway. She was wearing slippers and a dressing gown belted loosely over some kind of undergarment. Her hair, bright orange, showed grey roots. She held out her hand to him with surprising grace.

'Good morning sir. Avrilova. I am Avrilova.'

The way she said her name implied she thought it should mean something to him. He smelled the sweet perfume of mint and aquavit on her breath.

'They went out and left it like this?' he said.

'I mean, you've missed the other police. Or were they militia? What *is* the difference? Could you tell me please?'

'Madam ...'

'I told you, I am Avrilova. You must have heard me sing. Surely you did. I was at Mogen's for many years.'

'What did the police want here? The other police.'

'The same as you, of course. Looking for the Shaumian women.'

'And did the police do this to the door?'

'Of course not. Police don't break down doors. It was like that before. She's mad, the old one. She never goes out, but you hear her

147

all the time, shouting to herself. You wouldn't think she had the voice for it.'

'But she has gone out. She is not here now.'

'Well, obviously.'

Lom walked round the room some more. There wasn't much else to see. A bed. A few books. Poetry. That surprised him. And *Modern Painters of Mirgorod*, a cheap-looking edition with poor-quality plates. The author was Professor R. t-F. M. S-V. Vishnik.

When he looked up from the book Avrilova was still there.

'What does she shout?' he said.

'I beg your pardon?'

'You said you hear Madam Shaumian shouting to herself. So what does she shout about? What does she say?'

Avrilova shrugged. 'Does it matter? Rubbish. Craziness. I told you, she's mad.'

'Mad enough to wrench her own door off its hinges?'

Avrilova shrugged again. 'It would be a mad thing to do.'

'There must have been some noise when that happened to the door. Did you hear anything?'

'I sing every morning without fail. The house could blow up while I am singing and I'd know nothing about it.'

'Madam Avrilova, I need to talk to them. It's a police matter.'

'It's the daughter you want.'

'Why would you say that?'

'Well, she's the *trouble*, isn't she? She's the *intellectual*.'

'Do you know where she is?'

'Why ask me? Haven't you read the file? I've told Officer Kasso all about her several times. He gave me money and wrote it down.'

'What did you tell Kasso?'

'He knew the value of good information. Those other ones hadn't read the file either, but they gave me ten roubles. You only just missed them. You might catch them if you run. Then you could ask them, couldn't you? So many policemen for one broken door.'

Lom fished a handful of coins from his pocket.

'Madam Avrilova—'

'The daughter sews. At Vanko's. The uniform factory.'

39

Maroussia Shaumian worked without thinking, and that was good. She let the dull weight of work squat in her mind, smothering memory.

Vanko's uniform factory had been an engine shed once, but it was a hollow carcase now, a stone shell braced with ribs and arches of old black iron, the walls still streaked with soot, the high windows filmed with grease and dust. Parallel rail tracks sliced across the stone floor and the ghost of coal haunted the air, mingling with newer smells of serge and machine oil. The cutting machines clattered and shook under an old tin sign pitted with rust: MIRGOROD—CETIC AMBER LINE. From the iron arches Vanko had slung a net of cables sparsely fruited with bare electric bulbs, but he only switched them on when it was too dark to work by the dirty muted light of day. Vanko himself sat in his high glass cabin underneath the clock, warmed by a paraffin stove, drinking aquavit from a tin mug and watching the women work.

Maroussia was on buttons. The serge roughened and cracked the skin of her hands. She sat at a trestle with a tin of threaded needles and a compartmented tray of buttons – heaps of cheap brass discs and ivory pellets – while the endless belt of rubberised cotton jerked slowly past her. She had to pick a garment, sew four buttons on it, and replace it on the belt before the next one reached her. If she looked up, she saw the hunched back of the woman in front, who would add the next four. The row of women's bent heads and backs stretched away before her and behind, mirrored by an identical row across the conveyor belt, facing the other way. On the other side they worked pedal-powered sewing machines, black and shiny as beetles. They did pockets, collars, seams. Each woman worked in silence under the thin shelter of her own woollen scarf or shawl. You couldn't make yourself heard above the clatter of the belts and the cutting machines, and if you tried Vanko saw you and docked your time. He kept a plan of the tables on his desk and he knew the name of every woman by the number of their position.

'Hey!' Vanko's voice squawked on the tannoy. 'Get that old witch out of here! Who let her in? Blow away, Granny! Hey, Fasil! Where the hell is Fasil?'

Maroussia looked up. The small woman coming down the aisle was her mother. Her hair was a wild, sparse corona of grey, and she was clutching a small bag in both hands, holding it high against her chest as if it would defend her against the indifference of the women and Vanko's yelling. Scattered melting flakes of snow on her face and in her hair. She had no coat. Fasil was working his way towards her from the direction of the cutting machines.

Maroussia stood up, spilling a tin of pins across the floor. By the time she reached her, her mother had come to a bewildered halt.

'Mother? What are you *doing* here?' said Maroussia. 'Do you want to lose me my job?'

Her mother's eyes wouldn't focus properly. She was pressing the little bag to her breasts. Fasil was coming closer. Maroussia put her mouth against her mother's ear and shouted.

'Come on. We have to get outside.'

Her mother didn't move. She was saying something, but her voice couldn't be heard. Maroussia put her hands on her shoulders – they felt as soft and strengthless as a child's – and turned her towards the way out, pushing her gently forward. They had reached the door and Maroussia was pulling it open when Fasil gripped her roughly by the elbow and pulled her backwards.

'You're holding up the line. Will you pay for the pieces?' He turned to Feiga-Ita. 'Will you?'

'Look at her, Fasil. She's ill.'

Fasil pulled Maroussia closer against him. His cheeks were striated with fine red veins. His small eyes were narrowed, his mouth slightly open. There were damp flecks of stuff in his heavy tobacco-gingered moustache.

'Superior little whore,' he breathed. 'You think we're shit.'

'Fasil, please, I just need a moment …'

He moved his hand down her back. She felt him trace the curve of her spine down into the valley of her buttocks, probing with his fingers through the thin material of her coat.

'Whore,' he hissed in her ear. 'You can pay me later.'

Maroussia shoved her mother out and followed, pushing the door shut behind her and leaning against it, her eyes closed. Fasil was a bastard. There wouldn't be an end to that, now.

Her mother was talking rapidly.

'They've come for me. He's back. We have to go. Run. Hide.'

'What are you talking about?'

'He's alive. He's come back. He sent a message. He wants us. He says for us to go with her. To the forest, Maroussia. Back to the trees.' She held out the bag she was clutching. 'Take it,' she said. 'Take it. It's here. You can feel it here.'

Maroussia pushed the shabby little bag aside.

'You shouldn't have come here, Mother. I have to go back inside now.'

'No!' Her mother was pleading with her. She held the little bag forward again, her thin white fingers like frail claws. 'There were trees in the room. He wants you.'

'He's not in the forest! Josef is in Mirgorod. And he doesn't want us, Mother, of course he doesn't. And we don't want him.'

Her mother looked at her, puzzled. 'Josef? No. Not him – not Josef – the other one.'

Maroussia felt the door move behind her. Somebody was trying to push it open. She heard Fasil's voice.

'Go home, Mother!' It was hard enough without this. 'Please. Whatever it is, you can tell me later. At home.'

Maroussia turned and pulled the door open, surprising Fasil. She shoved past him and walked back to her trestle, looking neither right nor left, feeling the eyes of the women watching her. She picked a uniform from the line and began to work.

It took her two minutes, perhaps five, to realise that her mother would never find her way home by herself. It was a miracle she'd managed to get herself to Vanko's in the first place.

Maroussia picked up her coat and walked back down the aisle, out into the Mirgorod morning. There were other jobs. Probably.

When she got outside she looked up and down the street. There was no sign of her mother.

40

L om came round a corner against soft wet flurries of snow and stopped dead in his tracks. Twenty yards or so ahead of him two militia men were standing in the long alleyway that cut down between warehouses towards Vanko's. They had their backs to him. One of them was Major Safran.

The other had laid a hand on Safran's shoulder and was pointing out an elderly woman coming up the alley towards them, walking slowly, talking to herself. Her hair was a wild wispy mess and she was holding her hands cupped in front of her, carrying something precious. Safran took some papers out of his pocket – photographs – glanced at them and nodded. The militia men moved down the alley to meet the old woman. When she saw them coming she clutched her hands tighter against her chest and turned back.

'Hey!' shouted Safran. 'You! Stop there!'

She ignored him and walked faster, breaking into a kind of scuttling hobble. Safran took his revolver from his holster and levelled it.

'Militia! Halt or I shoot!'

'No!' shouted Lom, but he was too far away to be heard above the traffic noise.

Safran fired once.

The woman's legs broke under her and she collapsed. She was still struggling to crawl forward when Safran reached her. He hooked the toe of his boot under her ribs and flipped her over onto her back. She lay, her left foot stuck out sideways at a very wrong angle, looking up at him. Her other leg was shifting feebly from side to side. Safran compared her to the photograph in his hand, said something to the other militia man, and shot her in the face. Her head burst against the snowy pavement like an over-ripe fruit, spattering the men's legs with mess. The one with Safran flinched back in disgust, and dabbed at his trouser-shins with a handkerchief. After a cursory check that she was dead, they continued towards Vanko's.

Lom felt sick. Another senseless killing in the name of the Vlast. Another uniformed murder.

The woman's body, when he came close to it, was a bundle of rags. Around her broken face the cooling blood had scooped hollows in the snow, scarlet-centred, fringed with soft edges of rose-pink, and in one of the hollows lay the object she had held so tightly: a little bag of some thin, rough material. Hessian? Hemp? Lom picked it up. The side that had lain in the snow was wet with blood. He untied the cord that held the mouth of it pursed shut. Inside was a fragile-looking ball of twigs. He closed the bag and slipped it into his pocket

'Get away from her! Leave her alone!'

Lom looked round. Maroussia Shaumian was staring at him with wide unseeing eyes.

'She's my mother,' she said. 'I have to take her home.'

'Maroussia,' said Lom. 'I couldn't stop this. I was too late. I'm sorry.'

'I have to take her home,' she was saying. 'I can't leave her here.'

'Maroussia—'

'Perhaps I could get a cart.'

She was losing focus. He'd seen people like this after a street accident: together enough on the surface, but they weren't really there, they hadn't aligned themselves to the new reality. You had to be rough to get through to them.

'Your mother has been shot,' he said harshly. 'She is dead. That is her body. The militia killed her deliberately. They were looking for her. Do you understand me?' Maroussia was staring at him, her dark eyes fierce, small points of red flushing her cheeks. 'I think they're looking for you too. When they find you're not at Vanko's they'll come back, and if you're still here they'll kill you as well.'

'You,' she said. 'I know you. You did this.'

'No. I didn't. I wanted to stop it. I couldn't—'

'You're a policeman.'

He took her arm and tried to turn her away from her dead mother.

'I want to help you,' he said.

'Fuck you.'

'I'll take you somewhere. We can talk.'

She jerked her arm away. She was surprisingly strong. Her muscles were hard.

'I said *fuck you.*'

Safran had appeared at the far end of the alley.

'Maroussia, I want to help you,' said Lom. 'But you have to get away from here. Now. Or they'll do that to you.'

'Why would you help me? You're one of them.'

'No,' said Lom. 'I'm not.'

Safran was coming.

Maroussia looked at her mother, lying raw and dead under the high walls of the alley and the sky.

'I can't just leave her,' she said. 'The rats … the gulls …'

'Listen,' said Lom. 'You have to go now. I'll make time for you.'

'What?'

'Go now. Do you hear me? Don't go home. Go to Vishnik's and wait for me there.'

But she was glaring at him. Her face was hard and closed.

'You don't want to help me. You're a liar. Leave me alone. Leave my mother alone.'

Hey!' Safran had begun to jog, drawing his revolver as he came. 'Hey, you!'

Lom stepped into the middle of the alley and held up his hand, hoping that behind him Maroussia was walking away. Hoping that his own face wasn't on one of Safran's photographs.

'What the hell are you doing here, Lom?'

Safran's face was tight with anger.

'No mudjhik?' said Lom. 'Doing your own killing today?'

'Who was that woman? Teslev, stop her.'

'Wait,' said Lom. 'I want to talk to you. Both of you.'

Teslev ignored him and hurried after Maroussia, who had reached the end of the alley, walking fast. Her back looked long and thin and straight in her threadbare coat. The nape of her neck, bare and pale between collar and short black hair, was the most vulnerable and nakedly human thing Lom had ever seen. He felt as if a fist had reached inside his ribs and taken a grip on his heart, squeezing it tight.

41

Maroussia's legs were shaking so much it was hard to walk. Her spine was trickling hot ice, waiting for the impact of the militia man's bullet.

Keep going, she told herself. *Don't look back. Get out of sight. Think!*

Her world was compressed into the next few seconds. She imagined the bullets smashing into her spine. Her legs. Breaking.

Think! Do something! Now!

There were no limits. No rules. Just *do something.*

An alleyway opened up to her left, narrow between tall buildings. No one had been down it since the snow started. She knew where the alley went. Nowhere. A dead end. She cut into it. At least for a few moments she was out of their sight.

One side of the alley was a blank brick face, the other a wall of rough stone blocks stained with grime. Dark windows looked out over it, but high overhead, out of reach. No doors. The building was, she thought, an old warehouse. If she could get inside it … inside was better … she could run … weave … find a way out again … into the crowded streets … lose herself in the crowd …

She took a few steps into the middle of the alley, turned, ran at the wall, jumped … Her fingers stretched for the window ledge …

Her weight crashed hard against the wall. Her knee, her elbow, smashed against it. Her fingers scrabbled at the rough face of the stone, well below the window, and she fell.

She pulled off her shoes and forced the bare toes of one foot hard into the crevice between two blocks of stone, drove her fingers into the gap at shoulder level, and pulled herself up. It worked. She was off the ground, barely, her body flattened, her cheek pressed against the cold wall, her fingers trembling. She tried to dig them further into the stone, tried to gouge out holds by sheer effort of will. She raised her good leg, gasping as her weight pressed on her injured knee, lifted one hand, pulled herself a little higher. It worked. And again. She was almost half her own height above the snow and crawling slowly up the vertical face of the wall. She stretched upwards and got the fingertips of one hand onto the stone ledge of the window. With a desperate lunge she got the other hand next to it. Her feet slipped but she scrabbled with her toes and got purchase again, half pulling and half walking upwards until her backside was sticking out, her knees tucked under. There was a groove in the window ledge she could hook her fingers into. If she could just get one knee up there—

'Are you going to come down, or do I shoot you up the arse?'

42

Lom turned his back on Safran and walked over to the old woman's broken body. She had been so fragile. He could have picked her up and tucked her under his arm. It was taking all his effort not to look behind him, back up the alley, to see if Teslev was coming back.

'Who gave you the photographs, Safran? The pictures of the Shaumian women? Who turned you loose on them?'

Safran stared at him. 'This has nothing to do with you.'

'I mean,' Lom continued. 'You'd hardly come after them on your own initiative, would you? You probably don't even know who they are. I mean, who they really are.'

'What are you getting at?'

'I hope for your sake the order came directly from Chazia herself.'

'And who are *you* working for, Lom?'

Lom shrugged. He kicked at a stone. *Keep him off balance. Don't let him have time to think.*

'So did you find the object Chazia wanted?'

This time Safran looked genuinely puzzled.

'What are you talking about?'

'Never mind. Don't worry about it.'

The crack of a pistol shot echoed off the high walls. It sounded a few streets away.

Safran smiled. 'Teslev found her.'

Another shot. And then another.

'Ah,' said Safran. 'The *coup de grâce.*'

43

Maroussia, clinging to the window ledge, looked down under her arm and stared into the face of the militia man. He was standing below her, his pistol in his hand. He'd obviously been there a while, watching her trying to climb. He thought it was funny. It was in his face. She pushed herself away from the wall and crashed down onto him. He collapsed under her weight. The pistol fired. Something slapped, hard and burning, against her calf and her whole leg went numb.

'You. Stupid. *Bitch.*'

She was lying on her back on top of him. His breath was hot against her ear, his voice close, almost a whisper. She whipped her head forward and sharply back, smashing it into his face, and felt his nose burst. The militia man swore viciously and smashed his gun against the side of her head. And did it again. And again. She felt something jagged open a rip in her cheek. Then his other hand was scrabbling around in front of her, trying to pull at her, trying to roll her off him.

'I'm going to kill you,' he whispered. '*Bitch.*'

He was strong. She couldn't fight him. In another second he would be able to get his gun against her back or her ribs and fire without risk of hitting himself. She dug her hand back and under herself, pushing it down between their struggling bodies, scrabbling for his testicles, and when she found them she squeezed and twisted as viciously as she could. The militia man yelled and arched his back, trying to throw her off, trying to club at her hand with the pistol. She jerked her head backwards again and again, smashing it recklessly into his face. She felt it strike a sweet spot on his chin, smashing his skull back against the pavement. She felt him go slack.

Maroussia rolled away from him and raised herself up on her hands and knees. The militia man was lying on his back, trying to raise his head, his eyes struggling to focus.

'Bitch,' he mumbled. 'Bitch.' He raised his pistol towards her. It seemed heavy in his hand.

She grabbed at the pistol with both hands, twisting and wrenching it. It fired a shot but she barely noticed. She felt the man's finger snap and the gun came away in her grasp. 'Oh no,' he said quietly. 'No.'

She pressed the muzzle against his thigh and pulled the trigger.

44

In the mid-morning quiet of his apartment Raku Vishnik cleared his desk and spread across it a large new street plan of Mirgorod. The city – crisp black lines on fresh white paper – looked geometrical and rectilinear, a network of canals and prospects laid out like electrical cabling, connecting islands to squares and squares to islands; a civic circuit diagram for the orderly channelling of work and movement. It was nothing, or almost nothing, but wishful aspiration. A flimsy overlay of civilisation, the merest stencil grid over marsh and mist and dreams.

Next to the map Vishnik set out his neat pile of filled notebooks, a box file of newspaper cuttings, a sheaf of other maps and plans. The maps all showed the city or parts of it, and all of them were creased, much re-folded, and covered with faint pencil marks: lines and symbols and Vishnik's own cramped and scarcely legible annotations, from single words to entire paragraphs. The hatbox of photographs was on the floor beside his chair. On the other side of the window the city breathed and rumbled. Snow flurries smudged the distance, yellow and grey and brown.

He was looking for shape and pattern.

Methodically he sifted through his notes, looking for anomalous events. Times and places when the city slipped and shifted. Like it had in the Bakery Galina Tropina. Like it had in his photographs. Like it had when he went back to a familiar place and found it different. Others had seen such things in the city. He picked them up in newspapers usually, but also in conversations overheard on trams and buses, in shops, in the street. He'd kept a record of every one. They were in his notebooks. Date, place, time.

Ever since Maroussia Shaumian had come to him the other night a new idea had been taking shape in his mind. A new possibility. Maroussia had pushed him across a threshold. Until then it had never occurred to him that he could do more than accumulate notes and records. He had been an archivist of glimpses only. The thought had never struck him that what he was seeing had a cause. A source. That he could act.

But now, slowly, carefully, thoroughly, he went through the note-books, one by one, and for each event he made a pencil mark on the map. All morning he worked, attuning his breathing to the slow pulse of the rain and the city.

The pattern began to emerge. It started to resolve itself under his gaze like a photograph in a developing dish, a sketchy outline first, then the richer finer details. But he resisted it. He didn't want to jump to conclusions. He didn't want to mislead himself. He kept calm. He stuck to his method.

I should have done this long ago. This has always been here for the finding and I never thought to look.

By mid-afternoon he'd finished. He pinned the map to the wall and stood back. There was no doubting it. There could be no mistake. The spattering of pencil marks looked like a black sunburst, a carbon flower blooming, a splash – as if a ball of black flakes had been thrown at the city and splattered on impact. The rays of the sun-splash pattern thinned out in all directions towards the edges of the city, but at the centre they were clustered, overlapping, intense. They were concentrated around one place. It looked like an impact point, a moon crater, the focal point of an explosive scattering. It was the source. There was something there. Causing the surface life of the city to shift and tremble. And the effect was growing stronger. He had found it.

Vishnik went to the bookshelf by the stove and took out the old book with the sun-faded, water-stained cover. The spine was detaching itself, the gilt lettering rubbing away, the thin translucent pages grubby and bruised. It was a forbidden work now, under the interdiction of the Vlast for more than a century, ever since its existence had been noticed. He'd found this copy tucked behind a heating pipe in the library of the Institute of Truth at Podchornok more than twenty years ago. He'd shown it to no one, and he'd never found another copy since. No reference to it in any library. So far as he knew, his was the only one in existence. *A Child's Book of Wonders, Legends and Tales of Long Ago.*

Once more he opened it at the familiar page. Once more, sitting on the floor by his bookshelf in the dimming light of late afternoon, he began to read.

'How They Made The Pollandore.'

45

L om left Safran and the body of the executed woman, and walked.
Anywhere. Nowhere. He hated the city. He hated the way you
could just walk out of an alley and into the flow of crowds and
traffic. Faces in the street. Faces behind windows. Faces that knew
nothing about the dead body of an old woman a few yards away. That
was in another city, not theirs. He needed to *breathe*. Needed to *think*.

He bought a ticket and got on a tram at random. The circle line,
orbiting the city centre. The car was almost empty. Two thin men with
clean-shaven angular faces were talking about horses. Round-brimmed
hats, heeled ankle boots, woollen suits with trouser cuffs. Signs shouted
at him: CITIZENS! BEWARE BOMBS! REPORT SUSPICIOUS
PACKAGES! LEAVE NO LUGGAGE UNATTENDED!

A young man in the rear corner seat was staring at him. Frowning.
A long thin nose. High cheekbones. Greasy hair in thick strands across
his forehead. He had a book open but he wasn't reading. When his
gaze met Lom's he de-focused his eyes and pretended he was looking
past him, out of the window. Lom shrugged inwardly. Just a student.
He wondered what book he was carrying. It was heavy and thick and
looked old. Not mathematics or engineering, not with hair like that.
He considered going across to find out what it was. Shake the tree.
See what fell out. Once, not long ago, he would have. But not now.
Leave him be. Leave him to his thoughts. Lom realised he was staring,
and the young man was suffering under it: he'd buried himself in his
book, pretending to be absorbed in it, but his neck and the edges of his
cheekbones were flushed. When the tram stopped he would get up and
leave, carefully, avoiding eye contact.

The snow had stopped falling. Nothing but wet grey slush on the pavements already. Mirgorod unfolded on the other side of the window but Lom hardly saw it. It was too close, pressed right up against his face. It was too big and too dirty. It made no sense. What you saw from a tram window were the small things. Random, fragmentary things: a narrow alleyway disappearing between shopfronts; the sign of a drawing master's school; fresh perch on ice outside a fishmonger's; the hobbles on a dray horse; a bricked-up window. The city was vast beyond understanding. It replenished itself infinitely, teeming beyond count. People lived their lives in Mirgorod by choosing a few places, a few faces, a few events, to be the landmarks of their own imagined, private city. Interior cities of the mind, a million cities, all interleaved one with another in the same place and time, semi-transparent. Onion-layer cities, stacked cities, soft and intricate, all of them tied together by the burrowing, twining, imperceptible threads of the information machine. Flimsy cities, every one. All it took was a militia bullet, the hack of a dragoon sabre. But the tissue cities carried on.

And underneath them all, two futures, struggling against each other to be born.

Lom slipped his hand into his pocket and met something sticky and rough: Feiga-Ita Shaumian's bag, tacky with her clotting blood. He untied the cord and looked inside. It was like the hedge-nest of some bird, just the kind of thing a crazy old woman might carry around, but it wasn't a nest. The sticks were tied together with thread. He eased it out of the bag for a closer look. Some of her blood had soaked through and clotted on it, dark and viscous, and there were globs of some other stuff, some kind of yellow wax, and dry, maroon-coloured berries. He held it up to the light. There were fine bones inside, parts of the skeleton of some tiny animal. A mouse? A mole? A small bird? There was a strong scent too, some sweet warmth stronger than the iron of blood. He remembered the whiteless brown eyes of the soldier in the street in Podchornok, out in the rain.

Some instinct made Lom hold the thing up close to his face and sniff at it. And the world changed. It was as if the skin of his senses had been unpeeled. The hard line between him and not-him, the edge that marked the separateness of himself from the world, was no longer there. Until that moment he had been tied up tight inside himself, held in by a skin as taut and tense as the head of a drum, and now it was all let go. It was as if he had fallen into green water and gone down deep, turning and tumbling until he had no idea which way was up. At first he panicked, lashing out on all sides, struggling to get control, but after a moment he seemed to remember that you shouldn't do it like that. He stopped struggling and allowed himself to drift, letting his own natural buoyancy carry him back to the surface.

He was a woman in the woods in winter. He wasn't *seeing* her, he *was* her, crunching her way among silent widely-spaced trees, going home, tired and alive in the aftermath of love, her mouth rubbed sore, the man's semen pursed up warm inside her. She sniffed at her fingers. The scent of the man clung to them, as strong as memory. She remembered the weight of his belly on her, the warmth of his bed by the stove. Her collar, her sleeve, the fur of her hood, everything had soaked up the smell of his isba, rich and strong, smoke and resin, furs and sweat. Oh hell! *He* would notice when she got home! Even *He* couldn't miss the smell of him on her skin. Did she care? No! This was a new kind of madness and she liked it.

The vision faded. Lom closed his eyes and watched the patterns of muted light drift across the inside of his eyelids. Thinking was tiring. His thoughts were too heavy to lift. He stared out of the window, trying to think as little as possible. In the reflection he saw Maroussia Shaumian's wide dark eyes. Her long straight back as she walked away.

Three shots. There were three shots.

I've achieved nothing. Every thread I follow leads nowhere, or to a corpse.

No, not nowhere. To Chazia.

Kantor was Chazia's agent. All the killing, the bombs, the robberies, inspired not by nationalist fervour or revolutionary nihilism, but by the Chief of the Vlast Secret Police. Safran was Chazia's too. Chazia had sent him to kill Maroussia and her mother.

And I am Chazia's too.

Except that wasn't true. Not any more.

Chazia would kill him now for what he knew, and take the file back. She had sent the vyrdalak. It must have been her.

The file.

He saw it tucked away in the bathroom of Vishnik's apartment. He saw Vishnik beaten by militia night sticks. He saw Vishnik, dead in his room, bleeding from Safran's bullets.

The file. Shit. The file.

46

Josef Kantor followed Chazia along empty passageways seemingly cut through blocks of solid stone. They clattered down steep iron flights of steps lit by dirty yellow bulbs. The treads were damp and treacherous. She was leading him deep into the oldest, lowest parts of the Lodka, where he had never been before, down into ancient, subterranean levels.

'No one comes here,' she said. 'Only me. You're privileged, Josef. Remember that.'

When had she become so pompous? She was weaker than he had thought. Failing. Not to be trusted. She had agreed, reluctantly, to show him the Pollandore, but she had made him wait. 'Come back tomorrow,' she'd said. 'Let me prepare.'

Kantor felt suddenly annoyed with this terrible old fox-bitch who pushed him around. He wanted to bring her down a bit.

'Is Krogh dealt with, Lavrentina?'

She was walking ahead of him and didn't look round.

'You were right about him,' she said. 'He's an annoyance. It is in hand.'

'But not done yet, then. And what about the other matter?'

'The other matter?'

'The women,' said Kantor impatiently. Chazia had not forgotten – she never forgot anything – she was prevaricating. 'The Shaumian women. You were going to deal with them too. Is it done?'

'Oh that,' she said. 'Yes. Your wife is dead.' He caught a slight hesitation in Chazia's reply.

'And the daughter?'

Chazia said nothing.

'The daughter, Lavrentina?' said Kantor again.

'She is not dead. She escaped. We've lost her. Just for the moment. We'll find her again.'

'What happened?'

'She had help, Josef. Krogh's investigator was there.'

'Lom?'

'He interfered,' said Chazia. 'Safran let him get in the way. Your daughter shot one of Krogh's men and disappeared.'

'Did she, then?' Despite himself, he was impressed. But it would not do.

'You must kill them both,' he said. 'Krogh's man and the daughter. Do it now. Do it quickly, Lavrentina. And Krogh too. No more delays. Kill them all.'

Chazia turned to face him.

'Don't try to bully me, Josef. I won't accept that. Remember our respective positions. I have other things to do apart from clearing away your domestic mess. Today we are going into the Lezarye quarters. That will raise the temperature. And you have your part to play too. Remember that. The Novozhd—'

'You can leave that to me,' said Kantor. 'You don't need the details. Better you don't ...' He felt that Chazia was going to argue the point, but just then they reached a narrow unmarked door in the passageway, and she stopped.

'Here,' she said, reaching in her pocket for a bunch of keys.

The door looked newer than the rest. Shabby institutional paint, but solid and heavy with several good locks. Chazia opened it and Kantor followed her inside.

The first impression was of spacious airy dimness. Grey light filtered down from high – very high – overhead: muted daylight, spilling through a row of square grilles set into the roof. But they must have been far below ground level. The grilles were the floors of light wells, he realised: shafts cut up through the Lodka to draw down some sky. As his eyes grew accustomed to the dimness he saw that they were in a high narrow chamber that stretched away on both sides. He could not see the end of it in either direction. It might have been a tunnel. Parallel rails were set into the floor, for a tram or train.

The floor of the chamber was heaped with boxes and sacks and pallets. Large shapeless lumps of stuff shrouded under sacking and tarpaulins. And there were machines, on benches or on the floor. Some he recognised: lathes and belt saws, pulleys and lifting chains and other such contraptions. Others, the majority, meant nothing to him: complex armatures of metal and rubber and wood and polished stone. The impression was of a workshop, or a warehouse, but its purpose escaped him. There was an oppressive mixture of smells: iron filings, wet stone and machine oil. The atmosphere unsettled him. He felt on edge and slightly disoriented, as if there was a low vibration in the air and the floor, a rhythm and resonance too deep to hear.

'Where is it?' he said. 'Where's the Pollandore?' He didn't know what he was expecting the Pollandore to look like, but nothing he could see seemed likely to be it.

'It's not far,' said Chazia. 'I need another key.' She switched on a lamp at a work table and began to search through drawers. 'I haven't needed this for a while.' The table she was searching was spread with small implements, scraps of paper and chips of stone. Its centrepiece was a large brazen ball with tiny angled spouts protruding from its dented, fish-scaled skin. It floated in a dish of some heavy silver liquid that might have been mercury. Its surface shimmered and rippled faintly in the lamplight.

'So what is this place?' said Kantor.

Chazia glanced up. Light from the lamp glinted in her foxy eyes and slid off the dark marks on her face and hands. Did they cover her whole body, Kantor found himself wondering. He was beginning to feel uneasy. He felt for the revolver in his pocket.

'This is my private workplace,' said Chazia.

The lamp threw light into some of the nearer shadows. Kantor started. He thought he had seen someone else in the room, standing watchful and motionless against the wall. It was a shape, draped in oilcloth, almost seven feet tall. Curious, Kantor went across to it and pulled the sheet away.

At first he thought he was looking at a suit of armour, but it was much cruder, larger and heavier than any human could have worn and moved in. There was some kind of goggle-eyed helmet and clumsy-fingered gauntlets with canvas palms that made the effect more like a deep-sea diver's suit. The whole thing was a dull purplish red. He realised it was constructed from pieces of angel flesh. The woman had made herself a mudjhik! But one you could climb inside. One you could wear. He had underestimated her. Badly. His mind began to work rapidly. What you could do with such a thing, if it worked. If it worked.

'Come away from that,' said Chazia sharply.

She didn't want me to see this. So this is what she does. This is her dabbling.

'You *wear* this?' he said. 'You put yourself *inside* this thing?'

'It's nothing,' said Chazia. 'Come away from it. Do you want to see the Pollandore or not? We haven't much time. I need to get back. Come, it's this way.'

She led him to an iron door in the side wall, unlocked it and went through. Kantor followed her and found himself standing on a narrow iron platform suspended over space.

Whatever he had expected, it was not this. They were looking across a wide circular pit, a cavern, and in the middle of it was a wrought iron structure. It must have been a hundred and fifty feet high. In the depths of the Lodka. An iron staircase climbed up round the outside. There were viewing platforms of ornate decorative ironwork, pinnacles and spiracles, and within this outer casing an iron helix spiralling upwards. It reminded Kantor of a long thin strip of apple peel. And inside it, held in suspension, touching nowhere, the Pollandore.

The air of the cavern crackled as if it was filled with static electricity. It made Kantor's head spin. The Pollandore hung in blankness, a pale greenish luminescent globe the size of a small house, a cloudy sphere containing vaporous muted light that emitted none. Illuminated nothing. A smell of ozone and forest leaf. It revolved slowly, a world in space: not part of the planet at all, though it was following the same orbit, describing the same circumsolar trajectory, passing through the same coordinates in space and time, tucked in its inflated sibling's pocket but belonging only to itself. There was no sound in the room. Not even silence. The Pollandore looked small for a world, but Kantor knew it wasn't small, not by its own metrication.

He turned to say something to Chazia, who was standing beside him staring across at the uncanny, terrible thing. Kantor opened his mouth to say something to her, but nothing came out. The space in the cavern swallowed his words before they were spoken. He grabbed her arm and pulled her roughly back off the platform and pushed the door shut.

'We must destroy it,' he said. 'Get rid of that repellent thing.'

'Don't you think,' said Chazia, 'don't you think we have tried?'

47

Maroussia Shaumian sat on the slush-soaked ground under the trees at the end of her street, leaning her back against one of the trunks. Watching for uniforms. Watching for watchers. Her whole body was trembling violently. She had almost not made it. The militia man's first bullet had gouged a furrow of flesh in the calf of her left leg. It was a pulpy mess of blood, but it held her weight. Her knee, which had crashed against the wall in her first wild jump, stabbed bright needles of pain with every step, and the hair at the back of her head was sticky with blood – hers, and his. She could feel pits and flaps of skin where his teeth had cut her scalp. There was a ragged stinging tear in her cheek, wet with blood. Her neck was stiff. It hurt when she tried to turn her head. The pistol lay black and heavy in her lap.

She knew it was stupid to return home. The policeman. Lom. He had warned her not to. But then that was reason enough to do the opposite. Distrust of the Vlast and all its agents went deep. And yet … this one had helped her. He had let her get away. Without him she would already have been taken.

She could not think about that now. She needed to go home. Where else could she go? She needed to be clean of all this blood. She needed fresh clothes. She needed the little money that was there. She needed to rest. And she needed to think through her plan. She waited until the street was quiet, stood up stiffly and limped up the road to the entrance to her building.

There was a small bathroom up a flight of stairs at the end of the corridor. It had a basin and a bathtub and cold running water. A tarnished mirror. The walls were painted a pale lemon-yellow. Maroussia locked herself in, took her clothes off and washed herself, all over, slowly and without thinking. She let trickles of icy water take the blood and dirt from her skin. Out of her hair. She caught some water in cupped hands and drank from it: it tasted faintly of blood, but it was cold and sweet. She left her dirtied, bloodied clothes in a heap on the floor, wrapped herself in a thin rough towel and went barefoot back to her room as quickly as her stiffening injuries would let her, not wanting to encounter Avrilova on the stair. She found the door broken down, and assumed the militia had done it.

She dressed carefully, taking her time, not only because of her vicious and stiffening wounds, but also because she felt there was something ceremonious about it. *Here begins the new life.* She found clean under-wear. A cotton slip. A plain grey dress. A black scarf for her hair. Shoes were a problem: her left shoe was sticky with the blood that had run down her leg. Her mother had saved a pair of boots from better times. They would do. And there was a clumsy woollen coat, also grey, which her mother had left behind that morning. She must have frozen.

When she'd dressed, she wandered around the room stuffing things into a bag. A few spare clothes. Soap. Their bit of money, about thirty roubles. That wouldn't last long. After some thought she put in the book of Anna Yourdania's poems. Someone at the Marmot's had given it to her. *The Selo Elegies.* She loved the quiet, allusive, suffering voice.

The sun is dropping out of the sky, the orchard
breathes the taste of pears and cherries,
and in a moment the transparent night
will bear new constellations –
like salt berries – glittering – harsh.

Why are our years always worse?

Yourdania's son, who was nineteen, had died in the camp at Vig. Her husband was shot on the basement steps of the Lodka.

As she dressed and packed her few things, Maroussia went over her plan. Like so many people in Mirgorod, she had lived for years with the thought that one day such a time would come. The militia would come for her, and it would be necessary to run. She had decided long ago that when this day came she would make for Koromants, the Fransa Free Exclave on the Cetic shore, three hundred miles to the south of Mirgorod.

The whole world to the west of the forest was divided between Vlast and Archipelago, locked in their endless war. But wherever there was war, there must be bankers, financiers, traders in weapons – wars were fought on credit – and so the Fransa free cities, which belonged neither to the Archipelago nor to the Vlast, existed. Sealed off from the dominions by guarded perimeters. Everyone was stateless there, everyone was free, money and information the only power. Spies and criminals and refugees of every kind gravitated to such places – if they could get in, through the wire or over the walls. Exiled intellectuals gathered there to plot and feud, and she had heard of other, stranger figures, not human, forced out of the ghettos, margins and northern wildernesses of the Vlast, who found places to live in the older, darker corners of the Fransa exclaves. Ones who might understand about the Pollandore and help her.

The nearest Fransa port to Mirgorod was Koromants. Maroussia had seen a photograph once of the seafront there: a wide boulevard of coffee shops and konditorei looking out over clear dark waters, and behind it, rising against the sky, the sheer jagged mountains of the Koromants Massif. There, she had decided, that was where she would go, when the time came. Though how she would get there she didn't know.

Maroussia decided not to take her identity card. It would be no help where she was going. She placed it carefully on the table in clear view, for the police to find when they came. It was time. She had delayed too long.

She turned towards the doorway and saw the figure of madness and death standing there, regarding her with shadowed fathomless eyes.

'Maroussia?' it said. 'Maroussia. Are you ready?'

The paluba's voice was thin and quiet in the room, a breeze among distant trees. The air was filled with the scent of pine resin and damp earth. Flimsy brown garments shifted about the creature, stirring on a gentle wind. There was a mouth-shape in the hooded shadows that moved as it spoke.

The creature stepped forward across the threshold. Only it wasn't a step. The thing seemed to fall slowly forward and jerk itself backwards and upright at the tipping point. It appeared flimsy, held together by fragile joints. Its limbs were articulated strangely. Behind the creature another one came, its follower, its companion double, more shadowy, more shapeless, more airy, more … nothing. Just a shadow, waiting.

'What are you?' said Maroussia, at the ragged edge of panic. And hope.

'I can smell wounds here,' the paluba said. 'You're bleeding. You've been hurt.'

'Who are you?' said Maroussia again. 'What do you want from me?'

'You don't have to be frightened,' the voice said. 'I am your friend. Your mother's friend. But your mother wouldn't listen to me. Did she tell you nothing?'

'She's gone now. She's dead. The police killed her.'

'Oh.' There was a moment's stillness in the shadow where the paluba's face was suggested. Maroussia thought she could hear grieving in its voice. 'She took what we left for her. Did she give it to you?'

'No. She gave me nothing.'

'It was an invitation. A key. Your father sent it.'

'I never had a father.'

'Of course you did. Everyone does.'

'My father was a lie. I come from nothing.'

'Did she tell you that? Poor darling, it wasn't so. Do you want to know?'

'Know what?'

'Everything.'

'Yes.'

The paluba reached up and pushed back her thin hood, showing her beautiful, terrible face. Her waiting mouth.

'Kiss me, Maroussia.'

'What?'

'Kiss me.' In the shadow the companion stirred. 'Kiss me.'

Maroussia stepped forward and rested her hand on the paluba's slender shoulders. Sweet air was drifting out of its upturned mouth. It tasted of autumn. Maroussia put her own dry mouth against it, slightly open, and drank.

In the paluba's kiss there were trees, beautiful complex trees, higher and older than any trees grew, and everything was connected.

Maroussia was walking among them. She placed her hand on the silent living bark and felt her skin, her very flesh, become transparent. She became aware of the articulation of her bones, sheathed in their muscle and tendon. Eyes, heart and lungs, liver and brain, nested like birds in a walking tree of bone. A weave of veins and arteries and streaming nerves that flickered with gentle electricity.

She heard the leaves and branches of the trees moving. Whispers filling the air with rich smells. The trees reached their roots down into the earth like arms, and she reached down with them, extending filament fingers, pushing, sliding insistently, down through crevices in the rock itself.

And breaking through.

The buried chamber of the wild sleeping god was furled up tight but immense beyond measuring. The restless sleeping god, burdened with tumultuous dreams, had extended himself outwards and inwards and downwards, carving out an endless warren, an intricate dark hollowing. Its whorls and chambers ramified in all directions, turning and twisting and burrowing, spiral shadow tunnellings of limitless extent, unlit by the absent sun but warmed by the heart of the earth. It was all rootwork: the roots of the rock and the roots of the trees. It was matrix and web. Fibrous roots of air, filaments of energy and space, knitted everything to everything else in the chamber of the sleeping god's dream.

He was lying on his back and great taproots drove down through his ribs. A tree limb speared up out of his groin. Water trickled over him. Rootlets slipped down, fingering his pinioned body, brushing and touching gently. The roots of the great trees drank from the buried god as their leaves drank the sun.

Up in the light the trees mingled their crowns in one great leafhead and exhaled the good, living air of the world. The air she drank on the paluba's breath.

And there was a man walking among the trees. She knew that he was her father and he knew that she was there, and he greeted her, and she understood why her mother had loved him and why she had to leave and how the leaving had been her death.

48

L om sat bolt upright in his seat on the tram. The file! Chazia would come for it, and she would find Vishnik. Maroussia.
He had to do something. Now.

The tram had stopped. An anonymous place somewhere away from the centre of the city. Across the street was a hotel, a telephone cable running to it from a pole in the centre of the square. Lom ran across. THE GRAND PENSION CHESMA. Wet zinc tables under a dripping wrought-iron veranda. Steep marble steps up to a chipped, discoloured portico. A handwritten card propped in a small side window: *Closed For Winter*. Lom hammered on the door.

'Open up! Police!'

The paint on the door was peeling, revealing sinewy bleached grey wood. There was an ivory button in a verdigrised surround. BELL, it said. PORTER. He pressed it, more in hope than expectation, and kicked at the door.

'Police! Open or I break it down.'

There was a noise of bolts being pulled back. The door opened. A porter in sabots and a brown overall eyed him warily.

'You don't look like police.' *We wouldn't take you as a guest.*

Lom shoved the door open and shouldered his way past the porter into the dim hall. A suggestion of wing-backed chairs and ottomans draped with grey sheets. A smell of old cooking and older carpets. Dampness, dust and the sea. Lom unbuttoned his cloak.

'This is a uniform,' he said. 'And this is a gun. I need to telephone. Now.'

The porter led him into a back room. There was a phone on the desk. The porter lingered uneasily.

'Don't stand there gawking. I'm hungry. Get me some sausage. And a mug of tea.'

It took Lom for ever to negotiate his way past a series of operators, getting through first to the Lodka and then to Krogh's office. The private secretary's voice came on the line.

'Yes?' he said. 'Who is this?'

'It's Lom. I need to speak to him. Now.'

'Ah. Investigator Lom. The Under Secretary was beginning to wonder whether you might not have taken a train back to Podchornok. You haven't, have you? Where exactly is it you are calling from?'

'Just put me through to him.'

'I'm afraid he's not available at the moment. His diary is very full. If you'll tell me where you are, or give me the number, I'll arrange for him to return your call some time this afternoon. Unless you'd like me to make you an appointment to see him. I'm sure he would be most—'

'Stop pissing me about and put me through.'

There was a hiss of indrawn breath and the line went dead. *Fuck*.

He was about to hang up when he heard the tired dry voice of Krogh.

'Yes, Investigator. Something to report?'

'Can I speak?'

'Of course.'

'I mean, this call is private? Bag carrier not listening?'

'Just give me your report, Lom. I was playing this game when you were at school.'

'Perhaps you're getting complacent. Are you sure you're secure?'

'Of course I am, man. There are systems. Arrangements.'

'That's what Chazia thought, but she was stupid. She relied on the systems because she'd made them, but getting in wasn't even hard.'

There was a pause.

'What are you talking about?'

'Maybe she's listening now.'

'That's ridiculous. You're hysterical. Perhaps I made a mistake about you.'

'If she is, it doesn't matter. I'm not saying anything she doesn't already know I know.'

'What exactly *are* you saying?'

'Kantor isn't the story. Kantor's an agent. Chazia's agent. Chazia's the one moving all the pieces.'

'Can you prove it? Are you sure?' Lom listened for indignation. Disbelief. But there was only guarded interest in Krogh's voice. 'Is there proof, Lom? Certain proof I can take to the Novozhd?'

'Oh yes,' said Lom. 'I've got a bag full of proof. Her own files. Her own handwriting all over them. But she knows I've got them.'

'I see.'

'And if she is listening to your calls – and if I were you I wouldn't bet my life she's not – she knows I've told you. Of course, even if she doesn't listen to your calls, she'll assume I've told you anyway.'

'Ah. I see. Yes.' Pause. 'And how did you come by these sensitive papers?'

'I broke into her private archive and took them.'

'Did you, indeed? You've exceeded my expectations, Investigator.'

'And now you know, and she knows you know. So you have to do something about it. Action this day, Under Secretary. Action this hour.'

'What exactly did you have in mind?'

'You're her boss. Roll her up. Reel her in. Have her killed. I don't know – it doesn't matter – just get her, and do it now. Get her and you get Kantor too.'

'I'll need the proof. I'll need the papers.'

'There's no time for that. You need to move now. And I'd take care of your private secretary as well, if I were you.'

'That's wild talk, Lom.'

'Chazia had my personal file, Krogh. She had it from your office less than an hour after we met. Referred to her by your private secretary. He even signed the fucking thing out to her. They're running rings round you. They're so confident they don't even try to hide their tracks.'

'I still need to show the Novozhd the proof.'

Krogh sounded old and tired. The fatigue was seeping down the line. Lom remembered the big office. The plain neat desk. The windows. Quiet traffic noise. Long corridors. This wasn't going to work.

'I'll get the files to you, Krogh. But you can't wait for that. You need to act.'

'When can you bring me the files?'

'Soon. Soon. I'm not saying any more on this line.'

'Investigator Lom. Be calm. You're asking me to risk a huge amount – everything – on—'

'A telephone call from a junior policeman from Podchornok. Your rules, Under Secretary. You got me into this.'

'I did.'

'Oh, and there's one other thing.'

'Yes?'

'There's an angel in the forest somewhere beyond Vig. It's alive.'

'That's preposterous.'

'Chazia and Kantor – mainly Kantor, I think – are in communication with it. I just thought you should know.'

Lom hung up.

The porter brought a tray with a glass of black tea, a plate of rye bread and a length of dark purple sausage.

'The dining room is closed. You can take it here. Or there is the garden.'

'Forget it,' said Lom. 'You have it.'

There was half an hour yet till the tram to Pelican Quay. Back at the tram halt, Lom sat alone under the canopy, sick and dispirited. His clothes and skin stank of hopelessness and self-disgust and other people's blood.

Image: Safran killing the old woman in the street.

Image: Maroussia Shaumian walking away alone. Pistol shots. Three.

Image: Chazia overturning Vishnik's flat and finding the file.

Image: Vishnik dead.

All caused by him. His responsibility. His fault. Because every step he'd taken had been wrong. Because he'd been a blundering, half-hearted, self-indulgent, piss-poor idea of a detective, and now he wasn't even that. He was loose. He was alone.

It would take him hours to retrieve the file and get it to Krogh, even if it was still there. He had no confidence that Krogh would move against Chazia before he had the file in his hands, or even when he did have it. Lom had done what he could, but it hadn't been good enough. It hadn't been good at all. It had been shit.

The sky had grown dark and livid. Fat cold drops of rain began to explode on the ground, bursting at first like fallen overripe fruits but then like bullets from a mitrailleuse, rapid and hard and shattering, mixed with shards of ice. Over the sea a storm was coming.

*

Out in the Sound a high tide had been building. The two broken fragments of moon tugged at the weight of water, dragging its dark bulk
shouldering against the land. A twisting black surge of foam-flecked
ocean forced its way in through the Seagate towards the city, scouring
the foundations of the Halsesond martello forts as it came. The rivers
and canals of Mirgorod were already high and swollen, pregnant with
weeks of rain and snow. Inside Cold Amber Strand the column of
brackish tidal waters confronted and commingled with the rivers in
flood. In Mirgorod the waters rose quickly when they came.

49

The rain pounded the city and darkened the sky. Soaked, Vishnik stepped out of the shabby crowded street and closed the louvred door behind him, and the House on the Purfas enfolded him in its familiar melancholy civilised quietness. The entrance hall was faded, airy, spacious. Empty but for dust motes, pools of shadow and the sweetness of wax polish and age. Grey window-light and the sound of rain. Somewhere a clock was ticking slowly. Doorways and corridors opened in all directions, and a wide staircase climbed upwards into indistinctness.

Now, the House on the Purfas was home to the Lezarye Government in Exile Within, but once it had been the Sheremetsny Dom, a low expansive sprawl of wood and brick, skirted with peeling loggias and leaking conservatories. The country estate for which it was built had disappeared long ago under the tenements and courtyards of the ex-panding city, but for Vishnik the corridors of the House on the Purfas led away into the lost domain of his childhood. If he could go deeper into the house, he felt, he would be back among it all. Back in his own boundless childhood house at Vyra, with its world of passages and stairs. Daylight slanted in through high narrow windows panelled with stained glass, splashing lozenges of colour across dusty floorboards and threadbare rugs. The tall furniture and heavy fabrics of drawing rooms, salons, dining rooms, bedrooms, box rooms and attics. The strange devices and spiced air of kitchens, pantries and sculleries. If he went to a window in the House on the Purfas and looked out, he was sure he would see, not the Moyka Strel, but balustraded pathways, formal parterres, weathered statuary, great heaps and mounds of foliage overgrowing walls of old brick and, in the furthest distance, a slope of wooded hills.

There was a brass hand-bell on a side table. Vishnik picked it up and rang it. A woman in a black dress and a white cape came.

'Yes?' she said. 'Sir?'

A domestic servant. Another dizzying time-tumble. The whole place was a museum. A case of butterfly specimens, dried out and pinned; their dusty wings spread under glass in a parody of summer flight, but if you opened the glass and picked one up it would crunch and collapse between your fingers.

In the centuries after the coming of the Founder, the people of Lezarye had learned to accept the end of their annual migrations and settle into the static life of the Vlast. The elder families had absorbed the ways of the aristocrats, a choice that was only the latest in the long history of tragic turns and counter-turns that left them with nowhere to go when the Novozhd gripped power and the aristocrats fell.

'I need to see Teslom,' said Vishnik to the woman.

'What name shall I say?'

'Prince Raku ter-Fallin Mozhno Shirin-Vilichov Vishnik.'

'Will you wait in the library, please, Excellency.'

Teslom was the Curator of Lezarye. He kept the records of the old families and tended the artefacts, regalia and memories that survived from their proud ancient days of hunting and herding, and the long slow rhythms of their decline: the systole of assimilation, the diastole of segregation and pogrom. Although Vishnik had visited the House on the Purfas to consult Teslom several times before, he had never been admitted to the Curator's collection. No one who was not born into the long families ever was. The exclusion irked him. Lezarye had few enough friends in Mirgorod.

The room he was put in to wait was not part of the Collection, it was only the Secular Library. It was a dim quiet place of heavy bookcases shut away behind glass doors and curtains. Vishnik opened one of the cases and looked at the spines of the books. The ones here were merely miscellanea, marginal outriders of the true library, but still there were some things here that could be found nowhere else in the Vlast.

Lyrics From The Moth Border
Hunting Cold Beasts
Peace Of Mind Among Cold Beasts

Pigments, Tints
Life On The Water Ways
The Geometry Of Clouds, Steams and Vapours
Jurisprudence In The Archipelago

Vishnik took a book from a shelf, carried it across to a table and opened it. *Shaw's Atlas of the Archipelago.* It contained page after page of maps in muted colours and a gazetteer of place names: a world, but not his; other countries, other islands, strung out across the face of the blue, with vertebrae and ribs of snow-capped mountains. The poetry of unfamiliar shorelines. A great bridge had been built across the sea to join them, thousands of miles long, but it was broken in several places. The orthography of the place names was familiar, but the names themselves … He didn't recognise them – they were strange and wonderful. Morthern. Foerd. Mier. Gealm. The Warth. Horrow. Sarshalls. It was an atlas of elsewhere.

Teslom had come in quietly while he was reading. When Vishnik noticed him, the Curator made the formal gestures of acknowledgement and permission.

'Welcome, Prince Vishnik. The princes of Vyra and Turm were always friends of Lezarye in the former days of the long homelands. There is a place for you in our hearts and at our tables. How can I help you?'

Teslom was a small man, neat, spare, kempt, with dark-shadowed eyes behind rimless circular glasses and glossy brown hair flopped across his forehead. He wore a double-breasted suit of dark blue; a soft white shirt with a soft turned-down collar and faint pattern of squares; a dark tie held in place with a pin.

'I want you to tell me about the Pollandore, Teslom my friend. Every fucking thing you can.'

'The Pollandore? Why?'

'I found a story about this thing. It was in a book. An old and rare book. I asked myself, is it real? Is it true?'

'What story is this? Where did you find it? What book?'

Vishnik opened his satchel and handed it to him. *A Child's Book of Wonders, Legends and Tales of Long Ago.* Teslom took it carefully and opened it, his dark eyes shining.

'I had heard of it, but even we don't have a copy.' He held it close to his face, examining the stitch binding and inhaling its paper smell.

'Tell me about the Pollandore, Teslom, and I will give it to you. My gift to the People.'

Teslom handed the book back to him.

'A good gift. But why the Pollandore? There are other stories here.'

'Because of these.'

Vishnik opened his satchel again, took out a sheaf of photographs and spread them across the table. Teslom lit a lamp and studied them for a long time in silence.

'Where did you get these?' he said at last.

'They are mine. I took them. These things happen. I've seen them. This is the proof. And now I ask myself, what does Teslom know about this?'

'But what makes you connect these pictures with the story of the Pollandore?'

'Why? Always fucking why? Because it is a possibility, Teslom my friend. Because I have a feeling. A hypothesis. Because it would fit the case. So. What do you tell me? What do you say?'

Teslom hesitated.

'I would say,' he said at last, 'that you are not the first to come to this house and speak about the Pollandore. A paluba came here yesterday.'

'A paluba.'

'Indeed. From the woods. It talked of the Pollandore and now you come with these questions about the same thing.'

'The Pollandore is real then. It was actually made.'

'I don't know that. There is a record that Lezarye once held such a thing in care, that one of the elder families was appointed warden, but it was seized by the Vlast soon after the Founder came north. Attempts were made to destroy it in the time of the Gruodists, but they failed. That is what is said.'

'And this paluba spoke of it? That implies it exists.'

'It implies only that our friends in the woods believe so. Some of the Committee also think it is real. Others do not.'

'What else did it say, this paluba?'

'It asked to address the Inner Committee. It spoke of an angel, a living angel that had fallen in the forest and was doing great damage. The woods fear it will poison the world. The paluba wanted us to open the Pollandore. That is the way the legend goes, is it not? The Pollandore, to be opened in the last extremity, when hope is lost.'

185

'Exactly. Yes. Fuck yes. Do you see what this means, Teslom? Do you see?'

'The paluba also said the Pollandore itself was broken, or leaking, or failing, or something. The point was unclear, I think. I was not there myself.'

'What did the Committee do?'

'Nothing. They refused to countenance the paluba's message at all. They wanted nothing to do with it. They sent it away.'

'So …'

'I was appalled when I heard what they had done. But they're too frightened to act. The pogroms have begun again, worse than ever. Did you know that? The Vlast is clearing the ghettos. People are being lined up and shot. Lezarye is being rounded up and put on trains to who knows where. Whole neighbourhoods are being emptied.'

'I didn't know. I've seen the rhetoric in the papers, but I didn't … What are you – I mean the Committee …?'

'The Committee is too frightened to move. There is talk of arming ourselves and fighting back. Getting money and mounting a coup. Young men on the rooftops throwing down bombs on the militia. Others, of course, hope that if we keep quiet the troubles will fade away again, like they have done before. But already people are dying.'

'And you? The Collection?'

'My duty is to protect it. It has survived such times in the past. I've begun to pack it away, but … it is so much work for one man. The Committee offers no help. They will not consider departure.'

'Where would you go?'

'I don't know. Perhaps the woods, if I can find a way to transport the collection there. Or one of the exclaves. Koromants. Or maybe I will get it on a ship and go across the sea to the Archipelago. But with the winter coming …'

Vishnik held out the *Child's Book of Wonders*.

'Here,' he said. 'Take it.'

'But you know I can't … it may not be safe …'

'Take it, Teslom. Find a way. And if you think I can help you, my friend, ask me. Ask me.'

50

Maroussia must have fallen. She was lying hunched on the floor of her room. Aching, exhausted, she pulled herself carefully, with steady deliberation, up onto the chair. The feel of the trees, the buried sleeping god, swam in her head. The paluba was watching her.

'That's real,' she said. 'It's there. Isn't it? I didn't know.'

The paluba said nothing.

Maroussia saw it and the companion now for what they really were: a weaving of light and will and contained, living air. The moulded breath of forest trees. Trees rooted in the body of the buried god.

But her mother was still dead. The militia would come. They were already coming. That was real too.

'How long was I ...? I mean, when did you come? How long have I been lying here?'

The paluba shrugged jerkily. The question meant little to her.

'I've done what I can for your wounds. They will heal quickly now.'

Maroussia pulled up her skirt and looked at her leg. The raw gash had crusted over. The pain was dulled.

'Who was he?' she asked. 'The man I saw?'

'Your father?'

'Yes. My father. He must have a name.'

'Oh, he's Hasha.'

'Hasha?'

'Hasha. He can't come to you here. He can't leave the forest.'

'Will I ... Could I go there, to him?'

'Eventually. Perhaps. It is possible. But ... I'm sorry, there's something more.'

Maroussia stared into the paluba's wild, fathomless eyes. 'Show me.'

51

Rain was tumbling out of the sky. A heavy black downpour. Lakoba Petrov the painter had walked a long way, out to the northern edge of the city, no longer Mirgorod proper but the Moyka Strel, in the wider Lezarye Quarter, out beyond the Raion Lezaryet itself, an ageing halfway place where the houses were made of wood. Although they had been there for centuries, they were skewed, temporary-looking buildings of weathered planking, with shuttered windows and shingled roofs. Their eaves and porches and windows were mounted with strips of intricately carved wood, pierced with repeating patterns and interlaced knotwork. It was like embroidered edging. Like pastry. Like repeating texts printed in a strange alphabet. The woodwork was salt-bleached, and broken in places, but even so the houses looked more like musical cabinets or confectionery than dwellings. They were made from trees that had grown on the delta islands long before the Founder came.

Petrov had been born in this place, but he hardly knew that now. New thoughts filled him so full of wild energy that he could not keep body or mind still, he couldn't even walk straight. Uncontainable and superabundant, he tacked back and forth across the road, advancing only slowly and zig by zag in stuttering steps, muttering as he went, hissing random syllables under his breath in a new language of his own.

Lost in his fizzing new world, he walked smack into the line of soldiers that blocked his path.

In the face of one a mouth was moving, but Petrov heard no words, only the soft swaying of the sea and the hissing of the rain, until the soldier struck him in the shoulder with the butt of his rifle, hard, and he fell.

'Go down there. Get in line with the others.'

Petrov struggled to his feet, his shoulder hurting. The soldier who had hit him was young, not more than a boy, his face white as paper. He seemed to have no eyes.

'Get in line.'

'No,' said Petrov. 'No. I can't.'

The soldier jabbed the muzzle of the rifle hard into his stomach.

'Do it. Or we shoot you now.'

Some of the soldiers had circled round behind him. A hand shoved Petrov sharply in the back, so that he stumbled forward, almost falling again. The soldiers in front of him moved aside to let him through.

'Down there. Walk.'

Petrov realised then that he knew this place. It was a piece of waste ground, cut across by a shallow gully. Boys used to play there when he was one of them. They had called it Red Cliff, having never seen cliffs. There was a small crowd of people there now, lined up on the lip of the slope, in silence, in the rain. Soldiers to one side, waiting. Three army trucks drawn up in a line. Soldiers unloading stuff from the tarpaulined backs. An officer, fair-haired, neat and pale, was giving orders. Petrov knew he smelled of soap.

Some of the people were naked, and others were in their under-clothes. Some were undressing under the soldiers' gaze. Women crossed their arms over their breasts and shivered. The rain soaked them. There was a pile of rain-sodden clothes. Alone, at some distance, an earth-coloured mudjhik stood, sightlessly swaying, attendant. The soldiers were arranging their mitrailleuses in a row on a raised mound.

Petrov realised that one of the soldiers from the street had followed behind him, and was standing at his shoulder.

'Go over there and join the others, citizen,' the soldier said in his ear. His young voice was drab with shock. 'Leave your clothes on the pile. If we can, we will be quick.'

The people smelled wet and sour. They were as silent as trees. Petrov was aware of bare feet, his own among them, cold and muddy in the rain-soaked, puddled red earth.

Time widened.

Somewhere – distant – it seemed that someone, a woman, was

berating the soldiers with loud, precise indignation. Three echoless shots repaired the silence and the rain.

Then the mitrailleuses began to fire.

52

Maroussia was in a terrible place. The paluba's kiss had taken her there. A dreadful nightmare place in the shadow of a steep hill. Only it wasn't a hill, it was alive. It was an angel, fallen.

There were trees here too, but here the trees were stone, bearing needles of stone. Maroussia was walking on snow among outcrops of raw rock. In parts the earth itself, bare of snow, smouldered with cool, lapping fire under a crust of dry brittleness. Dust and cinders, dry scraping lava over cold firepools. Walking over it, Maroussia's feet broke through the crust into the soft flame beneath. Flame that was cold and didn't burn.

Stone grew and spread like vegetation. There were strange shimmering pools of stuff that wasn't water.

Everything was alive and watched her. No, not alive, but the opposite of life. Anti-life. Hard, functional, noticing continuation without existence, like an echo, a shadow, a reflection of what once was. But everything was aware of her. Everything.

The hill that was an angel had spilled its awareness. It was bleeding consciousness into the surrounding rock for miles. Like blood.

She wasn't alone. Sad creatures wandered aimlessly among the trees. Creatures of stone. Creatures that had become stone. They were broken, cracked, abraded, but they couldn't die. From the shelter of stunted stone birches, a great stone elk with snapped antlers and no hind legs watched her pass. There was no respite for it. It could only wait for the slow weathering of ice and wind and time that would, eventually, wear it away and blow its residuum of dust across the earth. But it would be watching, noticing dust. Cursed with the endlessness of continuation.

Stone giants were digging their way up out of the earth and walking across the top of it, breaking waist-high through stone trees. If they fell they cracked and split. Headless giants walking. Fingerless club-stump hands. Giants fallen and floundering in pools of slowed time.

The corruption was spreading, seeping outwards through the edgeless forest in all directions like an insidious stain, like lichen across rock, like blood in snow. It would never stop. It would creep outwards for ever. The forest was dying.

The angel had been shot into the forest's belly like a bullet, bursting it open, engendering a slow, inevitable, glacial, cancerous, stone killing.

The angel was watching her. The whole of the lenticular stone waste was an eye, focused on her. She felt the gross intrusion of its attention like a fat finger, tracing the thread from her to the paluba to the great trees of the forest.

It knew. And without effort it burst the paluba open.

The explosion of the paluba drove sticks and rags and meat across the apartment, smashing furniture and shattering glass. The air companion was sucked apart like a breeze in the hurricane's mouth.

Maroussia felt a scream in her head as the paluba tried to tuck her away in a pocket of safety. There were fragments of voice in the scream – the paluba's voice – desperately stuffing words into the small space of her head.

The Pollandore! Open it! Open it, Maroussia! You have the key!

And in the moment of ripping and destruction she also sensed the angel's fear. Fear of what was in Mirgorod waiting, and fear of what she, Maroussia, could do.

Maroussia walked out of her apartment and down the stairs. Out into the street and the rain.

53

Iakoba Petrov lay among the bodies of the dead. A dead face pressed against his cheek. The smell and the weight and the feel of killed people were piled up on his chest – he couldn't breathe he couldn't breathe he couldn't breathe – the trench was filling up with the bodies of the dead – one by one in rows they jerked as the bullets struck them and they died – they fell – they died. Water, percolating through the stack of the dead, brimmed in his open mouth. He coughed and puked. His mouth tasted bitter and full of salt.

The soldiers clambered among the bodies, finishing off the ones who were not yet dead, the ones who moaned, or hiccupped, or moved, or wept. Petrov, who had fallen when the firing began, untouched by any bullet, lay as still as the dead under the rain and the dead.

The soldiers began to cover the bodies over with wet earth. Petrov felt the weight of it and smelled its dampness. It was as heavy as all the world. He could not draw breath. He waited.

When the time came he pulled himself out from among the bodies and the red earth and turned back towards the city. But there was no escape: the dead climbed out after him in countless number; sightless, speechless, lumbering. Dripping putrefaction and broken as they died, they climbed out from the pit and followed him, walking slowly.

What he needed now could be got only from Josef Kantor.

54

By the time Raku Vishnik got home from the House on the Purfas he was soaked, but he hardly noticed the rain. He was certain that he had found the Pollandore. What Teslom had said confirmed it. It was real, it existed, he knew where it was. He wanted to tell someone – he would tell Vissarion – he would tell Maroussia Shaumian – they would share his triumph. They would understand. And together they would make a plan. His head was turning over scenes and plots and plans as he opened the door to his apartment and walked into nightmare.

The room was destroyed. Ransacked. His furniture broken. Drawers pulled out and overturned. Papers and photographs spilled across the floor. A man in the pale brick colour uniform of the VKBD looked up from the mess they were sifting when he arrived. Two other men were sitting side by side on the sofa. Rubber overalls and galoshes over civilian clothes. Neat coils of rope put ready beside them. Two large clean knives.

'My room,' he said. 'My room.'

It was the room he thought of first, though he knew, some part of him knew, that this was madness. When he'd arrived in Mirgorod twenty years before, to begin his career, he'd been able to obtain this small apartment, just for himself. The first time he closed the door behind him he had almost wept for simple joy. One afternoon soon afterwards he'd found on a stall in the Apraksin a single length of hand-blocked wallpaper – pale flowers on a dark russet ground – and put it up in the corner behind the stove. It was there now. And he'd accumulated other treasures over the years: the plain gilded mirror, only a little tarnished; the red lacquer caddy; the tinted lithograph of dancers. He looked at it now, all spilled across the floor.

'Fuck,' said Vishnik quietly, almost to himself. 'Fuck.' A tired resignation settled over him. None of it mattered now. He had known this time would come. He picked up the holdall, waiting packed by the doorway. 'OK,' he said to the VKBD man. 'OK. Let's go.'

The VKBD man took the bag from Vishnik's hand and shut the door.

'You won't be needing that,' he said. 'We're not going anywhere. All we need is here.'

'What?' said Vishnik.

'Where is Lom? Where is the girl? Where is the file?'

'What the fuck is this?' Vishnik was angry. Livid. 'Who the fuck are you, with your fucking questions? Look at my room. Look what you have done. You can go fuck yourself.'

'Where is Lom? Where is the girl? Where is the file? Please answer.'

'Number one,' said Vishnik. 'I don't know. Number two. What girl? Number three. What fucking file?'

The two men in rubber overalls were standing now. They picked up the couch and moved it to the middle of the room. The VKBD man repeated the questions. And then the fear came. Vishnik stumbled and almost fell. But he would not fall. He would not.

'You,' said Vishnik, 'can piss for it.'

The VKBD man indicated the couch in front of him.

'Sit down, Prince Vishnik. No, lie down. Close your eyes and think. We have plenty of time. Shout all you like. No one will come. The dvornik will have told them we are here and they'll keep quiet until we are gone. You know this is true. No one will come to help you. Now …' He put a hand on Vishnik's shoulder and propelled him gently forward. 'Please don't feel you must attempt to endure. Prolongation of your pain is needless and inconvenient.'

'Fuck you,' said Vishnik. 'Fuck you.'

55

L om's tram forced its way against the rising storm. The other passengers sat tightly silent, staring out through the rain-streaming windows. The air grew bruises, purple and electric. Wind burst upon the streets in panicky, erratic bellows. Ragged whorls and twisters of wind-lashed rain threw hard gobbets against roofs and windows. Within moments floodwater was gushing up through the gratings of the sewers.

The tramway was raised above it, running on embankments and viaducts. Lom watched the mounting flood through blurred glass. People caught in the streets wrapped their arms over their heads and waded for shelter. The embankments of the city overbrimmed. Canal barges and ferries were tipped out of their channels into the streets and surged about helplessly before the wind, thumping hollowly against the walls of buildings, smashing through the windows of shops and theatres and restaurants. Pale faces looked out from upper windows. Droshki drivers struggled in the teeth of the storm to cut their horses loose from their traces and let them swim. It was impossible to tell street from canal. Some people had taken to boats and sculled their way slowly between tenements and shopfronts. A few souls swam, making little progress against the currents and churn.

The tram trundled on, deeper into the city, until at last the inevitable confronted it and it lurched to a halt in a shower of sparks from the power cable overhead, up to its wheel-tops in mud-thickened surging water. In the aftermath of the engine's surrender, wind and rain filled Lom's ears. His first instinct was to wait where he was, but the driver was shouting at them that they had to get out.

'The water is rising! The car will tip!'

They could already feel her shifting uneasily under the pressure of the flood. One by one they climbed down. The water was almost up to his waist, brown and icy cold.

The passengers from the tram stood in a huddle in the water, ineffectually wiping at the rain streaming down their faces, at a loss. There was a small bakery nearby, its door open, the flood lapping dully at the counter lip. Baskets and sodden loaves and pastries floated low in the water. From an upstairs casement a man in a pink shirt was beckoning, mouthing, his words lost in the rain. The others moved towards the shop, but Lom ignored him. He had to get to Pelican Quay.

56

When Lakoba Petrov came to his room, Josef Kantor's first instinct was to shoot him out of hand. Petrov stank like shit in a ditch. He had shaved his head, and his body, always thin, was a bundle of sticks. He was sodden, weighted down with water, a drowned rat. There were smears of what looked like paint or ink on his face, as if he had been writing on himself. His pupils were dilated, wide and dark.

'You told the girl where to find me,' said Kantor. 'You are an idiot, a useless fool. What are you doing here now?'

But Petrov only looked puzzled.

'Girl?'

'The Shaumian girl.'

Petrov waved the issue aside.

'I have come,' he said. 'I am prepared. What we spoke of earlier. The great inflagration, when all things will burn. I have decided. Let it come.'

Kantor withdrew his hand from his pocket. He had been fingering his revolver, but he let it lie. Instead he sat back in his chair and regarded Petrov with an interested benevolence. He had given up on this plan, and intended to use Lidia or Stefania, but he had not been able to overcome his doubts about their reliability. Their commitment to the sacrifice that was required. If Petrov had come back to him, that was better. That would be much more satisfactory.

He smiled at Petrov.

'Good,' he said. 'Very good. I'm glad you came to me, my friend. Let us discuss what you need.'

57

Walking against the flood was a perilous business. The water was slicked with oil and foulness. A dead rat nudged against his chest and caught there. Lom slapped it away with a shudder. The cold numbed his feet; hidden kerbs and obstructions underfoot threatened to trip and duck him at every step; his cloak spread sluggishly about him on the water. There were fewer and fewer people about. The streets were being abandoned to the rising waters. Lom rounded a corner and saw a flat-bottomed boat making slow headway away from him. Lom surged ahead, shouting. The boat, already low in the water with the weight of hunched bodies, was being poled effortfully forward by a man standing in the stern. Someone saw Lom and tugged at the boatman's sleeve. He paused to rest and let Lom catch up. Lom grabbed the gunwale with both hands and hauled himself over the side, falling heavily into the bottom among feet and sodden belongings.

'Thank you,' he breathed. 'Thanks.'

'Fifty roubles,' said the boatman.

Lom fumbled for the money with chilled, clumsy fingers and leaned across to pay him – not fifty roubles, but all he had – rocking the boat and elbowing his neighbour. She glared at him in mute protest. The boat punted forward in silence, past the Laughing Cockerel Theatre and the sagging balconies of the Apraksin. The wind was getting up, whipping the rain into their faces, raising low, choppy waves and flecks of spray. Lom found himself shivering. At least the floods gave him time. Chazia's people couldn't move in this.

An argument broke out among the passengers. A group of conscripts wanted to be taken to the Armoury and were attempting to commandeer the vessel. The boatman had had enough and wanted to go home. He poled stubbornly onwards, ignoring the soldiers' attempts to issue orders and impress upon him the urgency of his duty. The rest of the passengers looked on disconsolately, having given themselves up to events, indifferent to where they were carried as long as they stayed out of the icy, dirty water. Lom kept out of it. Neither direction suited him.

The boat was crossing a wide inundated square when the arguing soldiers fell quiet. Lom followed the direction of their gaze. There was something in the water. A smooth coil of movement. It came again, and then again: a slicker, surer movement than the wavelets chopping and jostling in the wind. Lom glimpsed a solid, steely-grey, oil-sleeked gun barrel of flesh. He thought it was an eel, but larger. Blackish flukes broke the surface without a splash and a face was watching him. A human face.

Almost human. It was the almost-humanness of the face that made it so shocking, because it wasn't human at all. It was a soft chalky white, the white of human flesh too long in the water, with hollow eye-sockets and deep dark eyes, the nose set higher and sharper than a human nose, the mouth a straight, lipless gash. The creature raised its torso higher and higher out of the water, showing an underbelly of the same subaqueous white as the face, and heavy white breasts, with nipples like a woman's but larger and bruise-coloured, bluish black. Below the almost-human torso, the dark tube of fluke-tailed muscle was working away. The creature's face was watching him continuously. It knew he was there. It knew it was being watched. There was no expression on its face at all. None whatsoever.

The creature swam swiftly towards the crowded boat, its white face upturned, watching Lom intently. He saw its hollow dark eyes, its expressionless mouth slightly open. He heard a faint hiss, like an expulsion of breath. It came right up to the boat and put its hands up on the sides, and began to tug and rock it, trying to pull itself in. It had a smooth, square, white upper back, like a man's, with a faint raised ridge the length of its spine.

'Rusalka! Rusalka!'

The boatman was yelling, panicked, and striking at the creature with his long heavy pole. One of the conscripts shouted in protest and lunged across the thwarts to grab at his arm, but it was too late.

The boatman caught the rusalka a heavy blow full on its head, and it withdrew under the water.

The soldier jumped in after it.

'Come back!' he was shouting. 'Please! Come back!'

He splashed about until he was exhausted and sobbing and gulping for air. At last he let his companions pull him back into the boat. While the passengers' attention was distracted Lom slipped over the side and waded away towards the edge of the square.

58

Krogh barely looked up when his private secretary came into the office carrying another stack of files. As always, the files would be placed in the in-tray and the completed work from the other tray would be cleared. It would be done without speaking. That was the routine. Minimal disturbance. Krogh was slightly surprised when the private secretary lingered, and walked around behind the desk to stand in the bay and look out of the windows. The rain was pouring in sheets out of the ruinous, bruised sky.

'The floods are rising,' the private secretary said.

Krogh grunted. The interruption irritated him. He was already unsettled following the call from Lom.

'I won't go home tonight,' he said. 'I'll sleep in the flat. I may need to speak to the Novozhd later. There's no need for you to stay, Pavel. Go home now before the bridges are closed.'

'It's too late for that.'

There was something in the private secretary's tone that surprised him.

'Well,' said Krogh, 'get them to find a launch to take you. Tell them I said so. I don't want you any more, not till tomorrow.'

'There was a message from Commander Chazia.'

'What did she say?'

'That you were a stupid old fucker.'

Krogh realised too late how close behind him the private secretary had come. The loop of wire was round his neck before he could react. It tightened, cutting into the folds of his flesh. He felt it slicing. Felt the warm blood spill down his neck inside his collar. It splashed the papers on his desk. He tried to get his fingers inside the wire, but could not.

His fingers slipped on the blood. He felt the wire cut them. He tried to stand up, he tried to fight, he tried to call out, but the private secretary was leaning away from him, pulling at his neck with the wire loop, tipping him backwards, unbalancing him. He tried to throw himself sideways but the private secretary hauled him upright. No sound could escape from his constricted throat. He could get no air in. He felt the back of his chair digging into his head. It hurt. Then he died.

59

When Maroussia Shaumian reached the building where Raku Vishnik lived, she found the street door shut against the rising waters. She pushed it open and waded into the dim, flooded hall. Her splashing echoed oddly. She felt the weight of her sodden clothes dragging at her as she climbed the stairs to Apartment 4. The door was ajar.

'Raku?' she called softly. 'Raku? It's Maroussia.'

There was no answer. She pushed the door open and went in.

What was left of Vishnik lay on the couch, adrift on a sea of littered paper and broken household stuff. He was naked, on his back, his arms and legs lashed by neat bindings to the legs of the couch. There was blood. A lot of blood. Three fingers of his right hand were gone.

She must have made some sound – she didn't know what – because he turned his pulped and swollen face in her direction. He was watching her with his one open eye. She had thought he was dead.

She went across the room to him. He was moving his mouth. He might have been speaking but she couldn't hear him over the sound of the rain against the windows. She knelt down beside him. The water from her dress soaked the drift of notebooks and scattered photographs.

'Maroussia—' he said. 'I didn't . . .'

What should I do? she thought. *What should I do?*

'It's OK,' she said. 'I'll help you.' *What should I do?* She tried to undo one of the knots, but it was tight and slippery with blood. Her fingers tugged at it uselessly. 'What happened?' she said. 'Who did this? What can I do, Raku?'

'I found it,' said Vishnik. He was staring at her with his one remaining eye. They had taken the other one. 'It's here and I found it. I didn't tell them what I know.'

'It's OK, Raku,' she said. 'It's OK.'

'No. I want to tell you. I wanted to. I was going to.' He tried to raise his head from the couch. There was blood in his mouth. 'I found it. I found it. And they were here … But they didn't get it. Even they … even they are human. And stupid.'

'Raku?'

He laid his head back against the couch. His mouth fell partly open. His face was empty. He was gone.

Maroussia stood up. She was trembling.

I need to get out of here. I need to get out of here now.

The horror of the thing on the couch – what they had done to him … She could not stay. It was impossible. But the storm was raging outside, and the floods … She had almost not made it here. Where could she go? How?

She went to the window, parted the curtains and looked out into storming darkness. The casement was rattling in its frame; the reflection of the room behind her flexed as the panes bowed under the force of the wind. She pressed her face against the glass, trying to see.

The street lamps were out. The only faint light came from the windows of neighbouring houses, but she could see by their glimmering reflection on the waves down below that the flood had risen further. There must have been ten to fifteen feet of surging water in the street, whipped into choppy, spray-spilling peaks.

And there was a boat.

A diesel launch was nosing its way up the flooded street, half a dozen uniformed men in the open stern, hunching their shoulders against the rain, MILITIA OF MIRGOROD in white lettering on the roof of the cabin.

She heard a movement in the room behind her, and spun round, thinking wildly that it was Vishnik, raising himself somehow from the couch.

But it was Lom.

'We have to get out,' said Maroussia 'We have to go. They're outside now. They have a boat.'

'I know,' said Lom. 'I saw them.' He was looking at Vishnik. 'I came for him.'

'Raku's dead,' said Maroussia. 'He was ... He spoke to me when I got here, he said ... he said he told them nothing.'

'He had nothing to tell. They didn't need to do this.'

From down below there came the sound of hollow thumping, wood striking against wood, heavily. Glass breaking.

'There's no time,' said Maroussia. 'We have to go now.'

Lom stood looking at Vishnik for a moment.

'Take the stairs,' he said. 'Not the lift. Go up. In houses like this the roof space is usually open from house to house. All the way to the end of the row if you're lucky. Keep going up. You'll find a way.'

'What about you?' she said. 'Aren't you coming?'

'I'll keep them occupied. You can find a boat on the quay.'

'They'll kill you,' said Maroussia.

'They won't,' said Lom. 'Not straight away. They need to know what I've done. They need to be sure.'

Maroussia shook her head. 'Come with me,' she said.

'No,' said Lom.

Maroussia hesitated. There was another crash from downstairs. A shout.

'Shit,' said Lom. 'Just go. You need to go. Please.'

There was nothing else to say. She turned away from him and went out of the door.

60

When Maroussia had gone, Lom went to the lift cage and pressed the button to summon the car. The mechanism juddered loudly into life. The lift was on one of the upper floors, and it took agonising moments to descend. When it reached him, he pulled open the cage and stepped inside, pressed the button for the basement and stepped back out again. There was a splash when it hit the water below. It wouldn't be coming back, not with the weight of water inside it. That left only the stairwell.

He went to the top of the stairs. He would see down one flight and the landing below. He checked the gun. Checked it again.

A quiet voice. The sound of boots. A face peering up from the landing below.

Lom fired high. The shot struck the wall above the man's head, and he ducked out of sight.

'Lom?' It was Safran's voice. 'Lom? Is that you? What are you hoping to achieve?'

Lom fired another shot down the stairwell.

'Don't try to come up,' he called. 'I'll shoot anyone I see. I won't fire high again.'

'There are six of us, Lom. You haven't got a chance.'

'I've got boxfuls of shells. I'm very patient.'

'You're mad.'

Lom said nothing. The longer he could hold them here, the more time he would give Maroussia.

'We can rush you, Lom. Any time we want. You can't shoot us all.'

'Who's first then?'

'How's your friend, Lom? How's Prince Vishnik?' Lom felt the anger rising inside him. 'He liked you, Lom. Did you know that? He called your name a lot. When he wasn't squealing like a pig.'

'You bastard—' Lom stopped. Safran was goading him. He mustn't let it distract him. He waited. 'Safran?' he called. But there was no answer. The silence stretched. Nothing happened. Lom waited.

Someone appeared on the landing below. A face. An arm. Throwing something. Lom fired too late.

The grenade bounced off the wall and skittered towards him. Instinctively he kicked out at it, a panicky jab of his foot that almost missed completely, but the outside edge of his shoe connected. The clumsy kick sliced the grenade against the skirting board. It bounced off and rolled back down the stairs, two or three steps at a time. Lom lurched back, protecting his face with his arm.

The explosion sucked the air down the stairwell and then burst it back up. The noise was too loud to be heard as sound; it was just a slamming pain inside his head. Lom stumbled dizzily.

As he leaned against the wall, trying to clear his head, trying not to vomit, it dawned on him that the sawing, hiccupping sounds he was hearing were someone else's pain.

He looked up in time to see a uniform looming up the stairs. He fired towards it wildly and the uniform retreated.

Something – a sound, a glimpse of movement in the corner of his eye – made him turn. Safran was behind him, only a few yards away, his revolver raised.

Shit. The lift shaft. He climbed it.

As Lom swung round, he saw the satisfaction in Safran's pale eyes. There was no time to react. Safran clubbed him viciously on the side of his head. On the temple. And again.

Lom's world swam sickeningly, his balance went and he fell.

Two militia men were holding his arms behind his back. Safran's pale eyes were looking into his. Lom tried to tense the muscles in his midriff, but when the blow came, hard, he folded and tried to drop to his knees. The men held him up.

Lom hauled at the air with his mouth but no breath would go in. Safran pulled his head up by the hair to see his face and hit him again. And again. When the men dropped his arms, he went down and curled up on the floor, knees tucked in against his chin, trying to protect himself. At last he was able to suck in some air, noisily. A sticky line of spit trailed from his mouth to the floor.

'You,' said Safran, 'are nothing. You are made of shit.'

61

The room they left him in was stiflingly hot. It must have been somewhere deep inside the Lodka: there were no windows, just shadowless electric light from a reinforced glass recess in the ceiling. Some sort of interview room. A wooden table in the centre of the floor, two chairs facing each other across it, another two along the wall. Green walls, a peeling linoleum floor and, around the edges of the room, solid, heavy iron pipes, bolted strongly to the wall and scalding hot to the touch. Leather straps were wrapped loosely around them, and there were stains and dried stuff stuck on the pipes. There were stains on the floor too. Dark brown. Through the door came the sound of a distant bell, footsteps, muffled yelling and shouting. It was impossible to tell what time it was. Whether it was night or day.

Every part of him hurt. His left eye was closed. It felt swollen and tender to the touch. His fingers came away sticky with drying blood. His head was throbbing. There was a dull pain and an empty sickness in his midriff. A sharp jabbing in his ribs when he moved. No serious damage had been done. Not yet. He had been lucky or, more likely, Safran had been careful.

He tried the door. It was locked. He sat at the table, facing the door, and waited, trying to keep the image of Vishnik on the couch – what they had done to him – out of his mind. He would settle with Safran for that.

He found himself thinking about Maroussia Shaumian. Her face. The darkness under her eyes. She had been holding herself together but the effort was perceptible. There had been a ragged wound across her cheek. He hoped she was far away. He hoped he would see her again.

When he heard the key turn in the lock, he thought about standing up to face them, but didn't trust his body to straighten, so he stayed where he was. The man in the doorway was wearing a dark fedora and a heavy grey coat, unbuttoned, over a red silk shirt. His face was thin and pockmarked under a few days' growth of beard.

Lom had seen him before. In the old photograph on Krogh's file. In the marching crowd. As a statue half a mile in the sky, looking out across another Mirgorod, a city that didn't exist, not yet. The whisperers' Mirgorod. *His* Mirgorod. This was him.

The half-mile-high man laid his hat on the table, hung his coat on the back of the other chair and sat down facing Lom. His hair was straight and cut long, thickly piled, a dark of no particular colour, unusually abundant and lustrous, brushed back from his face without a parting. The red silk of his shirt was crumpled and needed washing. Close up, his eyes were dark and brown, with a surprising, direct intensity. It was like looking into street-fires burning. The man let his hands rest, relaxed and palm-down on the table, but all the time he was watching Lom's face with those deep, dark brown eyes in which the earth was burning.

'Kantor,' said Lom. 'Josef Kantor.'

'You're an interesting fellow, Investigator,' said Kantor. 'Stubborn. Clever. Courageous. A policeman who steps outside the rules.' He paused, but Lom said nothing. Every word was to be wrung from him. Nothing offered for free. He regretted he'd spoken at all. He'd given too much away already. In interrogations, there was as much to learn for the subject as for the interrogator. What did they know? What did they not? What did they need? The silence in the room continued. It became a kind of battle. Eventually, Kantor smiled. 'You react as I would,' he said. 'Observe, learn, give nothing away. That's good.'

Lom said nothing. Kantor leaned back in his chair.

'So. Here we are. I wanted some time alone with you before Lavrentina comes. She'll be here soon, I'm afraid, and after that it won't be possible for us to speak like this any more. Which for me is genuinely regrettable.' Kantor looked at his watch. 'You've impressed me. Do you want to know what time it is? Ask me, and I'll tell you.'

Lom said nothing.

'Would you like to smoke?' He laid a packet of cigarettes on the table. 'Oh please, say *something*. We both know the game. I've been beaten myself, in rooms like this one. You ask yourself, will I be brave? But it doesn't matter. It makes no difference. Lavrentina will come soon, and that won't be the kind of roughhouse you and I are used to.'

The strangest thing about Kantor, thought Lom, was that, despite all he knew about him, he was attractive. He turned interrogation into a teasing game. He made himself charming, fun to be with. You sensed his strength and power and his capacity for cruelty, but somehow that made you want him to look after you. He might kill you, but he might also love you.

'Perhaps you're still hoping you'll be able to deliver Lavrentina's stupid file to Krogh. Perhaps you're thinking, *Krogh is arresting Chazia even as we speak. He will come through the door any moment now and rescue me.* But that isn't going to happen.' Kantor paused, and looked into Lom's eyes with warm sympathy. 'We found the files in the bathroom. And Krogh is dead. She had to do that, didn't she, after that telephone call?'

Lom felt his defences crumbling. He was tired and scared and weak and sick.

'You killed him, actually,' Kantor was saying. 'Of course you did. You knew you were doing it at the time. At least, you were indifferent whether it happened or not. See why you interest me, Lom? I see something of myself in you, as a matter of fact. And you killed Vishnik too.'

'No!'

'What do you want to know, Lom? Go on, ask me something and I will answer, I promise, even if only to repay the pleasure of having finally got you to speak. I have to get something out of you before Chazia does. You have the advantage of me: you've seen my file. Tell me about it. What does it say?'

It was as if he had been reading Lom's thought processes in his face.

'Chazia thinks she can use you,' said Lom. 'But she's wrong, isn't she? You're using her. The question is, what for? What do you want, Kantor?'

'Ha!' cried Kantor. 'You wonderful man! You do see to the heart of things, don't you? You're right, that is the biggest question. No one, not even the angel, has asked it until now.'

'You owe me an answer.'

'I do.'

'So answer.'

'Have you ever wondered where the angels come from?'

Surprised, Lom shook his head. 'The stars, I guess,' he said. 'The planets. Outer space. Galaxies.'

'Exactly. And what about that? We hardly consider it, do we? They arrive, and we take them for signs and wonders. Messages about us. Who is justified, who not? What clever machines can we make of their dying flesh? It's all so narrow and trivial, don't you think? As if this one damp and cooling world with its broken moons was all there is. The Vlast looks inwards and backwards all the time. But we're see-ing angels the wrong way round. What they tell us is, there are other worlds, other suns, countless millions of them; you only have to look up in the night to see them. And we can go there. We can move among them. Humankind spreading out across the sky, advancing from star to star.'

'Impossible,' said Lom.

Kantor slammed his hand on the table. 'Of course it's possible. It's not even a matter of doubt. The engineering is straightforward. Like everything else, it is only a matter of paying the price. A few generations of collective sacrifice is all that's needed. The fruit of the stars is there to be harvested. That's our future. I know it. I've seen it in the voice of the angel. A thousand thousand glittering vessels rising into the sky and unfolding their sails and crossing the emptiness between stars. All it requires is ingenuity. Effort. Organisation. Purpose. Sacrifice. The deferment of pleasure. Imagine a Vlast of a thousand suns. That would be worth something. Can you see that, Lom? Can you imagine it? Can you share that great ambition?'

It seemed to be an honest question. It might have been a genuine offer, a door out of the torture room.

'No,' said Lom. 'No. I can't.'

'Ah,' said Kantor and shrugged. 'Pity.'

The door opened and Lavrentina Chazia came in.

Archangel unfurls his mind like a leaf across the continent.

The dead dig trenches to bury themselves.

The dead ride long slow cattle trains eastwards, the streets behind them empty, the walls fallen from their houses, their wallpaper open to the rain,

their home-stuff spilled across the streets. The smell of wet, burned build-
ings enriches the air.

Grey-haired young men with ears turned to bone.

A naked corpse lies at the foot of the slope; a lunar brilliance streams
across the dead legs stuck apart.

Conscripts in trenches kiss their bullets in the dark and drink the snow.

Corpses awaiting collection stiffen like thorn trees.

Men and women hang by the neck from balconies on long ropes, like
sausages in a delicatessen window.

I becoming We.

The clock and the calendar reset to zero.

Everything starts from here.

Archangel – voice of history, muse of death – reaches out across his
world – the is and the will-be-soon – touching its unfolding – tasting its
texture with his mind's tongue – testing it with his mind's fingers – it
is satisfaction – it is joy – it is hope. The stars are coming, and the space
between them.

And yet – and still – nearby but out of reach – the tireless egg of time
glimmers diminutively in the massy dark – his future tinctured still with
the edge of fear.

Chazia had brought a carpet bag with her, which she set on the table
and began to unpack. Lom watched as she unrolled a chamois containing an array of small tools: blades, pliers, a steel-headed hammer.

Kantor picked up his hat and cigarettes and withdrew to a chair at
the edge of the room. He laid the hat on his lap and folded his arms
across it. It seemed like an instinctive act of self-protection. It wasn't
deference. It might have been distaste.

'There is only one subject of interest to us, Investigator,' said Chazia.
'The whereabouts of Maroussia Shaumian, the daughter of Josef's late
wife. That is all. There is nothing else. The sooner we have exhausted
that topic, the sooner we can leave this unpleasant room.'

His flimsy constructions of hope and defence crumbled. He said
nothing.

'Major Safran saw you talk to her, and now we can't find her. I think
you know where she has gone.'

'He won't speak,' said Kantor. 'He's playing dumb.'

Chazia came round to Lom's side of the table and knelt beside him.

She began to bind him with leather straps like the collars of dogs. She fixed his hands to the legs of the chair, so that his arms hung down at his sides, and then she bound his ankles to the chair legs as well. Her face was close to his lap. Her breasts were pressing against the rough material of her uniform blouson. The patches on her skin didn't look like stone, they *were* stone. Angel stone.

She worked with methodical care, her breathing shallow and rapid. The fear was a dry, silent roaring in Lom's head. He wanted to speak *now*, to tell her *everything*, but his mouth had no moisture in it and he could not.

'You were a promising policeman, Investigator,' she was saying as she worked. 'Krogh thought he'd been clever, spotting you, but it was my doing, actually. Didn't you guess? I keep track of all Savinkov's experiments. You'd never have been able to get at Laurits if I hadn't let you. We fed you the evidence, of course. Laurits was lazy, and brazen with it. I thought it would be a good idea to let you take him down, if you could. Keep the others on their toes. I had it in mind to bring you to Mirgorod myself, if you succeeded. A career open to talent, that's what the Vlast should be. But Krogh got you first, and it has come to this. A pity.'

Lom tried to focus on her, but his vision was blurry. What was she saying? He wasn't sure. His gaze was drawn back to the line of implements ready on the desk.

'Oh no,' said Chazia. 'It won't be like that. Excruciation has many uses, but collecting information quickly isn't one of them. Torture is good for encouraging demoralisation and fear – for every one person put to pain, a thousand fear it – and it binds the torturers closer to us. But none of that is relevant in your case. Such methods were ineffective on your friend Vishnik, and I doubt they would be more so with you. On this occasion I require the truth quickly, and there is a better way. You may find the method professionally interesting.'

She took a piece of some dark stuff from her bag and pulled it onto her right hand. It was a long, loose-fitting glove made of a heavy substance something like rubber, but it wasn't rubber. She held it out for him to see. It had a slightly reddish lustrous sleekness like wet seal fur.

'Angel skin,' she said, though he knew that already. He had read of such things. This was a Worm. Chazia took a flask out of her bag and held it up to Lom's face. He jerked his head aside.

'It's only water,' she said. 'Drink a little if you like.'

He nodded, and she unscrewed the cap and held the flask to his dry lips, tipping it up to let him take a sip. He sluiced the water around carefully in his mouth and let it trickle down his throat as slowly as he could. Without warning, she tipped the rest of it over his head. It was ice-cold. Lom shouted at the shock of it.

'It helps,' said Chazia. 'I don't know why.'

She brought her chair round from the other side of the desk and sat beside him, placing her angel-gloved hand on his face. He flinched. His skin crawled.

'Ask him, Josef,' she said quietly, with suppressed excitement. 'Ask him.'

Kantor came and stood by him. His eyes were hard and dispassionately curious. The smouldering earth flickered deep inside them.

'Where is my wife's bastard daughter, Vissarion? Maroussia Shaumian? Where is she now?'

Lom felt something disgusting slithering about on the surface of his mind, and pushed it instinctively away. He closed his thoughts against it and concentrated on Kantor's face. He imagined himself drawing it, like a draughtsman, meticulously. He examined its lines, contours and shadows.

See it as an object. See the surface only.

Chazia grunted in surprise, and Lom felt her push the Worm harder against the defences he had built. Her hand inside the obscene glove tightened, gripping his face where before she had only touched. He shut his mind more firmly against her. Kantor asked the question again.

Fall back to the second line of defence. Tell them something they already know. Let them believe they are making progress.

He ignored Chazia and looked into Kantor's eyes.

I can do this.

'I saw Miss Shaumian this morning, for the first and last time. Or perhaps it was yesterday, I've lost track of time. I saw her on the occasion of the summary execution in the street of her mother, Feiga-Ita Shaumian, wife of Josef Kantor, by Major Safran of the Mirgorod Militia. Miss Shaumian also observed this execution, and afterwards she walked away. I do not know where she went. I have not seen her since.'

217

Kantor returned his gaze impassively. If the words meant anything to him he did not show it. Lom felt Chazia remove her hand from his face.

'Nothing,' she said to Kantor. 'Hold his head please.'

Kantor walked around the desk to stand behind him and put his arm across Lom's throat, under his chin, pulling him backwards until he was choking, and all he could see was the recessed light in the ceiling. Kantor's other hand gripped his hair so that his head was held firmly.

Chazia's face came into his line of view. He saw the fine blade in her hand, but it was only when she placed it against the skin of his forehead that he realised what she was going to do.

Repel! Repel!

He drove his mind against her with all his strength, trying to ball up the air in the room and throw it at her.

Nothing happened.

'The vyrdalak reported that you could do that,' said Chazia. 'No wonder Savinkov sealed you up.' She touched the stone rind in her face and smiled. 'Quite useless here, of course.'

He felt her begin to cut.

Chazia didn't find it easy to get the embedded piece of angel stone out of his forehead. She had to dig and gouge and pry with considerable force. She tried several different implements. The pain went on for ever. Lom choked and fought for breath and closed his eyes against the blood that pooled in their sockets and seeped under the lids. He might have screamed. He wasn't sure.

At last it stopped. Kantor released his hold on Lom's head and let it fall forward. Lom was gasping for breath. His eyes were blinded with blood and his nose was filled with it, but his hands were bound at his sides and he could do nothing about that. He hadn't fainted while it was happening, and he didn't faint afterwards. Fainting would have been easier, but it didn't come.

Kantor was leaning over him.

'Is that the brain in there?' he said to Chazia.

Kantor's finger probed the hole in his forehead.

'It's firmer than I would have thought.'

He jabbed harder. Lom felt no pain, only a deep, woozy sickness.

'Don't, Josef,' said Chazia. 'Don't damage it yet.'

Then Lom fainted.

62

'Now we must try again,' Chazia was saying, somewhere far away. Nothing had changed. It must have been only minutes. Seconds, even. 'Quickly, before we lose him.'

Still blinded, Lom felt the glove of angel substance on his face again, and this time there was nothing he could do to defend himself. She came right inside him, roughly. Invading. Violating. He was naked and broken.

He gave Chazia everything.

She was in there, inside his mind, and she *knew*. Nothing could be hidden from her. She went everywhere, and he gave it all up. Everything that had happened. Everything he had heard. Everything he knew. Krogh. Vishnik. The Archive. The massacre. The whisperers in the square. The Crimson Marmot. Petrov. Safran. The mudjhik. Maroussia. Everything.

'He desires her, Josef!' Chazia crowed with genuine wonderment and pleasure. 'The poor idiot desires her.'

And then – how much later was it? how much time gone? nothing seemed to take very long—

'He knows nothing,' she said. 'Nothing. He's of no use at all. Kill him.'

They left him alone in the interrogation room, still tied to the chair. After an unmeasurable amount of time it seemed that other men came and released him. He might have been sick. One of the men might have been Safran. He might have imagined that.

They were leading him along corridors. He could see from one eye: linoleum, worn carpet, flagstones, his own feet. It didn't matter.

A shock of cold and space and early morning light. The smell of water. A *bridge*. They were crossing a *bridge*.

He jerked himself out of the grip of the men, who were holding him loosely by the arms, and lurched away from them towards the bridge's low parapet.

For a moment, a half-second, no more, he looked down at the dark, swollen current. He wanted the water to wash the blood and mess and memory away. A clean, cold, private death. He tipped himself over the edge.

The water reached up to take him as he fell.

The moment between tipping over the parapet and hitting the water seemed to go on for ever. Lom hung head downwards in air. The surface of the river rose slowly to meet him, freighted with the debris of the flooded city. The water had a particular smell: dark, cold, earthy, cleansing.

He crashed into green darkness and the noise churned in his ears. The shock of the cold seized his lungs in ice fists and squeezed. Bands of freezing iron tightened around his head and his chest.

He tried to scrabble his way to the surface of the river, not knowing the direction where the surface was. His clothes, water-heavy, wrapped round his body. The weight of his boots pulled at his legs, slowing their struggle to a nightmare of running. His mouth fell open in a silent O.

And yet he was happy.

After the first rush of panic, he felt his pulse-rate slowing. The icy river reached inside his ribs with cool gentle fingers and cupped his heart kindly. Calmness returned. This was now, and he was alive, and the river was his friend.

He let the dark and freezing absolution of the Mir wash away the stink and shame and failure of the interrogation room. The river let him understand.

There is no blame. There is no judge but you. Forgive yourself.

He had been ... *violated* ... by alien, brutal intruding fingers. The fat, poking stubs of Kantor, Chazia's in her foul dead-angel glove. He had given up nothing. It had been ripped out and taken, that was all. And that was not the same.

The waters cleansed the hole in the centre of his forehead where the piece of angel stone had been ripped away and the river now entered.

He felt the cool currents of its touch directly against the naked cortex of his brain, bursting long-dead synapses into light and life. Unplugged at last, for the first time since childhood, Vissarion Lom perceived the world as it was, fresh and new and timeless, flooded with truth. He smelled the light and tasted the space between things.

The Mir was filled with watchful awareness and intelligence. Lom opened wide his arms and felt himself rising. He broke the surface into early morning air. His cloak unfolded and spread itself around him like a huge black lily pad, rotating slowly in the current. His face, upturned in the cloak's dark centre, was the lily's pale flower, opening to the grey light. Breathing.

The river was in full spate. As he turned slowly, tilted upwards, he saw the wharves and quays and rooftops of Mirgorod passing against the cloud-grey sky. Nearer to his face, pieces of wood and broken things came with him. He was the flagship of a debris flotilla, being carried towards the edge of the city and beyond it the sea, on the surge of the withdrawing flood.

Waves splashed against his face and trickled into the open hole in his forehead.

The sentient water had a voice that was speaking to him. It told him that the city was an alien tumorous growth, formed around the plug with which the Founder had tried to stop the river's mouth. Yet there had been a time before the city, and there could be such a time again: when it was gone, when trees grew up between the buildings, and moss and black soil breathed the air again.

The kindly waters of the Mir brushed against his skull and reached inside to calm his heart and whisper reassurance. The voice was telling him who he was. He was a man of muscle and lung and love and understanding. He was a vessel and a flowering on the seaward flow. There were people it was right to love and there were people it was right to loathe and bring to destruction.

Yes, if I have time. I need more time.

Only there was no more time.

As he rotated slowly on the current, the ice-cold waters of the river were draining all the feeling from his body. Lom no longer knew where his arms and legs were, or what they were doing. The muscles of his face were numbed into immobility, his mouth frozen in its permanent open O.

Helplessly, from a great distance, he observed the rippling water work at the bulges and pockets of air that had been trapped in the folds of his cloak. The movement of the river was easing them slowly to the edges of the heavy fabric. One by one they bubbled out and surrendered themselves to the sky.

There was nothing he could do.

What his lily-pad cloak was losing in buoyancy it gained in weight, and slowly it was sinking, and taking him down with it. The river was already lapping at his chin and spilling over into the waiting uncloseable O.

The river brimmed against his nostrils and covered them over. At last he inhaled the cold waters deeply and sank for the second and last time. It felt like sleep. As he closed his eyes he saw against the shadows the face of Maroussia, pale and calm and serious, looking down on him hugely out of the sky, like the moon made whole.

Close by (so close!) – but also not – neither in this world, nor very far away at all – the other O – the pocketful of second chances, the waiting second mouth, the tongue of different lives – is listening to the river, listening to the rain.

63

Maroussia Shaumian found Lom's body floating face down, lodged against a squat stone pillar of the Ter-Uspenskovo Bridge among planks and branches, lost shoes and broken packing cases. She tried to pull it into the boat but she could not. Several times she almost tipped herself into the river before she gave up and knotted a line to his leg and towed him, an inert, lifeless weight, to a place where there were stone steps in the embankment. All the time she worked, she expected the shouts, the bullets, to start.

She had found the boat – an open, clinker-built, tapered skiff, her oars neatly stowed on board – bumping against the wall at the end of Pelican Quay. Ignoring the oars, she'd crouched in the bottom and edged it slowly, hand over hand, along the house-fronts until she came in sight of Vishnik's building, and she'd watched from the shadows as Lom was taken into the militia vessel. When the police boat left, its searchlight stabbing the night, raking darkened street frontages and swirling water, she followed it all the way to the Lodka, and moored against a telegraph pole.

Cold and wet and shivering, she waited. She could have left, but she did not. Lom had saved her twice. She thought of Vishnik, his ruined body and his terrible lonely death. She thought of her mother, shot in the back in the street. She would not let the Vlast take another. Not if she could prevent it.

When dawn began to seep across the city and other boats began to appear, she felt it would be less conspicuous to be moving, and so she started a slow patrol, circling the Lodka through flooded squares and across re-emerging canals. It was sheer luck that she saw, from the cover of a stranded fire-barge, the uniforms come out of a side door, and Lom stumbling along in the middle of them as if he was drunk. She saw his lurch for the parapet and heard the warders' shouts and the splash when his body hit the water. But she couldn't go to look for him straight away. She had to wait, watching the killing party linger near the bridge, shouting to each other and shining torch beams on the dark water. It was fifteen minutes before they gave up and another fifteen before she spotted the sodden hump of his back floating low in the water among the rubbish.

She dragged the body up the steps and laid it on its back. Water seeped out and puddled on the stone. The eyes were open and glassy, the pupils darkly dilated. In the dim grey dawn the face and hands were tinged an ominous blue. She made a desperate, rushed examination. There was no pulse at the wrist or neck, and no breath from the stiffened, cyanotic mouth.

'He's *not* gone,' she said to herself. 'He's *not* gone.' She was surprised how much it mattered.

With a desperate energy Maroussia pumped the lifeless chest with the heel of her hand and forced her own breath into the waterlogged lungs. Every time she paused to rest, she saw the ragged-edged hole in Lom's forehead. It oozed a dark rivery fluid.

She worked and worked, pounding the inert chest, forcing breath into the cold mouth. At last she collapsed across him, her chest heaving.

It was no good.

But at that moment Lom gave a powerful jerk and twisted out from under her weight. He rolled over onto his side, retching and vomiting black river water.

Emptied of the river, Lom sank back into unconsciousness, but he was breathing now, and the blue of his face began to flush faintly in the rising light of morning.

Somehow she managed to heave him back into the boat. There was nothing else to do. She could not carry him, and she would not leave him.

She unshipped the oars and pushed the boat free of the landing place and out into the current. Pulling out into midstream she felt the force of the current seize her. The subsiding flood waters were pouring out of the city, down towards the marshes and the sea. The boat took its place among the detritus, the floating wreckage and the crewless vessels drifting, bumping and turning on the dark foam-flecked current. There was no need to row. It would be better – less conspicuous – if she did not. But Lom's body was icy to the touch. He needed warmth, and quickly, or he would die.

Maroussia pulled Lom's cloak over his head, stuffed it away at the stern, and got his shirt, boots and trousers off. His body, naked but for his underclothes, was white as chalk. She took off her own coat and dress and lay down next to him, pulling the clothes over them both and taking him in her arms like a lover. His body was cold, clammy, inert, like something dead, and the cold seeped from him into her. She shivered uncontrollably, but she pushed herself closer against him and closed her eyes.

The Mir surged forward in the cold of the morning, taking their small vessel in its grasp, carrying them onward, downstream on turbid waters under a dark pewter sky, past the waterfronts of the waking city.

Archangel probes a sudden strangeness, and realisation almost shatters him.

He is appalled.

He is brittle.

A new fact bursts open, flowering into his awareness, staining it with a rigid poison.

Blinded by the profusion of the millions – he has not noticed – not until this moment – the faint, brushing touches – the trails – the spraints – of those he cannot see. There are time streams, and people in them – story threads, small voices – that are not part of his future.

He begins to sense them now. He detects – faintly, peripherally – the tremor of their passing and knows what it means for him. Suddenly, disaster is near. At the very moment of his triumph, failure is becoming possible.

In the forest he heaves and struggles, desperate to release the embedded hill of himself from his rock prison. He pulls and shudders, straining at the crust of the earth. Stronger now, he feels the give of it, just a little, a fraction, and the snow roars and slides off his shoulders. For a moment he believes he might succeed. But it is not enough. He cannot move, he cannot rise, he cannot fly.

He sends his mind instead, the whole of it, the entire focused armoury of his attention forced down one narrow beam, ignoring everything except the hint of one small boat and its impossible cargo of change.

He cannot see them, he cannot find them, not himself: they are somehow hidden. But they are there, and there are – he reasons – others who will be able to see them with their jelly-and-electromagnetism oculars.

He bursts his way into first one human mind, then another, and another, a roaring angel voice.

WHERE ARE THEY? WHERE ARE THEY?

A sailor falls, bleeding from the eyes. Archangel jumps to another.

WHERE ARE THEY?

A typist collapses to the floor, fitting, speaking in tongues. Archangel jumps to another.

WHERE ARE THEY?

An engineer splatters vomit across the floor and tears at his ears until they hang in tatters and bleed. Archangel jumps to another.

Archangel leaps from mind to mind, faster and faster, finding nothing. Yet they must be found. Now. Before it is too late.

Part Two

64

The giant Aino-Suvantamoinen lay on his back on the soft estuarial river-mud of the White Marshes. It was almost like floating. It was more like being a water-spider, resting on the meniscus of a pool, feeling the tremor of breezes brushing across the surface. He kept his eyes closed and his hands spread flat and palm-downward on the drum-tight, quivering skin of the mud. He was listening with his hands to the mood of the waters, feeling the way they were flowing and what they meant. He drew in long slow lungfuls of river air, tasting it with his tongue and nose and the back of his throat. There was ice and fog and rain on the air, and the exhalations of trees. He knew the savour of every tree – he could tell birch from alder, blackthorn from willow, aspen from spruce – and he could taste the distinctive breath of each of the great rivers as they mingled in the delta's throat: the Smaller Chel, the Mecklen, the Vod, and above all the rich complexity of the Mir, with traces of the city caught like burrs in her hair. Everything that he could taste and hear and feel spoke to him. It was the voice of the world.

He was floating on the cusp – the infinitesimal point of balance – between past and future. The past was one, but futures were many, an endlessly bifurcating flowering abundance of possibilities all trying to become, all struggling to grow out of the precarious restless racing-forwards of *now*.

Aino-Suvantamoinen sat up in the near-darkness – his heart pounding, his head spinning – and scooped up handfuls of cold mud. Cupping his palms together, he buried his face in the slather for coolness and rest. There was something on the Mir that morning such as he had never known before. The river was excited, it was strung out and buzzing with promise. In three centuries of listening, no other morning like this one. A boat was coming, the river told him: a boat freighted with significance, freighted with change. New futures were adrift on the Mir, and also – astonishingly – he'd never felt, never even conceived of anything like this – a new past.

The giant picked himself up from the mud. He had to hurry. He had to reach the great locks and set his shoulder to the enormous ancient beams. He had to open the sluices and close the weir gates before the rushing of the flood carried everything past. Before it was too late.

65

Maroussia lay in the bottom of the skiff, wet and cold, holding the unconscious Lom in her arms. The boat rocked and turned in the current, colliding from time to time with other objects drifting on the flood: the bodies of drowned dogs and the planks of Big Side shanties. Maroussia kept her face turned towards the wooden inside freeboard, staying low and out of sight, risking only occasional glances over the gunwale. If anyone saw the skiff, it would look like one more empty boat adrift from its moorings. Lom was breathing loudly, raggedly, the terrible wound in the front of his head circled with a fine crust of dried blood and weeping some cloudy liquid.

The river had breached its banks in many places. The current was taking them west, towards the seaward dwindling of the city. They passed through flooded squares. Lamp posts and statues sticking up from the mud-heavy, surging water. Pale faces looking from upper windows. Later, at the city's edge, they drifted above submerged fields, half-sunken trees, drowned pigs. The swollen waters carried them onwards, out of Mirgorod, into strange territories. As the morning wore on, the waters widened and slowed, taking them among low, wooded islands and spits of grass and mud. By now they should have been following one of the channels of the Mir delta, but the channels were all lost under the slack waters of the flood. Maroussia couldn't tell where the river ended and the silvery mud and the wide white skies began.

Maroussia had been as far as the edge of the White Marshes once or twice, years ago. She remembered walking there, just at the edge of it, lost, exhilarated, alone. That's where the water would take them. There was no other choice.

It was a strange, extraordinary place. Inside the long bar of Cold Amber Strand, the huge expanse of Mirgorod Bay had silted up with the sediment and detritus of millennia, deposited there by slow rivers. The commingling waters of the four rivers and many lesser streams, stirred by the ebb and flow of the brackish water entering through the Halsesond, had created behind the protecting arm of the Strand a complex and shifting mixture of every kind of wetland, a misty tract of salt marsh, bog and fen. It was a place of eel grass and cotton grass, withies, reed beds and carr. Pools of peat-brown water and small shallow lakes. Winding creeks shining like tin. Silent flocks of wading birds swept against the sky, glinting like herring shoals on the turn.

The sun was hidden behind cloud and mist. Maroussia had no way of measuring the passing of time, except by growing hunger and thirst. Lom was breathing more easily, but she had no food or water. She needed to find a landing place soon. Eventually – it might have been early in the afternoon – she unshipped the oars and began to row. The little skiff was the only vessel to be seen, conspicuously alone in the emptiness. Cat's-paw ripples and veils of fine mist trailed across the flatness, ringed by the wide horizon only. Waterfowl flew overhead or bobbed in small rafts. A mist was gathering and thickening around them, and Maroussia was glad of it. Mirgorod was a fading stain on the horizon behind them. It began to seem to her that they were nowhere at all.

She rowed clumsily, learning as she went. At least the work warmed her and loosened her stiffened muscles. Lom lay at her feet in the bottom of the boat, heavy and still. Shorelines loomed at them out of the mist. The skiff seemed to be passing between islands, or perhaps they were following channels between mudflats. It was impossible to say. After a time – it might have been only an hour, it might have been much more – she began to feel that the shores were closing in around them. They were approaching slopes of mud and stands of tangled tree growth coming down to the water's edge. An otter slipped off a mudslope and slid away through the slow waters. A heron, motionless, regarded them with its unblinking yellow eye. At last she saw that, without realising it, she had been following the narrowing throat of a backwater, and now they had reached the end of the passage. They came up to a broken-down jetty of weathered, greyish wood. She managed to bring the skiff up against it with a gentle jolt, clambered up onto the planks with the bow line in her hand, and stood there, looking down at the inert shape of Lom, wondering how she was going to get him out of the boat. At a loss, she glanced back the way they had come.

A giant was wading towards them, waist deep in the dark waters.

In the city, in their labouring clothes, the giants were diminished and made familiar by the human context. This one was different. It was as if the river itself and the mud and silt of the estuary had gathered into human-like form – but twice as large – and risen up and started walking towards them.

The slope of the giant's belly broached the waters like a ship as he came. His chest was as deep and broad as a barrel, but far larger. Unlike the city giants, who wore their hair tied back in queues, his hair was long and thick and spread across his shoulders in dark, damp curls. The giant waded right up to them and gripped the gunwale of the skiff with both hands, steadying it. The hands were enormous. Fingers thick as stubs of rope, joined with pale webs of skin up to the first knuckle. Wrists strong and round as tree branches. His huge face was weathered dark and his eyes were large and purple like plums, with something of the same rounded protuberance.

'Your boat is named *Sib*,' he said. 'She's a good boat.'

His voice was deep and slow, with the cool softness of estuarial mud, but ropes of strength wound through it. His clothes were the silvered colour of mud, with a faint shimmer of grainy slickness. Brown or grey, it was difficult to tell the difference. He was neither wholly of the land nor wholly of the water, but in between, estuarial, intertidal, partaking of both.

'She's not our boat,' said Maroussia. 'I stole her. She was floating loose, so I took her. We needed her. Badly. My friend is hurt.'

'You make fast here,' said the giant. 'You climb out, and I will bring him.'

The giant scooped Lom up in his arms, settled him into a comfortable position against his chest and waded across to a place where he could climb out. The water sluiced off him. His legs up to the knee were sleek with mud. Maroussia hesitated. The giant walked a few paces, then stopped and turned. Maroussia hadn't moved.

'Well?' said the giant.

'What?' said Maroussia.

'Follow me.'
'Where?'
But the giant had already gone ahead.

66

Vissarion Yppolitovich Lom – that part of him which is not made of tissues and plasma, proteins and mineral salts – is floating out in the sea, buoyant, awash in the waves. And Vissarion Yppolitovich Lom – this is not his true name, he knows that now, but he has no other – is puzzled by his situation.

He is alive.

Apparently.

Evidently.

Yet he has no recollection of how he got here, how he came to be in this ...

Predicament?

Situation.

And he is ... changed.

This is not his body.

His body is elsewhere.

He is aware of it, distant, separate, yet not *entirely* detached.

And this sea that he is in, it is the real sea, but also ...

... not.

The sky is too clear. Too close above his head. There appears to be no sun in the sky. Everywhere he looks, it is ...

... just the sky.

Time is nothing here.

The sea shines like wet slate. Numbing slabs of sea-swell hammock and baulk him. He rides among the bruising hollows and feels the touch of salt water pouring over his face, and when he runs his fingers through it, it is like stroking cool hair. Fulmars scout the wave valleys and terns squall overhead. He sees the faint distant smudge of a cliff shoulder to the north, and the low beach-line curving away southwards into mist and indeterminacy. He sees the shore of Cold Amber Strand. He can see it, but he can't reach it. He lacks the strength to swim so far. It doesn't matter.

Time is nothing here.

His head is wide open – there is a hole in it – the sea is pouring in – and the fluid from inside him is seeping out, pluming away into the wider water. Part of him is part of the sea. Part of the sea is taking its place. And then ...

Time is nothing here.

The sea is slow and always. Days graze its surface and the sea's skin rises and falls with the barely perceptible pulse of the tide. He can feel the unseen pull of the moons: a gentle lunar gravity tugging at his hair and palpating with infinite slowness the ventricular walls of his heart. But days and nights touch only the thinnest surface of the sea, and all the while, below the surface, beneath the intricate, flashy caul, there is darkness: coiling and shouldering layers inhabited by immense, death-less, barrelling movers.

Time is nothing here.

He imagines he is already sinking. The abyssal deeps open below him like a throat. He dives, pulling the surface shut behind him, nosing downwards, parting the layered muscles of the dimming waters' body. Sounding. Depth absorbs him.

As he descends, the light fails. Layer by layer the spectrum is sucked dry of colour: first the reds fade and the world turns green, then the yellows give up the ghost and the world turns blue, and then ... nothing, only the fuliginous darker than dark, the total absence of sight.

The waters are deep. It takes only seconds to leave the light behind, but the descent will be many hours. Every ten yards of depth adds the weight of another atmosphere to the column of water pressing on his body. He imagines going down. Fifty atmospheres. A hundred. A thousand. More. More. The parts of his strange new body which contain air begin to rupture under the weight. Long before he reaches the bottom, his face, his chest, his abdomen, implode. Fat compresses and hardens. The finer bones collapse. Broken rib ends burst out through the skin.

He imagines he hears himself speaking to the hard cold darkness. 'You are the reply to my desire.'

67

Maroussia slept late the next morning, and woke in the giant's isba. It smelled of woodsmoke, lamp-oil and the smoked fish that hung in rows from the rafters. Rafters which, now that she looked at them up there in the shadow, weren't the branches of trees as she had thought, but salt-bleached and smoke-browned whale bones.

The isba was twice as tall as a human would make it, but it felt warm and intimate, lit with fish-oil lamps and firelight from the open stove. Although it was morning outside, inside was all shadow and quiet. The whale-skeleton frame was covered with skins and bark, the gaps caulked with moss and pitch. Iron boiling-pots and wooden chests stood along the sides. From the middle of the floor rose a thick pillar of ancient-looking wood, its base buried in the compacted earth. Every inch of it was carved with the eyes and claws and heads of animals – elk, horses, wolves, seals – their teeth bared in anger or defiance – and inscribed with what looked like words in a strange angular alphabet. The pillar seemed meant to ward off some threat, some doom that was waiting its chance. What kind of thing was it, out here in the marsh, that a giant would be afraid of?

The stove was made of iron, large and elaborate, with panels of white and blue tiles. It was the kind that had a place for a bed on the top of it. Lom lay on it now, breathing quietly. Inert.

Maroussia remembered the night before only in snatches and fragments. She had been too cold. Too tired. Too hungry. The giant had given her food, a broth from his simmering-pot. Fish, samphire, berries. Food that tasted of the river and the sea and wide open spaces. And then he'd left her and gone out into the night and she had slept.

When she woke, the morning was half gone, and she was alone with Lom.

She stood up stiffly and crossed the floor to look at him. The stove was taller than her but his face, roughened with a growth of reddish stubble, was near the edge and turned towards her. He wasn't sleeping, he was … gone. But his body breathed and seemed to be repairing itself. The giant had tended to the wound in the front of his head and left it bound in a cloth soaked with an infusion of bark and dried leaves. Now that she was close to him, the clean, bitter scent cut through the fish-and-smoky fug in the hut.

She had lain alongside him in the cold of the boat, the warmth of their bodies nurturing each other, keeping each other alive. That meant something. That changed something. She knew the smell of his body close up, the smell of his hair and skin, the feel of his warmth. She touched his face. Despite the stove and the furs he felt cool and damp, like a pebble picked up from a stream.

Wake up. Please wake up. We can't stay here.

She needed to go. She had something to do. It was a weight. A momentum. A push. What she needed to find was somewhere in the city. Vishnik had found the Pollandore. She was certain now, that's what he'd meant to tell her. He had died and hadn't told her where. Yet surely it would be in Mirgorod, if he had found it. She needed to get back there.

The giant came in, pushing his way between the skins across the entrance gap. His bulk filled the space naturally and made her feel that humans were small.

'Has the sleeper woken?' he said.

'No. No, he hasn't.'

The giant walked with a surprisingly soft and quiet tread across to where Lom lay, and looked down on him in silence. He placed a huge hand on the small head and put his huge face near Lom's small mouth, as if he were inhaling his breath, which – she realised – he was.

'He has been like this all morning?'

'Yes. He hasn't changed.'

The giant went to a wooden chest and took out something wrapped in dark cloth, which, sitting cross-legged on the floor by the stove, he unwrapped and began to eat. It looked like a piece of meat, except that it was dark grey, soft and satiny, with a strange oily sheen. He tore off a large chunk with his teeth and chewed it, his head on one side, his massive jaws working like a dog's, up and down.

'Does anyone else live out here?' Maroussia asked. 'In the marshes, I mean. I didn't see any sign … when we were coming here. It all seemed so empty. Are there villages?'

'Why?'

'I was wondering where the clothes came from.' He had found dry clothes for her, not city clothes but leggings and a woven shirt. Soft leather boots.

'There are no humans here now. There used to be a village on the smaller lake.' He waved his arm vaguely in no particular direction.

'You've been kind to us,' she said.

'The rivers brought you. Why would I not be kind?'

'I don't even know your name.'

'My name is Aino-Suvantamoinen, and yours is Maroussia Shaumian, and you are important.'

'What do you mean? How do you know my name.'

'You are someone who makes things happen. Different futures are trying to become. You have something to do, and what you choose will matter.'

She stared at him. 'You know?' she said. 'About the Pollandore?'

The giant made a movement of his hand. 'I know,' he said, 'some things.'

'You know where it is?'

'It was taken. Long ago.'

'Where is it now?'

'That I do not know.'

'I have to find it,' said Maroussia. 'I can't stay here. Time is running out.'

'Yes.'

'But I don't know what it is. I don't know what to do when I find it. I don't *understand*.'

'Understanding is not the most important thing. Understanding never is. Doing is what matters.'

The giant turned away and sat down in a corner to concentrate on his meat, as if he had said all he would say. It was like talking to a thinking tree, or a hill, or the grass, or the rain.

'What exactly is that stuff you're eating?' said Maroussia.

'Old meat,' the giant said. 'The marsh preserves. Trees come up whole after a thousand years. This meat … I put it in, I leave it, I find it again. It tastes good.'

'What kind of meat?'

He held the chunk at arm's length, turned it round, inspected it.

'No idea.' He took another bite. Then he laid it aside and stood up. 'Come with me,' he said. 'Let us walk.'

Maroussia looked at Lom, sleeping on the stove.

'What about him?' she said. 'Will he be all right on his own?'

'No harm will come today.'

Maroussia walked in silence beside the giant. The floods had receded during the night, revealing a wide alluvial land, a cross-hatch of creeks and channels punctuated by rocky outcrops, islands and narrow spits of ground. Reed beds. Salt marsh. Sea lavender and samphire. Withy, carr and fen. There were stretches of water, bright and dark as rippled steel. Long strips of pale brown sand, crested with lurid, too-green, moss-coloured grass. Reaches of soft, satiny mud. Wildfowl were picking and probing their way out on the mud. Maroussia knew their names: she had watched them rummaging on the muddy riverbanks near her home. Curlew, plover, godwit, redshank, phalarope. The quiet progress of geese at the eelgrass. A kestrel sidled across the sky: a slide, a pause, a flicker of wings; slide, pause, flicker of wings.

This was a threshold country, neither solid ground nor water but something liminal and in between. The air was filled with a beautiful misty brightness under a lid of low cloud. There was no sun: it was as if the wet land and the shallow stretches of water were themselves luminous. The air smelled of damp earth and sea, salt and wood-ash and fallen leaves.

'This is a beautiful place,' Maroussia said. 'It feels like we are in the middle of nowhere, but we're so near to the city. I didn't know. I never came this far.'

'It will be winter soon,' the giant said. 'Winters are cold here. The birds are preparing to leave. In winter the snow will lie here as deep as you are tall. The water freezes. Only the creatures that know how to freeze along with it and the ones who make tunnels beneath the snow can live here then.'

'But it's not so cold in Mirgorod,' said Maroussia. 'It's only a few versts away.'

'No. It is colder here.'

'What do you do when the winter comes?' said Maroussia.

'When the ditches freeze and the marshes go under the snow I will sleep. It will be soon.'

'You sleep through the winter like a bear? The giants in Mirgorod don't do that.'

'Their employers do not permit it. They are required to work through the year, though it shortens their lives.'

The giant fell silent and walked on. Maroussia began to notice signs of labour. The management of the land and water. Heaps of rotting vegetation piled alongside recently cleared dikes. Saltings, drained ground, coppiced trees. Much of it looked ancient, abandoned and crumbling: blackened stumps of rotting post and plank, relics of broken staithes and groynes, abandoned fish traps. The giant paused from time to time to study the water levels and look about him, his great head cocked to one side, sniffing the salt air. Sometimes he would adjust the setting of some heavy mechanism of wood and iron, a winch or a lock or a sluice gate.

They stopped on the brink of a deep, fast-flowing ditch. The giant stared into the brown frothing surge that forced its way across a weir.

'The flood is going down,' the giant said. 'Every time the floods come now, the city builds its stone banks higher. But that is not the way. The water has to go somewhere. If you set yourself against it, the water will find a way, every time.' He stooped for a moment to work a windlass that Maroussia hadn't noticed among the tall grass. 'I tried to tell them,' the giant continued when he had done his work. 'When they were building the city, I tried to tell them they were using too much stone. They made everything too hard and too tight. You have to leave places for the water to go. But I couldn't make them listen. Even their heads were made of stone.'

'You remember Mirgorod being *built*?'

'I was younger then. I thought I could explain to them, and if I did, then they would listen. They tried to drive me out, and every so often even now they try again.' He grinned, showing big square teeth. Incisors like slabs of pebble. Sharp bearish canines. 'I let them lose themselves.'

'What do you mean?'

'The marshes are bigger than you think, and different every day. Every tide brings shift and change. All possible marshes are here.'

'I don't understand.'

'Yes,' said the giant. 'You do.'

Maroussia hesitated. 'If you remember the city when it was being built—' she said.

'Yes.'

'—then you would remember the time before? You remember the Pollandore?'

'You don't need to remember what is still here.'

Maroussia hesitated.

'I need to go back,' she said. 'But I don't want to leave Vissarion. He helped me.'

'You should not leave him,' said the giant. 'He is important too.'

'What do you mean?'

The giant stopped and looked down at her.

'I don't know, and neither does he. But it is on the river, and the rain likes him. That's enough.'

'But what if he never wakes up?' said Maroussia. 'Or he wakes up but he isn't … right. He almost drowned, and there's that hole, that terrible hole, in his head.'

'He is not hurt,' said the giant. 'At least, his body is not. But he doesn't know how to come back.'

'I don't understand that either.'

'I can fetch him back, if you want me to. Tonight. After dark. When the day is over. Your choice.'

'Do it,' she said. 'Do it.'

68

Vissarion Yppolitovich Lom lies face down, floating on the glass roof of the sea. He presses his face against the water as if it were a pane of glass. Looking down into clarity. A landscape unrolls beneath him.

Time is nothing here.

This is the drowned, memorious land. Mammoths' teeth, the bones of bear and aurochs and the antlers of great elk litter the sea's bed. The salt-dark leaf mould of drowned forests. It is a woodland place. Lom sees the sparrowhawk on the oak's shoulder and he sees the bivalves browsing the soft stump's pickled meat. Sea beasts move across the floor of it. Their unhurried footfalls detonate quiet puffballs of silt as they go, slow without heaviness, shoving aside fallen branches, truffling for egg-purse, flatworm and urchin, their eyes blackened like sea beans and gleaming in the half-light.

Time is nothing here.

Except … something touches him. The merest graze of an eye in passing. An alien gaze, cold and empty, vaster far than the sea, star-speckled. It passes away from him.

And pauses.
And flicks back.
And takes him in its grip.

Lom closes himself up like a fist, like a stone in the sea, like an anemone clenching close its crop of arms, like a hermit crab hunching into its shell. He wants to be small. Negligible. He wants to pull himself tight inside and withdraw or sink out of sight. But it is hopeless. He knows the touch of the angel's eye for what it is.

Archangel begins to prise him open for a closer look.

No! Lom dives, pulling the surface shut behind him, nosing downwards, parting the layered muscles of the dimming waters' body. Sounding. Depth absorbs him. He is strong. Very strong. Stronger than he had ever known. Lom slips with a writhing kick out of the angel's grasp. He hears, very faint and far away, the yell of its anger. And feels its fear.

In his room on the Ring Wharf, Josef Kantor felt Archangel rip a hole in his mind and step inside. Archangel's voice filled his head. The cold immensity separating stars. He fell.

THEY ARE IN THE MARSH! THEY ARE IN THE MARSH! THEY LIVE!

KILL THE TRAVELLERS! DESTROY THE POLLAN-DORE!

As soon as he was able to stand and wipe the spittle from his face and stem the blood that was spilling from his nose, Kantor went to find a telephone. He needed to speak to Chazia.

69

Night came, a thick and starless black. Inside the isba the smoke from the burning bog-oak in the stove and the fumes from the boiling-pot made Maroussia's head swim. Afraid she would be sick, she tried to retreat into the shadows at the edge of the room and would have squatted there, watching, but the noises from outside drove her back. There were voices outside in the dark, voices that barked and growled and called like birds and argued in unintelligible words. The skin covering of the isba shook as if something was pounding on it and tugging at the door covering. She crawled back towards the centre of the room and crouched as near to the iron stove as she could get. Blue fire was burning hot and hard as a steam-engine's firebox, roaring heat into the air.

'Do not be alarmed by anything you see or hear,' Aino-Suvanta-moinen had said. 'But do not touch me. And do not go outside.'

Yet now he lay on the floor, immense, like a felled bull. His arms and legs trembled as if he was having a fit: their shaking rattled and clattered the antlers, vertebrae, pieces of amber and holed stones tied to his coat. The hood of the coat hid his face, but she could still see his eyes. They were open, but showing white only, as sightless and chalky as seashells. He'd put a piece of leather between his teeth, and now his mouth dripped spittle as he chewed and ground on it with an unconscious concentration that seemed like blank rage.

Lom lay on his back in the centre of the floor.

'No matter how bad it gets,' the giant had said, 'you can do nothing. Understand? Nothing. Whatever happens, do nothing. and do not touch me.' Yet he had been like this – collapsed, growling, fitting – for … how long now? Half an hour? An hour?

The wall of the isba bulged inward, as if some heavy creature outside had thrown itself against it. There was a screech of anger. Surely whatever was outside would break in soon. The carvings on the central pillar flickered in the fierce firelight as if they were alive and moving.

Five minutes. Five more minutes, and if nothing has changed . . .

Vissarion Yppolitovich Lom is lying on his back in the sea, looking up into the night sky. He feels the gentle pull of the moons in his belly. All around him the sea glows with a gentle phosphorescence. A fringe of luminousness borders his body. Light trickles down his arms when he holds them in front of his face.

The hole in the front of his head is open to the starlight. A little cup of phosphorescence has gathered there. So much has flowed in, and so much flowed out, washing across the folds of his cerebral cortex. He is merging with the sea. His pulse is the endless passing of waves. His inward darkness is the darkness of the deep ocean.

Time is nothing here.

He hears the sound of splashing. Rhythmical. Sweep, sweep, through the waves. It is a sound he remembers, but he cannot place it now. The drift of water through the kelp forests below him is more interesting.

Idly, with the last remains of merely human curiosity, he turns to look. Something very large and human-shaped, an outline darker than the sky, a starless mass against the stars, is wading towards him. That is what the sound is. Legs. Wading through water. Did he not once do such a thing himself?

The wading person is growing larger and larger as he comes closer. He is watching. He has a purpose. His purpose is to bring Lom back.

But Lom doesn't want to go back.

He gathers the weight of the sea and throws it against the giant in immense curling waves that crash against him. Lom fills the waves with the teeth and jaws of eels and the stings of rays. He tangles the giant's feet in ropes of weed. The giant stumbles and the undertow of the waves pulls at him, dragging him towards the edge of the deep trench that opens and swallows him.

The giant Aino-Suvantamoinen feels the viciousness of the sea's antagonism. Ropes of water form within the water and wrap themselves around his arms and legs, tugging him down towards the pit that is opening beneath him. Bands of iron water squeeze his ribcage, forcing the breath from his lungs. Ice-cold water-fingers grip his face, hooking claws into his nostrils, stabbing into his ears with water-needles, gouging his eyes, tearing at the lids. *This isn't how it is meant to be.* The man he is trying to bring home is fighting him. He's too strong. All the futures in which he will rescue this man and return home safe are fading and dying one by one. Something is putting them out like lamps.

I will drown here, and with me the marsh will fail.

With one last push of effort he begins to swim for the surface.

Pulling the water-fingers from his face he peers up and sees the dim light above him, the greenish star in the shape of a man, glowing dimly. It is not far. The giant kicks and hauls himself towards it. The seawater clamps itself about him, heavy and chill as liquid iron, squeezing like a fist. He fights it, dragging himself upwards out of the ocean pit. But it is too far. He is tiring. He cannot reach it. The thread of river-water that links him to his body in the isba is failing, and when it breaks he will be lost.

Desperately he lets go of a part of himself and sends it back up the river-thread, squirming and writhing for home like a salmon against the stream. The silver thought-salmon flickers its tail and disappears into the dimming green.

Maroussia was kneeling over the still body of the giant, her ear against his mouth. He was trying to say something.

'*Wake him ... wake the man ... call him back ... do it ... now ...*'

The hoarse whisper faded. The giant's face collapsed.

Maroussia lurched across to where Lom was lying and took his face in her hands, turning it towards her.

'Vissarion!' She was shouting to be heard. The voices outside in the night were screeching and yammering, hurling themselves against the walls of the isba. 'Vissarion! It's Maroussia! Listen to me! You have to wake up now! Oh, you have to. Please.'

Vissarion Yppolitovich Lom hears a voice calling, faint above the noise of the sea and very far away. He opens his eyes and sees against the shadows of the sky a face he knows, a familiar face, a face with a name he half-remembers, pale and calm and serious, looking down on him, like the moon made whole. He lifts his arm towards it, and as he does so he feels a tremendous blow against his back, lifting him up out of the water, and a huge fist seizes him by the neck and begins to pull him back towards the shore.

70

Lom woke in the giant Aino-Suvantamoinen's isba, aware of the warmth and the fire and the quiet shadows and the giant sitting near him, waiting, patient, large and solid. Lom knew where he was. Completely. He felt the moving water nearby, and grass, and trees, and the sifting satiny mud. The sea, some distance off, was still the sea, and the river that surged towards it was a great speaking mouth. The air around him was a tangible flowing thing, freighted with a thousand scents and drifting pheromone clouds, just as the space between the stars was filled with light and forces passing though. Everything was spilling myth, everything was soaked in truth-dream.

'You are awake,' said Aino-Suvantamoinen gently. His voice was slow and strong and estuarial.

'This will fade,' said Lom. 'Won't it? This will not last. Will it? Will it?'

He tried to raised his head from the leather pillow.

'No,' said the giant, 'this feeling that you have now will not last. But it will not altogether fade. There is no going back to the way you were before.'

'I don't want to.'

'You need to rest.'

'I hurt you, didn't I? I didn't want to come back, and I hurt you.'

'Yes.'

'I almost killed you.'

'Yes.'

'I'm sorry.'

'Not your fault. You were stronger than I thought. You did not know.'

'No.'

'I bear you no grudge. '

'But you are hurt.'

'Only tired now. I will recover. But I need to sleep. it will be winter soon.'

Lom tried to push the covers back and sit up.

'You can't sleep yet,' he said. 'You know that. There is something wrong. There's something coming. It's very close.'

'Ah. You felt that?'

When the giant left him, Lom went outside to sit by himself some distance from the isba, on a stump of wood. The stiffness of his bruises was scarcely noticeable. He touched his forehead tentatively. In the centre of it, just above the eyebrows, he found a small and roughly round hole in the bone of his skull, like a third eye socket. It had a fine, smooth covering of new skin, slightly puckered at the edge. With his fingertip he felt the fluttering of a pulse.

The world he had seen in all its oceanic myth-ridden fullness was already diminishing, but still he smelled the dampness in the air, the woodsmoke, and heard the flow of water in the creek, and he knew what they meant. It was all traces and memories now, a faint trembling of presences: possibilities almost out of reach. But still real. Still there. The plug in his head was gone, and he was alive.

The world and everything in it, everything that is and was and will be, was the unfolding story of itself, and every separate thing in the world – every particle of rock and air and light, every life, every thought and every event – was also a story, its own story, the story of everything becoming more like itself and less like anything else. The *might-be* becoming the *is*. The winter moths on their pheromone trails, intent on love and flight, were heroes. Himself, Maroussia, Vishnik, Aino-Suvantamoinen, they were all like that, or could be: living out the bright significant stories of their own lives, mythic, important.

But Vishnik was dead. Vishnik, what was left of him, mutilated and killed, his ruined body laid out naked on the couch; Chazia had done that.

Lom remembered Chazia and Kantor bending over him in the interrogation room – Chazia's knife, Kantor's indifferent finger poking at his opened brain. It was all coming back, riding a hot rushing tide of anger. He could not stay here, in this timeless watery place. He had to *do* something. He had to go back.

And then – only then – the question occurred to him. The last thing he remembered, vaguely, a blur, was throwing himself from the bridge into the flooding Mir. What had happened to him after he fell? How had he come to be here? He didn't know.

71

Elsewhere – far away, but not so far – in an empty side room in the Lodka, Lakoba Petrov was preparing himself for his one great moment. He had obtained all he needed – all the materials for his new, wonderful art – from Josef Kantor, impresario of destruction. And now the time was almost come for the performance.

From a canvas holdall Petrov extracted three belts of dynamite and nails, enwrapped his person with them, buckled the straps. Also from the canvas holdall he drew forth a capacious overcoat of dark wool, threaded the detonator cords through the sleeves so he could grip their terminations in his palms, and put on the coat to drape and obscure his death-belted torso.

Petrov did what he did with care. Fully. With absolute clarity and certainty of purpose. Every movement a sacrament. Every breath numbered. Rendered aesthetic. Invested with ritual luminance.

When he tugged the detonators, nails would fly outwards from him explosively. Omnidirectional. Flying in the expulsive, expanding, centrifugal cloud of his own torn and vaporised flesh. He would be the heart of the iron sunburst. Going nova.

And so I am become the unimaginable zero of form. The artist becomes the art. Total creation. Without compromise. Without hesitation. Without meaning, being only and completely what it is. The gap between artist and work obliterated.

His own unneeded coat he closed up in precise folds and set in the middle of the empty floor. Adjacent to this he placed the now-empty canvas holdall.

They would be found so. The only extant work of the Petrovist Destructive School: members, one.

A thought struck him. Awkwardly, on account of the bulk of the explosive girdles, he bent to withdraw items from his former coat. A tube of paint. A piece of polished reflective tin to use as a mirror. One final time, with the facility that came with practice, he inscribed his forehead. And then, with an unexpected flourish, one last tweak of originality, he unbuttoned his shirt and wrote on his bare, white, fleshless, hairless (because shaven) upper chest, the same two splendid words.

I, Petrov.

He was calm. He was prepared. All was ready.

At the other end of the same long corridor as the room in which Petrov prepared himself, in a much larger chamber, there was a large gathering of persons of importance. The Annual Council of the Vlast Committee on Peoples. Josef Kantor was there, thanks to the arrangements of Lavrentina Chazia. He stood anonymously at the back of the room, one more nondescript functionary among many, watching. Waiting for what would come. For what he knew would happen. His toothache, which had not troubled him for weeks, was back, and he welcomed it, prodding at the hurt again with his tongue as he examined the scene.

The large room was dominated by one long narrow heavy table of inlaid wood. A line of electric chandeliers hung low above it like frosted glittering clusters on a vine, and creamy fluted columns made an arcade along one side, where secretaries sat at individual desks with typewriters. For all its spaciousness the room was warm, and filled with muted purposeful talk. The places at the table were occupied by men in suits and full-dress uniforms, absorbed in their work, assured of their importance and the significance of what they did.

On the far wall from where Kantor stood hung a huge painting of the Novozhd, life size and standing alone in an extensive rolling late-summer landscape. Sunlight splashed across his face, picking out his plush moustache and the smile-lines creasing his cheeks, while behind him the country of the dominions unrolled: harvest-ready fields crossed by the sleek length of express trains, tall factory chimneys blooming rosy streamers of smoke against the horizon, the distant glittering sea – the happy land at its purposeful labours.

And beneath the portrait, halfway down one side of the table, sat the Novozhd himself, in his familiar collarless white tunic, drinking coffee from a small cup.

There was a shout from across the room.

'Hey! You! Who are you?'

Kantor looked across to see what was going on. It was Petrov. He was pushing past flustered functionaries, his shaven head moving among them like a white stone. He was wearing an oddly bulky greatcoat and there were fresh scarlet markings on his face. He was right on time. Kantor stepped back towards the wall. He needed to be as far away from the Novozhd as possible.

Petrov paused and surveyed the room for a moment.

The militia who lined the walls, watchful, were not approaching him. Those nearest him were retreating. Giving him room. They were Chazia's Iron Guard, every one: they would not interfere.

A diplomat near Kantor took a step forward. 'What is that man doing—?' he began.

'Stay where you are!' hissed Kantor. The diplomat looked at him, surprised, and seemed about to say something else. Kantor ignored him.

Petrov had seen the Novozhd, who had risen from his seat, cup in hand.

High functionaries were murmuring in growing alarm. A stenographer was shouting. There was rising panic in her voice. 'Someone stop him!'

Petrov moved towards the Novozhd, blank-faced and purposeful.

The ambassador from the Archipelago was on her feet, trying to push through a group of Vlast diplomatists who did not know what was happening and would not make way. She was shouting at the guards: 'Why won't you do something!' But the guards were moving away, as Kantor knew they would.

Petrov made inexorable progress through the crowd. When he got near the Novozhd, his arms stretched out as if to embrace him.

And the explosion came. A muted, ordinary detonation. A flash. A matter-of-fact thump of destruction. A stench. The crash of a chandelier on the table. Silence. More silence. Ringing in Kantor's ears.

Then the voices began: not screams – not shouts of anger – just a low inarticulate collective moan, a sighing of dismay. Only later did the keening begin, as the injured began to realise the awful permanent ruination of their ruptured bodies.

Pushing through the crowd, stepping over the dead and dying, Kantor found himself looking down at the raw, meaty remnants of the Novozhd, and Lakoba Petrov fallen across him like a protective friend. Petrov's head and arms were gone, and some great reptilian predator had taken a large bite of flesh from his side. The Novozhd, dead, was staring open-mouthed at the ceiling that was spattered with his own blood and chunks of his own flesh. His moustache, Kantor noticed, was gone.

Someone touched his arm, and Kantor spun round. He knew the guards would not bother him, but there was always the possibility. But it was only Chazia.

She leaned forward intimately, speaking quietly under the din and panic of the room. Her blotched fox-face too close to his.

'Good, Josef,' she said. 'Very good.'

Kantor took a step back from her in distaste. There was too much of angels about her. It was like a stink. She was rank with it.

'I do my part, Lavrentina. You do yours. What about the girl, and Krogh's man? Lom?'

'That's in hand,' said Chazia. 'It is in hand. Though I don't understand why you set so much store—'

Kantor glared at her.

'I mean,' Chazia continued, 'after today—'

'The angel needs them dead, Lavrentina,' Kantor heard himself say, and struggled to keep the self-disgust out of his voice. *It uses me like a puppet. A doll. A servant.* He was getting tired of the angel. More than tired. He feared and hated it. The situation was becoming intolerable.

I am bigger than this angel. I will make it fear me and I will kill it. I will find a way. I have killed the Novozhd and I will kill the angel. Kill Chazia too.

But now was not the time. He needed to prepare. He needed to focus on the future. Only the future mattered.

'Just get rid of them,' he said. 'Lom and the girl. Don't foul it up again.'

'I told you,' said Chazia. 'It's already in hand.'

72

It was night outside the isba, under clear stars. Aino-Suvantamoinen was a massive dark bulk crouching over the flickering wood-fire. It was crisply, bitterly cold, and the light of the moons was bright enough to see the shreds of mist in the trees at the edge of the clearing. A hunter's night. Lom sat wrapped in sealskin, drinking fish stew from a wooden bowl. He'd slept all day – a proper, resting, dreamless sleep.

'I can't stay here,' Maroussia was saying. 'I have to go back. To the city. There was a paluba. And someone else. She ... showed me ...'

The giant shifted his weight. 'You saw a paluba?'

'Yes.'

Lom watched her as she talked. She held herself so straight and upright, her face shadowed in the firelight. Lom saw her now as she was, a point of certainty, uncompromised, spilling the flickering light of possibilities that surrounded her. She was clear, and defined, and alive. She rang like a bell in the misty, nightfall world. She was worth fighting for.

'I have to do this thing,' she said. 'I don't have a choice.' She paused. 'No, that's not right. I do have a choice. And I'm choosing.'

She lapsed into silence, watching the fire.

'Maroussia?' said Lom.

'Yes?'

'I wanted to thank you.'

'What for?' she said.

'You came back for me, didn't you? You didn't have to.'

She didn't look round. 'You didn't need to help me either. But you did. Twice.'

'I'll come back with you to Mirgorod,' said Lom. 'If you want me to.'

She turned to look at him then.

'Would you do that?' she said quietly.

'Yes.'

73

Major Artyom Safran stood at the edge of the trees by the giant's isba, watching it from the moonshadow. Muted light spilled from a gap in the skins draped across its entrance. His quarry was inside. The mudjhik was motionless at his side, a shadow-pillar of silent stone.

Safran held the fragment of angel stuff that Commander Chazia had cut from Lom's head tight and warm in his hand. Using the mudjhik's alien senses he felt his way along the thread that still joined it to Lom until he touched the other man's mind with his own. He felt the faint, startled flinch of an answering awareness and hastily withdrew. Lom was unlikely to have known what the contact meant, if he had even registered it, but it was better to be cautious.

There were three of them, then. Lom, a woman – *the* woman, it must be – and something else: a strange, complex, powerful, non-human presence. He put himself more fully into the mudjhik, inhabiting its wild harsh world. The mudjhik needed no light to see by. It had other senses through which Safran felt the hard sharpness of thorns, the small movements of leaves on branches, the evaporation of moisture. Bacteria thrived everywhere, and the mudjhik was studying them with simple, purposeless curiosity. Something had died and was decomposing near their feet, under a covering of fallen leaves.

Safran felt the watchfulness of small animal presences pressing against him. One in particular was close by, drilling at him with a hot, bitter attention. A fox? No, something smaller and crueller. A weasel? Its mind was like strong, gamey meat. Every mind had its own unique taste, that was one thing he had learned. And here, in the wetlands, it was not only animals: ever since he and the mudjhik had entered the marsh territories, Safran had been aware of the semi-sentience of the trees themselves, and the rivers, even the rain. There was a constant, vaguely uncomfortable feeling that everything around him knew he was there and did not welcome his presence. He ignored it, as did the mudjhik, which disdained trees and water as beneath its notice. Safran, through the mudjhik's senses, probed the interior of the isba. The third presence was a giant, then. That too was unexpected.

For all its physical stillness, Safran sensed the mudjhik's eagerness to rush forward and attack. It enjoyed human fear and death. It fed on it. Some of the mudjhik's bloodlust leaked into Safran's mind. It made him hungry to charge and stomp and crush. He fought to keep the urge in check. He hadn't anticipated the presence of the giant. It could be done, of course, but the position was not without risk. It needed thought.

His target was Lom. Chazia had been clear on that. And the Shaumian woman, if he found her there. There had been no mention of others, human or giant, but the strategic purpose of his mission was to draw a line. No loose ends. No continuation of the story. What that meant was without doubt. Leave none alive.

Mentally he checked through his equipment: a heavy hunting knife; two incendiary grenades; the revolver that Chazia had given him (a brand new model, the first production batch, a double-action Sepora loaded with .44 magnum high-velocity hunting rounds, power that would stop a bear mid-charge). The Sepora should be enough to handle the giant. And then there was the Exter-Vulikh, a stocky and wide-muzzled sub-machine gun with a yew stock, modified to take hundred-round drum magazines, of which he carried four.

The Vlast employed killers who prided themselves on the precision and refinement of their technique: they affected the exactitude of assassins, with high-velocity long-range hunting rifles and probing needle blades. But Safran was not one of those. He preferred brutally decisive weapons, muscular weapons that did serious, dramatic damage. Handling the Exter-Vulikh gave him powerful gut feelings of pleasure. He liked the weight and heft of it, the fear it provoked, and the noise and mess it made. Just thinking about using it stirred a feeling in his belly like hunger. Desire. And with the mudjhik, it was even better: the strength of the mudjhik was his strength, its power his power. The fear it caused was fear of *him*. Safran loved the mudjhik, with its barrel head and reddish brown stone-hard flesh. It was the colour of rust and dried blood, but it could glow like warm terracotta in the evening sun.

Years of training and long experience had built the connection between Safran and his mudjhik, until their minds were so closely intermixed there was no longer a clear distinction between them. Most mudjhiks passed from handler to handler and brought traces – *stains* – of their previous relationships with them, including the memories of deaths, fears, failures, human aging; but Safran's had been a virgin, the last of them. Another reason to love it. But he feared it, too. Sometimes he dreamed it was pursuing him. In his dreams he tried to run and hide. In empty streets it followed him. Crashing through walls. Pulling down houses. Wherever he went it found him. In one dream he took refuge inside the Lodka itself, and the mudjhik was beating on the ten-foot-thick walls of stone, trying to break through. The *boom-boom-boom* of its heavy blows made the ground he stood on shake and tremble. He knew the mudjhik would never stop. Each blow chipped a fragment of the wall away. Hairline fractures opened and spread through the immense walls.

A mudjhik was tireless. If the man ran, the mudjhik would follow. Relentless and for ever. It was only a matter of time. There was no escape.

'You'll go alone,' Chazia had said. 'Travel light. Move fast. It'll be better.'

The march had taken longer than expected. The mudjhik kept sinking into the soft ground and floundering in streams and shallow pools. Safran had become confused about direction, distance, time. The territory seemed larger than was possible. A day's travel seemed to bring them no nearer the target. As time passed, Safran had felt his mind merging more and more completely with the mudjhik. He had thought they were close before, but this was overwhelming, as if the mudjhik were using him, not the other way round. It was a good feeling. He embraced it. He felt the Vlast itself, and all its authority and power and inevitability, flowing through him. He was not a single person any more. He was history happening. He was the face of the hammerhead, but it was the entire force of the arm-swing of the hammerblow that drove him forward. He didn't have questions, he had answers. And, at last, after uncountable days of arduous marching, the onward flow of angel-sanctified history and the piece of angel stuff he held in his hand like a thread brought him to the isba.

The mudjhik was restless, knowing its quarry was close. It wanted to wade in and crush his skull and stamp his ribs in. Now. Even in the dark it would not miss. But Safran was tired after the long days of marching. His hands trembled with cold and fatigue. He would not fail, he could not, yet he knew the dangers of overconfidence. Once again he surveyed the lie of the operational zone.

The isba stood, stark in the moonshine, on a slightly raised shoulder of ground in a clearing about a hundred yards across. On the far side of the clearing from where Safran stood some kind of canal or non-descript river was running. With the mudjhik's senses, he could smell its dark, cold and slow-moving current. On every other side of the isba there were thickets of thorn and bramble and low trees, cut through with narrow wandering pathways. Safran was satisfied that the targets could not escape. They could not cross the open ground without him knowing. In daylight, if they tried, he could cut them down with the Exter-Vulikh before they reached the cover of the trees. But in this light? The cloud cover was thickening, the last moonlight fading.

Working only by feel, Safran stripped down the Exter-Vulikh and reloaded the drum magazines one more time.

Wait. Let them sleep.

74

Lom was dreaming, dark, ugly, disturbing dreams of gathering hopelessness and death, and when the giant woke him he found them hard to shake off. Slowly he focused on the giant's heavy hand on his shoulder, the huge figure leaning over him, the dim face close to his, the deep soft voice whispering in the stove-light.

'The enemy is come. Wake up.'

'What?'

'You must go quickly. Both of you.'

'What? I don't ...' He struggled to separate reality and dream.

'There is a hunter outside in the trees. A killer. An enjoyer of death.'

'Yes,' said Lom. 'I know.'

And he realised that he did know. He'd felt the presence of them in his dream, and he could still feel it now.

'There are two of them,' he said.

'He has a *follower* with him. A thing like stone.'

A mudjhik? Could that be?

Lom, fully awake now, climbed down from the bed on top of the stove.

'You must make no noise,' said the giant. 'They listen hard.'

It was viciously cold. Lom stood as close to the stove as he could. He had the slightly sickened feeling of being awake too early. Maroussia was preparing with pale and silent efficiency.

'My cloak?' whispered Lom. 'Where is it?'

Aino-Suvantamoinen had it ready and handed it to him. Lom wished he could have felt the weight of the Zorn in its pocket, but that was still somewhere in the Lodka, presumably, where Safran and the militia would have left it when they brought him down. He'd lost his cosh too.

And then they were ready. But for what? He found he could sense the hunters outside in the darkness. They were out there watching. Waiting for dawn, presumably, a better killing light, and that would come soon. Lom considered their options for defending the isba, or getting to their boat, or escaping into the woods; but without weapons there were none. They were caught. Helpless.

Aino-Suvantamoinen stepped across to the great iron stove, pressed his belly against it and, stooping slightly, embraced it. The isba filled with the smell of damp wool singeing as the giant grunted, lifted the entire stove off the ground, spilling red embers against his legs, and carried it, staggering, a few paces sideways. The stove had been standing on a threadbare rug with an intricate geometrical pattern, much worn away and scarred by spills of ash and charcoal. The giant kicked the rug aside to reveal an area of rough planks. He knelt and fumbled at it, trying to get a grip with his huge fingers, then leaned back and pulled. The area of floor came up in his hands, releasing a chill draught of air that smelled of damp earth and stone. A patch of darkness opened like the cool mouth of a well.

'Go down,' he said. 'Quickly!'

'You want us to hide down a pit?' said Lom.

'Not a pit. A tunnel. The old lake people built souterrains. Follow the passageway until you find a side opening to the right. That will bring you out in the woods behind the enemy. When you are past them, then you run.'

'What about you?' said Maroussia.

'I don't fit down there.'

'So …?'

'So I will destroy our enemies if I can.'

'You can't fight a mudjhik,' said Lom. 'Not even you.'

'There are ways,' said the giant.

'You can run too,' said Maroussia. 'You don't have to fight. Not for us.'

The giant didn't reply. He lit a lamp from the stove embers and handed it to Lom. His face in the flickering light looked mobile, distorted and strange.

'You must be quiet,' he said, 'or you will alert the enemy. And you

264

must go now.' He knelt and scraped a heap of compacted earth from the isba floor and scooped it into the stove, dousing the flames and burying the embers. In the near-darkness they heard the swish of the entrance covers and knew that he was gone.

The souterrain passageway was narrow and low. Lom, stooping, the lamp flickering in his hand, went first. The walls and roof of the passage were lined with rough wet blocks of stone. The floor was of damp compacted earth. The feeling of immense weight above their heads, pressing down and pressing in sideways against the passage walls, was oppressive. Unignorable. It seemed impossible that there should be underground constructions at all in such a place of soft and shifting, saturated ground, but the tunnel they were following was evidently old. Perhaps even ancient. It had survived. Lom led the way forward as quickly as he could.

They felt the rush of scorching air almost before they heard the explosions. The surge extinguished the lamp in Lom's hand. The concussions themselves, when they came, were muted, abbreviated, like heavy slabs being dropped from a height, and it took them a moment to realise what they had heard.

'Oh, shit,' said Lom. 'Grenades. He's got grenades.'

There was a longer, liquid-sounding, sliding slump, another rush of hot air, then silence and profound darkness. The tunnel had collapsed behind them.

'Keep going,' said Maroussia. 'I'm right behind you. Don't stop.'

Lom edged forward, his right hand on the rough stone wall to feel his way along, his left hand stretched out ahead of him. The darkness was total. More than the simple absence of light, it was a tangible presence. It closed in around them and pushed against them, touching their faces with soft insistent fingers, pressing itself against their eyes, feeling its way into their nostrils, the whorls of their ears, slipping down their throats when they opened their mouths to breathe, thick with the rich and oppressive smell of being underground.

Lom kept moving. He had to push his way through the insistent jostling darkness, filled with the presence of the long-departed souterrain builders, alert, curious and resentful. He felt the hairs rising along the back of his neck.

There was nothing to measure their progress by, nor the passage of time, except the sound of their own bodies moving and breathing. Raw root-filled earth and rock were all around them now, just the other side of this thin skin of stone. This flimsy, permeable wall. The wall was nothing. Negligible. With one push he could put his hand through it and make an entrance for the slow ocean of mud. Why not? Mud was only a different air. They could breathe it, if they wanted to, like the earthworms did. They could swim through it, slowly, working their limbs through the viscous, slow-yielding, supportive stuff. They could do that. If they wanted to.

'Vissarion?' Maroussia's voice reached him from somewhere far away. 'Why have we stopped?'

He had lost the wall. He had taken his hand off it. When? Sometime. He waved his arms to left and right, over his head, and encountered nothing.

'Can you feel the wall?' he said.

'What wall?' she hissed.

'Either side. Any wall. Can you?'

'No.'

'Shit.'

Think. Figure it out.

They must have come into some larger chamber that the giant hadn't mentioned. He would have assumed they'd have the lamp.

He was standing on the very edge of a bottomless pit. A narrow tapering well. One more step . . . any step . . .

No. It was a tunnel not a cave. They were not lost, only disoriented. Taking a deep breath he turned to his right and began to walk steadily forward. Four or five paces, and he barked his knuckles against the cold damp stone. Its roughness was familiar now, and comforting.

There was another concussion. It made the ground sound hollow, and it seemed to have come from just above their heads. Then the ground shook again. And again. A rhythmical pounding that was obviously not grenades, not this time. Trickles of cold stuff fell across their faces and shoulders in the darkness. It might have been earth or water or a mixture of both. The pounding stopped, and a regular scraping took its place.

'It's the mudjhik,' said Maroussia. 'It's found us. It's trying to dig us out.'

*

Lom felt the mudjhik's presence. Felt the pleasure it was feeling. The anticipation. It would haul them out of the earth like rabbits. Burst their heads between its thumbs, one by one.

'Keep moving!' hissed Maroussia. 'Come on! There's no point waiting here till it gets through.'

Yes, thought Lom, *but which way?* He felt sour panic welling up at the back of his throat.

Which way?

His eyes were stretched wide, straining to see in the absolute dark that pressed in against them. When he realised what he was doing, he closed them.

We are too rational, he thought. *We overvalue sight.*

'Get low!' he hissed. 'Lie down and get out of the airflow. And keep still.'

'Lie down?' said Maroussia.

'Just do it.'

Lom breathed deeply, concentrating on the air around them, ancient and cold and thickened and still. Almost, but not entirely, still. The hole in his head was open, and he was open with it. He could feel the air circulating slowly in a hollow space, and he let himself ride with it, feeling its moves and turns. There was a current eddying slowly towards a gap in the wall. Another passageway. Sloping gently upwards towards an opening into the world outside. In the darkness he crossed directly to Maroussia and took her hand.

'Come on,' he said. 'Follow me.'

He was hurrying, almost running through the dark, pulling Maroussia behind him. She swore as she smashed her elbow against an outcrop of stone and almost stumbled, but he kept hold of her and pulled her on. Behind them the sound of the mudjhik's digging had stopped. It knew they were moving. Lom felt its uncertainty. Frustration. For the moment it was at a loss. But it would find them. And it would keep coming. It always would.

The walls of the passageway were closing in. The roof was getting lower. But Lom led them on at a desperate shambling run. Then there was light ahead of them. The grey light of dawn. Slabs of stone fallen sideways. A gap half-blocked with brambles and small trees. They pushed and scrabbled their way through, ignoring the scratching of thorns and the gouging of branches. And then they were out. Standing among fallen leaves in pathless undergrowth.

Lom looked for cover, any cover, any place to hide or make a stand against the mudjhik. Nowhere. Only a tangle of low trees and undergrowth and moss in every direction.

But what sort of stand could they have made? You needed a trench mortar to stop a mudjhik in its tracks. If it came, it came.

There was an acrid smell in the air. A big fire, burning. The isba!

Maroussia went crashing off towards the scent of burning. Lom was leaning against a tree, doubled over, gasping and trying desperately to get enough breath in to refill his spasming lungs.

'Shit,' he gasped. 'Shit. Wait!'

Maroussia stopped and turned.

'Come on,' she said. 'Just keep up.'

75

Minutes later they were crouched side by side among the trees at the edge of the clearing. The isba was in flames. Its skin covering was gone. The whalebone frame still stood, blackened and skeletal in the middle of a wind-tugged roaring fire of wood and furs and wool. White and grey smoke and clouds of sparks poured into the sky, swithering and whipping in the wind. The smoke was blowing away from them but they could smell it.

The mudjhik was a dark shape slowly circling the fire. From time to time it paused, its massive neckless head tilted to one side, as if it were listening to something. Sniffing the air.

There was no sign of Aino-Suvantamoinen. There was no sign of their human hunter either. They watched the mudjhik in silence.

Lom felt something dark touch his mind. It was the same intrusive triumphant contact he had felt in the souterrain. His hands prickled as if the flow of blood were returning to numbed extremities. His mouth was dry. He felt himself sinking into a pit of blank hopelessness. Despair.

The position is hopeless. We're going to die.

No. That's not my voice.

The mudjhik's blank face whipped around towards where they were hiding, driving its eyeless gaze into the tangle of branches.

'Fuck!' hissed Lom. 'It's seen us. Run!' He caught a glimpse of the mudjhik beginning to move towards them. A kind of lurching fall that was the beginning of its accelerating charge. They turned and fled.

They ran thoughtlessly, stumbling and crashing through the undergrowth. Lom's chest was tight, his stomach sickened. Already he was feeling the thud of the stone fist against the back of his head that would be the last thing he ever felt.

After twenty or thirty yards they broke out of the thorny scrub onto a path, a narrow avenue filled with pale dawn light like water in a canal. It led gently downhill between taller trees towards the mudflats. Picking up speed they ran along it. Lom had no plan, no hope, except the wild thought that if they could reach the soft expanses of mud the mudjhik would be unable to follow them. It would flounder and sink. How they themselves would cross the treacherous flats he didn't know.

He didn't look back. He didn't need to. He could hear the mudjhik following. The rhythm of its heavy footfalls shook the earth beneath them. And he could feel the taunting, the almost casual mockery of its leisurely pace. It would not lose them now.

Then Lom was almost knocked sideways off his feet by a slap of wind against his body. Flying leaves and small pieces of twig and thorn stung his face, half-blinding him. He half-felt and half-saw in the corner of his eye a small and indistinct figure flow out of the woods and back up the path behind them. It was almost like a woman except that she was made of twigs and leaves and twisting wind. Behind him he heard Maroussia cry out and stumble. He stopped and turned to grab her and pull her upright.

'Don't stop!' he shouted into the rising noise. 'Don't look back!'

The wind rose, dissonant and maddening: it was almost impossible to walk against it, let alone run. A heavy bough fell at their feet with a dull thud. It didn't bounce. Big enough to have killed them.

'Just keep going!' Lom yelled.

A series of tremendous crashes came behind them, one after another. Four. Five. Six. Accompanied by the squeal and groan of tearing wood. The wind died.

'Vissarion!'

It was Maroussia. He stopped and looked back.

There was an indistinct shape on the path, at once a woman and a vortex of air and tree fragments, standing on the air a foot above the earth. It seemed as if her arms were spread wide to embrace the wood. Beyond her, huge trees had toppled across the track. Half a dozen of the largest beech and oak lay as if hurricane-flattened. Swirls of wind still stirred among their fallen, near-leafless crowns. The mudjhik had almost managed to evade them, but the last of them had come down with the immense weight of its trunk across its great stone back. The mudjhik was trapped under it, its face pressed deep into the scrubby grass and dark earth. It was not moving.

The wind-woman let her arms drop to her sides in a gesture filled with tiredness and relief. Aino-Suvantamoinen stepped out of the woods. He was walking towards the mudjhik where it lay.

'No!' yelled Lom. 'Wait! Don't!'

The giant didn't hear him, or else he took no notice. He walked across to look down on the mudjhik's motionless head. Its face was pressed inches deep into the mud. It could not have seen or heard or breathed. But it did not need to. As soon as the giant came within reach the mudjhik's free arm whipped forward in a direction no human or giant could have moved. But it was not human or giant: it had no ligaments and skeletal joints to define the limits of its moves. Its fist of rust-red stone smashed into the front of the giant's knee and broke it with a sickening crack. The giant shrieked in shock and anger and pain as he fell. The wind-woman seemed to cry out also, and shiver like a cat's-paw across still water. A storm of twig-fragments and whipped-up earth clattered ineffectually about the mudjhik's half-buried head.

The mudjhik's arm struck out again, almost too fast to be seen, punching towards the fallen giant's body, but he was just out of reach. Groggily, Aino-Suvantamoinen began to crawl away to safety, shaking his great head and dragging his snapped and twisted leg. Lom could hear his laboured breathing, deep and hollow and harsh. He sounded like a huge beast panting, a dray horse or a great elk. The mudjhik was moving purposefully under the weight of the fallen tree. Unable to raise itself with the trunk on it back, it was rocking its body from side to side and scooping at the earth under its belly with its hands. Gouging a deepening groove in the ground. Digging its way out. Soon it would be free.

He turned to Maroussia, but she wasn't there. He looked around wildly. Where the hell had she gone?

Then Lom saw her. Up the path, at the edge of the trees. She was heading for the stricken giant. Aino-Suvantamoinen was waving her away, but she was taking no notice.

'Maroussia!' Lom yelled. 'Get down! Get out of sight!'

There was a sharp ugly rattle of gunfire. An obscene clattering sound, flat and echoless. *A sub-machine gun.* Lom saw the muzzle flashes among the trees up and to the left, on the side of the path away from Maroussia. Bullet-strikes kicked up the mud, moving in a line towards the crawling, injured bulk of Aino-Suvantamoinen. A row of small explosions punched into the side of the giant's chest from hip to shoulder, each one bursting open, sudden rose-red blooms in little bursts of crimson mist. The huge body shuddered at the impacts. Then the top of his head came off.

Lom heard Maroussia's sigh of despair. Then the gun turned on her. A spray of bullets ripped into the trees around her, splattering the branches like heavy rain. He saw a splash of blood across her cheek, red against pale, as she fell.

'Maroussia!'

She wasn't moving.

No, thought Lom. *Not her. No.*

He began to move. He needed to get to her. He needed to draw the fire. Give her time to get into cover. If she could.

The gunfire turned towards him. He yelled and threw himself sideways into the trees, falling heavily.

Silence. The firing had stopped.

Keeping low, expecting the hail of bullets to fall again at any moment, Lom began to slither along the ground, hauling himself along on his elbows, driving forward with his knees. He felt the low mat of brambles and the roots of trees scraping his lower belly raw. He winced as a sharp branch dug into him under his belt: it felt as if it had pierced his skin and gouged a chunk from his flesh. He ignored it. He was trying to work his way up the hill to where she had fallen. Keeping his head low, he could see nothing. Where was the gunman? Waiting for him to show himself. Moving to a new position? Coming up behind him? No point in thinking any of that. *Move!* The only thing in his mind was reaching Maroussia. He reached the shelter of a moss-covered stump. Pushing aside a thicket of small branches, he risked a look.

Twenty yards ahead of him, Maroussia, looking dazed and lost, was trying to stand. He saw her stumble into the cover of the trees.

And then the mudjhik was free of the fallen tree and on its feet, and coming straight towards him.

Lom ran, ducking low, ignoring the thorns and brambles that slashed his face and hands until they ran wet with blood, heading for where the trees grew densest, squeezing between close-growing trunks, wading brooks. Anything that would slow the mudjhik. Anything that would give him the advantage.

The mudjhik was relentless. It would not give up. It would keep on coming. But it could not move as fast as a man through a wood. Lom could hear it behind him, crashing its way through the trees, but he was getting further ahead. Widening the gap.

Lom ran. There was nothing before this moment, nothing after it; there was only *now* and the *next half-second after now*, where he had to get to, by running as fast as he could make his body run and by *not falling*. The world narrowed down to one single point of clarity, the hole through which he had to pass to reach the moment on the other side of now. Behind him was the hunter. Ahead of him … calling him, wanting him as much as he wanted it … the safe hiding. The dark place. The mothering belly. The hole in the ground.

Lom hunched in the souterrain. He was sweating and shaking with cold. Thick darkness pressed against his eyes and seeped into his skin. He could smell his own blood, smeared on his hands and face; he could smell the damp earth and stone; and he could smell his own fear. Fear, and despair. Where was Maroussia? For the third time he did not know. For the third time he had left her to face her enemies alone. Vissarion Lom, protector of women. His own death would surely come and find him here. The mudjhik would sniff him out and dig. Drag him out and snap his neck. He had a little time to wait. But no hope. The souterrain was not a refuge but a trap. A dark hand reached inside his skull with stone fingers and squeezed his brain in its palm. Cruel and stupid and certain. *I am coming. I will be with you soon.* Again Lom felt the prickling clumsy numbness in his fingers and the gut-loosening dread. *It will not be long.*

He repelled the touch with all his force and slammed his mind shut against it.. He had more strength than he had expected. This was something new. And good. He felt a moment of surprise, his adversary's mental stumble as he lost his footing, and then … silence. He was free of it.

Only when it was gone did Lom realise how long it had been there: the fear, the lack of confidence, the constant unsettling feeling of alarm and threat moving at the barest edge of his awareness. It had been with him ever since he'd woken in the giant's isba, but it was gone at last. He'd driven it out. He was stronger than he thought. Stronger than his enemies knew.

Lom waited a moment, collecting his strength. He took stock. The hunters knew where he was, and he couldn't keep the mind-wall in place for ever. But it was a chance. And Maroussia might be alive. She was alive. He was sure of it, though he couldn't have said how he knew. Somehow he could feel her presence out there somewhere in the woods.

It was time to fight back.

When he was ready, Lom called back all the feelings of defenceless-ness and despair. He let himself be defeated, hopeless, hurt. Bleeding and weeping and broken in the dark.

It is finished. Over.

He let the one thought fill his mind.

I am finished. No more fighting. No more running. Everything hurts.

And deliberately he lowered his defences and let the mudjhik in. He felt its touch flow into his mind, and let it feel his defeat.

And then – when he had it, when he felt its triumph – Lom began to edge away within his mind.

Carefully, slowly, reluctantly, so it would feel to the mudjhik like energy and will draining away, he slipped beneath the surface of his own consciousness, retreating behind a second, inner, hidden wall he had built there. Barely thinking at all, moving by instinct only, he began to crawl away down the souterrain passage, further and deeper into the earth.

76

Maroussia watched the militia man step past Aino-Suvantamoinen's body with relaxed, fastidious indifference. He was another uniform, another gun. After the mudjhik had lumbered off under the trees in pursuit of Lom, he had stepped out of cover. Coming for her.

He was casually confident now, the squat ugly weapon slung from his shoulder and held across his body, pointing to the ground. He stopped for a moment to look at the dead giant. A defeated humiliated hill of flesh. The carcase of an immense slaughtered cow. She could tell by the way the man held himself that he was pleased. Gratified by the demonstration of his own power. He was walking across to where she lay. Not hurrying. She was no threat to him. Simply a matter of tidiness. A job to finish neatly. An injured woman to kill, while the mudjhik hunted down the fleeing man. He was a man who had succeeded.

She saw him close up. He was bare-headed. She could see his pale, insipid face. Fine fair hair, close-cropped, boyish. A piece of angel stone in the centre of his head. Then it came to her. Like a blow to the head. Anger knotted its fingers in her stomach and pulled, tight, making her retch. *It was the same man.* The one who had shot down her mother was the same one who was sauntering across to her now to finish the job.

'No,' she said quietly. 'No.'

She began to crawl away towards the trees. She was not badly hurt. Splinters of wood, smashed from the trees by the machine-gun fire, had sprayed her face, leaving her stung and bleeding from small cuts, and something heavy had struck her on the back of the head, leaving her momentarily dizzy, but that was gone now. She could have stood up and tried to run, but the militia man would simply have cut her down. She wanted to draw him closer. Get him into the woods, where she could spring at him from behind a tree. Knock the gun aside. Claw at his eyes with her fingernails. She needed him close for that. Careful to make no sudden movement that might cause him to raise his gun and rake her down from where he was, she crawled with desperate slowness towards the thickets.

The image of her mother dead came vividly into her head. Another slack and ragged body lying in the pool of its own leaking mess. That was three of them. Aino-Suvantamoinen. Vishnik. Mother. Just three among many of course: the Vlast was heaping up the corpses of the dead in great hills all across the dominions, tipping them into pits with steam shovels and bulldozers, and no one was counting. Soon she would be another.

She was not going to make it to cover. Her chance was no chance at all. In less than a minute – in seconds – he would do it. It was his job. His function. He was an efficient man, and even here in the woods the day belonged to efficient men. She was about to get up and run, knowing it would only hasten the end, when she heard him cry out in anger behind her. The noise of his gunfire shattered the silence that had settled on the morning. But no bullets struck her.

She looked back. For a second she thought he had been surrounded by bees. Little black insects were swarming all over him and he was firing wildly, the gun held one-handed while he tried to protect his face with the other and beat the bees away. Only it wasn't bees. It was leaves and pieces of twig and thorn. He was at the centre of a wildly spinning vortex of wind. The woman-shaped column of air that she had glimpsed earlier was upon him. Embracing him with her arms of wind. The hunter was panicking, blinded, shouting in anger and fear, lurching from side to side, trying to punch the wind away, firing his gun at the air that was assaulting him.

Maroussia could see, as he could not yet, that the wind-woman was losing her strength. Dissipating. The man was keeping his feet. The wind-woman who had brought down huge trees on the mudjhik could not even floor him now. She was exhausted. But she had done enough. She had made time. Maroussia ran.

She pushed her way through the undergrowth, following a path she hoped was taking her back to the isba. It wound between trees and turned aside round boulders. Sometimes it failed altogether, and she had to squeeze between close-growing trees until she found it again. Or found a different path. There was no way of telling. She might have been doing no more than following random trails made by wild animals. She had a vague notion of where the isba lay, but no way of knowing whether she could trust her sense of direction in this world of moss and leafless branches and strange hummocks in the ground.

The wind-woman had given her time. She should use it. She stopped running. Stood. Listened. Heard the sound of her own ragged breathing, the beating of her heart, the air moving through the trees – a sound as ancient and constant as the sea. She rested her hand on the smooth grey skin of a young beech tree. Trying to feel the life in it. She could feel nothing, but she imagined the tree welcomed the effort. She felt that maybe the warm touch of her palm had quickened it somehow. Imagination. But it was a good thought anyway, her first good thought in a long time. Progress. The territory would help her if she let it. Her pursuer would not think like that.

Once more she followed the smell of burnt wood and bone and wool to the remains of the isba. Much of the whalebone framework had fallen, but a few blackened lengths stuck upwards out of the mess. Heaps of rug and fur still smouldered, clotted and blackened and ruinous. The smell of it caught at the back of her throat. The iron stove was canted sideways, heat-seared and filthy with ash and soot. Some of its tiles had fallen away. It looked diminished and pathetic. Everything looked smaller now. There had been so much room inside the isba when she was in it, but the burnt scar it had left on the ground seemed too small to have contained so much space. Maroussia had seen plots like this in Mirgorod, sites where condemned houses had been cleared away and new ones not yet built. The gaps they left always seemed too small. All interior spaces were bigger than their exterior. Living inside them made it so.

The *Sib* was still tied to the little jetty on the creek at the edge of the clearing where Aino-Suvantamoinen had brought it the day after they arrived, while Lom had lain lost in his fever and she had sat with him. She considered untying the skiff, climbing in and drifting away. But Lom was out there somewhere in the woods. Perhaps not dead. Perhaps the mudjhik had not found him.

What would the hunter do? Come here of course. Check the isba. Check the *Sib*. Maybe he was watching her now from the trees. Maybe the mudjhik was there. No. Not that. They would not wait. They would attack immediately. They were not here yet. But they would come.

Think.

The territory will help you, if you let it.

The hunter would come here. He would walk where she had walked. Cross the ground that she had crossed. Stand on the jetty where she had stood, to look down into the boat. Sooner or later, he must do that. How much time did she have? Perhaps hours. Perhaps minutes. Perhaps none.

Near the isba was a neat stack of Aino-Suvantamoinen's fishing gear, untouched by the fire. A hauled-out salmon trap. A mud-sled. Leather buckets for cockles. And, leaning neatly against a stack of firewood, a shaft of wood thicker than her arm and as long as she was tall, with a flat metal blade like a long, narrow spade, lashed firmly to one end. She tested the blade edge. It was sharp on both sides and at the end. She had seen implements like this before, in the whalers' harbour. Flensing tools, used to slice long ribbons of flesh from porpoises and small whales as they hung from hooks. This was the same, but bigger, of a thickness and weight for the giant to heft. Unwieldy for her. But it was all she had.

The territory will help you, if you let it.

There was a little inlet by the jetty, where a stream flowed into the creek. The ground all around it was flat, grassy, empty but for a few saplings all the way back to the isba and the wood's edge. But the bank of the inlet was undercut by the stream, creating an overhanging ledge a couple of feet above a small expanse of soft, grey, semi-liquid mud. Maroussia threw a stone out onto the mud and watched it slowly settle for half its depth into the slobs.

She threw the heavy flensing blade after the stone, marking its position by a large bluish tussock of rough grass. Then she took off her clothes. All of them. They would be useless for what she intended; they would only hamper her movements. Slow her down.

She shivered. The touch of the wintry morning raised tiny bumps on her skin. She would be colder soon, much colder, but that was nothing. She could ignore it. Rolling her clothes into a bundle she dropped them into the bottom of the boat and threw a tarpaulin over them. Then she went back to the overhanging bank and slipped carefully down onto the mud within reach of where the blade had sunk almost out of sight. She pressed it down with her foot until the mud closed over it.

Maroussia knelt on the mud. Her knees sank immediately into the chilly ooze. Its touch was soft and slightly gritty against her skin. She began to scoop out a narrow channel the length of her body, plastering the mud over herself. Water began to puddle in the bottom of the shallow trench. But she couldn't cover herself entirely with the mud. She couldn't reach her back. There was no time. She lay down in the hollow she had made and rolled, covering every inch of her pale skin with the cold grey mud. Rubbing it into her hair and over her face. She lay flat, trying to wriggle her body down into it as much as she could, until she was firmly bedded in. Lying still, she could feel herself sinking slowly deeper as the mud opened to take her down. Gradually she felt the cold softness rising higher. She had chosen a place where a notch in the bank gave her a view of the jetty ten feet away. It would have to do. She waited. The hunter would come.

Time passed. Maroussia felt her body stiffening in the cold. She felt the tiny movements of the soft mud oozing against her. Water puddling underneath. The mud on her back began to dry and itch. She closed her mind against it. *Do not move.* Slowly the terrain closed in about her, absorbing her presence until she was part of it. Scarcely there. A heron flapped along the creek on loose flaggy wings and alighted close by. She watched it stand motionless, a slender sentry, probing the water with its intent yellow gaze, oblivious of her only a few feet away. She could not let it stay. If she startled it later, when the time came, it would alert *him*.

'Go!' she hissed. 'Move it! Shift!'

The heron didn't react. She risked moving a hand. Flexing her fingers out of the mud. The heron's yellow eye swivelled towards the movement instantly, alert for the chance of a vole or a frog. Their gazes met. For a moment they stared at each other. Then the heron lifted itself slowly away to find a more private post.

Some time later – how long, she had no idea – an otter came browsing along the creek and passed near her face. It had no idea she was there.

And then the hunter came.

She didn't hear him until he was almost on her. He was good. He was taking care. She heard his boots in the grass when he was ten steps away. He was standing where she had known he would stand. Checking out the *Sib* as she had known he would. Holding the gun cradled and ready, as she had pictured him doing. With his back towards her.

The territory will help you, if you let it.

She took a firm grip on the heavy shaft of the flensing blade that lay alongside her in the mud. Now was the time.

She was certain that the sounds of the river masked the sound of her rising out of the mud – a thing of mud herself – and the tread of her bare muddy feet on the grass, but some peripheral sense must have alerted him He was turning towards her and raising the muzzle of the gun when she swung the blunt end of the flensing tool at his head. It caught him across the side of his face. The momentum of the blow knocked him sideways and his booted feet slid from under him on the wet planking of the jetty. He went down heavily, losing his grip on the gun, and ended up on his back, looking up at her, blankly surprised.

Afterwards she wondered whether it had been her startling appearance, naked and plastered with mud, her face distorted with effort and hate, that slowed his reaction, as much as the mis-hit blow and the awkward fall. But whatever the cause, he was too slow, and she had played this scene through in her imagination a thousand times while she waited, anticipating every variation, every way it might go. Without stopping to think, she reversed the tool in her grip, set the vicious leading edge of the blade against his neck between sternum and chin, and shoved it downwards with all her weight, as if she were digging a spade into heavy ground. It sliced into his neck with a gristly crunch. She felt it parting the flesh and lodging against his vertebrae. He tried to scream but could manage only a wheezing, frothing gargle. She pulled back an inch or two and thrust again. The shaft was at an angle now, and she leaned the whole of her weight onto it. She felt the blade find its way between two vertebrae. It was sharp. She pushed again. His head came clean off and rolled a few feet across the planking, leaving a mess of flesh and tubes and gleaming white glimpses of bone between the man's shoulders. A widening pool of purple blood.

77

Lom walked fast through the souterrain tunnels. There was no light, but he didn't need it: the fear had gone and he was strong. He was going back to where they had first come down, under the giant's isba. He knew the way. He knew how to avoid the earth fall caused by Safran's grenades. The tunnels weren't dark and cramped; they were bright, airy, perfumed, luminous, beautiful. He knew his way by the smell of the earth, the trickle of dislodged earth, the stir and spill of air across the dampness of stone. He felt it all – he felt the roots of trees in the earth and the sway of their leafheads in the wind – as he felt the rub of his cuff against his wrist, the sock rucked under his foot, the sting of the grazes on his belly. There were other things too, things he could not quite focus on, not yet, but he felt their presence: they were like flitting shadows, hunches, hints. He was a world in motion – a borderless, lucid, breathing world. The seal in his head was cut away. The waters of the river and the sea had washed him clear.

This would not last. He knew that. Aino-Suvantamoinen had said that. It would fade, but it would not altogether go, and it would come again.

As he passed through the dark tunnel without stumbling, he tried to reach out with his mind into the woods above him. He didn't know yet what he could do. What the limits were. Further and further he pushed himself.

He found Safran. Safran was nearby. Moving with careful confidence almost directly above him.

He found the mudjhik, pushing its way through thorns. It was hunting but it had no trail. It was lost.

Lom reached out for Maroussia, but he couldn't find her. He felt her presence, but she was ... withdrawn. Barely breathing. Waiting. Still. She was *hiding*. But not from him.

And then he felt Safran's death ...

Lom needed to get out of the souterrain. Now. He needed to get to Maroussia.

He came to the place where the giant had let them down, but when he pushed up against the wooden hatch it would not shift. It was high above his head: he could just about touch it with his hands but he couldn't get his full strength into the shove. It seemed as if there was something heavy on top of it – the stove had fallen across it, perhaps.

He needed to get out.

There was another way. Perhaps.

Lom gathered all his strength into himself. Breathing slowly, focusing all his attention on what he was doing, he reached out around him into the perfumed earthy darkness, pulling together the air of the tunnel, making it as tight and hard as he could. He waited a moment, gathering balance. The earth above his head was cool and dark and filled with roots and life. It was another kind of air. Thicker, darker, richer air, and that was all it was. And then he pushed upwards.

78

Maroussia sat on the edge of the jetty and considered her situation. She had killed a man. She thought about that. When she had shot the militia man near Vanko's, although she had not meant to kill him and didn't think she had, afterwards she had been filled with empty sickness and self-disgust. But this time, though she had killed, she hadn't felt that. There was only a pure and visceral gladness. Satisfaction burst inside her like a berry. She had wanted to do it. Now it was done. That was good.

She slipped off the jetty edge into the deep icy water of the creek. It came up to her chest and the coldness of it made her gasp. She wished she knew how to swim but she had never learned. She waded out into the middle of the stream, feeling the slippery mud and buried stones and the tangle of weeds beneath her feet. The strong current pushed at her legs. She ducked her head under the water, eyes open, letting it wash the clotted mud from her hair. Cleaning everything away, the mud and the fear and the blood that had splashed her legs. Surrendering herself, she let her body drift downstream, turning slowly, until she came to a place where the branches of a fallen tree reached out across the creek. There she climbed out.

When she got back to the jetty she kicked the severed head over the side. It fell in the water with a plop and disappeared. Then she put her clothes back on and prepared the skiff to leave: laid the oars ready in the rowlocks; made sure the lines were loosely tied so one tug would release them. She would give Lom till dusk to find her, and if he had not come, she would go alone. She drank a little water and wished there was something she could eat. She had not felt so hungry for days. But that was tomorrow's problem. For the moment it was enough to sit with her back against a jetty post and wait.

She tried to keep her eye on the edge of trees that enclosed the wide clearing, watching for any sign of movement that would signal the coming of Lom. Or the mudjhik. But her gaze kept being drawn back to the burned-out remains of the isba. The outward sign of her desolation and grief. Killing the militia man had not healed that. Not at all. Desultory snowflakes appeared, skittering in the grey air.

And then the wreckage of the isba erupted. It was as if a shell had fallen, or a mine exploded. A column of dark earth and roots and stone and the remains of the isba spouted ten – twenty – feet up and slumped back down in a crump of dust. She saw the giant's stove bounce and break open. A wave of dust-heavy air rolled over her, smelling of the raw, damp underground.

As the air cleared she saw something, a man-shaped figure, climbing up out of the earth. Its face was a mess of dirt and blood. A heavy cloak hanging from its shoulders. It stood for a moment as if dazed, looking around slowly, then it began to walk slowly towards her.

'Vissarion?' she said. 'Vissarion? Is that you.'

The figure stopped to wipe its face with its sleeve. It was Lom. He looked lost, disoriented, stunned. She saw that the wound in his forehead had opened. It was seeping blood into his eyes and down across his mouth. He kept wiping at his face, vaguely, again and again.

'Maroussia?' said Lom. 'There's dirt in my eyes. I can't see properly.'

'What ... what happened? Was that another grenade?'

Lom wiped his face again and looked at her, blinking.

'That?' he said. 'That was me.' He paused, and she saw that he was grinning at her. Grinning like a child. 'This is going to be fun.' Then his legs crumpled and he sat down heavily beside her with his hand to his forehead. 'Ow,' he said, looking at her balefully. 'My head hurts. You haven't got any water I could drink, have you?'

'Vissarion?' said Maroussia. 'Where's the mudjhik?'

79

Artyom Safran wondered where he was. Dead, certainly. But also … not. As the terrible flat blade had begun to slice into his neck and he knew that he would certainly die there, he made one last reckless throw of the dice. He grabbed at the mental cord connecting him to the mudjhik and hurled himself along it, all of himself, wholeheartedly, holding nothing in reserve. It was easy and instant, like jumping from a window to escape a fire. The mudjhik had been pulling at him insidiously for years, and the pull had been growing stronger all the time they were in the wetlands. More than once in the last few days he had felt himself slipping away, and it had required an effort of will to hold himself separate. Now he stopped trying, and threw himself instead at the door, and it was open, and he stumbled through. The mudjhik, reacting instantly, pulled him inside. Greedily. It felt like a great hunger being fed at last. In the last moment of his separateness, Safran had felt a surge of crude, ugly, inhuman satisfaction enfolding him.

What have I done?

It was his last purely human thought.

He was not alone. Dog-in-mudjhik came at him hard, scratching and tearing and spitting, before he had a chance to find his balance. Dog-in-mudjhik would tolerate no rival. It was a territory thing. Only the death of the interloper would do.

Safran tried to put up some sort of defence, but he had no time to work out how. He tried curling himself into a tight ball with his back against Dog-in-mudjhik's ripping jaw. Hugging himself to protect his vital organs. But it was the merest persiflage. Dog-in-mudjhik cut through all that. Dog-in-mudjhik was shredding him, tearing him off in chunks, snarling. Dog-in-mudjhik made himself as big as a house and started to dig. Safran was going to die a second time.

But the mudjhik's angel stuff knew what it needed, and it was not dog thoughts any more. In the gap between two instants the space inside the mudjhik that Dog-in-mudjhik occupied ceased to exist. It closed up completely, solid where space had been. Dog-in-mudjhik went out like a snuffed candle. Dog-in-mudjhik was extinguished, leaving only a faint and diminishing smell of dog mind in the air.

What had once been Safran lay still, curled up tight, quivering like hurt flesh. Trying to close himself off. Trying too late to renege on the deal. Far too late. The angel-stuff encompassed him, fitting itself around him until there was no space between them. Then it moved in.

Safran-in-mudjhik felt sick and dizzy with horror. He was in a cold red-grey world. Seeing without eyes, hearing without ears, overwhelmed and confused by the mudjhik's alien angel-senses, he couldn't grasp where he was. Or who. Or what. But even then, in the moment of his profoundest and most appalling collapse, he began to feel something else. A new kind of triumph. He sensed the first glimmerings of an immense new power. The angel stuff was feeling it, but so was he. He was going to be a new thing in the universe. A first. A best. Immortal. Safran-in-mudjhik was strong.

Experimentally he swept an arm sideways. It cracked against a tree and broke it. The tree toppled towards him and he fended it off effortlessly. A long-eared owl, half-stunned and dislodged from its roost, struggled to get purchase on the air with its wings. Safran-in-mudjhik caught it in flight and smashed it against his own stone chest. Felt it break. Felt it die. So good. This would be fun. There were so many things to do. Sweet freedom things.

First and sweetest, revenge.

Safran-in-mudjhik began to explore his new self. There were angel-senses here, and angel memories that Dog-in-mudjhik could perceive nothing of. The bright immensity between the stars. Existence without time. He could remember. He belonged there. And now he was on his way back.

Somewhere in the rust-and-blood-red corridors of his new mind he could feel the connection with Lom. Faint but still there. He fumbled towards it, but he was still too clumsy to hold on to it. He couldn't get it clear enough to know where Lom was. Not yet. But soon. Finesse would come. In the meantime, he certainly knew where she was. The Shaumian woman. The Safran-slicer. Creator of Safran-in-mudjhik. Kill her first. He turned towards the isba clearing and the creek. It was going to be a good first day.

80

The swollen river surged ahead, thick and brown and heavy. It carried the skiff onwards and widened as it went. Lom, cradling Safran's sub-machine gun, stared mesmerised at the surface. It was scummed with ragged drifts of foam, littered with dead leaves and matted rafts of grass and broken branches. He felt drained. His head hurt. The new skin across the hole in his skull had split, and though a crust of dried blood had formed, it throbbed in time with his pulse and wept a clear sticky liquid. It was sore, and all the muscles of his body ached. The effort of pushing his way out of the souterrain had exhausted him, and the world around him felt diminished, distant and separate. He wondered if such easy power would ever come back to him again.

Maroussia handled the oars. She had little to do but steer the skiff with occasional touches, avoiding the larger obstacles floating along with them and keeping them clear of eddies and backwaters.

'The waters are rising,' said Lom. 'It must have been raining in the hills.'

Maroussia shook her head.

'The giant is gone,' she said. 'Without him to work the sluices, the waters are running wild. All this wetland will go. There'll be nothing left but the city and the sea.'

A dark mossy floating lump of tree nudged heavily against the bow and rested there, travelling alongside them in the current. Lom stared at it. It was a mass of little juts and elbows of branch-stump and bark canker. Every crook and hole was edged with a dewy fringe of spider's web. Lom shifted the weight of the gun, which was pressing into his leg. The death of Aino-Suvantamoinen, and the weight of all the other deaths before him, had left him feeling numbed and stupid. The boat was taking them into a darker, emptier future.

Maroussia pulled hard at the oars, skewing the *Sib* sideways. She rowed in silence, looking at nothing. Lom watched her hands on the oars. Large, strong, capable. She'd pushed back her sleeves. Her hands were reddened but her forearms were pale and smooth. He could see the tendons and muscles working as she rowed. Her black hair was slicked with river mist: it clung to her face and neck in tight shining curls.

'It's not your fault,' said Lom.

'What?'

'The giant. It was Safran that killed him. Not you.'

'He tried to help,' said Maroussia.

'He thought it was important. So did Raku.'

'Yes.'

'So it is important.'

For a long time Maroussia didn't say anything. She just kept rowing. Then she looked up at him.

'I'm going to find the Pollandore,' she said. 'The angel is destroying the world. The Pollandore can stop that.'

Lom noticed how thin she was, though her arms were strong. As she rowed, he watched the shadow play on the vulnerable, scoop-shaped dip at the base of her throat. The suprasternal notch. She was human and raw and beautiful. She rowed in silence for a long time. Lom watched the empty mudbanks pass by. He wiped his weeping forehead.

'Vissarion?'

'Yes?'

'That thing in your head ...'

'It's gone now.'

'What was it? How did it get there?'

'I was young. I don't know how old. Eight maybe. Eight or nine. A child.'

'That man I killed ...'

'Safran.'

'He had one the same.'

'Savinkov's Children. They call us that. Ever heard of Savinkov?'

'No.'

'You should have. Everyone should know about Savinkov.'

'I don't.'

'He was provost of the Institute at Podchornok when I was there. Vishnik went there too. He was my friend.'

'But he didn't ... he didn't have anything like that.'

'No. Only a few of us. Before he came to the Institute, Savinkov was a technician of angel-flesh. His specialism was the effect of it on the human mind. Putting a piece of it in direct contact with the human brain.'

'They put that stuff in people's heads?'

'And the other way round.'

'You don't mean ...'

'It's common practice with mudjhiks to put in an animal brain: naturally they tried with human brains too, but it doesn't work that way. The mudjhiks become uncontrollable. Insane. But there are less dramatic methods than full transplant. Angel flesh has a sort of life. Awareness. It *affects* you. And it encourages loyalty. The sacrifice of the individual for the sake of the whole. It's a way of binding you to the Vlast.'

'But ... you ... They did it to you when you were a *child*.'

'That was Savinkov's subject. His research. Were children more or less susceptible? Did the effect grow or diminish with time? How could you measure and predict it? The skull insertion technique was Savinkov's invention. It used to go wrong a lot. The children died, or ... well, Savinkov put them to work. In the gardens. The stables.'

'But ... the *parents*?'

'We didn't have parents. None of us did. Savinkov used to take waifs and strays into the Institute for the experiments. I never knew who my parents were.'

'Oh ...'

'Savinkov saw nothing wrong with it,' said Lom. 'He had some successes too. Some of them became excellent mudjhik handlers and technicians with the Worm. Servants of the Vlast of great distinction.'

'But not you.'

'No. I was one of Savinkov's disappointments in that respect.'

Walls rose on either side of the river. The channel narrowed. A roar of rushing water. The skiff rolled and yawed, rushing ahead out of control.

'Hold on!' yelled Lom.

Maroussia almost lost the oars as the *Sib* pitched over a low weir and spun out into wide grey water. The Mir Ship Canal. The skiff settled, drifting slowly with the current.

It was a bleak, blank place after the edgeless mist and mud of the wetlands: a broad channel cut dead straight between high embankments of stone blocks and concrete slopes, wide enough for great ships and ocean-going barges to pass four or six abreast. Featureless. There was nothing natural to be seen, not even a gull in the sky. The trees were out of sight behind the great ramparts and bulwarks built by armies of giants and serfs. Built by the Founder on their bones. The water was deep: Lom felt it fathoming away beneath them, dark and cold. A bitter wind, freighted with flurries of sharp sleety snow, was pushing upstream off the sea, smelling of salt and ice, slowing their progress. It had been autumn when they entered the wetlands. It felt like winter coming now.

'It'll be easy from here on,' said Lom. 'Downstream to the sea lock. We can leave the boat there and walk back along the Strand to the tram terminus. Let me take the oars for a while.'

Maroussia wasn't listening. She was staring over his shoulder up towards the embankment. He followed her gaze. The mudjhik was standing on the crest, a smudge of dried blood and rust against the grey sky. Grey snow. Grey stone. It was watching them. As the current took them downstream, the mudjhik began to lope along the top of the high canal wall, keeping pace. Lom looked for an escape. On either side of the canal the embankments rose sheer and high. No quays. No steps cut into the stone. Nowhere to go. The mudjhik had only to follow them.

'Maybe we'll find a place on the far side where we can get out,' he said. 'It can't cross the canal before the sea lock. We can be miles away by then.'

As if in answer, he felt the dark touch of the mudjhik's mind in his. It felt stronger than before, much stronger, and different now. There was an intelligence there that had been absent before, with a sickening almost-human edge to it. It was almost a voice. No words, but a cruel demonstration of existence and power. It was a voice he recognised. *Safran*. But it wasn't quite Safran: it was something more and something less than he had been. Lom felt he was being touched intimately by something … disgusting. Something strong but inhuman, broken and foul and … wrong. A mind that stank.

He slammed his mind-walls closed against it. The effort hurt. His head began to ache immediately. He felt the pulse in the socket in his forehead flutter and pound.

'We have to destroy that thing,' he said. 'Somehow. We have to end it. Here.'

Safran-in-mudjhik considered the pathetic little rowing boat sitting there helplessly, a flimsy toy on the deep flowing blackness. The two frail lives it carried, cupped in its brittle palm, flickered like matchlights. He had shown himself deliberately so he could taste their fear. Their deaths would be … delicious. Especially hers. The one that had taken his head when part of him was in the man.

That part of him wanted to be back in the man. It wasn't happy any more. But it would learn, or he would find a way to silence what he did not need. The angel-stuff was coming awake. Learning to remember. Learning to think. Now it had learned it could soak up human minds, absorb them, grow, it wanted to do it again. The first one had come willingly. More than that, it had come by choice, pushed its way in. Regretted it already, though. Would have preferred extinction. Too late! Too late, impetuous companion! Stuck with it now. But willingness was not essential. There were many minds here. Take them. Harvest them. Fed with such nutriment, what could angel-stuff not become? It remembered swimming among the stars. Why not again? But better. Stronger. More dangerous.

Start with the two in the boat. There was history there. Bad blood.

81

Lom pulled hard on the oars, racing the skiff seaward, scanning the far embankment for a scaleable escape. There was none. His head was hurting worse: tiny detonations of bright light flickered in his peripheral vision; waves of giddiness distracted him. He couldn't maintain his defences indefinitely. He hadn't the strength.

Maroussia went through Safran's equipment. There was the pistol, useless against the mudjhik, but not negligible.

'Here,' she said. 'You'd better have this.'

Lom put it in his pocket.

There was also the Exter-Vulikh that had cut down the giant. Its magazine was half full and there were two more besides, but it was nothing that would worry a twelve-foot sentient block of angel flesh, not even for an instant. Maroussia laid it aside with an expression of distaste.

'Wouldn't it be better if we just stopped?' she said.

'What do you mean?'

'We could wait. I know we can't make headway upstream, but we could try to hold our position out here. Or maybe we could make the boat fast somehow against the far embankment. Sooner or later a ship will come along.'

Lom considered.

'Maybe,' he said. 'If there is a ship. We haven't seen any. Don't they try to clear port before the freeze? I think the season's over.'

'Something must come along, one way or the other.'

Lom turned the skiff and began to row against the stream.

The mudjhik understood what they were doing instantly. It stopped loping forward and began to jog up and down on the spot, stamping heavily. Then it bent forward and began to pummel the ground with its fists. For a moment Lom thought it was raging impotently, but it straightened up with a large chunk of stone in its hands and lobbed it towards them.

The first throw fell short. A boulder as large as a man's torso whumped into the canal, jetting up a column of white water. Short, but close enough for them to feel the sting of the spray on their faces. The ripples reached the *Sib* and set her rocking. The next shot was closer. The mudjhik was finding its range.

'Shit,' said Lom and turned the boat again.

As soon as the boat started heading downstream, the mudjhik halted its bombardment and went back to pacing them along the embankment.

'It's herding us,' said Lom. 'It could sink us anytime, but it wants to get in close.'

I will not let you touch her. Weak as he was, he tried to force the thought towards the mudjhik, against the flow of its onslaught. *I will bring you down.*

They heard the sea gate before they saw it. The light was failing. Twilight brought sharp fresh squalls of sleet off the sea. There were gulls now, wheeling inland to roost. The Ship Canal swung round the shoulder of a small hill and narrowed, channelling the flow of the Mir in flood into a bottleneck of concrete, and ahead of them rose the great barrier. On one side, the left as they approached it, were the lock gates themselves, three ship-breadths wide, and to the right a roar of gushing water hidden in a cloud of spray. The grand new hydroelectric turbine, turning the pressure of water into power to light the streets of Mirgorod.

The immense lock gates were shut against them. They could make out the silhouette of the Gate Master's hut at the far end, between the lock and the turbine, but no light showed there. Of course not. Night was falling. No shipping traffic would come now. None, probably, till the spring. They were alone except for the mudjhik, standing in plain sight next to the massive stubby gate tower, waiting for them.

Lom fought the surging water with the oars, but there was nowhere to go. The skiff would either be brought up hard against the bottom of the gate or carried into the turbine's throat.

'A ladder!' Maroussia shouted above the noise of the water. 'Over there.'

Lom could just make out in the gathering gloom a contraption of steel to the right of the turbine, away from the mudjhik, designed to give access to the weir at water level. All he had to do was take the *Sib* across the current without getting dragged into the churning turbine mouth.

He could see nothing of what happened under the curtain of spray. There would be a grating, probably, to sift detritus from the canal. Maybe that's what the ladder was for. To clear it. But even if there was a grating, the boat would surely be smashed against it. The whole weight of the river was passing through there: the force would be tremendous; nobody who went into that churning water would come out again.

He let the current carry them forward and tried to use the oars to steer a slanting course across it, aiming for a point on the embankment just upstream from the bottom of the ladder. His arms ached. His head was pounding. There would be no second chance. The mudjhik was attacking his mind hard, not constantly but with randomly timed pulses of pressure, trying to knock him off balance.

The skiff crashed against the wall, caught her bow on a jut of stone and spun stern-first away from the embankment towards the deafening roar and dark, blinding spray. Lom dug in with the left-hand oar, almost vertically down into the water, and turned the skiff again. She crashed against the foot of the ladder and Maroussia grabbed it. The boat kept moving. Lom crouched and leapt for the ladder. The impact jarred his side numb, but he managed to hook one arm awkwardly round a steel strut. He had slung the Exter-Vulikh across his back by its webbing strap and the Sepora was in his pocket. The *Sib* continued sliding away from under him. She left them both clinging to the metal frame and disappeared into the shouting darkness and mist. Lom scrabbled desperately for a foothold and barked his shin against a sharp-edged metal rung. Then he was climbing, following Maroussia up the sheer embankment side.

There was nowhere to go. They were standing on a railed steel platform overlooking the turbines. A narrow walkway led across plunging water and slowly turning turbines to the lock gate tower, and beyond that was the lock itself, and the mudjhik. There was no other exit.

Lom looked over the seaward side with a wild idea of diving into the sea and swimming for the beach. If there was a beach. But down there, there was no sea, only a cistern to receive the immense outflow from the turbines. It was a deep, seething pit of water. Hundreds of thousands of gallons burst out from the sluice mouth every second and poured into what was basically a huge concrete-walled box. You wouldn't drown in there, you'd be smashed to a bloody pulp before the air was gone from your lungs.

Across the walkway a door led into the lock gate tower. With a crash of masonry it shattered open and the mudjhik shouldered its way through. It stood there a moment. Its face was blank. No sightless eyes. No lipless, throatless mouth. Just a rough lump of reddish stone sat on its shoulders. But it was watching them.

Lom raised the Exter-Vulikh and fired a stream of shells into the mudjhik's belly. The clattering detonations echoed off the surrounding concrete, deafening even above the roar of the turbine sluice, but the shells had no discernible effect. Lom had not thought they would. It was a gesture. The magazine exhausted itself in a few seconds and he threw the gun over the rail into the water below.

For a moment nothing happened. Stalemate. The mudjhik watching them from its end of the walkway. Lom and Maroussia staring back. Waiting. Then the mudjhik turned sideways and began to edge its way across the narrow steel bridge, squeezing itself between the flimsy rails. Lom reached for Maroussia's hand – it was the time for final, futile gestures – but he didn't find it. Maroussia had darted forward, running straight at the mudjhik. Lom felt its surge of raw delight as it grabbed for her, reaching sideways, swinging its leading arm wildly. He felt it reaching for her with its mind at the same time. Opening itself wide. Drawing at her. It was like a mouth, gaping.

It's trying to suck her in.

Understanding slammed against Lom's head like a concussion. And with it another thought. Another piece of insight.

It's too confident. It fears nothing at all.

And he saw what Maroussia was trying to do.

The mudjhik's swing at her was too awkward a move for its precarious position on the walkway. She ducked and the arm missed her, sweeping through the air above her head. The impetus of the move overbalanced the mudjhik slightly. It stumbled and leaned against the walkway rail, which sagged under its weight.

Lom pulled Safran's Sepora out of his pocket and fired, again and again, aiming high to clear Maroussia, aiming for the huge eyeless head. The recoils jarred his hand and shoulder. He flung all his rage and defiance and disgust and hatred at the mudjhik's undefended, questing, open-mouthed mind. He was still tired and weak – the power of his push was nothing compared to what he had done under the ground – but he felt the jar as it impacted. It was enough. Together, the mental onslaught and the heavy magnum rounds confused the mudjhik and added momentum to its stumble. The narrow guard rail collapsed under its weight and the mudjhik fell into the churning, roaring waters of the cistern below.

82

Maroussia was lying on the narrow iron walkway. She wasn't moving. Lom ran across. He knelt down beside her and laid his hand on her head. She stirred, raised her head and looked at him.

'Is it gone?' she said.

'Yes. It's gone. Are you … are you OK?'

'If that thing is gone then we can go back. I need to go back.'

'It's almost dark,' said Lom. 'And it's a long walk back. There won't be any trams till the morning. We'll have to stay here.'

She sat up slowly. She looked dizzy and sick.

'No. I …' But she had no strength for a night journey. No strength to argue even.

'Just for tonight,' said Lom. 'We can stay in the Gate Master's cabin.'

The Gate Master's lodge was an incongruous wooden superstructure on the lip of the sea gates. The lock on the door gave easily at a shove from Lom's shoulder. Inside was near-darkness. The smell of pitch and lingering tobacco smoke and tea. Maroussia found a lamp and matches. In the yellow lamplight the interior had a vaguely nautical flavour: large-scale charts of the harbour and the inner reaches were pinned to the walls, and more of the same were spread out on a plan table under the seaward window, with instruments, pencils, a pair of binoculars. There was a chair, the kind with a mechanism that allowed the seat to revolve and tip backwards. A long thin telescope on a tripod stood on the floor; heavy oilskins hung from a hook on the back of the door; a pair of large rubber boots leaned against the foot of a neat metal-framed bed. The Gate Master had left everything prepared to make himself comfortable when he returned: firewood stacked in the corner, water in the urn, a packet of tea, a box of biscuits. Lom pulled the heavy curtains across the window while Maroussia lit the stove and the urn. There were even two mugs to drink from. Maroussia sat on the edge of the bed and Lom took the swivelling chair, leaning back and putting his feet up on the table.

'What if someone sees the light?' said Maroussia.

'There's no one for miles. Anyway ...' Lom shrugged. 'Shipwrecked mariners. Needs must.' But he took Safran's heavy revolver from his pocket and laid it on the table within reach.

'Any bullets left in that?'

'No.'

Maroussia was looking at him. Her eyes were dark in the lamp shadow. Uncertain.

'Before the mudjhik fell ...' she began, and stopped. He waited for her to continue. 'I felt something. Inside my head.' She paused again. Lom didn't say anything. 'I don't know ... There was a kind of sick feeling, like I was going to faint. Everything seemed very far away. And then ... it was like a fist, a big angry punch, but inside my head. It didn't feel aimed at me, but it almost knocked me over anyway. And then the mudjhik ... went.'

'What you did was crazy. Running at it like that. You were lucky. If it had caught you when it swung—'

'It was you, wasn't it? The mind-punch thing. It felt like you. You did it.'

Lom said nothing.

'And when you blew yourself out of the ground ...' said Maroussia. 'How do you do that? I mean, what is it?'

'I don't know. It's something I used to be able to do. When I was a child. Then it stopped when Savinkov sealed me up. But since the seal was taken – actually before then, when I came to Mirgorod. It's been coming back. I just ... I just do it.'

There was a long silence. Pulses of sleet battering at the window. Maroussia was examining the woollen rug on the bed. Picking at it. Removing bits of fluff.

'Who *are* you?' she said eventually. 'I mean, what are you? Where do you *come* from? I mean, where do you really *come* from?'

'I don't know,' said Lom. 'But I'm beginning to think I should try to find out.' He took a biscuit from the box. It was soft and stale and tasted of dampness and pitch. He swallowed it and took a sip of tea. Cooling now. Bitter. He chucked the box of biscuits across the room onto the bed next to her. 'Here,' he said. 'Have one.'

'No.'

'Sleep then. We need to clear out early tomorrow. You can have the bed.'

'What about you?'

'I'll take the floor.'

'We could share the bed,' she said. 'There's room.'

She was sitting in shadow. Lom couldn't see anything in her face at all. Another scatter of sleet crashed against the window. The door with the broken lock stirred in the wind.

'Yes,' he said. 'That would be better.'

83

L om lay on his back, pressed between Maroussia and the wall. He was tired but sleep hadn't come. As soon as he had got into the bed, Maroussia had pulled the blanket over them both, turned on her side, away from him, and apparently gone straight to sleep. He felt her long back now, pressed against his side, the length of her body stretched against his.

The wind and rain had died away. He could hear the slow rhythm of her breathing and the quiet surge of the sea. And it seemed to him that somewhere at the edge of his mind he could hear Safran under the water, crying in his pain. But if he tried to reach for the thread of it, it wasn't there.

'Vissarion?'

'Yes?'

But she said nothing more. Only the gentle ebb and flow of her breath. The rising and falling of her ribs against him. He turned on his side so that his face was against the back of her neck. He could smell her dark hair. The moment of rest at the end of the pendulum's swing, before it fell back and swung again. They would have time. Later. Or they would not.

The mudjhik lay pinned under a hundred thousand gallons a second. On its back. It pounded the concrete floor beneath it, the floor built to take the brunt of the Mir in flood, pounded it with its fists and heels and head. The mudjhik would never sleep. Never die. No matter how long, no matter what it took. It would pound its way out.

Somewhere, deep inside the angel-stuff, what remained of Safran wanted to scream but had no voice. Wanted to weep but had no tears. No mouth. No eyes.

They overslept. Lom surfaced eventually to the sound of Maroussia making tea. She had drawn back the curtains and filled the cabin with grey dawn light. Lom stumbled out of bed and found the Gate Master's shaving kit – a chipped bowl for water, soap, a razor and a small square of mirror – all set out neatly ready for use. He washed and shaved for the first time in ... how long? He had lost count of the days. The mirror showed him the hole in the centre of his forehead with its crust of blood. He washed it clean and watched it pulsing faintly with the beating of his heart. He touched it with his finger. The new, healing skin felt smooth and young. The pulse inside it was a barely palpable fluttering.

'Here.'

Maroussia nudged him gently and handed him a mug of strong, sweet tea. She had found sugar. As he sipped it, she kissed him, once, quickly, on his freshly shaven cheek. He caught once more the scent of her hair and felt the cool bright touch of her mouth fading slowly from his skin.

With the Gate Master's razor he cut a strip of cloth from the bottom of his shirt, knotted it bandanna-fashion round his head to hide the wound of the angel mark, and checked the result in the mirror. The effect was odd but not unpleasing. Gangsterish. Buccaneering. Conspicuous, but not as instantly-identifying as a hole in the head. After a moment's hesitation, he folded the Gate Master's razor, slipped it into his pocket and turned to find Maroussia appraising him.

'You'll do,' she said. 'I've seen worse.'

'And you look ... fine,' said Lom. She had washed her hair. It was damp and lustrous. Her cheeks were pink. 'But you're going to freeze out there.'

'I'm too hungry to notice.'

'We'll find a café,' he said. 'When we get back. We'll have breakfast.' Coffee. Eggs. Pastries. That would be normal. That would be simple and good. Then a thought struck him. 'Have you got any money?' He had none. Nothing but a razor and an empty gun.

Maroussia dug in her pockets and came up with a few coins. Enough for tram fares to the city, perhaps. Not much more.

'I wanted to leave something,' she said. 'For the Gate Master.'

'We'll send it to him,' said Lom. 'Afterwards.'

They stood for a moment in the middle of the neat cabin. They had set things as straight as they could, and Lom had made a temporary repair to the lock. It would hold.

'We'd better go,' said Maroussia.

'Yes.'